## About the

**Clare Connelly** was raised in small-town Australia among a family of avid readers. She spent much of her childhood up a tree, Mills & Boon book in hand. She is married to her own real-life hero in a bungalow near the sea with their two children. She is frequently found staring into space – a surefire sign she is in the world of her characters. Writing for Mills & Boon Modern is a long-held dream. Clare can be contacted via clareconnelly. com or on her Facebook page.

**Melanie Milburne** read her first Mills & Boon at age seventeen in between studying for her final exams. After completing a Masters Degree in Education she decided to write a novel and thus her career as a romance author was born. Melanie is an ambassador for the Australian Childhood Foundation and is a keen dog lover and trainer and enjoys long walks in the Tasmanian bush. In 2015 Melanie won the HOLT Medallion, a prestigious award honouring outstanding literary talent.

**A.C. Arthur** was born and raised in Baltimore, Maryland where she currently resides with her husband and three children. Determined to bring a new edge to romance, she continues to develop intriguing plots, sensual love scenes, racy characters and fresh dialogue; thus keeping the readers on their toes! Arthur loves to hear from her readers and can be reached through her contact form or via email at acarthur22@yahoo.com

# Billionaire Christmas Nights

CLARE CONNELLY

MELANIE MILBURNE

A.C. ARTHUR

MILLS & BOON

First Published in Great Britain 2024
by Mills & Boon, an imprint of HarperCollins*Publishers* Ltd,
1 London Bridge Street, London, SE1 9GF

www.harpercollins.co.uk

HarperCollins*Publishers*
Macken House, 39/40 Mayor Street Upper,
Dublin 1, D01 C9W8, Ireland

ISBN: 978-0-263-34497-4

MIX
Paper | Supporting
responsible forestry
FSC
www.fsc.org
FSC™ C007454

This book contains FSC™ certified paper and other controlled sources to ensure responsible forest management.

For more information visit: www.harpercollins.co.uk/green

Printed and Bound in the UK using 100% Renewable Electricity
at CPI Group (UK) Ltd, Croydon, CR0 4YY

# BOUND BY THEIR CHRISTMAS BABY

## CLARE CONNELLY

To my fabulous South Australian Romance Association friends: smart, supportive and kind women who sparkle like ornaments all year round.

# CHAPTER ONE

GABE WAS BORED. He always was at these damned things, but they were part and parcel of his life. His job. His all. And he'd never been a man to walk away from a challenge.

God knew Noah—his business partner and best friend—wasn't going to step forward to attend a damned investors' dinner. A party in a club, sure. Noah would be there in an instant. But this kind of entertaining fell to Gabe, and Gabe alone. He looked around the table, smiling blandly, wondering how much more he had to endure before he could make his excuses and leave.

There were a thousand better ways than this to spend an evening.

He hadn't been to New York in a year, and the last time? Well, it had been a spectacular disaster. No wonder he'd avoided it like the plague. Too much melancholy at Christmas, that was the problem. He'd actually allowed himself to feel lonely, to feel alone, to feel sorry for himself. That was why he'd been stupid enough to fall for her ploy.

'Calypso's going to be game-changing,' Bertram Fines said with confidence. 'You've done it again.'

Gabe ignored the flattery. People were all too quick with praise now that he and Noah had established the foremost technology company in the world. It was the early years when they'd been without friends, without funds, and still made it work through sheer perseverance and determination. He reached for his glass. It was empty. He lifted a hand in the air, summoning a waiter without lifting his gaze.

'This is the culmination of a lot of innovation, and even more research. Calypso isn't just a smartphone, it's a way of life,' he said with a lift of his shoulders. It was the culmination of an idea he and Noah had years earlier, and they'd worked tirelessly to get it to this point—almost to the market. Calypso went beyond the average smartphone. It was smarter. More secure, guaranteeing its users more privacy.

His spine straightened with a *frisson* of alarm when he recalled how close he'd come, a year ago, to compromising the project. How close he'd come to seeing Calypso's secrets taken to one of his business rivals.

But that hadn't eventuated. He'd made sure of that. His eyes glinted with the ferocity of his thoughts, the strength of his resentment, but his smile was all wolf-like charm.

'How can I help you, sir?' A woman appeared to his left. A brassy redhead with a pleasing figure and a smile that showed she knew it. Once upon a time, Gabe might have smiled back. Hell, he'd have done more than smile back—he'd have laid on the charm, asked what time she finished her shift, and then he'd have seduced her. Bought her a drink, taken her for a drive in his limousine before inviting her to his hotel room.

But the last time he'd done that, he'd learned his lesson. He would never again invite a wolf in sheep's clothing to his bed, nor a woman dressed like a temptress who'd come to betray him. Before he had met Abigail Howard, Gabe couldn't have imagined going a month without the company of a beautiful woman between his sheets, but now it had been a year. A year since Abigail, a year without women, and he barely cared.

He named a bottle of wine, one of the most expensive on the menu, without smiling, and turned his attention back to his table of guests. Conversation had moved onto the cost of midtown realty. He sat back, pretending to listen, fingers in a temple beneath his chin.

The restaurant was quietening down. Despite the fact it was one of Manhattan's oldest and most prestigious spots, it was late—nearing midnight—and the conservative crowd that favoured this sort of establishment were wrapping up their evenings.

Gabe let his eyes run idly around the room. It was everything he'd come to expect in this kind of place, from the glistening chandeliers that sparkled overhead to the sumptuous burgundy velvet curtains adorning the windows, to the menu and wine list that were both six-star.

The waitress approached with the wine and he gestured that she should fill up his companions' glasses. For Gabe's part, he wasn't a big drinker, and certainly not with men he hardly knew. Discretion was the better part of valour—another lesson he'd learned a year ago. No, that wasn't true. He'd known it all his life. She'd just made him forget.

His eyes wandered once more, this time towards the kitchens, concealed behind large white doors that flapped silently as staff moved quickly through them. Inside, he knew, would be a hive of activity, despite the calm serenity of the restaurant dining room. The doors flicked open and for the briefest moment Gabe was certain he saw her.

A flick of white-blonde hair, a petite figure, pale skin.

He gripped the stem of his empty wine glass, his whole body stilled, like a predator on alert.

It wasn't her. Of course it wasn't.

In the kitchen? Had that been a dishcloth in her hand? Not possible.

He homed back in on the conversation at the table, laughing at a joke, nodding at something someone said, but every few moments his eyes shifted towards the doors, trying to get a better look at the ghost of Christmas last.

Gabe wasn't a man to leave things to chance. He'd experienced enough random acts, enough of fate's whimsy, to know that he would never again let life surprise him.

She had surprised him though, that night. What was it about the woman that had got under his skin? She was beautiful, but so were many women, and Gabe wasn't a man who let a woman's appearance overpower him. In fact, he prided himself on being more interested in a woman's mind. Her intellect. The decency of her soul and conscience.

And yet she'd walked into the bar of his Manhattan hotel and their eyes had sparked. Then he'd held his breath for the longest time, waiting for her to say something, needing to hear her voice and to know all about her instantly.

What madness had overtaken him that night?

It hadn't been a random spark though. Their meeting had been planned meticulously. He forced himself to return his attention to his guests, but his mind was on that long-ago night, a night he usually tried not to remember. A night he would never forget. Not because it had been so wonderful—though at the time he thought it had been—but because of the lessons it had taught him.

Don't trust anyone. Ever. Except for Noah, Gabe was alone in this world, and that was the way he wanted it.

Still, the mystery of the vision of Abby remained, so that, as the night wore on and cars were called for the investors, he gestured towards the maître d'.

'How has your evening been, Mr Arantini?' the man asked with an obsequious bow. Gabe might have grown up dirt-poor, but he'd been phenomenally wealthy for a long time now; such marked deference was not new to him. He'd even come to find it amusing.

Gabe didn't answer the question. There was no need. If he hadn't found the evening a success, the maître d' would have heard about it well before then. 'I'd like to speak to Rémy,' he said silkily.

'The chef?'

Gabe lifted a brow. 'Unless you have two Remys working this evening.'

The maître d' laughed a little self-consciously. 'Not at all, sir. Just the one.'

'Then I'll let myself into the kitchen.' He stood and spun

on his heel, stalking towards the doors without allowing the maître d' a reply.

At the doors, though, he hesitated for the briefest moment, bracing himself for the likelihood that he might come face to face with her once more. And the greater likelihood that he would not.

So?

Why did that bother him?

If he'd wanted to see Abigail Howard again, he'd had ample opportunities. She'd called him relentlessly, desperate to 'apologise' for her part in the scam. Desperate to see him, to make amends. Didn't she realise how futile those efforts were? As if Gabe could ever forgive such a betrayal! He'd left her in little doubt as to how he felt when she'd turned up at his office in Rome—for heaven's sake—demanding to see him.

That had been six months ago. Six months after she'd bargained her innocence for a glimpse at top secret Calypso files on behalf of her father. His blood still curdled at what that night had been about—at what she'd been willing to give up for commercial success.

He'd known a lot of manipulative characters in his time, but none so abhorrent as she'd been.

The satisfaction of having his security remove her from his office had been immense. She'd come to Rome to see him and he'd made it painstakingly obvious that he'd never see her again.

So? What was he doing now? Hovering outside a restaurant kitchen because he thought he'd caught a glimpse of her? And how could he possibly have recognised her in the brief moment the blonde had walked past the doors? It wasn't physically possible, he told himself, all the while knowing he *had* recognised something about the woman. The lithe grace of her walk. The elegance of her neck as she turned her head, hair that was like clouds at sunset, glowing with the evening's rays.

Great.

Now he was becoming poetic about a woman who'd seduced him with the sole intention of ruining him.

He tightened his shoulders and pushed into the kitchen. It wasn't so busy as he'd thought earlier. The dinner rush was over, and now there were chefs prepping for the next day's service, some cleaning, some standing around talking. His eyes skimmed the kitchen and his stomach dropped unexpectedly.

She wasn't here. This was a men-only zone at present— something he'd never allow in any of his hotels or restaurants. Within his and Noah's company, Bright Spark Inc, they demanded equal gender representation across the board. They invested heavily in STEM projects for schools—they were both passionate about playing fields being levelled as much as possible, having been on the dodgy end of their own playing fields for a long time.

'Rémy,' he said smoothly, striding across the kitchen.

'Ah! Arantini!' The chef grinned. 'You like your dinner?'

'Exceptional.' Gabe nodded, annoyingly put out by having come into the kitchens and not found the woman he'd seen.

'You had the lobster?'

'Of course.'

'Always your favourite,' Rémy chuckled.

Gabe nodded, just as the cold room door opened and the woman stepped out. Her head was bent, but he'd have known her body anywhere, any time and in any clothes.

True, the night they'd met she'd been dripping in the latest couture, but now? She wore simple jeans, a black T-shirt and a black and white apron tied twice around her slender waist. Her hair was pulled into a ballerina bun and her face, he saw as she lifted it, was bare of make-up.

His gut twisted and a strong possessive instinct hammered through him.

She'd been his in bed. That hadn't been just about Calypso. She'd wanted him. She'd given him her virginity, she'd begged him to take her, and he'd thought it a gift. A special, beautiful moment. He'd never been anyone's 'first' before.

She placed the containers she was carrying onto the bench and then lifted her eyes to the clock above the doors. She hadn't seen him, and he was glad for that. Glad to have a moment to observe her, to remember all the reasons he had for hating this woman, to regain his composure before showing her how little he thought of her.

When he'd had her evicted from his office in Rome, he'd told himself it was for the best. He never wanted to see her again, and nothing could change that. But here, in this six-star Manhattan hotspot, looking nothing like his usual romantic quarry, Gabe knew he'd been lying to himself.

He'd wanted to see her again and again. He drank in the sight of her, knowing it could only ever be this minute, this weakness, this moment of indulgence, before he would be forced to remember that she'd planned to ruin him.

Bright Spark Inc wasn't just a business to him. It was his and Noah's life. It had saved them when their own futures had been bleak and they'd been desperate for a fresh start.

And she'd wanted to destroy it. She'd come to him specifically to steal Calypso's secrets. It was a crime for which there could never be sufficient repentance.

'Rémy.' He spoke deliberately, slowly, and loud enough that she heard. He had the satisfaction of seeing her head jerk towards him the moment the word was uttered, saw shock flood her huge, expressive green eyes, saw the colour drain from her face and the telling way she pressed her palms into the counter. 'You have a traitor in your midst.'

Rémy frowned, following Gabe's gaze across the restaurant. 'A…traitor?'

'*Sì*.' Gabe moved across the room, closer to where she stood. She was trembling slightly now, her expression unmistakably terrified. His own expression remained cool and dismissive, the aloofness he was famed for evident in every line of his hard, muscular frame. No one in that kitchen could have known that beneath his autocratic face and strong body was a pulse that was rushing like a stormy sea.

'What are you talking about?'

'This woman,' Gabe said with quiet determination, 'isn't who you think.' He flicked his gaze from her head to her stomach—which was all he could see of her, owing to the large bench she stood behind. 'She's a liar and a cheat. She's no doubt working here to pick up whatever secrets she can from your customers. If you care at all about your reputation, you'll fire her.'

Rémy moved to stand beside Gabe, his face showing confusion. 'Abby's worked here for over a month.'

'Abby…' Gabe lifted a brow, his expression laced with mockery. It was the name she'd given him too. Far more endearing than Abigail Howard—billion-dollar heiress. 'I think *Abby* is having a laugh at your expense.'

The woman swallowed, the slender column of her throat moving overtime as she sought to moisten her mouth. Gabe caught the betraying gesture with a cynical tilt of his lips.

'That's not true, I swear,' she said, her fingers trembling when she lifted them to her temple and rubbed. Gabe's eyes narrowed. She looked tired. As though she'd been run off her feet all day.

'Oh, you *swear*?' he drawled, moving closer, pressing his palms against the bench. 'You mean we have your *word* that you're telling the truth?'

The words were dripping with sarcasm.

'Please don't do this,' she said softly, with such an appearance of anguish that Gabe could almost have believed her. If he hadn't personally seen what she was capable of.

'Did you know this woman is worth a billion dollars, Rémy? And you've got her, what? Ferrying things from the cold rooms?'

Rémy's surprise was obvious. 'I think you've got the wrong idea about Abby,' he said with a shake of his head, dislodging the pen he kept hooked over one ear.

Gabe's laugh was a short sound of derision. 'I know, better than most, what she's capable of. And, I can tell you, you don't want her anywhere near your patrons.'

'Abby?' Rémy spread his hands wide. 'What's going on?'

She opened her mouth to say something and then shut it again.

Rémy pushed, 'Have you met Mr Arantini before?'

Her eyes flew to Gabe's and, damn it, memories of her straddling him, staring into his eyes as she took him deep within her, spread like wildfire through his blood, burning him from the inside out. He didn't want to remember what she'd been like in his bed. He needed to recall only the way it had ended—with her taking photographs of top secret Calypso documents when she'd believed him to be showering.

His jaw hardened and he leaned forward.

'Tell him how we met, Abigail,' he suggested, and a cold smile iced his lips, almost as though he was enjoying this. He wasn't.

She blinked her eyes closed. 'It doesn't matter,' she muttered under her breath. 'It's ancient history.'

'If only it were,' he said softly. 'But here you are in my friend's kitchen and knowing you, as I do, I can't help but believe you have an ulterior motive.'

'I needed a job,' she said with a shake of her head. 'That's all.'

'Yes, I'm sure you did.' Gabe laughed, but it was a harsh

sound, without any true mirth. 'Trust funds are so hard to live off, aren't they?'

'Please—' she focused her energy on Rémy '—I do know this man…' Her eyes shifted to Gabe and her frown deepened. She was an exceptional actress. He could almost have believed she was truly feeling some hint of remorse. Pain. Embarrassment. But he'd been wrong about her once before and he'd never make that mistake again. 'A long time ago. But that's not relevant to why I'm here. I applied for this job because I wanted to work with you. Because I wanted to work. And I'm good at what I do, aren't I?'

Rémy tilted his head. 'Yes,' he conceded. 'But I trust Mr Arantini. We've known one another a long time. If he says I shouldn't have you working here, that I can't trust you…'

Abby froze, disbelief etched across her face. 'You *can* trust me.'

'Like you can trust a starving pit bull at your back door,' Gabe slipped in.

'Monsieur Valiron, I promise you I'm not here for any reason except that I need a job.'

'Needing a job? Another lie,' Gabe said.

'You don't know what you're talking about.' She glared at him and the heat in that look surprised him. The vehemence of her anger. It was as though she were driven to defend herself by something other than pride, by true desperation. He'd felt it often enough to recognise it.

'You forget how well I know what I'm talking about,' he said smoothly. 'You're just lucky I didn't press charges.'

She drew in a shaky breath. 'Mr Arantini,' she said crisply, 'I've moved on from…that…how we met. And you obviously have too.' She blinked her eyes and he had a sinking feeling in his gut that she was trying not to cry.

Hell. He'd never made a woman cry, had he?

Even that night, when he'd accused her, she'd been shocked and devastated, but she hadn't cried. She'd taken his tirade, admitted that her father had asked her to contrive a way to meet him, to get close to him and find out all she could about Calypso, and then she'd apologised. And left.

'I'm not asking you to forgive me for what happened between us.'

'Good,' he interrupted forcibly, wishing now he had a glass of something strong he could drink.

'But please don't ruin this for me.' She turned back to Rémy. 'I'm not lying to you, *monsieur*. I need this job. I have no plans to do anything that will reflect badly on you...'

Rémy frowned. 'I want to believe you, Abby...'

Gabe turned slowly towards his friend, and his expression was cold, unemotional. 'Trusting this woman would be a mistake.'

Abby was numb. It had nothing to do with the snow that was drifting down over New York, turning it into a beautiful winter wonderland, nor the fact she'd left the restaurant in such a hurry she'd forgotten to grab her coat—or her tips.

She swore softly, her head dipped forward, tears running down her cheeks. What were the chances of Gabe Arantini walking into the kitchen of the restaurant she happened to work in? Of his being friendly enough with her boss to actually have her fired?

A sob escaped her and she stopped walking, dipping into an alleyway and pressing herself against the wall for strength.

She'd never thought she'd see him again. She'd tried. She'd tried when she'd thought it mattered. She'd tried when she'd thought it was the right thing to do. But now?

Another sob sounded and she bit down on her lip. He hated her.

She'd always known that, but seeing his cold anger filled

her with doubts and fears, making her question what she knew she had to do.

When had he come to New York? Had he been here long? Had he thought of her at all?

She had to see him again—but how? She'd tried calling him so many times, and every call had been unreturned or disconnected. Emails bounced back. She'd even flown to Rome, but he had two burly security men haul her from the building.

So what now?

It would serve that heartless bastard right if she didn't bother. If she skulked off, licking her wounds, keeping her secrets, and doing just what he'd asked: staying the hell away from him.

But it wasn't about what she wanted, nor was it about what Gabe wanted.

She had to think of their baby, Raf—and what he deserved.

Her chest hurt with the pain of the life she was giving their son. Their tiny apartment, their parlous financial state, the fact she worked so hard she barely got to see him, and instead had to have a downstairs neighbour come and stay overnight to help out. It was a mess. And Raf deserved so much better.

For Raf, and Raf alone, Abigail had to find a way to see Gabe—and to tell him the truth.

And this time she wasn't going to let him turn her away without hearing her out first.

# CHAPTER TWO

'THERE'S A MISS HOWARD here to see you, sir,' Benita, his assistant, spoke into the intercom.

From the outside Gabe barely reacted, but inside he felt surprise rock him to the core. She'd come to his damned office? What the actual hell? How many times did he have to tell her to stay away from him?

He reached for his phone, lifting it out of the cradle. 'Did you say…?'

'Miss Howard.'

He tightened his grip on the receiver and stared straight ahead. It was a grey day. A gloomy sky stretched over Manhattan, though he knew at street level the city was buzzing with a fever of pre-Christmas activity.

It was on the tip of his tongue to tell his assistant to call the police, when he remembered a small detail. The way Abigail had been two nights earlier, her eyes wet with unshed tears, her lip quivering. As though she really *did* need that menial job.

He knew it to be a lie, of course. But what was the truth? What ruse was she up to? What game was she playing? Was she looking to hurt Rémy? Or was her latest scheme more complex?

He owed it to his friend to find out. But not here. His office was littered with all manner of documents someone like Abigail would find valuable.

'Tell her I'm busy. She can wait for me, if she'd like,' he said, knowing full well she would wait—and that he'd enjoy stretching that out as long as possible.

He stayed at his desk for the remainder of the day. Hours passed. He caught up on his emails, read the latest report from his warehouse in China, called Noah. It was nearly six when Benita buzzed through.

'I'm all done for the day, Mr Arantini. Unless there's anything else you need?'

'No, Benita.'

'Also, sir, Miss Howard is still here.'

His lips flattened into a grim line. Of course she was.

'Tell her I'm aware she's waiting.'

He disconnected the call and picked up the latest report on Calypso's production, but struggled to focus. Five hours after she'd arrived, the suspense was getting under his skin.

With a heavy sigh, he stood, lifted his jacket from the back of a conference chair and pushed his arms into it, before pulling the door between his office and the reception area open.

It was still well-lit, but the windows behind Abigail were pitch-black. The night sky was heavy and ominous. Despite the fact Christmas was a month away, an enormous tree stood in one corner, and it shone now with the little lights that had been strung through its branches. They cast an almost angelic glow on Abigail. An optical illusion, obviously. There was nothing angelic about this woman.

Her eyes lifted to him at the sound of his entrance, and he ignored the instant spark of attraction that fired in his gut. He was attracted to character traits—intelligence, loyalty, strength of character, integrity. She had none of those things. Well, intelligence, he conceded, but in a way she used for pure evil.

'What do you want?' he asked, deliberately gruff.

She seemed surprised—by his tone? Or the fact he'd actually appeared?

'I didn't think you were going to see me,' she said, confirming that it was the latter. 'I thought you must have already left.'

'My first instinct was to have you removed,' he said.

'You know I'm capable of it.' Now heat stained her cheeks, and her chin tilted defiantly towards him. 'But then it occurred to me that I should find out what you're planning.'

'Planning?'

'Mmm. You must have some reason for working in my friend's kitchen. So? What is it?'

She shook her head. 'Gabe…'

'I prefer you to call me Mr Arantini,' he said darkly. 'It better suits what I think of you and how little I wish to know you.'

She swallowed, and the action drew his attention to the way she'd dressed for this meeting. That was to say, with no particular attempt to impress. Jeans again, though she did wear them well, and a black sweater with a bit of beading around the neckline. She wore ballet slippers on her feet, black as well, but scuffed at the toes.

Her eyes sparked with his, emotions swirling in them. 'Gabe,' she repeated, with a strength he found it difficult not to admire. Not many people could be on the receiving end of Gabe's displeasure and come out fighting. 'The night we met, I was…'

'Stop.' He lifted a hand into the air, his manner imperious. 'I do not want to rehash the past. I don't care about you. I don't care about your father. I don't care about that night except for one reason. You taught me a lesson I'll never forget. I let my guard down with you in a way I hadn't done in years. And you reminded me why I don't make a habit of that.' He said with a shrug that was an emulation of nonchalance, 'Now I want you to get out of my life, for the last time.'

'Listen to me,' she said.

'No!' It was a harsh denial in a silent room. 'Not when every word that comes from your mouth is a self-serving lie.'

She clamped her lips together and his eyes chased the gesture, remembering how her pillowy lower lip had felt between his teeth. A kick of desire flared inside him. Desire? For this woman?

What was wrong with him?

Celibacy, that was what. He should have found someone else for his bed before this—why had he let the ghost of Abby fill his soul for so long?

'You traded your body, your looks, hell, your virginity, because of what it could get you. That makes you no better than...'

He didn't finish the sentence but his implication hung between them, angry and accusing.

'I wanted you, Gabe, just like you wanted me. Calypso wasn't a part of that.' She blinked up at him, and he felt it. The same charge of electricity shot from her to him that had characterised that first night, their first meeting. It was a bolt of lightning; he was rattled by heavy, drugging need. God, would he forgive himself for acting on it? For leaning down and kissing her, for pushing her to the floor and making her his one last time before kicking her out of his life for good?

No.

She had used him; he wouldn't use her.

That wasn't his style. And, no matter how great the sex had been, he sure as hell wasn't going to compromise his own morals just because he happened to find her desirable.

He jerked his gaze away and thrust his hands onto his hips with all the appearance of disregard. 'I don't want you now,' he lied.

'I know that,' she said, a hint of strength in the short words.

'So? What's your plan, Abigail? Why work for Rémy?'

'I need the job—I told you.'

'Yes, yes.' He rolled his eyes. 'You think I'm stupid enough to buy into your lies for a second time?'

She looked startled. 'It's not...it's complicated. And I

can't tell you what I came here to say with you glaring at me like you want to strangle me.'

He almost laughed—it was such an insane accusation. 'I don't want to strangle you,' he said. 'I don't want to touch you. I don't want to see you. I'd prefer to think you don't exist.'

She let out a slow, shuddering breath. 'You actually hate me.'

'*Sì.*'

'Okay.' She licked her lower lip. 'I get it. That's…actually strangely good to know.'

'You didn't know this already?'

She shook her head and then changed it to a nod, before pacing slowly across the room. She jammed her hands into her pockets, staring at the shining doors of the lift.

Gabe's impatience grew. He couldn't have said if it was an impatience to be rid of her or a need to know what the hell she'd come to him to say. Why had he been able to ignore her for a year and now suddenly he was burning up with a desperate need to hear whatever the hell she'd come to him for?

Because he'd seen her again. And he'd felt that same tug of powerful attraction, that was why. He needed to exercise caution—it was a slippery slope with Abigail, almost as though she were a witch, imbued with magical powers to control and contort him. There was danger in her proximity. The sooner he could be free of her, the better.

'So?' he demanded when she didn't speak. 'What's going on? Why are you here? What do you want this time?'

She was wary. 'Well, I'd like my job back,' she said, somewhat sarcastically.

'Pigs might fly,' he said. 'You're just lucky I didn't tell Rémy the full sordid story of how we met.'

'Would it have mattered? He fired me anyway.' She narrowed her eyes. 'Did that give you satisfaction? To see me embarrassed like that? To see me thrown out?'

He considered it for a moment, his expression hard. 'Yes.'

She squeezed her eyes shut and tilted her head towards the ceiling, breathing in, steadying herself. 'You're a bastard.'

'So I've been told.'

He looked down at her again. She was slim. Too slim. Her figure had been pleasingly rounded when they'd met, curves in all the places Gabe—and any red-blooded man—fantasised about. Now, she was supermodel slender.

Her body was a minefield of distraction, but he'd been down that path before. No good would come from worshipping her physical perfection. He refocused his attention on the matter at hand: the sooner they dealt with it, the sooner she'd be gone and this would be over.

'Why does it matter?' he demanded. 'We both know you don't need to work—even if poor Rémy was foolish enough to believe your act. So, what's the big deal?'

'You're wrong.'

'Rarely.'

'I needed that job. I needed the money.'

'Your father's company?' he asked, frowning, a hint of something like genuine interest colouring the words. 'It hasn't gone bankrupt?' He'd have heard, surely.

'No—' she shook her head '—I think he's holding it together. But I don't know. I haven't spoken to him in a long time.'

'Oh?' Gabe was no longer losing interest in this. His blood was racing through his body and he took a step towards her, unconsciously moving closer. 'Why is that?'

She swallowed, and appeared to be weighing her words—something Gabe hated. Liars always thought about what they wanted to say, and she was an exceptional liar.

'He threw me out,' she said, the words tremulous even though her eyes met his with a fierce strength.

'He…threw you out?' Gabe, rarely surprised, felt that emotion now. 'Your father?'

'Yes.'

Why was he so shocked? He knew enough of cruel fathers and their ability to abuse their children's affections to know Lionel Howard was capable of everything Abigail claimed.

'Because of me?'

She nodded.

Gabe's curse was softly voiced but forceful, and it filled the room. 'Your father threw you out because you didn't have photos of the Calypso project?'

'No.' She shook her head, her skin pale. 'Not exactly.'

Gabe waited, but his impatience was making it difficult.

'I mean, he was furious that morning. Furious that I had come back empty-handed. But it was a fury born of desperation, you know? He was desperate, Gabe. My dad isn't a bad person, he's just…'

'Why,' he interrupted coldly, 'do you think I want to talk about your father?'

'You have to understand…'

She was quicksand. He'd let her in and now he was sinking—back into her web of lies, her intriguing fascination. What a fool he'd been to think he could talk to her and not fall down this rabbit hole of desire.

'No, I don't. I don't "have" to do anything where you're concerned. I don't know why you're here. I don't know why I didn't have you escorted from the building. But I'm done. This is over.'

'Wait.' She licked her lower lip and then lifted her hand to her hair, toying with the ends in an unmistakably nervous gesture. 'I'm trying to explain.'

'Explain what?'

'That night—it wasn't what you think. I mean, I know I came to you because of Calypso, but from the minute I met you, that was just about you and me, and the way we felt.'

'And yet you still took photographs. You thought you could have your cake and eat it too? A night with me *and* the chance to salvage your father's company thrown into the mix?'

'No. I didn't think it through, obviously.' She pulled a face. 'I know it's no excuse and it must sound pathetic to someone like you. It's just… I've always done what he asked of me. It's hard to rewire that.'

'He asked you to do something borderline illegal.'

'I know!' she growled—a growl born of self-disgust. 'I wish, again and again, I could undo that night.' Her cheeks flushed. 'I mean, not *all* of it.'

'Ah,' he said with dangerous softness. 'Here we differ. Because if I had my way I would go back in time and *never* meet you. Never set eyes on you, never kiss you, never ask you to my room. I would undo every little bit of what we shared. I regret *everything* about knowing you.'

Her mouth dropped open. He'd hurt her. He'd shocked her. Good. He recognised, in the part of his brain that was still working properly, that he liked that. He liked seeing that pain on her face. She deserved it. It was only a hint of how he'd felt when he'd discovered that his lover was actually some kind of corporate spy.

'And now,' he said, 'if you'll excuse me, I have a date.'

Yes. He'd definitely landed that blow successfully. She physically reeled, spinning away from him in a poor attempt to conceal her reaction.

'When I told Dad I hadn't met you, he was angry. Angry because he'd told me exactly where you'd be. Angry because he thought I hadn't tried hard enough.'

'Yet you're an accomplished liar,' Gabe pointed out. 'So I'm sure you managed to win him over.'

She didn't react. Her eyes were glazed over, as though she were in the past. 'Not really. I mean, he stopped being mad with me, but his business worries grew. He was losing his market share to you; he has been for years—'

'It's not *his* market share. It's anyone's for the taking. And the only reason Bright Spark is at the top of the ladder is because we release better products than our competitors.'

'I know.' She nodded, almost apologetically. 'I'm just explaining his mindset.'

'Whatever his mindset, you are your own person. You made a decision to manipulate me...'

'I'm talking about after that,' she said with quiet determination. 'You know I've been trying to contact you.'

He tilted his head. 'Apologies are fruitless, Abigail. There is no apology you could offer that would inspire my forgiveness. You're a liar and a cheat.'

She shook her head but didn't say anything. 'It was bad at home. I was worried about him, and I didn't feel well.'

Gabe lifted his brows.

'When did you not feel well?'

'A few months after we...after that night. I'd been tired—yet not sleeping.'

'Guilt will do that to a person. Then again, I don't know if you're capable of feeling guilt.'

'Believe me, I am,' she promised, the words steady, so that he was at risk of believing her despite everything he knew her to be. 'I've felt a bucketload of it since I met you. Anyway, I went to the doctor and...you can probably guess where I'm going with this.'

'No,' he said with a lift of his shoulders. 'And frankly I'm bored of our conversation.'

'Right, you have your date,' she said, the words almost manic.

'Yes,' Gabe lied. Well, not strictly a lie. There were any number of women he could call. Just because he hadn't done so in over a year didn't mean they wouldn't jump at the chance for a night with Gabe Arantini. He stared at Abigail for one long moment and then made to walk past her, only she reached out and grabbed his arm. 'Gabe, stop. You need to let me say this.'

'Why do you think I owe you anything?'

'I was pregnant,' she said, arresting him in his tracks completely. His eyes locked onto hers and in his face was a torrent of emotions. There was anger, disbelief, confusion, fury and, finally, amusement.

'Nice try, Abigail, but I don't believe you. You think this is a way to extort money from me? Or ruin me somehow? Is this your father's idea?'

'No!' She was pale and shaking. 'Gabe, I'm not making this up. I went to the doctor and they ran some tests. I was pregnant. You're the only man I've ever been with.'

His eyes narrowed.

'I didn't tell Dad until I was five months along and I started to show. He demanded to know who the father was and when I told him he…'

Gabe could barely keep up, but somehow he answered calmly. 'Yes?'

'He kicked me out. He cut me off. I haven't seen him since.'

Gabe felt as though he'd been punched in the solar plexus. He couldn't speak.

'It's why I need that job. Why I'm working nights. I have a good babysitter who sleeps over, so I can work at night. And in the days I'm with Raf.'

His eyes flew wide. 'Raf?'

'Rafael,' she said with a small, distracted smile. 'Our son.'

Silence fell, heavy and caustic, in the room. Gabe processed what she'd said, but it simply didn't make sense.

'We used protection.'

'I know.'

'It's not possible.'

'The three-month-old I have at home would beg to differ,' she said calmly, even when her nerves were jangling.

Gabe nodded, a coldness to his expression. 'What is this? You want money? Or something else?'

'I thought you should know,' she said with hauteur, reminding him of the silver spoon she'd grown up with.

'You thought I should know that I'm a father. That supposedly the night we were together, you fell pregnant. How convenient!'

'Not particularly,' Abby said with a soft laugh.

'Do you think I am this stupid? That I'll listen to these lies? I should have followed my first instincts and had you kicked out. What the hell are you playing at?'

'It's the *truth*,' she said. 'I have a son. His name is Raf Arantini and he's the spitting image of his father.'

Gabe glared at her. She'd even used his name? Could it be true?

Presumably she hadn't been on birth control, but he never slept with a woman without protection. And he'd never had any consequences come from his sex life before. So why now? And why this woman?

Because she was a liar. And though he couldn't see the full picture, he knew with confidence that there was more to this story than she was telling him. It *couldn't* be the truth. There was no way on earth he had a baby.

He needed time and space to think, and he sure as hell couldn't do that with her in the room.

'Get out of my office, Abigail. And don't contact me again.'

He walked to the lift and pressed the button; it pinged open almost instantly.

She walked slowly and as she passed him he caught

just a hint of her sweet vanilla fragrance. His whole body clenched.

'You don't believe me?' she asked.

'Do you blame me?'

Tears welled in her eyes but she met his eyes with obvious defiance. 'It's the truth.'

'I don't think you'd know the truth if it bit you on that perfect little arse of yours.'

# CHAPTER THREE

ABIGAIL STARED OUT of the window, unseeing. It was a cold, snowy night, but she hadn't put the heating on. Raf was bundled up in a fleecy suit and wrapped in blankets, fast asleep, and she was wearing about six layers. She wrapped her hands around her hot chocolate—it was a pale imitation, seeing as she'd taken to making it with water instead of milk, but it was still sweet and warm—desperately necessary after the day she'd had.

She'd gone over her conversation with Gabe all evening—while he was no doubt out at some glamorous restaurant or bar with an equally glamorous woman. He probably wasn't even giving her a second thought. Why would he be? He'd made it clear he despised her and, more importantly, didn't believe her. So why would he be thinking about a baby he didn't believe existed?

She should have shown him a photograph, but Abigail hadn't been thinking straight. A photograph would have convinced him of his paternity. They were so alike—Raf had Gabe's dark eyes, his strong determined brow and curling black hair, though the dimples in his cheeks were all Abby's. She curled up in the armchair by the window and watched as a child dressed as an elf ran past, followed by a happy-looking mum and dad, also wearing elf hats.

Fliers had been up in the street for weeks—tonight was one of the local school's Christmas concerts—which explained why there'd been a procession of Wise Men and reindeer shuffling around her Brooklyn neighbourhood since she'd returned.

While Abigail hadn't expected Gabe to be doing cartwheels about the fact he was a father, nor had she expected his reaction—utter disbelief.

For months, she'd tried to find a way to tell him about the baby they'd conceived. First, when she'd been pregnant, and then once Raf had been born. It had never, not for an instant, occurred to her that he wouldn't believe her. She had run through almost every contingency—but not this one.

The coldness of his expression as she'd stepped into the lift and turned back to face him would always be etched into her mind. He *hated* her. He'd said as much, and in that moment she knew it to be true.

So, what was she going to do?

She looked around the apartment, empty save for a threadbare chair, a plastic table, a lamp that she'd bought at a thrift shop, and she felt hopelessness well inside her.

Even with her job, she'd barely been making ends meet. Now? She had forty-seven dollars in her bank account, rent was due and her baby needed formula and nappies. Before long, he'd need actual food and bigger clothes, and then what?

She couldn't keep living like this. Raf deserved so much better.

She finished the hot chocolate and placed the empty cup on the floor at her feet and then curled her legs up beneath her.

Exhaustion was nothing new to Abigail. Pregnancy had been exhausting and she'd been sick almost the whole time. But then Raf had been born and she'd discovered that motherhood was a little like being hit by a truck. She was bone-weary all the time.

Her eyes were heavy and she was so tired that even the thought of getting up, showering and changing for bed seemed too onerous and so she stayed where she was, telling herself she'd just sleep for a moment. Just a little rest. Then she'd go to bed, wake up in the new day and scour the papers for help wanted ads. She'd get a new job. Gabe couldn't have her fired from every place in the city.

A knock at the door woke her after drifting off. It was persistent and loud—so loud she was certain it would wake Raf if she didn't act quickly. She scrambled up and moved towards the door, yanking it inwards without taking the precaution of checking who was there—a foolish risk given that the downstairs security door had been busted for weeks.

Still, she had thought it might be the upstairs neighbour, Mrs Hannigan, who seemed to always need something at inconvenient times. Even this though—nearly midnight—was a stretch for her.

Abby hadn't expected—foolishly, perhaps—to find Gabe Arantini on her doorstep, his handsome face lined with emotions she couldn't comprehend.

'Gabe?' The word was thick with sleepiness. She ran the back of her hand over her eyes in an attempt to wake up, but it only induced a yawn. 'What are you doing here? How did you find where I live?'

His response was to brush past her and step into her apartment.

'By all means, come right in,' she snapped sarcastically. But the tart emotion disappeared almost as soon as it had arrived, swallowed by a sense of self-consciousness for him to be seeing her threadbare apartment.

'Where is he?'

'I… He's sleeping.'

'Of course he is,' he said, the same thread of incredulity in his words now as had been there earlier that day.

He still didn't believe her? How was that possible? She would just show him a photo. Her phone was on the chair. She'd get it and show some pictures to him. Then he'd have no doubt that she was telling the truth. She moved in that direction but his voice stilled her.

'Stop, Abigail.'

She froze, turning around to face him once more. He was right behind her, his body close to hers, his angular face filling her vision.

'No more lies.'

'I'm not lying to you.'

He lifted a finger and pressed it to her lips. 'I think you don't even realise you're doing it,' he said. 'I think you've lost sight of what's true and what's not.'

'I...'

'Shh...' he said again, shaking his head. 'I didn't come here to hear more lies...'

'Then why...?'

His eyes held hers and Abigail grabbed a deep breath because she knew what was coming and she had about two seconds to decide what she would do. Step backwards, away from him, or surrender to the intimacy of his kiss, even knowing it was stupid and wrong and wouldn't achieve anything?

But oh, how she craved him. Ached for him. Desperately longed for him.

He was going to kiss her and she was going to let him. Heck, *she* was going to kiss *him* if he took much longer. The air around them seemed to hum and crackle with anticipation, their eyes locked, their lips parted. Time seemed to stand still. It was madness, but hadn't it always been for them?

He dropped his head infinitesimally closer and she pressed a little higher, waiting, her mind blanked of the myriad reasons she shouldn't let this happen.

Then he blinked and straightened.

'What the hell is that?'

The question jolted her, dragging her out of the sensual fog.

'Raf!' She shot him a look of frustration and sanity

began to seep back in. Gratitude too. How could she have let herself get sucked back into his sensual, distracting appeal?

In the seconds it took her to compute the situation, Gabe was already moving to the hallway. There was a bathroom on one side and a bedroom on the other. He followed the sound of the crying and pushed into the bedroom. He stood just inside the door, staring at the crib as though he'd never seen a baby in his entire life.

'Excuse me,' Abby said, moving past him to scoop up Raf. He nuzzled into her and she stroked his head, her eyes lifting to Gabe's with a hint of triumph in their depths.

'What is this?' he finally asked, dumbfounded.

'What do you think?'

'It's a baby.'

She could have laughed; it was so absurd. 'Yes, it's a baby. This is your son. You may remember I told you about him this afternoon?'

'I…' Gabe stared at the child with a look of utter confusion.

'He needs to go back to sleep,' she said, nodding towards the door. And purely because he was at such a loss he did as she suggested and stepped out of the room, leaving her to settle Raf on her own.

When Abby emerged a few moments later, Gabe was in the centre of the tiny living room, his expression grim.

'You were telling the truth.'

'Yes!' she said emphatically. 'Why would you think I wasn't?'

He frowned. 'You need to ask that?'

'Gabe, I made a mistake that night. Admittedly, a big one. I get why you're mad. But it was a *mistake*. A stupid decision. Contrary to what you might think, I don't make a habit of lying to people.'

He rubbed his palm over his face and shook his head. 'How is this even possible?'

'Really? You need me to explain how that works?'

'I mean, we used protection.'

'Yeah. The doctor said that's not infallible.'

He grimaced. 'It was your first time. This shouldn't have been possible.'

'Okay, you need to stop saying that. You're the only man I've ever been with and nine months after that night, almost to the day, Raf was born. So, whether it should or shouldn't have been possible, that's what happened.'

'You should have told me,' he said, harsh judgement in the statement.

Abby made a primal noise of irritation, a growl born of pure annoyance. She would be the first to admit she'd messed up the night they'd met, but she wasn't going to be tarred with that brush for evermore. 'I tried to! Damn it, Gabe, why did you think I was calling you?'

He paled visibly beneath his tan. 'You... I presumed to apologise, or make up excuses.'

'No. I mean yes to the apology thing, but mainly, Gabe, I needed to tell you about Raf.'

'You're saying you didn't keep him from me intentionally?'

'Are you serious? Do you really think I'd do something so immoral?'

His eyes locked onto hers and she sighed.

'I guess you do think me capable of that. But Gabe, I would never, ever keep someone from their child. He's your son. I had no intention of doing this alone. That's why I went to Rome...'

'Rome.' His eyes swept shut, anguish on his features. 'You knew you were pregnant then? You came to tell me?'

'Yes!' Pique at his reaction darkened her expression. 'And you had me dragged out like some kind of criminal.'

'*Madre di Dio*, Abigail. I didn't know.'

'Yes, well,' she said stiffly. 'If you'd given me a minute

of your time, you'd have seen for yourself the evidence of my condition.'

'What do you mean?'

'I was six months along.'

'And they just dragged you out of the building?'

'Well, they told me in no uncertain terms to go before the police arrived,' she conceded.

'I asked them to do that,' he admitted darkly. 'I didn't want to see you. I was so angry you'd come.'

'I know.' She lifted her chin, defiance radiating from her slender frame. 'But don't you dare accuse me of intentionally keeping Raf from you.'

He shook his head, as if to clear the memory. 'I cannot believe I have a son.'

What could Abby say to that? It was the truth. She waited for something—perhaps an apology. A commendation of how well she'd done? An admission that she'd *tried* to do the right thing, to tell him the truth?

And got instead: 'And you're raising him here? Like this?'

Her spine straightened and she squared her shoulders. 'What's wrong with it?' she said.

'It is a hovel.' He glared at her. 'How can you live like this?'

Her jaw dropped. His assessment wasn't wrong but how dare he?

'It's fine,' she said through gritted teeth. 'And I'll find something better before he's big enough to notice. For *now*, this is fine,' she amended.

'This isn't *fine* for a pack of rabid dogs, let alone my *son*.'

She stared at him as though he'd called her the worst name in the book. 'I'm aware that it's not ideal. I'm not blind. But it's the best I could do at short notice and with very limited means.'

A muscle in his jaw throbbed and Abby stared at it, fas-

cinated by the pulse point there. 'So when your father discovered you were pregnant with my child, he turned you
out of his home?'

She winced. 'It was more complex than that. I mean, it
proved that I'd lied about that night. That I'd let him down.'

'Let him down?' Gabe repeated incredulously. '*Dio!* He
is unbelievable.'

'I know that,' she said. 'I never thought he'd react like
this. I mean, I thought he'd be angry, but not…'

'To remove all financial support from his pregnant
daughter, just because he hates me?' Something in Gabe
shifted and he was very still, his expression faraway, as
though completely consumed by unpleasant thoughts.

Abby waited, her breath unconsciously held, for him
to elaborate.

But in the end he shook his head. 'It doesn't matter. You
are no longer his responsibility.'

'I'm no one's responsibility,' she said stiffly, instantly
rejecting that assessment.

'Wrong, *cara*. You are mine.'

'No.' Abby's denial was swift.

'You are the mother of my child.'

Her hackles rose. 'I'm a woman you spent one night
with, a year ago.'

'*Sì*. And you fell pregnant. I should have prevented that.
I was experienced. This is my fault.'

'Your fault?' Now her maternal instincts roared to life.
'I don't consider Raf anyone's *fault*. He's a blessing.'

Gabe grimaced, uncharacteristically on the back foot.
'I didn't mean that the way it sounded.'

But she wasn't to be placated. She had to set the record straight while she had a chance—if she didn't control
this, the situation could quickly move beyond her control.
'You don't owe me anything, Gabe. I'm not asking for a
handout.'

'You live like *this*,' he said slowly, gesturing around the room, 'and you think I don't owe you anything?'

Frustration burst through her. 'I know this place isn't...'

'It's a dump.'

The insult hurt. 'It's home, for now.'

He crossed his arms over his chest, his expression intractable.

'You say you wanted to tell me about the baby?'

She nodded.

'And what did you expect me to say?'

Abby frowned, but her silence only seemed to spur him on. He took a step closer, his expression grim.

'What did you want from me?'

She swallowed, and tried to find the words of the speech she'd imagined she'd give him, if ever he learned the truth. 'Raf is your child too, and I respect the fact you might want to be involved in his upbringing.'

'Oh, yes?' he murmured, but there was a sharpness to the response, an underlying firmness she didn't understand.

'Your life is in Italy and we live here, but I mean, you visit the States and I guess, when he's older, he could come over...'

Her sentence tapered off into silence. His eyes held hers for a long, icy moment. Then, with a guttural sound of disgust, 'Look at this place, Abigail!' He glared at her. 'Why is it so cold? Why is the heating off?' He stalked into the kitchenette and ripped open the fridge. 'What are you existing on? I see two apples and one bread roll. What did you have for dinner?'

She bit down on her lip and ridiculous tears moistened her eyes. She dashed at them angrily. 'I'm not crying because I'm sad,' she clarified. 'I'm mad! And I'm tired! And you have no right turning up on my doorstep at midnight only to throw insults at my feet!'

'What did you think I would do? How am I supposed to react?'

'I…' She glared at him. 'I don't know. I just had to tell you.'

He dipped his head forward in silent concession. 'I'm grateful that you did. And for the fact you haven't used our son to attempt to blackmail me.'

'Blackmail you?' she repeated, aghast, flicking her fair hair over one shoulder. 'What would I blackmail you for?'

His laugh was short and sharp. 'Oh, I don't know. Money. Power. Calypso prototypes?'

Abby had never hit a man in her life—or anyone, for that matter, but her fingertips itched to strike his arrogant face. 'You're a jerk.'

'I'm the father of your child and, like it or not, I'm in your life now.'

She was very still, waiting for that thought to make sense. But it didn't. 'In my life how?'

Gabe shut the fridge door and moved to the pantry. It was almost empty, save for a tin of spaghetti and a bag of pasta.

'How quickly can you pack a suitcase?'

'Huh?' She watched as he stalked back into the small living room.

'Your wardrobe looked small. I presume you don't have much. Is there a bag somewhere?'

'I… No.' She'd sold her designer set of luggage as soon as she'd moved into the apartment.

'Fine. I'll have one sent over.'

'Gabe, wait.' She lifted a hand in a determined appeal for his silence. 'I don't need a suitcase. I'm not going any-where.'

He ignored her, speaking as though she hadn't. 'It's too late to depart now. You should go to bed. I'll…take the chair. We can leave in the morning.'

'And where exactly do you imagine we're going?'

'Italy.' He reached for his phone and, before she could respond, he began speaking into it. She had not a hope of comprehending as he spoke in his native tongue, but she picked out a few words—*bambino…andiamo…subito.*

He disconnected the call before giving Abby the full force of his attention.

'The plane will be ready in the morning. My car is downstairs. Tomorrow, Abigail, we will leave.'

She shook her head emphatically. 'No!'

'Yes.'

'I'm not going to Italy. This is my home. *His* home. And you… I know you're his father, but I didn't tell you so you'd take us away! I just wanted you to know because he's your child and at some stage he or you might want a relationship. I don't believe in secrets like this, okay? I have no right to keep a father from his child. But that's the end of it. I've done my part. I told you about Raf, and when he's older I'll tell him about you.'

His eyes narrowed and his chest lifted with the force of the deep breath he sucked in. 'Get ready. This is non-negotiable.'

'You're right. It's non-negotiable. We're staying here.'

'Make no mistake about it, Abigail, my son is coming to Italy. I am giving you a chance to come with him. The decision is yours.'

Panic flared in her gut but she hid it behind anger. 'There's no way you can do that.'

'Do you want to test that theory?'

'You seriously think I'm going to move to a foreign country with a man I hardly know?'

'No. I think you're going to move to a foreign country with the man you're going to marry.'

Her eyes flew wide and for a moment she thought she must have misheard. 'What did you just say?'

His jaw tightened. 'You heard me.'

'But that's crazy.'

He jerked his head in silent agreement.

She blinked. 'But why?'

Something like anguish shifted through his dark gaze, showing how clearly he wished this step weren't necessary. 'Because it's the right thing to do.'

'Right, how?' she demanded, wondering if she'd slipped through the looking glass into a bizarre parallel universe.

'Because of what I can offer him, and what I can offer you. The security, the comfort, the support.' He took a step closer. 'I'm offering you the world, Abigail. The world for you and our son.'

Her heart twisted painfully inside her chest. She was like an outsider looking in. In that moment, she realised that marrying Gabe Arantini would have, in another lifetime, constituted a fantasy. If things had been different between them, if they'd met under different circumstances and they'd been allowed to enjoy getting to know one another.

'This is the twenty-first century. People don't get married just because of a baby.'

His eyes narrowed and she had the strangest sense that he was holding back on saying what he really wanted to say. Through teeth that were bared like a wolf's, he said, 'My son is going to grow up with two parents.'

'Who hate each other? Do you really think that's best?'

'No.' His eyes glowed with silent warning. 'But it's the best decision you can make. I have a son, Abigail. A three-month-old boy I knew nothing about. If you think I am leaving this country without him, if you think I have any plans of walking out of his life, even temporarily, then you are deranged.'

She sucked in a breath but her lungs didn't fill sufficiently. She dug her fingernails into her palms, taking strength from the gesture. 'Then stay here,' she said after a moment, the words sounding reasonable and calm despite the tremors taking over her central nervous system.

He looked around the room with scathing contempt.

'Not *here* here,' she amended. 'In New York.'

His eyes locked onto hers. 'I have no intention of raising my child anywhere other than Italy. We will go there tomorrow and as soon as possible we will marry. Raf will grow up believing that he is wanted.'

'He is wanted by me!' she shouted and then winced at the very real possibility that such loud arguing would wake their son.

'And by me,' he said warningly.

'No. I think it's time for you to leave, Gabe. We can discuss this in the morning when you're thinking straight.'

'Do you think you have any right to dictate to me after what you've done?'

'What I've done?' she demanded, taking a step closer, wishing she were taller so that she didn't have to crane her neck to look up at him. 'And just what am I supposed to have done?'

'You set all this in motion when you came to my hotel last year. Even if there had been no baby, no Raf, you have still shown yourself capable of making very poor decisions.'

'You got that right,' Abby muttered. 'Sleeping with you was the biggest mistake of my life.'

She swept her eyes shut, instantly wishing she could retract the words because of course she could never really regret anything that had resulted in Raf. Besides, even without Raf, she'd be hard-pressed to regret what she and Gabe had shared. Only that her father's machinations had been the cause of it.

'I feel exactly the same way.' The coolly delivered response slammed right into her heart and suddenly all the emotions of the previous year filled her up, like water in a bathtub.

'Oh, go to hell,' she muttered, slumping back against the wall and dipping her head forward.

'I think I'm already there.'

The volley landed squarely in her chest, twisting her organs and supercharging her blood. She swallowed, but her throat was drier than the desert.

Two days ago she'd been working as a kitchen hand for one of New York's most renowned chefs. She'd been exhausted and lonely but she'd been making it work.

And now she had this man, this handsome, arrogant billionaire who she couldn't be in the same room as without breaking into a full-blown fight, demanding that she move halfway around the world and become his wife? Mrs Gabe Arantini?

She couldn't marry him! God, what a nightmare! Why had she ever thought she had to tell him about his son? At least without seeing a lawyer first! Why had she been so naive? She should have kept Raf hidden from him. She should have moved heaven and earth to avoid this.

What an idiot she was!

'I won't marry you,' she said angrily, her blood simmering. 'I can't. It would never work.'

'Believe me, the last thing I *want* is to legally bind myself to you—or your father, for that matter.' His eyes glazed with determination. 'But it is the only way this will work. These are my terms, *tempesta*.'

'It makes no sense.' The words were stoic when her chest was crushing under the weight of his demands.

He stared at her long and hard. 'I told you, I want our son to have a family. That's…very important to me.' The words were spoken with an iron-like determination but, even without that, Abby found the concept dug deep into her chest. A family? What would that be like? It had been so long since her mother had died, she could barely remember a time when they'd been a collective. Her father had emotionally shut her out many long years before he'd finally cut their ties altogether.

Abby was alone in the world. Her beloved mother was dead, her father had slammed the door on her, and now Gabe was threatening to take Raf away. She couldn't lose her son; she wouldn't let her son lose her either!

But, far from losing him, what if she could give him exactly what Gabe was offering? What if she could give Raf a real family?

'A marriage born of hate cannot work,' she said dubiously, her eyes flicking to his before skimming away.

He spoke softly, considering each word. 'There is love too. I saw my son and loved him instantly. You are his mother. That means something to me, Abigail. No matter how I feel about you personally, I wish you no ill. I want to take care of you as well. Raf deserves that—to know that his father will protect his mother.' Deep emotions rang through that last sentence, as though he'd dredged it up from deep within his soul.

She wanted to fight him. She wanted to tell him that what she most needed protection from was the power Gabe wielded over her, and the ease with which he could hurt her. She wanted to shout at him and rail against him but the last year had been long and draining for Abigail, and all the pluck she'd once held in her armoury had been dulled to the point of non-existence. Her fight had been washed away; sleeplessness and loneliness, abandonment and discord with her father had made her heart sore and heavy. She wanted to fight Gabe, she wanted to fight him so badly, but every day had been a battle and she found—in that moment—she had very little fight left.

What he offered was so tempting. She swept her eyes shut, desperately trying to rally some strength, some fight, some determination to keep him at a distance.

'I don't know how it would work.'

'We don't need to discuss semantics now.'

'It's not semantics!' she insisted, reaching out a hand and wrapping her fingers around his wrist. 'This is my life. Mine and Raf's. You can't expect me to just *marry* you.'

He expelled a sigh, a sound of impatience. 'Why not?'

'Seriously? Why not? I could give you a thousand reasons.'

'I'm not interested in a thousand. Give me a single good one.'

His manner was imposing at the best of times but now, in this conversation, she could barely scrape her thoughts together.

She clutched at the first straw she found. 'I hardly know you.'

'How is that relevant?' he said with a shake of his head.

'You're asking me to move to Italy and become your wife…'

'I'm suggesting you choose the best-case scenario in this *situation*.' He stared at her resolutely. 'It is, of course, your decision.'

Her heart sank.

Her decision?

She was broke, alone, and hardly ever saw her tiny baby because of the hours she had to work just to get by. Everything she did was for Raf; wouldn't she hurt her son by denying him all that Gabe could offer?

She was terrified of the way this man made her feel, but wasn't motherhood about putting your child's needs above your own? All she had to do, in order to make this decision, was ignore her own needs and wants and think of what was best for Raf.

Then the decision was a simple one.

She wanted Raf to have the best life in the world—she wanted to give that to him. She just had to dance with the devil…

Living with Gabe wouldn't be a walk in the park, and nor would marriage to him. But for Raf? What wouldn't she do? With a look of fierce strength and resolve, she nodded. 'Fine. You win. We'll come to Italy.'

'You'll marry me.' It wasn't a question, but he clearly wanted her to answer.

'On one condition.'

He arched a brow, but said nothing.

Abby hadn't been sure what she wanted to say, only that she knew she had to demand something of him—anything—to assert her position as an intelligent woman. Yielding power to him would be a disaster. 'If I move to Italy and marry you—'

'When,' he interrupted, his expression daring her to disagree.

'When I marry you,' she agreed with soft defiance, 'you'll be a good father to him. You'll spend time with him. He's not a trophy son to be loved on Christmases and birthdays. I'm only doing this for Raf, so he'll have what I…'

The sentence tapered off, a sense of betrayal forestalling her from adding: *what I never had.*

But Gabe knew. He understood what kind of father she'd had, or rather hadn't.

'I will be a hands-on father, Abigail. You can rest assured on that score.'

She expelled a soft breath. He *would* be a good father; she had no doubts. He might hate her, and perhaps with good reason, but she could see how much he wanted this, how much he already loved their son.

'Fine,' she said, holding his gaze even when she wanted to squeeze her eyes shut and blot out reality for a little longer.

There was a brief glimmer of triumph in the coal-dark depths of his eyes, but then he nodded. 'We'll leave in the morning.'

# CHAPTER FOUR

'WHERE ARE WE going to, Mamma?' Gabe asked, his six-year-old self huddled beside Marina's slim frame.

'On an adventure, darling. Far from here. To a happy place, full of sunshine and oceans and friendly people.'

'Sunshine *all the time*?'

'Yes, Gabe. Somewhere life will be kind, where you will be happy, and me too.' She crouched down, her eyes meeting his. 'And your father.'

'Papà?'

'*Sì.*'

'He's going to come with us?'

'He'll visit.' She smiled mysteriously. He didn't see Marina smile often. It was nice. He was glad.

'I'll get to meet my father?'

'You will.' She reached into her pocket and pulled out a sweet. 'He gave me this, for you. For the flight.'

'We're going on an aeroplane?'

'Oh, yes, Gabe. Australia is far away, across many oceans. It will take a long time to get there, but it's worth it.'

'How do you know?'

'Because when I was a little girl, I lived there, and I loved it. And because your father says so, *dolci*, and he's never wrong. He's going to take care of us from now on. No more struggling, no more worries. Just sunshine and happiness for you and me.' She kissed his head and ruffled his hair, and then smiled in a way he hadn't known her capable of. 'Pack your bag, little love. It's time to go.'

He slept in the lounge. Abby hadn't expected that, but at one point during the night, having tossed and turned for hours, she got up to get a glass of water and saw Gabe's broad sleeping frame huddled in the dilapidated recliner nearest to the window. It was a tatty chair, but it was her favourite spot to curl up in and read a book.

The sight of his body crumpled into it arrested her in her tracks. She froze, just inside the kitchenette, her eyes hungrily devouring every single detail in a way she'd never have allowed herself to do were he awake.

He'd stripped off his suit jacket and discarded it over the back of another chair, and his tie too. His shirt was un-buttoned at the neck, revealing the strong, thick column of his neck, and his sleeves were pushed up to reveal tanned forearms.

He breathed deeply, his broad chest lifting with each inhalation.

In the year since they'd been together, she'd dreamed of him often. But they were never coherent dreams, nor were they sensible. They were fractured memories. His body over hers, their eyes locked, fingers entwined, lips meshing. Their breathing in unison, laughing, his voice as he whis-pered Italian words into her ears, words that she couldn't understand but became addicted to hearing.

The way he'd held her tight as he'd pushed past her in-nocence, reassuring her with his words and his body that she would be all right. That he would keep her safe.

She swallowed and took a step closer to him without re-alising it. He shifted in the chair and she froze, swallowing guiltily, heat spreading through her cheeks.

He was a beautiful specimen of masculinity. When she'd met him, she'd been rendered speechless by the strength and power that emanated from him. There was confidence and control in every breath he issued. He was inherently remarkable. But now, in repose, there was something even more fascinating, even more appealing.

There was a raw vulnerability in his face as he slept,

almost as if she could peel back the layers of time and see Gabe as he'd been years earlier, as a child. Had he always been confident in a way that bordered on arrogance? Had he been feted and worshipped in those early years of his life, so that the seeds of self-belief had been firmly planted in the make-up of his soul? Or had he become like this later? In his teens? Twenties? Had something happened that had shaped him, such as his phenomenal success?

Abigail discounted it instantly. He and his business partner were self-made success stories. To achieve what they had took a huge amount of confidence, as well as intelligence and ability. Success hadn't shaped him—he'd reached for success with both hands. That determination and grit was fundamentally Gabe.

'You're staring.'

She was startled, her eyes flying back to his face, heat intensifying in her cheeks as she realised he was awake, languidly watching her—watching her watch him. Embarrassment curdled her blood.

'I…thought you might be cold,' she lied huskily. 'Do you need a blanket?'

His lips curled derisively, showing he understood exactly why she'd been staring at him.

'I'm warm enough.' There was a mocking challenge in his expression.

'Good.' She swallowed.

'You cannot sleep?' he prompted after a moment.

She shook her head. 'My mind can't stop spinning. I can't stop thinking about the madness of what I've agreed to.'

He made a soft noise. 'There's no point thinking about what is already done.'

'It's not done, though,' she said with a shrug.

'Are you trying to tell me you've changed your mind?'

Was she? She stared at him, her heart still thundering

through her body like a runaway horse in a storm. She bit down on her lip and closed her eyes, trying to sift through her wants and needs, her certainties and doubts.

'Raf deserves what you can give him,' she said finally, with a shake of her head. 'I know that.'

'I'm going to take care of you both, Abigail.' The words held a strange other-worldly quality. 'You will have nothing to worry about from now on. *Capisce?*'

She carried his assurance to bed, strangely warmed by it when she had no real reason to trust him.

The next morning broke over New York cold and bleak.

'Are you packed?' Gabe was waiting when Abby stepped out of the bathroom.

She stared at him, her heart jolting at this version of Gabe. All arrogant, in-control tycoon once more, dressed in his suit, his dark hair pushed back from his brow. This was not the man who'd issued lazy promises to take away all her worries. This was the man who was worth billions, who took over businesses like most people changed underwear.

'It won't take me long.' She gestured towards her bedroom door. 'Raf's still sleeping. I didn't want to disturb him.'

Gabe's eyes narrowed. 'We're leaving soon. Disturbing him is inevitable.' And then, after a pause, 'I'll hold him.'

Abby jerked her attention to his face. 'Seriously?'

Gabe's smile was slightly mocking. 'He's my son, *no*?'

She arched a brow, her surprise obvious. But he was right, and hadn't she wanted him to be a good father?

When she walked into her bedroom, it was to discover that the little boy was already stirring, his back arched, his head pushed upwards and his lips pouting as he stretched the sleep away. She smiled instinctively and pulled him into her arms, pressing a kiss to his soft little head. 'Your daddy's here, Raf.'

Gabe was watching her initially when she stepped into

the lounge, but then all of his attention, the full force of him, was channelled towards their son.

Abby didn't have a camera handy, but she didn't need one anyway. She would always, always remember the tortured look on Gabe's face in that moment. He wore an expression of such deep feelings, such pain, that she almost forgot all the reasons she had to keep him at a distance.

She almost forgot the way he'd treated her after the night they'd shared—she almost forgot the way he'd ignored her, refused to allow her to apologise or explain, refused to give her the dignity of so much as a simple conversation so that she could tell him about the baby.

She almost forgot that he was, in many ways, the enemy.

She longed instead to wrap her arms around his waist, to lift up onto her tiptoes and press a kiss against his lips. To whisper into his mouth that he could make up for the three months he'd missed—that he had a lifetime to be in his child's life and it was all about to start.

She didn't, though.

Sanity and the reality of who they were to one another prevented her from weakening, even a little. She handed Raf to Gabe, careful not to touch him more than she had to in order to effect the transfer, and then stepped back with a crisp nod. 'I won't be long.'

Gabe didn't answer; she couldn't have said if he'd even heard. He was in his own world—just him and Raf. She watched, and tried her darnedest to ignore the strange prickling impression that she was an outsider.

Abby had grown up with money, she was used to this rarefied way of living, and yet she still felt a tremble of anxiety as she moved up the metallic stairs and into the body of the private jet.

There were markers of understated luxury everywhere she looked, from the sleek white leather seats to the highly polished woodgrain meeting table and the small cinema space at the back of the plane.

It took her a moment to realise that they weren't alone. Three women and one man were seated at the back of the plane, and there were the two men in dark suits who'd lifted the luggage from the car.

Gabe walked towards the people at the rear of the plane, his grim expression not lifting. For lack of knowing what else she should do, Abby fell into step behind him.

One of the women stood at his approach, a smile on her face. Abby liked her instantly. She was tall and slim, in her forties, Abby would have guessed, and while she was dressed in beautiful clothes, her glossy brown hair was braided down her back and she wore no make-up. She had a nice face. Smile lines and bright eyes that spoke of a quick wit and good humour.

'Hello, little one,' she cooed as Gabe approached and, to Abby's surprise, he passed their son to the other woman.

She watched, trying to make sense of this development before reacting.

'You must be Abigail,' the other woman said, her tone soft, her eyes not leaving Raf's face.

'Abby, please,' Abigail murmured, her voice sounding hoarse. She cleared her throat softly.

'I'm Monique.'

Perhaps reading the look of confusion on Abby's face, Gabe explained, 'I have engaged Monique as Raf's nanny. This is her team.' He nodded to the others. Apparently, they didn't need names.

But Abby barely noticed. How could she? Not when the hiring of a nanny was a reality still detonating in her brain.

'What did you say?' Anger fuelled the words. She didn't particularly want to argue in front of the nice-seeming nanny, but her maternal instincts were twisting inside her.

And he understood; he easily read the emotions that

were about to burst from her. His eyes sparked with Abby's and he put a hand on the small of her back, his touch none-too-gentle.

'Come with me.'

He propelled her down the aisle and only the knowledge that no harm could befall Raf when she was only on the other side of the aircraft meant she went with Gabe without complaint.

But as soon as they were far enough away she whipped around and hissed, 'You can't just hire a nanny without talking to me!'

His expression was unyielding. 'Why not?'

'Because!' Finally she gave into the impulse to lash out at him, lifting a hand and pushing his chest, hard. He didn't move. Not even a little. He was like a stone wall to her ricocheting emotions.

'Because that's something I want to be consulted on. Who is this woman? What experience does she have with children? You're asking me to hand my son over to a stranger! I should have been able to review her résumé. Besides, how good can she be if you were able to organise her within a *day* of finding out you have a son? Or do you just keep nannies waiting in the wings in case you discover you have a secret baby somewhere?' Her brain kept firing and new possibilities detonated sharply. 'Oh, God, do you have other children? Has this happened before?' Abby felt light-headed, and not just because of her tirade but because her palms were resting against Gabe's chest and her fingertips were tingling with the contact, sending little barbs of electricity through her veins, making her knees tremble.

She didn't want to be aware of him physically! Not in this moment! Not when she should be simply enraged.

'No,' he responded, his own word filled with barely restrained anger. 'Raf is a first for me.'

'So?' Abby wasn't placated. 'Where did you find this

woman? What are her credentials? How dare you hire someone without taking the time to make sure it was safe or right?' Her eyes shifted to the back of the plane, but thick grey curtains had been drawn, partitioning the staff from Abby and Gabe.

He wrapped his fingers around her wrists, removing her hands from his chest and holding her arms down by her side. 'He is my son. I would *never* do anything that might put him in harm's way.'

'Like engaging a nanny you know *nothing* about?' Abby retaliated, her gaze smarting.

'Monique has worked for the Italian ambassador for six years. I have met her a number of times in that capacity and she comes with excellent references. Her security clearance is the highest imaginable. I trust her implicitly, or I wouldn't have hired her.'

He released his grip on her wrists and stepped backwards, the distance and lack of physical contact immediately frustrating to Abby.

His reasonable response was like a pin popping her anger and yet still she said, 'You should have spoken to me about it. This kind of thing should be my decision too.'

'And?' he said, crossing his arms over his chest, drawing her attention to the breadth of his torso—a torso that had been naked above her, that made her ache to feel his body weight once more. She looked away, her mouth suddenly dry. 'Would you have wanted her, Abigail?'

'I'm raising my son,' she said wearily, taking a step back from him, finding a seat and easing herself into it. She curled her legs up beneath her and gnawed on her lower lip, the deluge of emotions that was flooding her quite unwelcome.

'Yes.' He took the seat opposite, his long legs spread between them. 'And you are raising him still. It is not a crime to have professional help.'

Tears clogged her throat and she was afraid of speaking in case he heard the emotions in her voice.

'If you decide, after a month or two, that you don't want that help, I am open to re-evaluating the situation.'

It was a concession she hadn't expected. Abby flicked her glance to him, but whatever she'd been about to say flew from her head. He was looking at her lips, focused intently on them, and her pulse began to drum hard and hot, filling her ears, her body, gushing through her in a way that made her insides clench together. Warmth flooded her and she held her breath.

His eyes lifted briefly to hers and heat seared her, and then his attention moved lower, as if drawn of its own accord. She was wearing a shapeless sweater and a pair of jeans, hardly the stuff of expert seduction, and yet, the way his eyes lingered on the soft curves of her breasts, she felt as though she were wearing the latest designer lingerie.

But when he returned his attention to her face, a face that was flushed courtesy of his slow, possessive scrutiny, there was nothing but determined resolve in his look. Nothing to indicate he'd been at all affected by his languid inspection. Whereas Abby felt as if she might need an ice-cold shower to get her wayward thoughts under control...

# CHAPTER FIVE

GABE STARED AT the snow-covered fields on either side of the car and, beyond them, the twinkling night sky. His lips were set in a grim line of determination and his mind was focused on avoidance.

Avoiding the consequences of what he'd just manoeuvred.

Avoiding the realities of marriage to a woman like Abigail—a woman he'd sworn he never wanted to see again.

Avoiding the fact she was still fast asleep in the seat opposite, her pale blonde hair like gold across one shoulder, her body languid even in repose, so that he wanted to stare, but to stare only as a prelude to touching her.

'Abigail.' He spoke with a coldness that was completely at odds with the thoughts that had been simmering through his body, tightening him, hardening him, making him remember the softness of her breasts between his palms.

She stirred a little, but remained asleep.

'Abigail.' More loudly, more emphatic, as they passed the turn-off for Fiamatina, the small village at the foot of his land. She blinked her eyes open slowly at first, relaxed, unguarded, and for a few moments she frowned with apparent confusion. Then she looked at him and straightened instantly, her expression wary, her body on alert.

'Where's Raf?'

Her jumper had risen up a little, exposing an inch or so of flesh at her waist. He looked at it without even realising what he was doing until she reached down and straightened the fabric, clearing her throat. 'Gabe?'

He couldn't mistake the desire that was running rampant through his system. That he still wanted her physically was a complication he needed like a hole in the head. 'In the car behind.'

'The car behind?'

'You were asleep,' he said with a shrug. 'I didn't want him to wake you.'

Abby's eyes flicked to the window, then back to Gabe. 'You shouldn't have done that. I don't… How long have I been asleep?'

'A few hours. You drifted off about an hour before we landed.'

She stared at him, surprise obvious. 'I don't even remember landing.' Her cheeks flushed. 'Or getting into the car.'

'I carried you.'

Her body had been soft and warm against his, pliant to his touch, and she'd made a small sigh as she'd curled in closer, her lips so close to his throat that he could feel her breath.

'Why?' She pressed back further in her seat and crossed her arms. Her body language told him she wanted to be anywhere but in his car, anywhere but with him.

'You were obviously exhausted,' he said softly.

She didn't answer, nor did she see the way his eyes stayed focused on her face for several long seconds.

'We're almost home.'

Her eyes swept shut at that pronouncement and a twist of guilt tightened in his gut. He'd made this happen, and it had been the right thing to do. He was nothing like his own father; he was the complete opposite. He'd proved that by manoeuvring Abigail into his life, into this marriage.

He'd meant what he'd said in New York: he would take care of her; he would take away her worries.

He would be everything his father wasn't—Raf would know how much Gabe loved him; that fact would never be in doubt.

This was the *right* decision, he reassured himself, ignoring the insistent pounding of doubt.

Abby couldn't help the small gasp that escaped her when the car pulled off the road and began to ascend a narrow, curving drive. It was night-time, but against the black velvet sky she could make out enormous pine trees capped in white, their big, fluffy branches cloud-like with snow. In the distance, there looked to be a small village, perhaps a town, the buildings glowing warm and golden. The car moved higher and, as they rounded a bend, a scene that could have been straight from one of Abby's girlhood fantasies lifted almost as if magically from the earth.

'It's a castle,' she whispered, moving closer to the window so that she could see better. The building looked to be quite ancient. In the light that was cast by the moon she could see it was built of stone, perhaps a yellow-coloured stone? It was four storeys high, with a central turret and lots of little balconies. She could make out the detail more clearly as they drove nearer—the castle was well-illuminated. In fact, it looked as though every light was on, the place appearing almost to glow.

'You live here?' She turned to face him, her surprise obvious.

His nod was a short confirmation.

'But it's so beautiful…'

'You have not realised I like beautiful things?'

She had no reason to suspect he was talking about her and yet her cheeks warmed and her heart tripped in her chest. 'I just hadn't expected this.'

'What did you expect?'

She shrugged. 'Some super-modern apartment in Rome?'

'I have a place in Rome,' he conceded with a dip of his head. 'I stay there for work sometimes.'

'But you prefer it here,' she said softly, turning to face him.

He studied her for a long moment before shrugging. 'It's quiet.'

'It's…lovely.' The word felt insufficient, hugely so. But it was also very, very apt. Beauty was *everywhere*. She was in a snow-covered wonderland, like the snow globe her mother had brought back one year after a concert season in Vienna.

A moment after the car had drawn to a stop the door was pulled open but, before Abby could step from the car, Gabe put a hand out, arresting her with his touch. It was just a light contact, his fingers pressed to her knee. Abby froze instantly, turning to face him with eyes that were huge in her face.

'It's cold out,' he said thickly, reaching beside him and handing her a black woollen overcoat.

'Thank you.' Just a murmur when, inside, her heart was racing at the thoughtfulness of the gesture. She was less grateful when she pulled the coat on and realised it was his. It swam on her; she could easily have fitted herself into the thing twice. Worse than that, it was filled with his intoxicatingly masculine fragrance so that her hormones tripped in her body, responding instantly to the memories of their night together, reminding her of the way they'd made love.

She ignored the recollections, focusing her attention instead on the castle. She was no expert in Italian history but she would have guessed the castle to be fifteenth or sixteenth century. It looked too rustic to have been influenced by the Renaissance movement, though that didn't mean it wasn't beautiful. In fact, it was the most beautiful thing Abby had ever seen. The windows were cathedral in shape and the door, at the very middle of the castle, was at least twice Abby's height and made of thick, ancient wood. She'd put money on the wood having been sourced from one of these enormous pines—the forest that surrounded the castle must be hundreds of years old too. She breathed in deeply and tasted Christmas.

It was an odd thought for a woman who hadn't celebrated the holiday in more than the most perfunctory of ways for many years. But if she could write Christmas as a fairy tale it would be set somewhere like this. A bird flew overhead, a night bird with wide wings and a soft song. Abby's eyes were drawn upwards, following its progress and then remaining on the jewel-encrusted sky.

No matter how beautiful the setting, Abby needed to remember that it wasn't, in fact, a fairy tale. Being here with Gabe might have been the answer to many of her problems but she was pretty sure it would bring with it a whole raft of new worries. She just couldn't bring herself to deal with them yet.

The crunching of tyres called her attention back to earth and the present moment. She spun, the jacket warm around her, to see a mini-van arrive. Monique stepped out first, Raf nestled in her arms.

He was awake, but looking perfectly calm in the face of all these changes. He was still so tiny, just a very wrapped-up little bundle with a tiny face poking out the top.

Monique smiled at Abby, crossing to her. 'He did very well on the flight, Abigail. Barely a peep, except when we landed, and a pacifier soothed him right back.'

Abby nodded, though she couldn't help feeling like the worst mother ever for not even hearing her child's distress. Raf hadn't been interested in pacifiers before, though she'd tried to introduce them, to buy peace and quiet when he was at his most inconsolable. A niggling doubt that maybe she hadn't tried hard enough, or simply hadn't known enough, spread like wildfire.

She reached out a finger, touching her little one's forehead, and, though it was absurd and made no sense, she didn't try to take him from the nanny. For some strange reason, she almost felt as if she didn't have any right.

Perhaps sensing her ambivalence, Monique smiled kindly. 'I will take him inside and bathe him. Would you like me to give him his bottle or...?'

'No.' Abby shook her head, grateful that the other woman seemed to understand that she was generally a very hands-on mother. 'I'll do that.'

Monique nodded and moved back to the others; they went as a group towards the castle but Abby held back a little, watching as they disappeared through the enormous timber doors.

She felt balanced on a precipice, one foot in her old life and this new existence beckoning her. It was a reality that shimmered like a reflection in a pond; she could see it and fathom it, but its edges were rippled and the exact nature of it was too hard to properly understand.

If she took a step, and then another, would she disappear for ever beneath the surface? Would she be a part of this world only?

She swallowed, thinking of Manhattan. The father who'd disowned her years ago. Oh, he'd made it official only recently, but his heart had turned cold to Abby much earlier than that.

She thought of her apartment, the tiny space and life she had tried to carve out for herself. She thought of the fridge that was full of bills and emptied of food, and the heating that was too costly to use, and the difficulties of juggling the need to work with trying to make everything good for Raf, and she swept her eyes shut, as if she could dissolve the image of America so easily.

'Come.' His voice was gravel. 'I'll show you around.'

Snow was thick on the ground everywhere except for the driveway that led to the front entrance; someone must have cleared it very recently because it was already beginning to fall again. Abby paused at the door, turning around to survey the setting once more. The village twinkled in the distance, the pine trees loomed large, fragrant with their alpine scent, and the air was so clear and bright that Abby would swear she could make out the shape of the stars. It was a place that seemed almost to have been carved from heaven.

'Well?' His impatient word cut through the serenity of the moment. 'I know you've been living in an ice box but perhaps we could move inside before freezing to death.'

'I'm sorry I'm not moving fast enough for you.' The words were laced with tart acidity. 'I just wanted to get my bearings.'

He ground his teeth.

'That is Fiamatina, a small village that formed around this castle. The closest city is Turin, about two hours that way. The alps, obviously—' and he nodded to his right. When she turned, she gasped again. They *were* obvious and yet she hadn't yet noticed them, so awestruck had she been by the castle. If she'd thought the sky glistening, she had been ill prepared for the sight of the Italian alps, snow-covered, on a bright moonlit night. They looked to have been cast from silver and diamond dust, yet, for all their beauty, there was something simultaneously frightening about their dramatic, looming presence. They were hard and defined, sharp against the night sky. Abby ran her gaze across them, as far as the eye could see in one direction; her shiver was involuntary.

'Do you have your bearings now, Abigail?'

'Yes,' she responded sharply, though she would have liked to stand out there for longer.

Gabe was right to chivvy her along; Raf would be hungry and she was desperate to hold her little boy, to cuddle him and reassure them both that, for all the changes, life was still normal; they were still together.

A family.

Just like Gabe had said.

He walked into the castle as though it were completely normal, and yet Abby needed another moment to take stock, this time of the interior. The entranceway was high, with vaulted ceilings, and all of it mosaic—the floors a cream and white swirling pattern and the walls with an emphasis on black and grey. There were armchairs to one side, creating a sort of lounge foyer that wouldn't have been out of place in an exclusive hotel. At some point the building had obviously been heavily modernised. The lighting was like an art gallery, all concealed and elegant, and the heating was excellent. She shrugged out of her coat, surrendering to the cosy warmth of a building that was so utterly enormous. The staircase in the middle of the entrance hall, though made of old terracotta tiles, looked to have been remodelled at some point in recent years.

'There is a kitchen here, though you will not need to cook, of course. I have a team of domestics who take care of castle operations.'

Her father had never believed in servants. They'd only had a nanny when she'd been younger, and a cleaner as she'd got older. He'd said he didn't like the way it felt to have people hovering around his home, touching his things, watching him breathe. She wondered if she'd ever get used to the omnipresence of an invisible brigade of helpers.

'I will show you the back of the house tomorrow; there is a garden you might like to explore. Somewhere Raf can play. It is fenced, so you need not worry he will escape.'

'Okay.' She nodded, but her head was swimming. The house—no, it wasn't a house—the *castle* was sumptuous.

He led her up the staircase, moving quickly, so she almost had to jog to keep up with him. At the landing, he split in one direction and she followed him. It was on the tip of her tongue to implore him to slow down when he did just that, so she had to halt abruptly or risk bumping into him.

'This is Raf's room.' He stepped back to allow her to precede him, and his eyes glowed with an emotion she couldn't immediately understand.

It was defiance, she realised, when she stepped over the threshold and saw the way Gabe had furnished it. He was telling her that he was right—that he had been right to insist she accompany him.

Abby had no idea what the room had been in the past, but it was now a child's paradise. There was a bassinet and a cot, a small chair—something he wouldn't need for many months yet. There was a baby jumper, a walker, shelves and shelves lined with age-appropriate toys, a rocking chair, a narrow bed that an adult could use. Abby walked around the room, her breath held as she fingered many of the objects, her mind sagging when she tried to calculate what this must have cost him. A year's rent for her, certainly.

There was a doorway on one side; she went through it and discovered a large bathroom to one side and a bedroom to the other.

'The nannies will take it in turns to be on duty overnight. Whoever is watching Raf will sleep here.'

'And the bed in his room?' she asked softly, her eyes swept shut.

He shrugged. 'If he's sick. Has nightmares.'

It was the kind of thoughtful inclusion she wouldn't have expected of him.

'How did you *arrange* all this so quickly? It must have been hard to source so many items…'

'Not particularly.'

Of course it wasn't. For someone like Gabe, this would have been easy. Just a click of his fingers, a flex of his wallet, and all was arranged.

'Where's my room?'

He regarded her for several seconds before turning away and stalking through Raf's comfortable suite. Abby followed. Gabe walked past several doors that must have led to other bedrooms, and eventually he paused at the end of the hallway.

Until he opened the door, Abby hadn't realised she'd been holding her breath, fully expecting—hoping—that Gabe would insist they share a bedroom...and a bed! Deep, deep down, she'd been preparing for the likelihood and, in the back of her mind, trying to fathom how she would respond to that.

But the room he gestured towards was definitely not his. It was furnished in neutral décor, for one thing, with a couple of flower arrangements on the bedside table and a dressing table. It was devoid of personal details.

'My room,' she said with a confident nod, as if telling herself, reassuring herself.

'My own is next door,' he said, the words giving no indication that this affected him in any way.

But for Abby? Knowing he would be so close made her heart throb inside her and her pulse pounded in her veins, rushing hard and fast, demanding attention. Colour bloomed in her cheeks and when she lifted her eyes to Gabe he was watching her intently.

'Unless you'd prefer to share my room,' he prompted silkily, and Abby's knees began to tremble.

One night.

Her only night with a man.

The feelings he'd invoked had tormented her, the memories strong and vivid in her mind, demanding more, craving more. But there'd been no more. No Gabe, only memories.

And now?

She blinked at him, her expression unknowingly panic-stricken. But it wasn't fear of being with him; it was fear of showing him just how much she wanted and needed that!

It was fear of the fact she did want him, even now. That, no matter what she'd promised to herself, she knew she wanted Gabe in a way she couldn't—wouldn't—ignore. Did that make her foolish or brave? And what point did a definition serve?

She was hungry for him, desperate for his touch, despite knowing she might very well regret succumbing to that hunger. She felt instinct take over, changing the course of her determination with ease.

'Relax, *tempesta*. It was a joke. I think we both know one night together was one night too many.'

Gabe was just a boy again and his mother, Marina, was dying. Not of any illness, but because of the drugs she slid into her veins until she was no longer coherent. She was dying and he couldn't save her.

He remembered the fear of those times, the pain of trying to hug her and make her laugh. Of having her bat him away from her legs, push at him and say, with fury, 'You are just like *him*!'

How she'd hated Gabe when she'd been high. Gabe was like his father, Lorenzo, and that was something his mother couldn't forgive.

Raf wouldn't know that pain. He wouldn't know the anger that was a by-product of paternal estrangement. He wouldn't have a father who rejected his mother and made her miserable. Raf would be spared what Gabe had seen and lived—Raf would have everything, including a mother who was cared for by his father.

Gabe just had to find a way to forgive Abigail for who she was and what she'd done—he wouldn't let their son feel the measure of Gabe's antipathy. At least, he hoped he wouldn't.

# CHAPTER SIX

THE DREAM HAD disturbed him and some time around dawn he woke, sweat beading on his brow, his eyes heavy with angry emotions. Jogging was something Gabe had long indulged in, particularly when he needed to blow off steam. He ran for six miles and then came back to the castle, restless and as irritable as he'd been for days.

Without knowing what he was doing or where he was going, he found his feet moving towards the stairs and then taking him upwards. One hand curled around the balustrade, part securing him, part deterring him.

At the door to their son's room, he hesitated only a moment before pushing in. The child was awake. Lying in his crib, his huge eyes open and staring at the mobile that hung above it.

A powerful instinct fired inside Gabe's gut. Possession, fierce pride and love. Yes, love. He'd never felt it before but now it flooded through him, unmistakable and all-consuming. He hovered above the cot, unsure what to do at first.

Then Raf made a gurgling noise and lifted an arm, his eyes locked to Gabe's, and Gabe followed his instincts, reaching down into the crib and lifting the little boy.

He made a guttural noise of surrender as he cradled Raf to his chest, pressing his face to the boy's sweet, downy head, breathing in his intoxicating baby fragrance.

'You're my son,' he whispered, the words not entirely even. 'And I am going to take all the care in the world of you.' He breathed in once more. 'I love you.'

It was a freezing cold morning and Abigail had risen at dawn. In part owing to jetlag and in part owing to dreams that had been causing her nerve-endings to reverberate, making her ache to do something really, really stupid.

She'd tiptoed past Gabe's room, even when she'd been tempted to push his door inwards and climb into his bed. To seek his body, not caring for how pathetic that made her. How needy and desperate.

There was only one activity that ever helped soothe Abby in times of stress. She'd had to abandon ballet for the last few months of her pregnancy and since Raf had been born she hadn't had much energy for anything other than a bit of stretching. But an urge to go back to her roots now drove her with a wild desperation.

She didn't need much. Just a room that was lightly furnished, a bit of floor space and privacy, and she would have put money on this castle having something to fit the bill *somewhere*.

The perfect room happened to be just opposite the kitchen. A space that might have been a sunroom at one point and which now offered an almost blank canvas. Just a few chairs against one wall, glass doors that opened onto a deck and views of the alps in every direction. She ignored the beauty outside. Looking out only reminded her of where she was—and why—and she needed to forget for a moment. She loaded up a piece from *The Nutcracker Suite* and stretched for the first few minutes, and then she closed her eyes and let the music wash over her, sweeping her into a trance-like state, filling her with a sense of who she was, who her mother had been, what she'd loved about ballet. She danced and felt her worries shift away; she felt safety and security, reassurance and bliss.

She danced the entire song, and then another, but, as the third began to play, something on the periphery of her vision caught her attention and she spun sharply, breaking a pirouette mid-way with surprise, to find Gabe watching her.

No. Staring at her, as though he could eat her with his eyes, his attention finely homed in on every single minuscule shift of her body. A *frisson* of awareness rushed through her. She ignored it, staring back at him unapologetically, trying desperately to match the coldness he could so easily convey.

'Did you want something?' she asked impishly, crossing her arms over her chest, glad she hadn't gone with her first instinct and pulled on her old leotard and tights.

'What are you doing?'

The question was a strange one. Did he really not recognise ballet?

He frowned thoughtfully, shaking his head, as though he realised the stupidity of what he'd said. 'You're a ballerina?'

'No.' Abby remembered the angry conversations with her father, his remonstrations at her 'quitting'. 'I just like to dance.'

'Is it not the same thing?'

'No.' The word held a bone-deep finality. She wasn't going to discuss the career she might have had. Nor the way her father had taken her decision not to pursue it as some kind of personal affront—a perceived rejection of Abby's mother—instead of what it really was: Abby's realisation that she wanted different things from life.

'You...move as though you are part of the song.'

Abby's eyes swept shut. She had been told often enough that she was gifted, and by a variety of people, to know that it was true. That had only added to the outrage at her decision to walk away from the stage.

'Thank you.' It was a curt dismissal.

He blinked, as though clearing his mind of the vision of her dancing. 'I am going into Fiamatina. Do you need anything?'

'The village?' she asked, a natural curiosity twisting inside her.

'*Si.*'

Abigail eyed him warily. 'I'd like to go with you.' It would mean a car trip with Gabe, but the chance to explore was something she didn't want to resist. The lure of a snow-topped Italian village did something strange to her tummy.

'Fine. If you wish,' he said, shrugging his shoulders in the same indolent manner he'd employed the night before. 'But I'm leaving soon. Get ready.'

Abby shot daggers at his retreating back; his high-handed manner did funny things to her tummy and knees, making her ache to run up to him and turn him around and demand that he not be so cold to her when she knew a flame was going to combust between them.

'Get ready,' she mimicked under her breath, rolling her big green eyes as she moved through the castle, noting details she hadn't seen earlier. Ancient bricks that formed a vaulted ceiling in the corridors, walls that had been rendered at some point, that were now a charming mix of stone and concrete, walls that told stories. Windows framed views of the alps, snow-covered and magical, each vista like a post-card. She drifted towards one, staring out for a moment, mesmerised by the view.

Was this little slice of heaven on earth really to be her home?

She closed her eyes and breathed in deeply, trying to re-member the bedroom in her father's house, the cafés she'd go to for brunch at the weekend, the sound of New York traffic and commuters, the smell of diesel and bitumen heavy in the air; it all seemed so far away.

There wasn't time for reflection; she kept going, taking one wrong turn in the enormous castle before finding her way to the corridor that led to their bedrooms. She paused at Raf's door, listening for noises, and smiled when she heard voices.

She pushed in without knocking and found one of Monique's staff changing Raf's nappy, smiling down at him with all the adoration a mother could wish from someone who was entrusted with their child's care.

'Good morning,' she said, smiling. Raf turned his head. He was only young but already strong and alert, and a big toothless smile appeared on his face, digging dimples into his cheeks.

*'Buongiorno,'* the young girl said. 'I'm Rosa.'

She was obviously a native Italian, her accent heavy even on the single word 'I'm'.

'Abby.' Abigail stroked Raf's head, smiling back at him, before placing a kiss on his brow. 'How did he sleep?'

'He slept well,' Rosa answered, lifting Raf off the changing table, cradling him to her hip. 'And now he is going to eat. Would you like to give him his bottle?'

Guilt sliced through Abby and for a moment she wondered if she was doing the wrong thing to abandon her son, even if for only a couple of hours. Yet he seemed so happy, and she wouldn't be long. Besides, if this was to be their home, the sooner she got to grips with their locale, the better she'd be able to make them truly comfortable here.

'I'm on my way to Fiamatina,' she said, shaking her head regretfully. Mother guilt, she'd felt it often, always agonising over whether she was making the right decisions for her child. 'You'll call me if there are any problems?'

'Of course! Raf is a very contented baby, though. We'll be fine.'

Abby nodded, but she was thinking of how difficult he had been in New York, how he had seemed far from content on many occasions. Before she escaped to her own room to ready herself for the trip, she reached for Raf and snuggled him close to her chest, wrapping her arms around him, pressing a kiss to his forehead and breathing him in.

This was all for him. Being here with Gabe, living in the lion's den, that was because she knew Raf deserved what Gabe could provide.

She had to make this work.

'I'll be back in a few hours.' She returned Raf to Rosa and prepared to face the morning.

There was a petulant child inside Abby who wanted to dally over getting ready but, alas, she'd never been someone who took time over her appearance. Besides, there was an excitement coiling inside her, as if she was about to set off on an adventure, to discover the village at the foot of the castle. She showered, marvelling at the heat, not only of the water but of the bathroom, as well. Underfloor warmth greeted her bare feet when she stepped out of the shower— it must have been triggered by the lights, she supposed. She dressed in a pair of jeans and a shirt, pulling on a big grey sweater and a bright pink scarf before reaching for the only jacket she'd brought, a black knee-length coat that buttoned up to her neck.

Gabe was waiting at the bottom of the enormous staircase, the elegant seating area to his left glowing with the milky sunshine from outside. As with before, in the morning light she was able to observe much more of the castle's details than she'd been capable of doing after the strange discombobulation of the day before. The stairs were slightly uneven, worn through the middle by centuries of use. The railing was softened by touch as well, so that she slid her hands over hundreds of years of other peoples' lives, and a shiver ran through her.

But when she reached the bottom and her eyes met Gabe's, all thoughts of the castle and its provenance skittered from her brain. There was only him and her. Even the air seemed somewhat thin, making breathing difficult.

'You will be cold,' he said, eyeing her coat.

It wasn't what she'd expected him to say. 'I'm fine.'

'It's below zero...'

'It's not like I'm not used to the cold,' she interrupted. 'I grew up in New York.'

'Fine,' he said with a shrug, but his obvious disapproval irked her. He was so superior, so arrogant, she yearned to take him down a peg or two.

'Our son is fine, by the way. Thanks for asking. Your concern is truly touching, particularly given the way you uprooted us from our lives so unceremoniously.'

His brows lifted and an electrical current surged from him to her. 'I'm well aware he is fine. I gave him a bottle before coming in search of you this morning.'

Just like a tower being demolished, Abby's moral high ground gave way beneath her, leaving her feeling churlish. Worse, she felt like someone who'd used their baby to score points, something she'd sworn she'd never do.

Refusing to apologise, she stared at a point over Gabe's shoulder. 'Rosa said he slept well.'

Gabe could have continued their spat but he didn't, and she was glad. 'Yes. Perhaps it is the Italian air that agrees with him.'

'Perhaps.'

They walked side by side from the castle, through the enormous wooden door at the front. The icy temperature hit her like a wall. It was *much* colder than she'd expected. The castle had been so cosy she hadn't been able to grasp that beyond its walls was a sub-arctic breeze. She didn't respond visibly though; he didn't need to know he'd been right. Next time she'd have to add another layer or three beneath her coat.

In the daylight, everything was clean and shiny, glowing white against a leaden grey sky. It wasn't snowing, but it had done so overnight. The freshly fallen powder had been recently pushed aside and a sleek black sports car was parked at the foot of the steps. It was exactly the kind of car she would have expected Gabe to drive. Expensive-looking, undoubtedly powerful and very expensive.

She pulled open the passenger door, sliding into the warmth of the vehicle with relief, buckling up and pressing back against the leather of the seat.

A blast of ice-cold air hit Abby as Gabe slid into the seat beside her, his powerful frame taking all the spare space, his presence a force to be reckoned with and conquered. The engine throbbed when he started it, like a beast beneath them. He steered it away from the house, his driving expert. Once they cleared his long winding driveway and entered the streets there was thick snow, but Gabe and the vehicle had no problem manoeuvring across it.

'You don't need to grip the door as though you are about to die,' he said, tilting his face sidelong to regard her with sardonic amusement before returning his attention to the road. 'You are safe.'

Safe? She didn't feel safe. In the road sense, she did, but the reason her nerve-endings were pulling taut had more to do with the man beside her and the anxiety his proximity kindled within her.

'Have you lived here long?' she asked to ease the tension within her.

He arched a brow, turning his handsome face towards her. 'Small talk?'

'Curiosity,' she corrected. 'If I'm going to marry you, I figure I should know a bit more about you besides the fact you're a judgemental douche.'

'A judgemental douche?' he repeated and, despite the cynicism in his tone, there was the hint of a smile at the corner of his mouth.

'Yes.' Abby wasn't laughing.

He sobered. '*Va bene.*'

'So?' she said after a long moment of silence had

stretched between them. He slowed the car to a halt. 'Why have you stopped?'

He jerked his head and Abby followed the direction of his gaze. Two deer were making their way across the road, picking their way slowly through the snow, their inky-black eyes alert as they eyed Gabe's car warily. It looked like a scene from a Christmas movie. All that was missing were bells around their necks and elves at their sides.

'I've lived in the castle about five years.'

'Why? It seems so remote.'

'I like remote.'

'Yes,' she drawled. 'I can see that.' Again, she was sure she saw his lips twitch. The deer moved off the road and Gabe started to accelerate gently, continuing their journey.

'I have a helicopter for when I need to get to my office in Rome.' He frowned and when their eyes met she wondered if he was imagining her in his lobby. Pregnant and desperate to talk to him. Was he remembering the way he'd had Security remove her from the premises? Did he feel guilty? He turned his attention back to the road. 'But I have all the facilities I need to work from here.'

'The castle is amazing,' she agreed. 'I can see why you were drawn to it.'

'I doubt that,' he said under his breath.

'What do you mean?'

He was quiet for a moment. 'It doesn't matter.'

Curiosity exploded inside her. Was there more behind his purchase of the castle? Suddenly, she wanted to know everything. She wanted to pick Gabe's brain, to understand him completely and unequivocally, but she suspected he wouldn't willingly accede to that.

He turned at a large pine tree and the snow-covered road gave way to one that was ever so slightly less so, as though it had been swept clear an hour or so earlier. Just the lightest dusting of white had fallen over it since.

'The castle was the heart of this village. It was once a great agricultural stronghold and supported all of the people who lived here.'

But Abby heard Gabe's words in the very back of her mind. She was leaning forward in her seat, her breath held, as she stared out of the windscreen at Fiamatina. It was, without doubt, the most charming and exquisitely beautiful place she had ever seen. The buildings all looked to be very, very old and, like the castle, they were built of stone. Mostly, they were joined together, forming rows and rows of cottages with ancient windows, creating streets so narrow that two cars couldn't have been accommodated at the same time. In deference to this, or perhaps to allow Abby to see everything they passed, Gabe went slowly, winding the car through street after street. Swathes of greenery were hung between the walls, covered in snow now, giving the Christmas decorations even more of a hint of festivity. The shops they passed were decorated too, and Abby was itching to explore properly.

When Gabe turned the corner again, the village opened into a square with a large Renaissance statue in the centre—the Virgin Mary and Baby Jesus, also topped with snow. A garland had been laid at their feet recently enough that it was still fresh.

Gabe brought the car to a stop. 'I will be a few hours. I presume you will be able to entertain yourself without getting into any trouble, for that short space of time?'

Abby lifted her eyes to his, frustration zipping through her. 'This doesn't exactly look like the kind of place that invites trouble.'

'Still, you are particularly good at finding your way into it,' he said, his words not showing a hint of humour or kindness. 'Try not to seduce any of the local businessmen, *tempesta.* You will not find their secrets worth keeping. Nor their wealth worth having, compared to mine.'

She sucked in an angry breath, her chest burning with the unfairness of his accusation. 'I didn't seduce you...'

He laughed and then shook his head as if sobering with the speed of lightning. He reached across and gripped her chin between his forefinger and thumb. 'You seduced me a year ago, make no mistake. But I have your measure now; you will not find me so foolish again.'

She wanted to tell him to go to hell, that she wouldn't touch him with a ten-foot bargepole for a million dollars, but already her body was making a liar of her, warming beneath his touch, filling with remembered pleasures.

His eyes roamed her face, dark emotions spiralling through them. 'Did you make a habit of doing your father's bidding?'

A soft sigh fell from Abby's lips. 'I love him,' she said simply. 'He's my dad.'

Something flickered in Gabe's expression and he dropped his hand. 'He's a fool.'

Sadness began to ricochet through Abby. 'It's not that simple,' she demurred with a small shake of her head. 'He's just... Since losing Mom, the business is all he has. He's so proud of his company but since Bright Spark came onto the scene it's been so hard for him.'

'My products dominate because they are, simply, better.'

His arrogance was no less galling because it was the truth. 'I'm trying to explain that he would do anything to succeed...'

'Including sending his only child to bed with a man she barely knew.'

'God, don't be so... You make it sound so sleazy,' she said with a shake of her head. 'It wasn't like that.'

'No?' Snow had begun to fall and it was blanketing the windscreen, removing the square from their view and vice versa. In the distance, she could hear beautiful Benedictine-type music, those lovely melodious chants, and she wondered if there was a church nearby.

'What *was* it like then?'

Abby swallowed, drawing her gaze back to Gabe's. 'He just wanted me to find stuff out about Calypso,' she said, her eyes falling away again almost instantly. His fury and contempt were not easy to face. 'The going to bed with you thing was all me.'

'So you remained a virgin until twenty-two, only to fall into bed with someone you barely knew? That sounds unlikely.'

It sounded preposterous. How could she explain that he wasn't like *anyone* she'd ever known? That he had been bone-meltingly perfect and every cell in her body had rec-ognised that they were meant to sleep together, that he was what she'd been waiting for?

The thought was one she certainly didn't appreciate.

Abby wasn't going to share that train of thought with Gabe. He was looking at her with the kind of mockery that made her want to lash out—to diminish what they'd shared in the same way he had.

'I was a twenty-two-year-old virgin,' she heard herself say, laughing. 'I just wanted to sleep with *someone*.' The lie was weird in her mouth but she was glad for it when she saw the way his face paled beneath his tan. Good. 'Anyone would have done, but you happened to be there…'

He swore, bringing his face closer to hers. 'You are not what I thought,' he said darkly.

'No? Well, that's mutual. My dad was definitely right about you.'

If she'd known him better, she would have understood that the wolfish smile on his face held a warning.

'I'm almost certain he was,' Gabe agreed. His face was dangerously close to Abby's but she didn't back down; she barely even noticed. She was lost in his gaze.

'So you slept with me because you wanted to have sex.'

'Yes.'

'Despite having waited...'

'I didn't wait for any magical reason,' she snapped. 'I just didn't get around to it...'

'Until you met me.'

'Look, Gabe.' She aimed for irreverent amusement, but the words sounded strangled. Now that she'd committed to this, she had to keep going. 'I was embarrassed by my virginity, okay? I wanted to be like any other woman my age.'

He stared at her long and hard and then shook his head, his expression cold. 'You failed. You are not like any woman I have ever met.'

# CHAPTER SEVEN

GABE SLAMMED THE car door shut with more force than he'd intended. Their argument—her admissions—had got under his skin and he couldn't, for the life of him, say why! He had long since ceased thinking anything but the worst of his son's mother, so why should he be surprised that she'd used him simply to get rid of her unwanted virginity?

Because it hadn't *felt* like that. The night they'd shared had been different for Gabe. Despite the fact he had been with many women in his time, he'd never had the privilege of being a woman's first. That she'd trusted him had meant something to Gabe. How foolish!

She'd had an itch, that was all, and she'd used him to scratch it.

'I've never done this before,' she'd whispered, her eyes not meeting his. Moonlight had filtered into the apartment, casting her naked body in silver dust.

'You've never done what? Slept with a man you've just met?'

She'd shaken her head and then met his gaze, her eyes locking onto his as though drawn to them by threads of biological imperative. 'Slept with any man.'

The confession had robbed him of breath. 'How is that possible?' He'd pulled her closer to his body, seeing the way desire flushed her skin as his arousal pressed hard to her body.

She'd groaned, rolling her hips in an innate instinctive need to be close to him. 'I just didn't get around to it before.'

He'd nodded, an unusual uncertainty shifting through him, causing him to pause. 'We don't have to, Abby. Your first time is…special…a gift.'

'I want to,' she'd whispered, lifting onto her tiptoes to kiss him. 'Please, Gabe. I want you to be my first.'

*Liar.*

She had told him the truth originally, only he hadn't listened. *I just didn't get around to it before.* That was the real reason for her virginity. For whatever reason, she'd not had sex. That was her choice, just as sleeping with him had been her choice. But it hadn't been a gift; it simply hadn't *mattered* to her.

And now it didn't matter to Gabe. If possible, his opinion of Abigail Howard sank even lower. His mouth was a grim line as he stormed through Fiamatina. There was nothing for it; he would marry her but he certainly didn't relish the prospect. Not one bit.

The condemnation rang in her ears—and there was no other way to describe the tone of his voice, the words he'd chosen. He hadn't meant the parting shot—that she was unlike any woman he'd ever known—as a compliment. He had intended to hurt her. Or perhaps he hadn't; perhaps he'd simply been speaking his mind and it was Abby's feelings that were making her vulnerable to his judgement.

His words consumed her, so that she walked through the village for at least an hour before realising that she was freezing cold, and also that she'd been so wrapped up in her tortured reflections she'd barely seen a thing. With a soft sigh of frustration, she pushed Gabe from her mind, or resolved to try, and made herself look at her surroundings. She'd wandered in a circle and was now in a street that was at the end of the square where he'd parked his car. He'd told her to meet him back there in two hours, meaning she had a little over an hour left to explore.

Warming up was also a priority. The street she was in was lined with shops. A few were closed but the third she passed was open and she pushed inside, realising when she entered that it had a collection of gifts. Nothing gaudy or touristic though; the items assembled were all of the highest quality.

'*Ciao, signorina!*' the shopkeeper called from behind a counter. Abby looked in his direction with a small smile. He was in his fifties, pleasingly rotund and short, with a thick white beard that fell to the second button of the grey shirt he wore. Red suspenders held his trousers in place. He was the picture of an Italian Father Christmas.

He said something in Italian and Abby shook her head. 'I'm sorry, I only speak English.' Something she'd have to remedy if she was going to make a go of life here.

'American?'

'*Sì.*'

'Welcome.' His English was heavily accented, his smile bright. ''Ave a look around. If I can help, you say, okay?'

She nodded. 'Okay.'

The shop was a marvel. She looked at statues first, tiny enough to fit in the palm of her hand, carved out of marble, all the details and intricacies perfect despite their miniature size. There were different coloured candles and Christmas ornaments made of wood, the like of which she'd always associated with Germany. Nativity scenes mostly, set at the base of elaborate shapes that, when candles were lit, would spin a fan at the top, causing the arrangement to move. Music boxes were also in evidence.

'It's all so beautiful,' she said to herself.

'Eh?'

'*Bella,*' Abby supplied, waving her hand towards the shelves. Her eyes fell on something in the corner and she moved towards it with a greedy hunger for everything this quaint little shop could offer.

The shelf was laden with Christmas decorations, but unlike anything she'd ever seen. They were spherical in shape, made of blown glass so fine that it was almost like a wisp of cloud. Each had been etched with a festive scene, some of the nativity, others with Santa and his elves, and inside each there was a bell, so tiny that when Abby lifted one ornament it made the most beautiful little noise, almost like a sigh.

'Oh…' She turned to the man, wishing she could convey to him how perfect they were.

But he understood. '*Aspetti*,' he said, then his brow beetled. 'Wait. Wait.'

He disappeared behind a thick velvet curtain and when he returned it was with a younger woman at his side. She wore an apron and had her dark hair pinned up into a loose bun. She brought with her the faint hint of gingerbread and a kind smile.

'My daughter,' the man said, his pride obvious. Abby's heart lurched. When was the last time her father had looked at her with anything like pride? Affection? Never.

'*Ciao*,' the woman said. 'You are American?' She spoke English more comfortably.

'Yes.' Abby nodded.

'You like the decorations?'

Abby nodded. 'They're…exquisite.'

The man said something and the daughter translated Abby's summation. He smiled. '*Sì, certamente.*'

He seemed gratified by Abby's appreciation.

'They're unique to this area,' the woman said. 'When our village formed, some craftsmen from Murano were amongst the first townspeople. They brought their skills with them, and these became the specialty. Each… How you say it? Father to son to father to son?'

'Generation?' Abby supplied after a moment.

'Yes! Each generation has learned from their father. There are only three people left in the village who make them, and they make only fifty each per year—to keep them special.'

Abby doubted she'd ever seen anything more beautiful.

'They are said to bring luck and wishes,' the woman continued. 'But I don't know if this is true. I think they are just pretty.'

Abby nodded her agreement. She could see them on a big green tree, with fine fairy lights twinkling amongst them, making them sparkle with tiny reflections. Though Abby hadn't celebrated Christmas with any degree of enthusiasm since her mother had died, she now felt a jolt of enthusiasm at the prospect. Why shouldn't she decorate a tree this year? It was, after all, Raf's first Christmas and that meant something, didn't it? 'How much are they?'

'*Quanta costa?*' the woman asked her father.

He named an amount that had Abby's heart sinking. They were beautiful and rare—what had she expected? She thought of her bank balance with a hint of desperation.

'I'll take two,' she said, thinking it was still an extravagance she could ill afford.

'Two,' the woman said with a nod, lifting her fingers to her father to translate. 'Enjoy them.' She waved her hand in farewell, disappearing back behind the curtain to the business of baking and domestic happiness.

The shopkeeper wrapped the decorations with care and placed them in a bag. When she handed over the money, he gripped her hand and smiled, a smile that was filled with genuine care. 'They give luck, *sì?* You have the luck now.'

Abby nodded, though of course she didn't believe in such superstitions. In any event, she'd need more than luck to make it through her marriage to Gabe Arantini unscathed.

She checked the clock in the town square—she still had fifteen minutes to spare. She pulled her coat tighter around her waist and walked down the street, looking in the shop windows—not risking going into any others! She couldn't *afford* to succumb to the charming wares of this part of the world.

She was freezing cold though. She jammed her free hand into her pocket and moved back towards the square. The alps loomed large in the background, so beautiful, like something out of Narnia. There was a heavy sense of magic and spells in the air of Fiamatina; even the people she saw seemed to be otherworldly, somehow.

'You're finished?' Gabe's voice came from behind her and Abby turned to see that he was carrying several shopping bags and wearing a mask of disapproval. A hangover from their conversation in the car?

'Yes,' she said with regret. If she were dressed more appropriately, she would have wanted to stay all day.

He nodded, clicking a button so that the trunk of his car pushed itself open. 'You're cold.'

He lifted something out of one of the bags. 'Here.'

It was a coat, clotted cream in colour. It looked to be made of luxurious wool, and inside it was lined with fleece. 'Put it on,' he said with impatience, 'before you turn into an ice block.'

'You bought me a coat?'

'And gloves, a hat and scarves,' he enumerated impatiently. 'While it would solve some problems for me, I don't actually wish you to die of hypothermia.'

She glared at him. He could be such a bastard sometimes! Sometimes? Try all the time. Default setting: rude.

'Gee, thanks,' she said, making it obvious she wasn't at all grateful. Even though the moment she slipped out of her old coat and into the new one, her body temperature raised by several degrees.

She buttoned it up all the way and when she lifted her gaze to his face she saw his attention was fixated on the buttons. Particularly the ones at chest height. He looked at her in a way that made her pulse soar.

'Gloves,' he said thickly, turning away and reaching into his car. The moment was over so quickly that she almost wondered if it had happened at all, but the swirling of her blood was all the confirmation she needed.

'But before you put them on—' he handed her a small box '—start with this.'

It was said so unceremoniously that she had no reason to suspect what she'd see when she lifted the lid, so she did so without care.

But inside was a ring—an engagement ring, apparently. A huge green emerald was at the centre and a circlet of white diamonds surrounded it, then ran down either side and around the diameter. It was beautiful, it was huge, it was *expensive*.

'Oh.' Abby blinked at the ring and then up at him. 'What is it?' she asked. Stupid question, but she was blindsided.

'What do you think?' He lifted it from the box and placed it in her palm. 'I hear they're part of the deal.'

'Deal?' She arched a brow.

'The getting married deal.'

Abby nodded, still not putting the ring on. 'But this is… too much. A simple band would have been fine, right?'

A muscle jerked in his jaw. 'A simple band is not the kind of ring I would buy for the woman I want to spend the rest of my life with. If we want people to believe this is a real marriage, then you'll have to convince them. Starting with the ring you wear.'

She frowned. 'Do we care what people think?'

A muscle throbbed in his jaw and his face was loaded with obvious derision. 'I care for our son's sake. I will not have him be subjected to gossip and cruelty because his parents cannot act like mature adults.' When she didn't react, he sighed heavily. 'Just put the ring on.'

She arched a brow. 'Gosh, seeing as you asked so nicely.' The words were uttered facetiously. Still, she didn't do as he said. Not to be ornery, but because she was truly miffed by the point he was making.

'Not for nothing, I don't think children get teased for having unmarried parents in the twenty-first century.'

'We won't know for sure, will we, because Raf will have two parents who love him, and are apparently happy together.'

Abby looked down at the ring, her own green eyes reflected in the colour of the central gemstone. Her heart stuttered with the brief consideration that perhaps he'd chosen it for that reason. But it was absurd. He'd probably just picked the first ring he'd seen when he'd walked into the shop. That it happened to be this one was a coincidence.

'Are you having second thoughts about our arrangement?' he asked silkily. Her heart began to race. Internally, she rejected that very idea. She knew already that living here with Gabe was the right decision—the advantages to Raf were abundantly clear.

'No,' she said thoughtfully. 'But I think we should talk about what kind of marriage we're going to have.'

He looked as if he was about to say something—to argue with her—but then he angled his head. Was it a nod? An agreement?

'It makes sense,' she said firmly. And, knowing what would motivate Gabe, she pulled out the big guns. 'It's best for Raf.'

'Fine,' he said, retrieving a bag from the trunk and then closing it. 'Let's talk.' He spoke the word with obvious reluctance, as though it were the very last thing he wanted to do, yet at least he had conceded something.

He began to walk away from her and she followed with a frown, ring in one hand, shopping bag in the other. 'Gabe? Where are you going?'

He stopped walking, his expression frustrated. 'You wanted to talk?'

When she was close enough, he reached for her hand and unfurled her fingers, then slid the ring into place. His nod of approval showed that he, at least, was happy with the way it looked, even though it felt curiously heavy to Abby.

'There is a *caffè* around the corner.'

'Oh.' She nodded, for some reason having thought they would simply speak in the car on the return trip.

'I'm hungry,' he said, as if that explained his choice.

He held the door to the *caffè* open for her, and it took Abby a moment to see past her distracted thoughts and appreciate the beauty of the place. It was charming, only ten or so seats at a few tables, with bay windows that looked out onto the ancient street. Festivity was in abundance here. A tree was set up at one end of the room and it had been decorated with burgundy ribbons and gold tinsel. A small train ran in circles around its base. Carols played overhead, Italian words set to familiar tunes, so that Abby's mind hummed along even when her heart was cold.

'Have a seat,' he prompted, pointing to a table in the corner.

Abby shot him a look that straddled amusement and irritation. 'Would it kill you to *not* boss me around?'

He lifted a single dark brow. 'Probably.'

She fought the temptation to poke her tongue out and made her way to the table, sitting down at it heavily. Even the beautiful decorations she held couldn't cheer her up. She resisted an impulse to pull them from their packaging and look at them. That would be her special reward when she got back to the castle.

She turned towards Gabe unwillingly, noting the deference with which he was treated by the couple behind the counter. They seemed completely inspired by him, nodding as he gestured to various foods, speaking in rapid-fire Italian.

He was such a native of these parts, and yet she knew he'd spent a large part of his life in Australia. He spoke

English like it wasn't his first language, still shying away from easy contractions and idioms.

He turned towards Abby unexpectedly. Their eyes locked and her pulse began to hammer hard inside her veins. She looked away, focusing her attention on a little scratch in the table top as though it were the most fascinating detail she'd ever observed.

'You wanted to talk,' he said, taking the seat opposite her. 'So?'

'Well...' She bit down on her lip, forcing her thoughts into order. 'Our marriage... I mean, you want people to think it's a real marriage, but...'

'Yes?' he prompted, his expression droll.

'It won't be.'

'No.'

She should have felt relieved by his rapid agreement, but she didn't. Something strange twisted inside her. 'So you don't...expect us to...'

'Sleep together?' he mocked, putting her out of her misery.

'Right.' She nodded jerkily. The woman from behind the counter appeared, placing two short black coffees down onto the table before swiftly disappearing.

Abby cupped one of the small glasses, simply to have something to do with her hands. It was warm and strangely comforting.

'As I said last night, sleeping together isn't on the agenda.' The words were so cold that Abby couldn't doubt their truth. 'My preference would have been never to see you again, after that night. As you know.' He paused for a moment. 'But I'm prepared to put that aside for our son. I truly believe this is the right decision.'

Abby nodded, though she could no longer separate sense from stupidity. A thousand and one questions raced through her mind. If they weren't sleeping together, would he sleep with someone else? Would her life include putting up with a series of Gabe's mistresses? What if he fell in love with one of them? What if he wanted to *marry* one of them? And they sued her for custody of Raf and won?

Suddenly her heart was thumping too hard, too fast, and she knew she had to fight her natural reserve to do what was best not just for Raf but also for herself.

'But there'll be no one else,' she said, her chin tilted forward defiantly.

His smile was smug and condescending. 'Does the idea make you jealous?'

'No,' she said. 'You're the one who's worried about exposing Raf to gossip. Don't you think extramarital affairs might qualify?'

He eyed her thoughtfully. 'I have every intention of doing what is right for our son, at every step of the way.'

It was strangely worded and yet his statement reassured Abby. It hadn't been a promise, yet she trusted him. She believed him.

Did that make her a fool?

'And for how long?'

He lifted a brow in silent enquiry.

'How long do you see this "marriage" of ours lasting?'

'As long as he needs us,' Gabe said, and something in the words pierced Abby's heart. 'At some point in the future we will separate. When he is older, when he's happy and settled. It's impossible to say now when that time will come.'

Abby nodded, wondering why his words didn't offer more relief.

'Rest assured, *tempesta*, I will not keep you at my side longer than is necessary.'

He threw his coffee back, oblivious to the way Abby's face went ashen at his throwaway sentence. She hid her reaction quickly, grateful when a waitress appeared with food. There were *piadini* and *zeppole*, *biscotti* and fruit.

He hadn't been kidding about being hungry—he'd ordered enough to feed a family of five.

But her appetite had diminished; his final statement had left Abby with a sinking feeling deep in her gut. He hated her, he hated that they were marrying, yet he was prosaically willing to accept it—but only for so long as was absolutely necessary.

'How long did you study dancing?' he asked, changing the subject neatly.

Her ballet career was a subject she generally took great care to avoid. But with Gabe Arantini? She was emotionally disorientated.

'A while.'

'A year? Two? Five?'

'Does it matter?'

He leaned closer and surprised her by putting his hand on hers, his fingers grazing over the top of the engagement ring. 'We are going to need to get better at pretending we don't dislike one another,' he said softly. 'It is natural that I should know this about you. So?'

He was right, and that annoyed her. 'Eleven years,' she said quietly. And then, surprising herself, she continued to speak, her eyes trained on the table top, her lips moving without her consent. 'My mother was a prima ballerina, so beautiful and graceful. I wanted to be just like her.'

He nodded. 'How old were you when she died?'

She'd mentioned this on their first night together, though she'd been careful to omit any details that might give away her identity.

'I was eight,' she murmured, the memories heavy on the periphery of her mind. 'It was a month before Christmas. A traffic accident. Very unexpected.'

'I'm sorry.' His civility surprised her.

'And you began to learn ballet after she died?'

She nodded. 'My father knew I wanted to be like Mom.

But it was more than that. *He* wanted me to be like her. I look like her,' she said quietly. 'And I move like her.' That was a lie. Abby had been told several times by careless, callous people that her mother's talent had been *nothing* to Abby's. As though that were praise and not a dagger through a grieving daughter's heart.

'What happened?' he asked, shifting a little in his seat.

'It was a child's dream,' she said, ignoring the lurch of pain in her chest.

'You grew out of the dream?'

That wasn't precisely true. And, though she generally didn't speak about her ballet career, she felt compelled to make Gabe understand, to explain the truth. 'It's a funny thing, being good at something.' Her smile was just a ghost. 'I *was* good at ballet, Gabe. Very good. Exceptionally good.' She spoke without even a hint of bragging. She was simply admitting the truth. 'I was given amazing opportunities. I danced with some of the world's best.'

'And then?' he prompted when she took a pause to bite into a strawberry.

'I broke my leg,' she said, a smile curving her lips at the reminiscence.

He waited for her to continue.

'And I could no longer rehearse. I had to rest. For the first time in my life, I had time to explore new diversions, and I discovered, much to everyone's displeasure, that there were things I loved more than dancing.'

He nodded thoughtfully. 'So you quit?'

'Yes.' She nodded slowly. 'A friend brought me *Jane Eyre* one evening. It was supposed to be a joke. He teased me that I was a bit like Bertha in the attic, and I wouldn't understand until I'd read the book.'

She laughed.

'It was silly—he was playing on the fact that I was "locked up" by Dad, but of course that wasn't true. Anyway, by the time I finished it I was hooked, and I devoured anything I could get my hands on. I realised there was so much more to life than dancing. Books, for one thing. I wanted to read everything ever written.'

Abby fingered one of the cinnamon doughnuts, her mind far away.

'I just… I didn't want my whole life to be consumed by ballet any more. My every waking thought given over to the act of dance. Oh, no. I wanted to be in the ocean, aboard the *Pequod*, or in ancient Troy by Agamemnon's side as he fought Achilles, I wanted to be at Manderley and Thornfield Hall, I wanted to be twenty thousand leagues under the sea. I thought breaking my leg and missing re-hearsals for so many months was an ending, but it was a beginning. The world opened up to me in a way I had never even hoped it would.'

Gabe's lips were tight. 'Yet you still dance?'

'Oh, I'll always dance,' she agreed. 'I love it as a hobby, but I don't want to spend my life pursuing it as a career.'

'You said your father wanted you to be like your mother. How did he take your decision to abandon professional ballet?'

Abby dropped her head forward, not wanting to answer. Her father had behaved appallingly; it was impossible to convey that to Gabe without allowing him to condemn her father, and it wasn't that simple.

'He got over it,' she said stiffly.

'I'll bet he didn't.' Gabe eyes narrowed. 'Yet you still adore him enough to do his bidding?'

She swallowed. How could she explain that, in part, guilt at disappointing her father had motivated many of her de-cisions, including the one that had brought her to Gabe's feet? A desperate, soul-deep need to impress a man who was, perhaps, impossible to impress?

'He's my father.' She shrugged. 'It's hard to explain. I know he has his faults,' she whispered. 'But I love him.'

'And you'd forgive him anything?'

'I guess,' she said, bright green eyes meeting his glittering black. 'Wouldn't you do the same?'

Gabe's laugh was a scoff. 'No, *tempesta*. I destroyed my father at the first opportunity I had and I would do the same a hundred times over.'

# CHAPTER EIGHT

ABBY STARED AT RAF, a frown etched on her face. In the two weeks since the morning in Fiamatina, she'd barely spoken to Gabe, yet his statement had continued to play on her mind, making her wonder to the point of distraction.

He'd destroyed his father?

She thought of what she knew of the man who was to become her husband. He'd been raised by foster parents in Australia. That was how he'd met his business partner, she knew, because he'd mentioned it in passing only a week or so earlier, as though it hardly mattered. He'd gone into the foster system at eight—she'd remembered because it was the same age her own life had been turned on its head when her mother had died.

But before that?

She had no idea, and now she *wanted* to know.

She could ask him, but Gabe hadn't seemed at all forthcoming after he'd dropped the bombshell. He'd skated around the topic, talking instead about logistics for the wedding—the licences that would be necessary, given that she was American. It could take time, he'd warned.

That was fine with Abby. It wasn't that she regretted having agreed to marry him, but a little time to adjust to her new circumstances would be good.

Necessary.

Essential.

Only she'd barely seen him for two weeks and she was beginning to suspect that he was avoiding her.

Fighting an urge to reach down and cuddle Raf, she slipped out of his room, making her way to her own bedroom. She didn't think of Gabe as she passed his door; it was too dangerous.

From her room, she spied the forest that surrounded the castle and suddenly she remembered the idea that had occurred to her weeks earlier in Fiamatina. Perhaps the conversation with Gabe had pushed all else from her mind, because she'd barely thought of the delightful Christmas decorations either. They were still sitting in the shopping bag. She pulled them out now, setting them on her dressing table with reverence, smiling as she observed how beautiful and special they were. And they would look even better on a tree!

Surely they deserved a tree?

With renewed determination, she grabbed the coat Gabe had given her—several more had been added to her wardrobe since then, arriving in boxes from Milan, Venice, Paris and Prague. It was a thoughtful gesture but Abby resented feeling like a beneficiary of his patronage.

She'd come to know many of the household staff well, including Hughie, a young Irishman who'd taken over much of the work in the grounds around the castle. It was Hughie who cleared the snow several times a day. She liked him best, perhaps because he spoke English and so they were able to converse easily. He also had a soft spot for Raf, which was instantly endearing.

'Hughie?' She found him bent over the fireplace, stocking it with fresh wood.

He lifted his head and grinned, a smile that would bring most women to their knees. Unfortunately for Abby, only one smile in the world had the ability to set her pulse racing and she had to rely on her memories of it. She hadn't seen a lot of Gabe's smile since she'd come to Italy.

'Do you think you could help me with something?'

'Anything.' He stood up and wiped his hands on the

worn fronts of his jeans. 'You look like you've got mischief on your mind,' he said, wiggling his brows.

'Definitely,' Abby laughed. 'I want to put up a tree.'

'A Christmas tree?'

'Yep. No shortage of trees to choose from, right? But I don't have an axe. Or experience with felling trees, come to think of it. And I thought…'

'Oh, yeah, sure.' Hughie grinned. 'I'll bring one down for you right now, before the dark settles. Come on. You can even pick it.'

It was the first real fun Abby had had in a long time. They walked through the dense woods for half an hour, talking about Hughie's family back home—six sisters and parents who adored their brood—which made Abby incredibly jealous.

He was moving onto describing his oldest sister, Daphne, when Abby froze.

'It's *perfect*,' she squealed, jumping up and down on the spot.

'Sheesh!' Hughie grinned. 'You couldn't 'ave chosen a tree closer to the castle, huh?'

'Sorry…' She winced. 'Can we have this one?'

'Yeah, I reckon we can.' He lifted the chainsaw. 'Stand back, then.'

She did, watching with admiration as he chainsawed through most of the thick trunk and then gave it a kick, felling the tree easily.

Once it was down, Hughie rigged a rope around the tree's base and then began to drag it through the soft snow.

'Won't that break the branches?' she asked. 'It'd be a shame to get it back to the house and find it's only half-perfect.'

'You'd just have to display it facing outwards,' he teased. 'Nah, it's soft needles, see.' He stopped walking so she could feel them. He was right; they were luxuriant beneath her touch. 'They'll be fine.'

They walked towards the house and Abby was so relieved to simply be having a normal conversation with someone that all of her attention was focused on Hughie. She didn't see Gabe glowering down at them from one of the upstairs windows. If she'd looked up, she would have seen his expression was one of utter fury.

He had forgotten how beautiful she was. No, that wasn't true. He'd remembered her beauty, but he had trained himself to look beyond it, to remember that her heart was quick to manipulate and lie. Every time he saw her smile and wanted to smile back, he remembered the photographs on her phone. The pictures of the Calypso design files that she'd snapped to show to her father—to bring his company down. It was easy to harden himself to her charms in the face of such obvious duplicity.

Every time she hummed under her breath and the song wound around his chest, tying him up in Abigail knots, he reminded himself that he'd had every reason to walk away from her and refuse to see her again.

When he woke up in the middle of the night in a cold sweat at dreaming of her pregnant and alone, wishing he could reach out and touch her, comfort her, know her, he reminded himself that *her* lies, *her* deceit had made that impossible.

He'd taught himself to ignore her beauty.

Only watching Abby as she was now, laughing with Hughie, he couldn't help but notice. Her smile, her dimples, her sparkling eyes, the grace and fluidity of movement that were as much a part of her as were her arms and legs.

He'd kept her at a distance this last fortnight, and he'd been glad. As if every day that passed without more than an occasional civility, a brief greeting, proved that he was up to the challenge of being married to Abigail and not capitalising on the chemistry that flashed between them.

Hughie's face was animated. He said something low and Abby had to lean closer to hear it properly. Her body, wrapped in one of the coats he'd bought her, made Gabe's pulse throb. She tucked her hair behind her ear, her expression serious as she concentrated on what Hughie said, and then she laughed again, reaching a hand out and touching his forearm. Their eyes met and Hughie's look of admiration was obvious.

Gabe swore into his office and dragged a hand through his hair.

She was serious now, her expression almost haunted, her eyes focused on the house, and Gabe's heart shifted in his chest. She was beautiful when she laughed, and enigmatic when she was sombre. Both emotions seemed to call to him in a way he utterly resented.

Just the sight of another man looking at Abby like Hughie was stirred a dark, possessive lust within Gabe's bones.

She was the mother of his child, the woman who'd given her virginity to him. She was *his* in so many ways… He just had to remind her of that.

'Where do you want it?' Hughie asked, straightening the tree as though it were simply a bunch of flowers.

'I suppose the study?' Abby murmured, thinking of the room that had the comfortable leather lounges and a view of the alps.

'The study is nice,' Hughie said. 'But it's out of the way, and I'm not sure this beast you've chosen will fit. It might have to be the entrance hall.'

He was right. Here at the house, without the other enormous trees dwarfing it, Abby could see the tree she'd chosen was actually quite large.

'Okay.' She nodded in agreement, equally pleased with the idea of the tree being set in the midst of the beautiful armchairs and sofa that sat in the foyer.

'Abigail?' There was a coldness in Gabe's voice. She turned to face him slowly, marshalling her expression into one of dispassionate curiosity, ignoring the kaleidoscope of butterflies that had begun to beat against her insides.

Why did he have to be so handsome? Even now, wearing dark jeans and a black pullover, he looked like a piece of art.

'I need you for a moment.'

'Oh.' Abby chewed on her lip. 'We were just about to set up the tree…'

'I can see that,' Gabe responded with barely suppressed anger.

'You're all right, Abby,' Hughie interrupted with a grin. 'I can wrangle this monster on my own.'

She was sure he could, but that wasn't the point. She'd been looking forward to helping. She shot Gabe a look of impatience but when she saw the dark, almost tortured emotions in the lines around his eyes, her own emotions ebbed. Had something serious happened?

'Okay.' She had a sense of urgency about her now. 'I'll be back soon.'

When she was level with Gabe on the stairs, he began to move upwards and she did her utmost to remain as far away from him as possible.

When they reached the landing though, he put a hand in the small of her back and steered her down the hallway at speed.

'I can walk just fine by myself, thank you,' she said tersely.

He threw her a fulminating glare.

'What the heck is going on?' she asked, coming to a stop halfway down the corridor.

'I would prefer to discuss it in private.' He nodded

pointedly towards a door and, curiosity growing, she went with him.

'Fine, we're in private now,' she said once they were ensconced in her bedroom. She determinedly tried to ignore the presence of the bed.

Gabe shut the door.

'You tell me you're worried about rumours of infidelity, but at the first chance you get you're out there flaunting yourself for all the world to see.'

Abby froze. 'What?'

'You were practically fawning over Hughie just now.'

She gaped, speechless, lost for words.

He prowled towards her. 'You actually think sleeping with a member of our household staff is appropriate?'

'He's not "our" household staff, he's yours,' she snapped.

'An unimportant distinction.'

'And I'm *not* sleeping with him,' she denied hotly. 'I like him, okay? He's nice to me and we speak the same language. He's the only other person I've actually been able to talk to since I moved to Italy. He's *nice* to me, unlike a certain other someone I could mention and, newsflash, Gabe, it's refreshing to spend time with someone who doesn't look at me like I'm dirt on the sole of their shoe.'

He glared at her, his expression darker, if possible. 'I don't care that he's *nice* to you,' Gabe snapped. 'He's off-limits. I don't want to see you talking to him again.'

She made a scoffing sound. 'You can't click your fingers and just *forbid* me from having a friend.'

'No? But I can fire him,' Gabe responded, taking another step towards her, his expression mutinous.

'Don't you dare.' Abby pushed at his chest but he caught her hands, holding them in place, and when her eyes met his now, sparks of another variety flew, like their own localised fireworks display, erupting between their chests.

'Don't you tell me what I can and can't do. I'm not

going to have you carrying on with whoever you decide you want...'

'Oh, grow up,' she said, pushing at his chest again. He pulled her hands down, holding them by her side, his breath heavy. 'I'm not sleeping with your gardener. I'm not sleeping with anyone! I haven't slept with anyone since you, so you can just go to hell with all your stupid accusations.'

Gabe's expression shifted momentarily and then it was fiercely intense and, before Abby knew what was happening, he was kissing her.

No, it wasn't a kiss, it was so much more. It was a mark of utter, unquestionable possession. It was a raging, desperate connection. His lips mashed to hers, his tongue slid inside her mouth and she made a noise of surprise and then surrender, low in her throat, her hands pulling free of his grip and reaching under his shirt, connecting with his bare chest, skin she remembered so intimately.

It had been over a year since they'd done this and yet it felt as if no time had passed. Or was it that they—this— existed outside the bounds of time and space?

'You won't be with anyone else,' he grunted, ripping his shirt over his head so she could marvel at his naked chest. He crushed her to him, kissing her desperately once more, his hands lifting to her hair and tangling in its length. It was still cold from her time in the snow and perhaps that reminded him of what they'd been fighting about, because he made another darkly guttural noise before stepping out of his trousers and pants so that he was completely naked.

'You are mine,' he said, pushing her shirt off, his expression deadly serious.

'I'm *not* yours,' she snapped. 'How can I be? You don't even speak to me. You don't look at me. I'm not yours.'

'I'm looking at you now.' He pushed at her jeans at the same time she stepped out of them. She wasn't his, but she was sure as hell desperate for him.

There was a vital difference, she told herself.

'I don't want you to just look at me,' she said boldly.

His laugh was hoarse. 'That's just as well.'

He ran his hands over her back, his fingertips gliding trails of goosebumps over her skin.

'You are too beautiful for your own good,' he groaned. His mouth came down on her breast, taking a nipple deep in his mouth, rolling it with his tongue, teasing it between his teeth so that shards of pleasure and pain shot through her body like little lightning bolts. His fingers toyed with her other breast, his palm wrapping around her, holding her weight, his thumb and forefinger rubbing over her nipple until she was crying out, moaning his name over and over again.

'You want me?' he asked, something grim in the question.

'Yes.' She wasn't afraid to admit that; she was afraid of what would happen if she didn't. She was afraid of this coming to an end when she needed Gabe, in that moment, more than she'd ever needed anything from anyone.

'Good,' he growled. 'Because I intend to make your body so desperate for mine that you cannot go a day without feeling me inside of you.'

She gasped at the promise, excitement flooding her veins.

'I thought you didn't want to touch me.'

'Apparently, I was wrong,' he admitted, lifting her up and wrapping her legs around his waist. His arousal was so hard and so close to her that she tried to push down, to take him deep inside her but he made a tsking noise. 'Be patient, *tempesta*.'

He placed her on the bed, his kiss pushing her back so that his weight was on top of her. He disappeared, but only for a moment, and when he returned it was with a foil square in his hands. He sheathed himself and she held her breath, needing so desperately to feel him.

'Is this what you want?' he asked, pressing his arousal to her womanhood gently, teasing, so that she nodded, her brow fevered, her eyes hungry.

'Say please,' he commanded.

'Please,' she whimpered, arching her back.

'Tell me again that I am the only man you've slept with,' he demanded, pushing himself a little deeper inside her, so that she groaned softly.

'Yes, yes.' She lifted her hands over her head.

He pulled out completely. 'Say it.'

Her eyes jerked open but she nodded. 'I haven't been with anyone since you.'

His smile was grim but he gave her what she needed, thrusting deeper into her feminine core. Still not deep enough, but she let out a low, soft moan as pleasure rippled through her.

Her fingernails dug deep into his back, scoring his shoulders as she lifted her legs, needing to wrap around his waist, to hold him closer, but he caught her knees and held her apart, kept her at a distance, his control and mastery of her body absolute.

'Please,' she cried out, desperate for release, for pleasure, for Gabe.

He dropped his mouth to her breast and flicked her nipple with his tongue, then ran his mouth down her body, over her flat stomach, across the dip of her navel and the apex of her thighs.

She gasped when his mouth connected with her most intimate flesh. 'Has a man ever touched you here?'

She whimpered and shook her head, digging her fingernails into the bed sheets.

His tongue ran across her seam and perspiration dampened her brow, her nipples pushed hard into the air, her whole body covered in goosebumps.

'I've changed my mind,' he said against her, his fingers running over her hips, finding her thighs and spreading them, giving him greater access.

'What about?' The question was panted, the words husky.

'I want you in my bed every night. Like this. Begging for me.'

She arched her back, her brain unable to engage and function, her mind non-existent.

'I need you,' she cried out.

'Then say you agree,' he said, his tongue dipping inside her so that she lost the ability to speak as well as to think. She was incandescent with desire, so completely overcome by the consuming need of him, so fully in the moment that she couldn't respond at all.

He lifted away from her and she let out a guttural noise of impatience.

'This is torture,' she snapped, pushing up on her elbows, panting, her long hair across her face.

He nodded. 'Yes.' He brought his body back to hers, his weight pleasing, his absence from her body not. 'I will torture you until you admit to me what you want.'

'I have,' she groaned, wrapping her legs around his waist.

As with before, he pushed her knees downward, shaking his head. 'I'm not having a wife who runs around with a gardener, or anyone else. Not when we make such sense together in bed.'

Through the fog of sensual desire, the words pushed into her brain. He was acknowledging that this was special, different and addictive, for him as well.

'Well,' she said, the word husky, thick, angry. 'That goes both ways. I won't have a husband who runs around with *anyone*.'

His eyes sparkled with something like an acknowledgement and he nodded, bringing his hard, firm arousal back to her feminine core. 'Deal,' he said, sliding inside her, thrusting hard, so that she let out a cry of relief when he finally took possession of her, his body everything she remembered and so much more.

His fingers laced through hers, pushing them above her head, and he kissed her, his possession absolute. He stoked flames in her she hadn't known existent, his body was, in that instant, her reason for being. Every movement, every thrust, every touch, every kiss, sent her closer and closer towards the edge of sanity until she was crying out, pleasure like a single point of bright light in her brain, blinding her utterly.

'Gabe.' She whispered his name and he broke the kiss to look at her. 'Is this normal?'

She had no experience outside of what they'd shared, but if sex was like this—enough to tear you apart at your cosmic core—then how did people ever get anything done?

In answer, he pulled out of her, something like iron in his expression, his desertion intense, but then he thrust into her anew so that she bucked her hips hard, meeting his demands—more than meeting them, conquering them.

'No, *tempesta*.' The admission seemed ripped from the depths of his being. 'Nothing about this is normal.'

Among the desire, the longing, the pleasure and the delicious, sensual heat, Abby knew she felt relief at that. She was glad this was different, even for him. She wanted to ask more, to ask him if he'd ever felt this, if he'd felt this the first time they were together, if he could tell her why it was so incredible between them.

But then he kissed her again and she surrendered to the moment completely, lost to the pleasure of their connection and the power of his body.

Pleasure began to spin in her gut, slow and insistent, before bursting through her whole body, promising delight and release, and she called his name over and over, arching her back, welcoming his every movement, taking him in deep, kissing him as though her life depended on it.

His hands sought her breasts, palming them, moving over them, and her release didn't abate, she was building anew, wave after wave of pleasure dousing her until she almost couldn't bear it.

At the moment she began to fall apart, he joined her, swearing under his breath as he thrust into her so deep and hard that it tipped her completely over the edge. She wasn't conscious of how loud she was being until he laughed, a choked sound, and pressed his lips to hers. Not a kiss of passion so much as to silence her.

Their breathing was in unison, just the inhalation and exhalation of two bodies that had been torn apart by sensual heat.

It had been the most intense pleasure of her life. Abby only realised now that he had been gentle with her in New York. That he had taken her innocence slowly, softly, subjugating his own desires to meet her own, initiating her into the way of lovemaking and desire in a way that would enable her to feel maximum pleasure.

But now?

No-holds-barred sex, and it had rocked her world to the core.

'That was amazing,' she sighed.

His body was still heavy on hers, his breathing deep, and she wondered if he'd fallen asleep until he shifted and his eyes met hers. 'You are mine,' he said darkly, seriously, reminding her of the argument they'd had before they'd slept together. 'I do not want to see you talking to Hughie again, as though he is your lover...'

'Gabe—' Abby smiled, trying to hold onto the threads of what they'd just shared, needing to be enveloped by intimacy for a little longer '—how can you think about any-one else after that? How can you think I am?'

'You forget, Abigail, that I know what you're capable of. That I have no reason to think the best of you.'

And the desire that had made her body so warm gave way to ice-cold regret. Remorse.

She pulled away from him, pushing him off her at the same time she jack-knifed off the bed, her face pale, her expression mutinous.

'How dare you throw insults at me after what we just shared?' she demanded through teeth that were chattering.

'We just shared sex,' he said with a nonchalant shrug. 'Albeit fantastic sex, but it doesn't change who you are.'

Abby shifted away from him, her eyes seeking her clothes, needing, desperately, to shield herself from him. 'You don't know anything about me,' she said, finding her underpants first and sliding them up her shaking legs, grate-ful for the modesty they afforded.

His short, sharp laugh was a dismissal that twisted her heart painfully in her chest. 'I know *everything* I need to know,' he corrected.

'Oh? Enlighten me,' she demanded, finding her jeans and turning them so they were the right side out.

'I don't need to enlighten you. You're not stupid.'

'Oh, I'm so glad that's not something you can fault me for.'

Gabe frowned, his expression one of true bemusement. 'After the way we met, I cannot change how I feel about you, nor what I think you are. But this—' he gestured to the bed '—this is a silver lining.'

'God—' she reached for her jumper, holding it in the palm of her hand '—you're such a bastard! You're cold and ruthless and heartless and so, so cruel. How can you think this marriage will ever work when you speak to me like that?'

'Have I said anything that's not true?'

'You don't know me,' she said, frustrated. 'You don't even try to know me!'

'You conned me into bed. Took photos of highly guarded, top-secret blueprints. You planned to pass them off to my competition…'

'I know all that,' she said on a small sob. 'But if you took a second to understand my relationship with my dad…'

'We all have a history.' Determination fired his veins. 'We all have baggage. You allowed yours to control you.'

He was right and she knew it. That angered her even further. She ripped the jumper through the air, shaking it pre-emptively and pulling it on, so she didn't see the way his face shifted, the way guilt momentarily glanced across his features. Regret too. The way he looked as if he hated that they were arguing and wasn't sure how to defuse it—to wind back his careless remark so that they were still entwined. Two bodies post-passion.

The sleeve of the jumper flew wide and as Abby jerked it over her head she heard a delicate, unmistakable breaking noise that mirrored the breaking of her heart.

'Oh, no!' For she knew immediately what had happened.

She spun around and, sure enough, one of the decorations had crashed to the ground, the other balancing precariously. She pushed it back to safety and then fell to her knees, her fingertips reaching for the tiny, fragile shards.

'Stop it.' Gabe swore, jumping from the bed and crouching beside her. But Abby didn't hear him. She blinked back tears that threatened to fall.

'Now look what you made me do,' she snapped, but the words lacked conviction.

'What is it?' He batted her hands away as she tried to pick up the pieces but she refused to comply, her fingertips seeking each shard as though she could somehow put them back together again.

'Stop,' he said softly, urgently. 'You're going to hurt yourself.'

Just as he said it, a piece of glass punctured her skin and a perfect droplet of crimson blood fell to the floor.

'Damn it.' He gripped her wrists and pulled her to standing. 'Sit here.'

He arranged her on the edge of the bed and disappeared into her bathroom. He returned with a wad of tissues, handing them to her. 'Press them to your skin.'

She pulled a face at his retreating back, refusing to watch while he cleaned up the vandalism of the perfect little decoration.

Only once the floor was clear of glass, the tiny bell resting on the edge of the dressing table, did he come back to Abby. He crouched down in front of her, his eyes holding hers.

'What was that?'

She sniffed, refusing to meet his eyes.

'Abby?'

His use of the diminutive form of her name did something to her and she flicked her gaze to his, her own vulnerabilities unconsciously displayed in the lines of her beautiful young face. 'Christmas decorations,' she said softly. 'They were perfect.'

He looked towards the dressing table. 'Where did you get them?'

'A shop in Fiamatina,' she hiccoughed.

'So?' It was obvious he didn't comprehend. 'You can buy another one, *tempesta*.'

'No, I can't,' she sobbed, shaking her head then dropping it into her palms.

'Why not? Were there only two in the whole shop?'

'No, there were quite a few but...' She clamped her lips together, sucking in a deep breath.

'But?' he prompted.

'They were expensive, okay? I could only afford two. And I loved them. They were special and rare and I was going to put them on the Christmas tree for Raf's first Christmas and every Christmas after and now it's all ruined. Everything is ruined.'

# CHAPTER NINE

GABE WATCHED THEM from his office, every cell held taut. They hadn't spoken again since he'd left her room the day before. Her anger had been disproportionate to the perceived crime. No, not crime. It hadn't been his fault. She'd knocked the decoration herself, and yet she'd blamed him. She'd been so cross with him—he hadn't known her capable of that anger.

When they'd argued in New York, she'd been passive. She'd taken his remonstration, she'd accepted what he'd laid at her feet and she'd been sad, apologetic. She had known how wrong she'd been. Yes, he had seen shame in her eyes—remorse too—and she'd been reasonable enough not to argue in the face of his anger.

Yesterday, *she'd* been enraged.

And not about the decoration. Not really. It was more than that. The way he'd treated her, the things he'd said.

Regret perforated the lining of his gut.

He'd been shocked by his weakness—shocked by his very emotional response to seeing her with Hughie. It had been an innocent conversation and he'd acted as though he'd caught them *in flagrante*. He'd taken her into her bedroom, knowing that if they didn't have sex he'd be driven almost insane by possessive need.

And then he'd done what he could to turn back time, to remind them both of why they were enemies more than lovers.

An unfamiliar sense of shame flooded him. He hadn't enjoyed hurting her. He hadn't liked seeing her shock, feeling her withdraw from him, physically needing to distance herself from him.

He closed his eyes, flashes of their time together running before him. Her passion— a passion that had been unmatched in his experience—the way she'd given herself to him completely. What cruel twist of fate was it that a woman he despised had turned out to be his perfect partner in bed? More than that, she was the mother of his child and he was committed to spending his life with her, to making their child happy.

He couldn't do that if he spent the whole time berating her for the sins in her past, yet he couldn't move beyond those sins until he understood her better. He had every reason to be careful with his trust—his childhood had been a baptism of fire and he'd developed the necessary defences. That included being careful who he admitted to his inner sanctum—which so far just included Noah.

Now, there was also Raf.

He opened his eyes and his gaze instantly pinpointed Abby, a bright shape against the white backdrop of snow. He studied her. She was smiling and despite the fact their child, so bundled up he was three times his usual size, couldn't possibly comprehend her, she was talking as she built an enormous snowman. His cheeks were ruddy from where he sat propped in a stroller.

Gabe watched as Abby pinched a small amount of snow in her fingertips and pressed a tiny bit to Raf's cheek. Their baby's eyes flew wide and then the little boy smiled. She smiled back. Something within Gabe squeezed. What must it be like to have that kind of affection?

Maternal love was a foreign concept to him.

Any love, really.

Abby had it to give in spades, apparently.

She turned back to the snowman and kept building, fattening his belly until her arms couldn't wrap around him. Some time later, when she was happy with the construction, she reached into the bottom of the stroller and pulled out something red and white. A scarf! She wrapped it around the snowman's neck and tied it in a knot, then she reached for something else. A Santa hat.

She was making a damned Santa snowman on his lawn, with their son. Was this what it would always be like for him? On the periphery of something—a family—and not being able to reach for it? Was this the lasting legacy of his own childhood?

He didn't believe in love—even as a boy, witnessing the way love had slowly deadened his mother's soul, he swore he'd never get married, never have children. He hadn't wanted either. The necessity of loving wasn't something he'd ever craved.

Did that excuse his behaviour?

Did anything?

Making sure Abby married him was one thing; using her innocence and desire against her to keep her in his bed was another. He had kissed her and she'd quivered. She'd said she hadn't been with anyone else and he believed her. It wasn't as if she'd had a multitude of opportunities since she'd been so sick while carrying his baby. But if he hadn't brought her to Italy? No doubt she would have found someone to share her life with.

The very idea filled Gabe's mouth with acidity.

In bed she was putty in his hands and there was so much he could teach her, so much he could do to help her forget how imperfect their situation was. Keeping her in a sensual fog so that she never stopped to question the madness of what they were doing. Was he really capable of that? Could he stoop so low?

His expression was grim because, deep down, he knew that as long as she was under his roof, with his ring on her finger, he would do whatever it took to have her.

He would never love her—never trust her—and nor would he ever forgive her; but he would make love to her often because they both wanted that. That was the only part of this whole plan that made sense—the rest was a minefield...

She laughed again with Raf, and certainty formed as a rock in his gut. *She was his.*

'I have to go to Rome.' His voice came from the door to her room and Abby paused her reading, pressing a finger against the page of her book and looking up in the hope it wasn't obvious what effect his appearance was having on her.

Had it only been a day ago that they'd made love? For confirmation, her eyes flew to the dressing table where a solitary ornament remained.

'Rome?' She sat up straighter in bed, her heart hammering against her ribcage. He was wearing a suit, just like the first night they'd met, and he looked so damned handsome it was impossible to remember that she was still frustrated with him. With great difficulty, she did, though.

Her voice was cool. 'Well, have fun.'

Gabe stepped into her room, closing the door behind him and striding across to the bed. Abby's pulse accelerated.

'I would have more fun here,' he admitted gruffly. His strong, confident hands caught her thighs and pulled her to the edge of the bed; Abby's breath caught in her throat and she stared up at him with such obvious passion that she knew he must see it, must comprehend.

'Do you remember what we discussed?' he asked, moving his head closer to hers so only an inch separated them.

She shook her head, merely because she couldn't think straight and needed to buy time.

He lifted a finger and pressed it to her cheek, then ran it down her jaw to her neck, and to the pulse point hovering at the base of her throat. 'You are mine,' he said simply.

She opened her mouth to argue, to say something to assert herself, but he took the opportunity to kiss her, his lips taking hers, pressing her back to the bed so that his body was on top of hers and she moaned into him, such a sweet sound of innocence that his gut twisted.

'I want you to share my room,' he murmured, the words seductive, as was the way he moved his kiss to her throat, nipping her with his teeth while his hands ran over her body, finding the flesh beneath her shirt. She wasn't wearing a bra; he was easily able to cup her breasts, to feel their warm sweetness, her tight nipples.

She made a noise of acquiescence, a garbled sound of pleasure.

'You'll move in with me,' he said, a little more confident now but still miles from his usual arrogance.

'I *have* moved in with you.' She said the words into his mouth, kissing him, her ache to be possessed by him profound.

'You know what I mean.'

He seemed to be asking, to *want* something from her without simply demanding it. She tilted her head to the side. 'I'll think about it.'

He lifted his head and his eyes glowed, but he wisely chose not to push the point.

Distance knifed between them and she wanted to bridge it, but he was already straightening, pulling further away from her.

'How long will you be gone?' She tried to make the question sound casual when in fact she was irrationally bothered by the idea of him so far away.

'A day or so.' He took a step back, his eyes holding hers, the rapid shift of his chest the only sign that he had been at all affected by the kiss they'd just shared.

'Be good while I'm gone. And, just to save you some time, there are *no* Calypso files in the castle, so you don't need to go looking behind my back.'

She glared at him but he shook his head.

'It was a joke. A bad one.' His smile was tight. 'I'll see you soon.'

It had been a joke but the words stung, in the way that only the truth could. When she looked back to that night in New York, she could scarcely believe what she'd done. It was as if someone else had temporarily taken over her body.

And now she'd have to face that misstep for the rest of her life. Or for as long as this charade of a marriage continued.

When he was out of sight she picked up her book and continued to read, but without seeing a single word. Less than an hour later, she heard the helicopter take off and moved—as if on autopilot—to the window. It was shiny black; it looked like a huge eagle, all sleek and elegant, as it moved away from her and the castle.

She told herself she was relieved he was gone, that it would give her time to make sense of what was happening between them. But, in truth, relief was nowhere near the top of what she felt.

She dropped her head to her pillow and breathed in deeply. It still smelled of him.

She groaned—she didn't have to analyse her feelings to know that she had them, and to know that it was inherently dangerous to feel *anything* for a man like Gabe Arantini. Particularly given that he had made it obvious he didn't like her and would never trust her.

And yet...

Yes—and yet. Apparently, her heart hadn't got her brain's memo, for it was already softening and turning, allowing Gabe more space inside her mind than she knew was wise.

Telling herself she was going to make the most of this opportunity to explore, she didn't want to acknowledge that she was actually marking time however she could.

She woke early the next morning and, wrapped up in her warmest clothes, went to explore the forest to the side of the house. She found pine cones which she could spray-paint silver and use to decorate the tree, and she counted seven squirrels as she went.

She imagined Raf when he was older. She imagined the way his face would light up at the sight of the bushy-tailed creatures, the way he'd laugh and try to chase them. Her chest heaved.

It was right that she was here in Italy, here with Gabe. She'd hated Gabe for sweeping into her life and expecting her to fall in with all these changes, but when she thought of the tiny apartment in Manhattan with no heating she knew their son would be happier here.

And her? She pushed that question aside.

Reliving the time they'd spent together in Manhattan, she played with Raf, noticing every little detail about him anew. She lay with him on his tummy, she read to him, she watched him sleep and she got to know the nannies who also looked after him.

Gabe had told Abby she wouldn't need to cook but to distract herself she dug out a recipe book from the castle's library and made gingerbread dough until the whole kitchen was fragrant with the spiced aroma. And though she'd never attempted anything so grand as a gingerbread house, she figured she was already way outside her comfort zone so what was one more brave attempt?

It was almost dark by the time she was finished, the house hardly a work of art but at least structurally sound. She went back upstairs but instead of returning to her bedroom, she went to his.

He'd asked her to move in. Was that what she wanted?

She padded into his suite, hovering on the threshold as though she were crossing some invisible barrier before pushing deeper inside. His room was larger than hers, with a king-size bed at its heart, two sofas to the side and a bay window that overlooked the gardens. She wondered what these gardens would be like in summer. It was hard to imagine while they were completely blanketed in snow.

There were no marks of personal possession in this room, besides his clothes in the wardrobe and toiletries in the en suite bathroom. No photos hung on the walls, no artwork to show his aesthetic preference. There was a flat-screen television mounted on the wall. She flicked it to life distractedly—the Italian news was on. She sat on the edge of the bed, watching for a while, wondering if she'd ever comprehend the fast-moving language.

Hours later, she accepted that Gabe wasn't coming back to the castle.

The wave of disappointment was unwelcome, but she recognised that feeling well.

She showered and dressed in a pair of wintry pyjamas before curling up in her own bed.

She fell asleep dreaming of Gabe and woke with a start some time in the middle of the night, sitting up straight. She was disorientated, as though she might have been in his room after all, as though he might be with her.

A cursory inspection with the light of her lamp showed that not to be the case. She was alone in her own bed.

She dropped back against the pillows and stared at the ceiling until the oblivion of dawn or sleep came first.

In the end, it was dawn. Morning light broke across her room and she was grateful, if somewhat exhausted, to step out of bed, shower and dress.

Her previous day's distractions had only worked so much.

She spent an hour with Raf and then pulled on some leggings and a form-fitting shirt and went to the room near the kitchen.

Ballet would help.

She chose a piece from *Les Petit Riens* to punish herself. The choreography included seven back-to-back *fouettes* then a double *pirouette* and she loved it for its intricacy. The hardest dances always looked the most beautiful, the most deceptively effortless, when they were performed well.

She breathed in deeply, her eyes closed as she felt the music, and then she began to move, her eyes remaining closed as she lost herself to the emotion of the Mozart piece, performing the *fouettes*—one of the most difficult steps in ballet—as though she were simply walking.

*You're going to be a star, Abs. Just like your mom.*

The words pushed against her and she frowned, slowing to a stop, dropping her head forward. Tears sparkled in her eyes when she thought of her father, when she thought of the fact that he was alone in America, that he was such a stubborn ass he'd let her go. No, he hadn't let her go. He'd pushed her—hard—out of his life.

She made a grunting noise, forcibly removing such thoughts, and continued to dance, pushing herself harder and harder, performing a *grande jeté* high in the air before landing gracefully on her feet and pushing up *en pointe*.

Had she known he was watching?

No.

Yet the sight of Gabe, draped against the door, as he had been the first time she'd practised in here, didn't surprise her. Their eyes met and everything inside her coiled tight like a spring. She was very still as the music swirled around them, enveloping them, throbbing with tension.

'Don't stop.' The words were more than a gravelly command. They were a hoarse, desperate plea.

She didn't like the way he told her what to do—her cheeks flushed because deep down she liked it very much—but she wanted to show her free will as much as possible. She felt his desperation, the lure of his need, and turned back to the dance, once again feeling it as though it were a part of her.

She didn't close her eyes though. If he wanted to watch her, then she wanted to watch him, to see the play of emotions on his face as she pirouetted around the room. For a moment she remembered what it had been like to perform, wearing the beautiful yet hard and scratchy costumes, the feet that had ached, the rapturous attention of the audience, the adoration from the other dancers. Though she'd come up against some jealousy, Abby moved so beautifully, so instinctively, that most ballerinas had simply accepted she was different to the rest of them.

After half an hour the piece came to a stop and Abby paused with it, remembering the last movement of choreography as though she'd learned it only the day before. The *attitude derrière* was the final step and she held it long after the last note had throbbed around them, her eyes meeting Gabe's, locking to his, before she eased her foot down and returned to standing.

She waited, her breath held, uncertain what he would say, only feeling that something powerful had shifted between them, something new and interesting.

'You...' He frowned, the words apparently stuck deep inside him. His voice was hoarse and she was glad because she knew it was emotion that did that. He had watched her and he'd *felt* something. That was the point of ballet, wasn't it? 'That was incredible.'

The praise, though not the most lavish she'd ever received, made her heart soar because praise wasn't something Gabe Arantini offered often.

'Thank you,' she said, even more pleased when she sounded calm in the face of her racing heart. 'How was Rome?'

He dipped his head forward and she had no idea what the gesture was supposed to convey.

'How is Raf?'

She smiled; she couldn't help it. 'Delightful.'

He arched a brow. 'You seem well. Less tired.'

'Well, having round-the-clock nanny care will do that for a mom,' she pointed out.

He nodded. 'I think he is settled here too.'

'Well, it's only been a few weeks. But yes. He seems to be settling in well.'

He frowned, and she had the sense that he was trying to find words, that he was looking for what to say. But he didn't speak, and so Abby did. 'I…guess I'll go take a shower.'

He nodded but when she was almost at the door he reached out, wrapping his fingers around her wrist. 'Did you sleep in my bed?'

She blinked, the question unexpected. 'No.'

He made a small tsking noise. 'And here I was, imagining you there.'

She swallowed. 'It felt weird.'

He scanned her face intently and then nodded. 'No matter. There is tonight.'

Her stomach rolled with anticipation.

'I have to catch up on some work. Have lunch with me later? There's something I need to discuss with you.'

If she'd been planning on refusing, the last short sentence scuppered that intention. Curiosity fanned in her chest. 'Okay.'

She took a step towards the door but, instead of letting her go, he pulled her back to his body, firm, and she felt then that he was so hard, all of him, and she groaned softly under her breath.

'Did you miss me?' he asked softly, lifting his hand to her hair and tangling his fingers in its length.

'You were only gone for a night,' she pointed out.

'Was I? It felt like longer.'

# CHAPTER TEN

THE BUTTERFLIES IN her stomach were rampant, swishing their delicate wings against her sides, making it difficult to concentrate on anything. She barely noticed the beautiful table she was led to, in a part of the castle she was yet to explore. A balcony beyond would be beautiful in warmer weather, but for now it remained sealed off, thick glass doors keeping the cold out but allowing an unimpeded view of the alpine scenery. A light dusting of snow had begun to fall and some of it settled on the railing as she watched. The table was round, large enough to comfortably accommodate six, but only two place-settings had been laid, and with the kind of cutlery and glassware one would find in a six-star restaurant.

She sucked in a deep breath, telling herself it was ridiculous to be nervous. The engagement ring Gabe had given her sparkled on her finger and Abby tried to draw strength from the beauty of its design—and failed. It was so lovely and perfect that it only added to her nervousness.

The domestic who'd shown her to the table had poured a glass of wine and Abby took a sip now, grateful to have something to occupy her hands. The alcohol was cold and yet warmed her insides. She closed her eyes and drew in another deep breath; when she blinked them open Gabe was striding into the room, a large black shopping bag held in one hand, so handsome that her breath snagged in her throat.

'I was held up,' he said by way of explanation rather than apology.

A wry smile touched Abby's lips.

'It's fine. I've only been here a few minutes.'

He nodded, taking the seat opposite her. Out of nowhere another domestic appeared, pouring Gabe some wine. He looked at the man with a frown. 'We can manage. I'd prefer not to be interrupted.'

The man said something in Italian, smiled at Abby and then disappeared.

Abby's frown was instinctive. 'You don't strike me as a man who would like having staff.'

He lifted a brow. 'Forty thousand people work for me.'

'I don't mean in a professional sense,' she said with a small shake of her head. 'I mean household staff.'

'You get used to it.' He shrugged.

'I don't know if I ever could.'

'You mean, if you ever *will*,' he corrected.

She nodded slowly.

'You must have had servants?'

'God, no.' She laughed, having no idea how beautiful she looked as the creamy midday sun bounced across her blonde hair, causing it to shimmer. 'My father hated the idea of having people in our home. He's very private.'

At the reference to Lionel Howard something between them shifted, a darkness descending on the table.

Gabe spoke first with a heavy sigh. 'Tell me how it started.'

Abby lifted her shoulders. 'How what started?'

'You, coming to meet me. What did your father say to you?'

Abby's tummy twisted. She couldn't meet his eyes. 'Is that why you wanted to have lunch with me?'

Gabe's frown was infinitesimal, but she caught the tail end of it.

'It's natural you'd be curious,' she rushed to add.

'I wasn't. But seeing as you've mentioned him…'

She nodded. Hadn't she decided that she needed to be

honest with him, to help him understand why she'd done what she had? Of course he felt the same need to know.

'I told you—' she spoke slowly, every word considered '—my father was destroyed when your company launched.' Her grimace was an acknowledgement of the fact that this was an awkward conversation to have. 'I'd heard about you for years, you know.'

She felt Gabe stiffen without looking at him.

'He came to blame you and...your foster brother...for every single business problem he had.' She closed her eyes, finding it insufficient simply to look away from Gabe now and needing instead to block him out completely. Her slender throat shifted as she swallowed.

'You are not saying anything I had not deduced for myself,' he said. The words were offered with his usual degree of detachment but Abby felt them—she felt them right in the centre of her heart. 'You are fortunate your father targeted me rather than Noah.'

'Why?'

Gabe thought of his best friend and his frown deepened. 'Because Noah is...'

She waited, her interest obvious.

'Noah and I are very similar. But he has no interest in pretending to be civil. He would have chewed you up and spat you back out again if you'd tried your trick on him.'

'It wasn't a trick.'

He ignored her. 'Noah would have seen through you too. He's always been a better judge of character than me.'

She paled.

'He would hate you, I think, for what you planned to do.'

Abby gripped the fork tightly, her brain hurting. 'I'm sorry to hear that. He's your best friend, right?'

'He's my...yes.'

'Have you told him about us? About Raf?'

Gabe's eyes held Abby's. 'No.'

'Why not?'

'He's…' Gabe looked towards the window for a moment, his expression tight. 'He's got his own stuff going on.' It was vague enough to create more questions than it answered, but Abby didn't push him. Gabe had clammed up and she knew him well enough to know that he would only speak when he was ready to share.

'My dad didn't *target* you,' she said softly, bringing them back to the topic.

Gabe spun back to face her, lancing her with his eyes.

'He wanted information. He never meant to hurt you.'

'He wanted to destroy my business. You don't think that would have hurt me?'

'He didn't think about it like that,' Abby insisted. 'You were irrelevant. All he cares about is his own success. For years he was at the top of his game, and then you came along…'

'I am hardly irrelevant, given that he sent you to spy on me.'

She brushed past his interruption impatiently. 'But do you understand what I'm saying?'

'I understand the excuses you're offering.' His eyes glittered with an emotion she didn't understand and then, as though the words were being dragged from him, 'I believe you were motivated by love for your father rather than hatred for me.'

'Hatred?' That jolted her eyes to his and she reached across the table, curving her palm over his. 'It was *never* about hatred for you. Even before I met you I was *fascinated* by you, Gabe. Your…dynamism and success, your work ethic, your lifestyle.' She blushed. 'You were my polar opposite in every way. It didn't take much convincing when my dad suggested I meet you…'

He swallowed, his throat bunching beneath her gaze. 'And yet you still came with the intention of finding whatever information you could and taking it back to your father?'

She bit down on her lip, nodding slowly.

At his look of disapproval, she rushed to add, 'But only at first. Gabe, fifteen minutes into knowing you and there was no way I was going to go through with it.'

She withdrew her hand, the intimacy feeling discordant suddenly. 'I slept with you because I wanted to,' she said with quiet insistence.

'You wanted me? You wanted Calypso.'

'No!' She shook her head to emphatically refute him. 'Gabe, you have to believe me. Us sleeping together, that was… Didn't you feel it?'

'Feel what, *tempesta?*' he challenged stonily, every cell in his body closed to her, the definition of immovable.

Still, having come this far, Abby urged herself to be honest. 'A connection,' she said, her eyes landing on his. 'I felt something for you the instant you spoke to me, the second we first touched, when you made me laugh… I *wanted* you to be my first lover,' she promised. 'Because of who you were to *me*, not to Dad, nor to the world.'

He was quiet, appraising her words from every angle.

'You told me you simply wanted to rid yourself of your tiresome virginity,' he pointed out.

Inwardly she winced, wishing she could take back that excuse. She'd said it to save some pride, but now she wanted to dispel that idea. 'You don't think I'd been smiled at by handsome men before?' she asked. 'You don't think I'd had ample opportunities to "rid myself" of my virginity in the past?'

He stared at her long and hard, his cheeks darkening with a flush of emotion. 'I don't know.' He shrugged. 'It made little sense to me on that night; it still doesn't.'

'I had no interest in sex,' she said simply. 'I was too busy with ballet—my schedule was pretty intensive—and then, by the time I gave it up, when it came to intimacy I felt like a fish out of water. All my friends had been in several relationships, and the guys I met were obviously way more experienced. I was…embarrassed.'

'You weren't with me.'

'Because I felt like I knew you,' she said with urgency. Had he truly not felt that same sense of familiarity?

'Abigail—' he sighed heavily, dragging his fingertips through his hair '—I think you need to be careful here.'

'Careful how?' she prompted.

'You speak like a classic romantic,' he said, his smile bordering on mocking. 'A connection. As though I was some fated Prince Charming riding into town to win your heart.' He laughed, a harsh sound, but that same heart ratcheted up a gear, his description unknowingly hitting on how she *had* felt at the time. 'We are going to get married, *for our son*. The last thing I want is for you to get hurt—even if a small part of me thinks you are simply reaping what you sowed a year ago.'

Pain scored Abby deep in her heart and her veins turned to ice as crisply cold as the snow outside. 'I've tried to explain—'

'Damn it! Abigail, listen to me.' He softened his tone with obvious effort. 'You will never be able to explain what you did. What you intended to do. I appreciate that you didn't follow through with what your father wanted, but you came to me with one purpose—betrayal. Nothing that happened beyond that matters. Had you not fallen pregnant, if we didn't share a son, we wouldn't be sitting across a table having this conversation. Or any conversation. You understand that, don't you?'

She sat frozen to the spot, her heart thumping inside her the only sign of life. His words were shredding her into tiny pieces and uncertainty lurched all around her. 'How can you say that?' she asked quietly, digging her finger-nails into her palms. 'After what we shared the other day?'

His smile was almost sympathetic. 'For your own good, try to remember that sex and love are two very distinct sides of a coin.'

His words ran around her head like an angry tornado. She didn't believe it was *love*, necessarily, but it was more than just great sex. When they were together she felt as if she could trust him with her life; she felt as if everything made sense. Didn't he feel that too? Or did he always feel that?

'I guess I wouldn't know,' she said after a moment, hoping she didn't sound as confused as she felt. 'You, on the other hand, have plenty of experience.'

'Yes.' The word was a crisp agreement. He reached over and topped up Abby's wine; she hadn't even realised she'd been sipping it as they spoke. 'Was he angry when you went home empty-handed?'

It took Abby a moment to realise that Gabe had returned to their original topic of conversation. 'Yes.' She didn't feel like talking about her father though. 'You were fostered in Australia?' she asked, the question catching Gabe off-guard. His face shifted into a mask of displeasure but he covered it quickly enough.

'Yes.'

'But you were born here? In Italy?'

'Yes.'

Abby frowned. 'So how did you end up in Australia? I would have thought you would stay in your own country when you lost your mother…'

'She had recently emigrated to Australia,' he said matter-of-factly. 'It's where she was from, and she still had family there. A cousin, at least. It made sense to go home.'

'How did she die?' The question sounded insensitive even to Abby's ears. She blamed the wine and the fact she was still reeling from the ease with which he'd limited their relationship simply to sex...

'A drug overdose,' Gabe said, the words cold.

'I'm sorry.' She reached over, cupping her hand over his. 'That must have been awful.'

'Awful?' He looked at her hand as though it were a foreign object, something unexpected and strange on the table. 'Awful is one way to describe it.'

'Were you close to her?'

Gabe's eyes lanced Abby. 'Aren't all children close to their mothers?'

Abby nodded. 'I guess.' She was quiet as she contemplated her next question.

'You can ask,' he prompted, understanding that she was holding back.

'Had she taken drugs for long?'

'No.' He reached for his wine and took a sip. The silence around them was another presence at the table, heavy and sad, all-encompassing.

It was broken by the arrival of a domestic, wheeling in a trolley laden with food. Plate after plate was placed on the table and silence didn't give way. Abby watched Gabe from beneath shuttered lashes, studying him, trying to imagine him as a heartbroken eight-year-old.

When the servant left and the food was offering delicious, tantalising aromas, Abby spoke again. 'Did you know she had a substance abuse problem?'

Gabe was stiff. 'I was only a child,' he said, his broad shoulders lifting with self-recrimination. 'I suppose I knew something was wrong, but I had no way of knowing exactly what. It started about a year before we moved to Australia.' His expression was taut, his whole body wound like a spring. 'It got worse once we arrived.'

Abby shifted in her chair and, beneath the table, her toe inadvertently rubbed against his calf. His eyes seared hers with the heat that was always simmering just below the surface for them.

But Abby didn't want to be distracted by what they felt physically. She sensed that she was on the brink of understanding something important. Something important about Gabe that she *needed* to know.

'Why?'

She felt the depth of emotion in him and wanted to reach inside him and hold it, to reassure him and comfort him. But she couldn't without knowing what motivated it.

'You want me to explain addiction?' he asked, but the question didn't come across as flippant as Abby knew he'd hoped. It was desperate. Angry. She could see the eight-year-old he'd been now, feel his sense of rejection.

'Your mother's addiction,' she said quietly. 'Do you know why she took drugs?'

He sat straighter in his chair, as though remembering that he was Gabe Arantini, one half of the multi-billion-dollar Bright Spark Inc, a man renowned the world over as a ruthless CEO. 'I know why she was miserable.'

'Why?'

His eyes pierced hers then and she shivered because there was such cold anger in his gaze that it scored her deep inside. 'Because she made the phenomenally stupid mistake of falling in love with my father.'

She felt his words resonate strongly: a warning to herself.

'They weren't happy together?' Abby pushed. The feeling that she was on the brink of something very important held her still.

'They weren't together at all, period.'

Abby frowned, remembering threads of past conversations. 'You told me that you destroyed your father...'

'Yes.' He nodded once, a cold jerk of his head.

'He hurt her?'

'He ruined her life,' Gabe grunted.

'How? Why?'

'Because I hardly fitted into his plans, *tempesta*.'

'He didn't want to be a father?'

'He was already a father,' Gabe corrected. 'A grandfather too.'

Abby frowned. 'I don't understand.'

Gabe expelled an angry sigh, and now his eyes held resentment. 'My mother was a cleaner. Here. In this castle.' He waved a hand around the room. 'My father was a lecherous jerk who liked to get his hands on the maids when his wife wasn't looking—which was pretty often.'

Abby frowned, but she didn't say anything. She didn't want to interrupt him. Not now that he'd started to open up.

'She *loved* him. When she found out she was pregnant, she was overjoyed,' Gabe spat, his derision for that emotion obvious.

'He wasn't overjoyed, though,' she surmised.

'No.' Gabe sipped his wine then turned his head, his eyes running over the view through the window. The snow was still falling—a thicker layer had settled on the railing now. 'He paid her to have an abortion. And fired her.'

Abby gasped. She couldn't help it. 'You're not serious?'

He didn't answer. Her question had been largely rhetorical.

'She took the money and tried to make a life for herself in a nearby village.' His eyes shifted to Abby's for a moment. 'It was tough. Being a single mother to an infant is not easy, as you are well aware.'

Something was prickling at the edges of Abby's brain, something she didn't want to think about until later. But it offered darkness and doubt and complications she hadn't been aware of when she'd agreed to this.

'What did she do?'

'She blackmailed him,' Gabe said softly. 'He paid a small

amount to keep her quiet and refused to see us. I don't think she even wanted the money,' he said. 'She wanted him to be in our lives. She really did love him. He was forty-five years older than her and he'd had a string of affairs. He was an out-and-out bastard to her, by all accounts. Apparently love makes people act like fools.'

'Eventually, as he grew older, I suppose he became worried about what would happen when he died. Would my mother seek a share of his inheritance?'

'She'd have been entitled!' Abby snapped, ignoring the parallels between her own situation and that of Gabe's mother.

'Yes.' His gaze narrowed thoughtfully on Abby. 'But she wouldn't have tried. As I said, she loved him.'

'So what happened?'

'He convinced her to go back to her home. He bought her ticket, told her he would come and see us, that if we were over there it would be easier for him to visit and be in our lives. He offered her a lot of money to leave Italy.'

Gabe's face was taut with anger. 'He lied to her. He wanted her gone. He knew he would never visit, but he also knew that once she was in Australia it would be harder for her to come here.'

'But he gave her money…'

'He *promised* to give her money. It never eventuated. Once she landed he broke it off.'

'Oh, God.'

'So I can only presume it caused her to do whatever she could to blot out the pain.'

'Gabe…' Abby's heart was swelling with sympathy and sorrow for both his mother and him—then and now. 'That's awful.'

Gabe's nod was a sharp dismissal. 'He was a bastard, as I said.'

'But he must have had a change of heart,' Abby said thoughtfully. 'To leave you the castle...'

'Leave it to me?' Gabe let out a harsh laugh. 'He was in his nineties when I bought it from him. His finances had been draining for years. The castle was all he had left.'

Something like pure hatred flashed in his face. 'I took it from him for her, you know. I wanted my father to die knowing that I was living here.'

'Oh, Gabe...' She squeezed her eyes shut. 'I'm so sorry.'

'Why? I did what I needed. I made him pay. I avenged her life and death, her abuse at my father's hands. I only wish his wife had lived to learn about me.'

A shiver ran down Abby's spine; Gabe's hatred and animosity were formidable. She couldn't imagine being on the receiving end of that degree of rage. It made his anger with her, her intention to deceive him, pale in comparison.

'Did he know she'd died? That you were left alone out there?'

'Yes.'

Abby's eyes swept shut. The rejection was awful and astounding.

'So you see why it is very important to me that Raf grows up knowing his parents love and want him; why I want him to see that I live to protect him, to protect you both. I never wish him to have a reason to doubt that.' His frown deepened. 'You must also understand that if I had known about him sooner I would have done everything I could to spare you the pain and financial burden you carried. I would have made sure you were comfortable and cared for, that you had all you needed. I would never allow a woman to experience what my mother did.'

Abby nodded, but it was impossible to take any comfort from his words. He wanted to do right by her but not because of who she was, nor because of the connection she was convinced they shared. No, this was all because of what had happened to his mother. The concern she'd allowed herself to see, to hope might be a sign of burgeoning feelings specifically for her, was simply a commitment to a duty he knew his father had neglected.

Tears sparkled on her lashes and she blinked them away hurriedly, but not fast enough to escape the notice of Gabe.

'It was a long time ago,' he said softly, misunderstanding the reason for her emotional response. 'Getting upset won't change what happened then.'

She nodded, dashing at her cheeks with fingertips that weren't quite steady.

'You met Noah through foster care?'

'Yes. I'd been in the system a long time by then,' he said, the conversation obviously one he wasn't overly thrilled to be having. 'The day he arrived at the same house was a turning point for me. And for him.' He shifted in his seat. 'Eat something, Abigail. You are too slim.'

She frowned. Was she? She had always been petite— her ballerina build partly genetics as well as from diet and exercise. But since having Raf she'd been stretched emotionally and financially. 'I don't always get time to eat,' she admitted.

'You've been busy. Raising a child on your own must have been difficult.'

Gabe reached for some serving spoons and began to heap various portions onto her plate. She watched with a frown. 'You could say that.'

'And the pregnancy?'

She blinked. 'Hard. I was sick often.'

He shook his head. 'I should have been there.'

'You couldn't have done anything to stop me from being ill,' she pointed out, her heart thumping hard in her chest.

'I tried to tell you,' she said, though they'd discussed it before. 'About Raf. I *wanted* you to be involved.'

His eyes locked onto hers and something strong and

fierce surged between them, an electrical current that flooded her body with sensations. 'I know that.' He compressed his lips into a grim line. 'And it's just as well. I can't think how I might have reacted if you'd chosen to conceal my child from me. I think that is something I would *never* have been able to overlook.'

She swallowed. 'You'd probably feel a little like I did when I was dragged out of your office in Rome,' she said tartly.

He winced. 'A grave error on my part.' His eyes held hers. 'I am sorry, *tempesta*. I should have listened to you.'

How could she fail to be moved by his apology? She lowered her lashes to the meal and speared a piece of vegetable, but inside she was warming up from the centre.

But not for long.

'I could have killed your father, you know,' he said, so conversationally that Abby almost laughed. Except it wasn't funny—not even remotely.

'He was the man who should have been there for you, who should have loved you, and he was no better than my own father. He threw you out into the cold—and threw Raf out too. How you can *not* hate him is beyond me.'

She shook her head sadly. 'Because he's my father,' she said simply. 'And I see him for what he is. Flawed, yes. Broken, undoubtedly. But there is goodness in him too, and kindness. He's just been too battered by life's ill winds to remember that.'

Gabe let out a noise of frustration. 'You make excuses for him because you are not brave enough to face the truth and accept that he is a disappointment. You are too frightened to live in a world in which you reject your father.'

'I think it takes more courage to fight for who you love,' she said with quiet strength. 'To hold onto the truth of what you believe, deep in your heart, even when all evidence is to the contrary. I *know* my dad. I know how he feels. I understand why he acts as he does. And I forgive him that.'

He swore. 'Do me a favour, Abigail? Never say such things about me. Never make excuses for me as though I need them. I know I am cold and ruthless and cynical—my father's son in many ways—and that I am—and always will be—a loner in this life. I am happy with that. I don't need you digging deeper and pretending there is more to me.'

'A loner?' she murmured, the smile on her lips heavy. 'Hardly. You're a father, and soon to be a husband.'

'Yes,' he said with a curt nod. 'But our marriage is not about love; it is about common sense and practicality. Isn't that proof of my coldness?'

# CHAPTER ELEVEN

ABBY BARELY TASTED the scampi, though she was sure they were delicious. Everything looked to have been prepared with care and using only the finest ingredients, but her mind was reeling.

It shouldn't have surprised her. She knew that what Gabe said was true. And yet her own visceral sense of despondency forced her to look deeper and acknowledge what she'd probably known all along.

Why had she been willing—no, desperate!—to go to bed with him? Because the connection she'd felt was that mythical, much talked about love at first sight. She'd looked at Gabe and known that they were meant to be together. That there was more to their meeting than a random happenstance and her father's financially motivated manipulations.

It was him and her.

Fate had conspired to give them a baby, linking them for ever. Surely there had been something predestined and magical at work there, for now that she knew the story of his parentage she didn't doubt that Gabe would *always* take great care not to conceive a child.

'I'm sorry you have been worried about money,' he said, apparently having no idea that Abby was still brooding over his revelations.

'Yeah, well, working in a kitchen doesn't pay very well.'

'I don't mean in New York,' he said. 'I'm talking about here in Italy.' His frown was grim, self-condemnatory. 'I overlooked this detail, and I truly regret that.' He reached into the bag beside him and pulled out a black wallet, slender and long.

'I've had cards drawn in your name.' He passed the wallet to Abby and she opened it reflexively. 'You'll have no spending limit, of course. Buy whatever you need.'

The words were said without any expectation of a response but Abby sharply rejected the sentiment.

'There's cash too.' He nodded, indicating a huge wad of hundred euro bills. 'And I'll have one of my assistants take on your workload. Anything you need—money, holidays booked, cars, if you wish to go back to America and see... your father, or anyone, she will arrange.'

A shiver ran down Abby's spine. The delineation was clear—she was his wife in name only. Oh, and in his bed. But when it came to troubling himself with her concerns, he was washing his hands of it.

Abby folded the wallet and placed it in the centre of the table. 'I don't need any of that.'

He leaned forward. 'You have already proved to me that you are not mercenary, but think this through, Abigail. Do you want to come and ask me for money any time you want to book a trip? To go on holiday?'

She swept her eyes shut. She had thought, of course, stupidly, that they would do such trips together. But of course Gabe was setting out a life that was far more private. Separate.

*A loner in this life.*

Her heart twisted. Just like that, the difficulty of her position became glaringly obvious. She had fought it, she had resisted, but such efforts had proved impossible. She was in love with him and he felt *nothing* for her, beyond responsibility. He was trying to right the wrongs of the past, to prove to himself that he was different to his father, Lorenzo.

Her future yawned before her, long and cold, save for the love of their son. Raf alone could make this bearable for her.

'I want you to make a life here with me,' he said gently, so that her heart ached. 'A real life. You aren't to feel like a guest. This is your house, your money. Our son binds us, *tempesta.*'

'*Tempesta,*' she said distractedly. 'You call me that often. What does it mean?'

'Storm.' His lips twisted sardonically. 'I thought it the first night we met—that you had the power to move through me like a hurricane. I feel that still.'

She wouldn't let those words come to mean anything. They were insufficient, meaningless.

'Have you told your father we are to marry?'

Abigail shook her head. 'I didn't have time before I left and...' The words trailed off into nothingness.

'You don't want him to know,' Gabe concluded.

'He'd hate this,' she said simply. 'I'd worry that it would be the last straw for him. You know? Since losing Mom, he's just been so...caught up in the company and a huge part of that is...'

'Hating me,' Gabe supplied with a drawl.

'Yes.' No sense denying that. 'When he found out I was pregnant with Raf, that you were the father, it was like I'd shot him.'

Gabe's eyes narrowed.

'Knowing that I've moved in with you... I don't want to do that to him.'

Sheer cold anger met her gaze when she looked at him. He was furious—but why? 'Do you expect our marriage will be kept out of the public eye? I am a well-known figure, and you are too. At some point the media will discover our union. Isn't it better for your father to hear it first from us?'

'No.' She shook her head quickly. 'Absolutely not. It's best of all if he *never* knows.'

'But I've just pointed out how unlikely that is.'

'Unlikely isn't definite,' she said urgently. 'There's still a chance.'

\* \* \*

The noise was shrill, panicked. He sat bolt upright, rubbing a hand across his face, trying to work out what the hell was going on. He turned around and saw her. Abby, crying out in her sleep. He stared at her and an adrenal response fired in his belly. He reached for her, shaking her shoulder gently. 'Wake up, Abby.'

She pulled a face in her sleep but didn't open her eyes. 'You're dreaming.'

She mumbled something, words he didn't hear, so he did the only thing he could. He kissed her, swallowing the panic, tasting it, and returning it as passion. She responded instantly, wrapping her arms around his neck and, when he lifted his head a little, her eyes were open. Groggy and thick with passionate entreaty.

His own body stirred in response, but his curiosity over what had upset her was greater. 'You were having a nightmare.'

'Was I?' Her eyes flicked away from his, a small frown playing about her lips. He dropped a finger to them, touching her gently. 'That happens sometimes.'

That adrenaline response was back. 'Does it?'

'Not for a long time.' She cleared her throat. 'It started when my mom died.'

Gabe dropped onto the pillow beside her, propping himself on one elbow so he could see her face. 'Are the nightmares about your mother?'

'Yes and no.' She slid her gaze to him warily. 'She's always in them, but out of reach. Like watching me from behind a window or talking to me but when I look for her I can't find her. Does that make sense?'

He shrugged. 'Dreams rarely do.'

'I haven't had one in a long time.' She swallowed. 'But I've been thinking about her a lot lately. She would have loved Raf, you know.'

He smiled, but inside he felt as if she'd hit him hard. No, not her, it was life. He didn't want his wife to be miserable; he didn't want her to be mourning a mother she'd so obviously loved. He couldn't fix that, though. Death was life's most final act—what could be done to remedy it?

'Do you...?' Abby swallowed. 'You must miss your mother.'

Gabe shrugged a single shoulder. 'I miss the role she might have played in my life.'

'It must have been so hard for you.' Abby lifted a hand and traced an invisible circle on his shoulder, almost against her will. 'To have seen your mother so miserable, to have known your father to be the cause...'

'She was the cause,' he said softly. 'She should have seen what he was doing to her and fled. She should have taken whatever money he'd given her and left him, and started a new life.'

'Starting a new life isn't easy. And it sounds like your father led her on, like he led her to believe he might love her too.'

'Yes.' Gabe's eyes sparkled with renewed determination. He was nothing like his own father—he had never led Abby on. In this way, they were vitally different.

'Go to sleep, *tempesta*. And try to make your dreams sweet.'

And though she had a habit of creeping to her own bed in the middle of the night, he slid his arm beneath her, rolling her onto his chest so he could feel her breathing and hold her tight. He couldn't bring her mother back to life but, with any luck, he could forestall the nightmares.

That, at least, was within his power.

Gabe stared out of his study window without seeing the vista. He was used to it and, despite the fact he had, once upon a time, thought this to be the most beautiful place on earth, he had grown accustomed to its charms now. Did that diminish it, somehow?

He had also grown accustomed to having Abby in his bed. He was used to all of her belonging to him, utterly and completely, though it had only been days since his return from Rome.

She didn't hide how much she wanted him, and he was glad for that.

He had worried she would mistake their chemistry and marriage for love, but she seemed to understand that theirs was a transaction and only certain parts of him were on the table.

But at night, oh, how he craved her.

He doubted that need would ever fade, his appreciation for her curves and undulations unlikely to diminish with exposure.

In fact, the opposite was true. The more that he was with her, the more he wanted her. He woke up aching to pull her close, but with the sun's rise came the reality of their situation and everything shifted between them. She pulled away from him, presenting him with a cool smile and a terse nod, showering in her own en suite bathroom, away from him, away from his touch and kiss and eyes that were hungry for more glimpses of her beautiful body.

She spent much of her time with Raf, even just reading in his room. He knew because Monique had become worried for Abby.

*'She seems distracted and tired. She doesn't need to exhaust herself with the baby—she must have more important things to do! Weddings don't plan themselves.'*

But Abby had no interest in planning a wedding.

She had told him outright that she was happy to organise things, but that her preference was for as small a ceremony as possible, just the two of them and Raf, with a couple of domestics as witnesses. No guests, no dinner.

When he'd suggested a honeymoon she'd blanched and pointed out in a brittle voice that they were already living as a married couple. Besides, she'd added with a poor attempt at a smile, where in the world could they go more idyllic than the castle?

He'd analysed the feeling low in his abdomen for days, wondering at its root cause, but now he had to admit it. He was ill at ease.

He'd brought Abigail to Italy with the belief that it would be best for her, and him, as well as Raf, and she seemed to be fading away before his eyes. She'd thrown herself into the Christmas spirit, adding little touches throughout the house, like green garlands along the staircase, the Christmas tree she'd decorated with the lone bauble, food that she baked that had an unmistakably Christmas aroma. That had been the only sign she was settling into life in Italy. That she was making her peace with being here, with him.

What had she said the day they'd argued about Hughie? *He's nice to me...*

Something uncomfortable shifted inside Gabe. Nice? He wasn't sure he knew how to be *nice*. He wasn't sure he knew how to be anything Abby needed.

A knock at his door roused him from his thoughts. He turned around, expecting to see one of his staff. Only it was Abby and, as always, his body responded instantly to her appearance. His blood began to rush through him, tightening him, making him throb and ache for her anew, and his eyes ran over her hungrily, needily, desperately.

She blushed beneath his inspection.

'Am I interrupting?'

'Not at all.' He indicated the seat opposite him, but she shook her head.

'This won't take long.'

'What is it?' He came around to the opposite side of the desk and propped his hips against it. He saw the way her eyes darted to his haunches and the way his trousers had strained across the muscles there, and something like relief filled him.

She wanted him.

And she always would. In bed, she wasn't cold—ever. She begged for him and dragged her nails down his back and nipped at his flesh; in bed she was a fever in his blood, because that same fever raged in her blood.

It wasn't *nice*. It was so much better.

'I know Raf is only little, but this will be his first Christmas and I want it to be special. He won't remember it, I know,' she rushed on, countering her sentimentality before he could. That she knew him so well worried him.

'But he'll have photos—we can have photos, I mean, get them framed and put them in his room. You want him to have a family—' now she forced her eyes to his and he felt their defiance '—and I do too. I want him to know we've been a family since he was born.'

He nodded thoughtfully.

He'd been doing that a lot lately.

Thinking.

Thinking about Abby and the things she'd said. She was like a fever in his blood and he resented her for that, even while knowing it was hardly her fault. He simply had to try harder to regain control of the situation.

'Anyway—' she was awkward '—I wondered if I could somehow get to Fiamatina today, or tomorrow, to buy him a little gift.' Colour filled her cheeks, two dots of pink on either side of her lips. 'I don't mean anything grand, just a book or a little toy. He doesn't need much, obviously. It's more about giving him something we can keep for him.'

Gabe was struck by this—more so by the fact it hadn't even occurred to him, despite the way she'd turned his house into Santa's Grotto, that Christmas might mean something to Abby. That, unlike his terrible memories of this time of year, she might actually *want* to mark the day in a manner that was different to any other.

'Fiamatina.' He jerked his head. 'I'll take you.' And if he had any luck he'd find the perfect present for her. She should have something to open, seeing as the day meant so much to her.

'Oh!' Her surprise was obvious, so too her dismissal. 'You don't have to take me. You're busy. I can drive.'

He laughed, a grim rejection of that idea. 'Do you have any experience of driving on snow or ice, Abigail?'

Her eyes met his, annoyance brimming in their depths. At least that was better than coldness. 'No, but I'll be careful.'

'You must be mad if you think I would let you risk your life like that.'

'*You* must be mad if you think I'd ever do anything dangerous, that I wasn't capable of. I'll be fine.'

'I intend to make sure of it.' He put a hand at the crook of her elbow. 'Are you ready?'

'Have I told you how bossy you are?'

'I think so.'

She glared at him. 'You're busy and I have to learn to drive here at some point—'

'Perhaps. But not today.'

She fired him a fulminating glare and he ignored the jolt of pleasure in his gut. The relief of seeing her emotional response. He'd take her anger over ice-coldness any day of the week.

He liked her being emotional; he liked knowing he'd caused that. He was addicted to it.

With a throaty sound of need, he curved his hand from her elbow to her back, pulling her to him, and when her eyes flew wide in surprise and her lips parted on a gasp he kissed her, pushing her back against the door to his office, his body holding hers.

She was his in an instant, her hands lifting to link behind his head, her hips moving, swaying in time to their kiss and the sensual fog that always pursued them.

She was wearing a dress, thank God, as opposed to her usual jeans, and he lifted it desperately, finding the sweet curve of her bottom, cupping it in his hands and lifting her so that her legs wrapped around his waist and his arousal pressed hard to her, hungry for her as always.

He spoke in Italian, words he couldn't have recalled later, words that came from deep within him, whispering them in her ear as his fingers pushed her underwear aside and found the heart of her warmth, sliding inside her until she bucked against him.

'Please,' she groaned, breaking the kiss to look into his eyes. 'I need you, Gabe. I need this. Please.'

He understood and it was instinct alone that pushed him, his hands freeing his arousal from his trousers, just enough to take her, to hold her to him, to bind them together.

She was panting against him, kissing him frantically, her hands running over his shoulders and arms, her body trembling until finally they both exploded in unison, one singular, perfect release for the *tempesta* that had been raging between them—and probably always would.

'Oh, my God,' Abby murmured as sanity began to seep back into her passion-addled brain. 'What just happened?'

Gabe straightened, his smile one of such indulgence that her heart tripped heavily inside her. 'Well, we've done it before. Quite often. I presumed you understood...'

'We didn't use protection.' She dipped her head so that her forehead was pressed to his shoulder. 'That was so stupid.'

'Stupid? I can think of other words to describe it.'

'You don't understand,' she groaned. 'I'm not on any form of contraception.'

Comprehension dawned, but apparently produced a very

different reaction for Gabe. 'So?' he asked, a brow lifted. 'Then we have another baby.'

'Another baby?' Her words were a sharp rejection of the idea. She pushed away from him, placing her feet on the ground and straightening her dress with fingers that shook. Panic seared her belly.

'Yes, another baby. Two more. Three more. We already have Raf. We're getting married. Why not more children?'

'How can you be so cavalier about this?'

'Calm down, *tempesta*. You're acting as though this is the worst thing in the world. You don't even know if there will be any…complications…'

'It *would* be the worst thing in the world!' Abby shouted, the stress and the confusion of the last few weeks beginning to mount inside her, so that she was pale, her eyes flashing with emotion.

In contrast, Gabe was completely frozen, his expression like granite. 'Why, may I ask, is that?'

She bit down on her lip and looked over his shoulder. How could she explain how she felt? How could she put into words the misgivings she had? About this wedding, their marriage, the ability to raise Raf in a way that wouldn't completely mess him up? Another baby would be heaven on earth if they were a real couple. 'It's irresponsible to bring another baby into this environment,' she said crisply. 'Raf happened, and we're getting married to give him a family. But there's no sense compounding that with any more children. Raf is enough.'

# CHAPTER TWELVE

GABE USED VOICE-COMMAND to call his best friend.

'Noah?' His voice was gruff when the call connected.

'Gabe. What's up?'

Gabe swallowed, staring at his desk. An excellent question.

'I just wanted to see how you are,' he lied anxiously. Noah had enough going on in his life—he didn't need Gabe adding to it.

'Fine. I'm cured, remember?'

Gabe frowned. The therapy he'd made Noah enter might have been paying dividends. But wasn't it too soon? Gabe silenced the doubts. He wanted to believe his foster brother was improving. He wanted to feel some degree of relief.

'I'm glad.' Gabe sighed heavily. 'I'm...' He clamped his lips together. What did he want to say? *I'm getting married.* No. Too problematic. Noah would want to know what the hell had happened. Gabe had sworn until he was blue in the face that he would *never* marry. He'd promised himself repeatedly that emotional commitments were for fools; he'd sworn to be smart.

And he *was* being smart. This marriage wasn't about emotion.

'Do you ever wonder what the Sloanes are doing?'

'Those bastards? No. I never think of them.' The anger in Noah's voice made a liar of him. Their foster family had influenced both their lives, no matter how they wished that weren't the case.

Gabe pushed back in the leather chair, his eyes closed. 'Why? Do you?'

Gabe frowned. 'I was with them a lot longer. They're

almost the only family I remember.' The words were defensive and immediately a response came to him. He saw, in his mind's eye, the mother of his son. The woman he would marry. And his gut twisted. He'd been given a family at birth—a father who didn't want him, a mother who resented him.

He'd been taken in by a family—they hadn't wanted him either.

And now? A sense of unease tripped through him. Being unwanted was the running theme of his life—and now he was marrying a woman who wanted more than he could give her. He was marrying a woman who deserved more.

'They were bastards,' Noah grunted. 'I hope they got what was coming to them.'

Gabe's lips compressed. 'I don't.'

'You always were a soft touch.'

At that, Gabe laughed. If only Noah knew what he was about to do. Abby had been cast out of her life, left pregnant and impoverished, abandoned by her father, orphaned by her mother, and he'd strong-armed her at every point. He'd swept aside her objections. He'd insisted on this—and he'd been right. Marriage was the only option. But suddenly the idea of joining himself legally to Abby seemed absurd. She didn't want him, not as he was, and he didn't want her. Did he?

They'd slept together a long time ago, and that had been a mistake. She had used him, she had lied to him, she had gone to him specifically to further her father's business interests. He had no business wanting her—other than physically.

This marriage wasn't about anything other than practicality, and giving their son what he deserved, just like Abigail had said. Raf wouldn't grow up wondering about his father, resenting his father, hating his father. He wouldn't feel for Gabe as Gabe had for Lorenzo. No, Raf would feel loved. He would feel cherished and he would feel wanted.

And he just had to hope he wouldn't ruin Abby's life in the process. No matter what she'd done, no matter how he told himself he'd never forgive her, he knew the truth. He didn't want to hurt her; he didn't want to ruin her life.

He wasn't his father, he reminded himself, even when his doubts made his conviction waver. They would marry and Gabe would make sure she had a good life. A great life.

He wouldn't be the kind of husband she wanted nor deserved, but eventually she'd get over that. Wouldn't she?

Christmas morning at the castle was spectacular in all ways but one. Snow had begun to fall overnight and Hughie, who'd gone home to see his family, wasn't around to clear it, which meant the place seemed even more magical than ever, as though it had risen from the edge of the mountains. A little family of squirrels ran across the field and Abby watched them, an enchanted smile on her face as they scampered up a tree. As for their Christmas tree, the lights glistened in the early morning sunshine as the smell of coffee filled the hall.

Raf slept in a bassinet at Abby's feet as she lost herself to the pages of *Persuasion*—her favourite of all the Austens. There was something about Captain Wentworth's enduring love for Anne Elliot that had always spoken to her.

No doubt, Gabe would accuse her of over-sentimentality, but she had always adored the idea of such permanence. The idea that years spent apart, with one at war and the other marooned by a cold, unemotional family, couldn't destroy true love.

Abby's eyes lifted to where Gabe sat, reading a newspaper on his tablet, apparently absorbed. Yes, it was all spectacular, save for the tension that was zapping between them.

Her heart raced and her skin goosed all over. She drew

in a deep breath and told herself she'd be fine, that she could do this. Reminding herself that they were celebrating for Raf.

She was the one who'd put this in motion—now wasn't the time to start having regrets.

Their marriage would work just fine. The longer they were together, the better she'd get at pretending not to feel anything for Gabe.

He'd put presents beneath the tree, though, and her heart skipped a beat. Were they for Raf? Surely they must be. Not for her...

Her eyes strayed to the tree, a frown on her face. Nothing was labelled. 'Yes, *tempesta*. It's for you.'

'Oh!' She spun to face him, her cheeks flushed. 'I didn't get you anything.'

'It's a gift for both of us.'

She frowned. 'Shall I open it now?'

Something glowed in his eyes. 'Raf is awake. Why don't we get that photo you wanted before he drifts off again?'

Abby nodded. 'All the staff are upstairs. Shall I...'

'I can take it.' He pulled his cell phone from his pocket and propped it on a ledge near the door, then stepped back towards Abby. She held Raf in her arms, smiling down at him, leaving Gabe to take the space beside her. Using his watch, he set the timer going. A light on the phone flashed faster and faster.

'Ready?' Gabe asked after a moment.

She nodded and forced a smile to her face, breathing in her husband, her baby, their first Christmas together. The phone clicked, just like an old-fashioned camera, taking the photo, so they'd always have a photograph with which to remember this moment. Abby didn't break the pose though. Just for that small fraction of time, she let herself pretend that this was all real. Normal.

That Gabe was marrying her because he wanted to, that

Raf had been conceived in love. Emotion hitched, heavy, in her throat. It was Christmas; couldn't she wish?

'Gabe…' She looked up at him, not entirely sure what she wanted to say. Their eyes locked and she felt the force of her emotions throbbing around them, so strong and urgent that she wasn't sure she could ignore them. She knew she didn't want to.

'Open your present,' he suggested, taking Raf from her arms. He held their baby so naturally, as though he'd been doing it all his life, and Abby could only watch, those same emotions intensifying at the proof of Raf's parentage.

'He's so like you.'

'He's my son.'

She nodded, spinning away from him. The cloying feelings were heavy inside her, swirling like the hurricane he often called her. Now that she knew how she felt about him, it was impossible not to be conscious of it whenever they were together. She walked towards the gift—it was large in size. A box of something?

'Open it,' he said again, close behind her.

Her fingers were trembling when they reached for the ribbon. It was store-wrapped, she noted, pulling at it so that the bow gave easily. She slid her fingers under one edge of the paper and then the next, and finally opened the slit at the back, unpeeling the gift with interest. The back of the box was white, giving no hint of what it contained. But when she turned it over it had a thick plastic window, showing cream lace.

She lifted the lid and stared inside, her lips tugging downwards.

Though the dress was folded into a neat rectangle, there could be no mistaking what Gabe had given her.

'A wedding gown?' She lifted it from the box so that she could see it at full height.

It was incredibly beautiful, just what she might have chosen for herself. Lace, long, like something from the twenties, with beads down the back and slightly off the shoulder.

But why was he giving it to her?

She bit down on her lip, turning to face him, her expression quizzical.

'You wanted to make today memorable,' he said, the words oddly lacking any emotion whatsoever. Only his dark eyes showed a hint of intensity. 'So? What do you say? Shall we get married?'

Abby stared at him, her blood rushing so fast she was sure he must hear it. 'We are getting married.'

'I mean now.'

'You mean…today?'

He laughed. 'Yes, today. Well, once Raf has had another nap perhaps,' he said as the little baby yawned in Gabe's big, strong arms. 'Will that give you enough time to get ready?'

Abby was numb. She nodded, but everything was going too fast, as if she'd inadvertently stepped into quicksand. She draped the wedding dress over a chair and when she smiled at Gabe she didn't meet his eyes.

Everything she wanted was before her, but it was a poisoned chalice. Marrying Gabe, knowing the limits of what they were—it was like being dragged beneath the ocean.

'I'll take him upstairs.' She held her arms out for Raf, the words stilted, but Gabe shook his head.

'I'll do it. You go. Start to prepare.'

Prepare? Could she ever?

'A priest will be here just after lunch,' he said with his trademark confidence. 'Monique and Rosa will witness the wedding for us. Just as you wished.'

Abby nodded, but her whole body was resisting. Not because she didn't want to marry him, but because marrying him like this would break her.

She needed him to see that! Because if he didn't, she knew her heart would be a lifelong casualty.

But Gabe was walking away, talking in soft Italian to Raf as he carried him up the stairs. Abby watched them go, her heart sinking further. On autopilot, she lifted the dress, carrying it carefully up the stairs and into her bedroom.

Why was this turn of events so hard to process? They'd discussed the wedding several times before. She'd known he wished to marry sooner rather than later. This made sense.

She was just overthinking it—hoping for a fantasy, praying for a miracle, when she should have known better. There was no such thing, was there? Christmas notwithstanding, theirs was not a fairy tale; there was no happily ever after in store for them.

She showered, long and slow, deliciously warm, lathering herself in soap, breathing in its floral aroma. The dress was visible through the door; she tried not to look at it.

Once she had dried herself and styled her hair into an elegant chignon, she began to apply her make-up. Only halfway through, she wondered if she should have put the dress on first?

She wasn't good at this; she needed someone to help her. Someone who knew about weddings. It was probably why brides usually got ready for their weddings surrounded by their friends—their mothers.

She walked towards the dress and the moment she touched it tears welled in her eyes. Her own mother should have been with her. Or her father. Certainly some of her friends. But they'd all dropped away when her father had disowned her. Without the financial means to keep up with their lifestyle, Abby had found herself completely alone.

Now? She had a baby and a fiancé. Soon a husband. But there was no love there. She'd been wrong before to think she could make do with the sensible, practical justification for this wedding. It would be the loneliest marriage imaginable.

A sob racked her slender body and she wrapped her arms tightly around her waist.

It was useless.

She *couldn't* do this. She couldn't marry Gabe. Everything about it felt wrong; she was suffocating. Dying. Drowning.

She had to tell him how she felt. He might be angry but she couldn't let that stop her. She wouldn't marry him like this. He still hadn't forgiven her for what she'd done—and he probably never would. There was no way she could have a husband who despised her—and especially not when she loved him with all her heart.

Abby had no choice: she went in search of Gabe, certainty growing with each step. She found him in his bedroom, wearing a tuxedo that made her bones melt and her pulse race.

'You look…amazing,' she said honestly, clicking the door shut. Her breath was burning in her lungs, torturing her with every exhalation.

'Thank you.' He frowned as he took in the jeans and sweatshirt she was wearing.

'You didn't like the dress?'

'The dress is beautiful,' Abby whispered hoarsely. 'But, Gabe…' More tears moistened her eyes. 'God, Gabe, I can't… I can't marry you.'

She squeezed her eyes shut, her heart breaking into a thousand pieces.

'Abigail?' He crossed the room but didn't touch her. He was close to her though; she could feel his warmth and strength and it thawed her, just a little, but enough. She opened her eyes, dared to face him, to meet his gaze head-on.

'What's happened?'

Her expression was pinched. 'Tell me why you want to marry me.'

'You know why we're marrying,' he said with a deep frown. 'We've gone over that.'

'In New York,' she said with a shake of her head. 'That feels like a long time ago.'

His frown deepened. 'Nothing's changed since then.'

'Are you so sure of that?' she murmured.

He frowned.

'We were different people then,' she said urgently.

'In what way?'

'*I* was different,' she amended, rubbing her palms together, lost in thought. 'I was exhausted and scared, and angry and hurt. I was so, so tired. So worried about money. And I wasn't thinking clearly. I truly believed I was making the right decision in coming here with you. That I could marry you as easily as I could slip on a new winter coat or…' her eyes dropped to her hand '…an engagement ring.'

'It is easy,' he said firmly. 'We have a son together, and now we'll marry.'

'That makes it sound black and white. What about all the grey in between?'

'What grey?'

'All of this is grey,' she said emphatically. 'You were so angry with me in New York—and now? I don't know what you are. We're together at night but in the day we're like strangers in this huge castle. I can't… I just can't marry you if this is what our life would be like.'

His eyes sparked with hers, dark emotions obvious in their depths. 'I see.' The words were a grim indictment.

'You don't want to marry me either,' she pointed out with a tight grimace. 'Do you?'

'Do I strike you as a man who would do anything he didn't wish?'

'I mean if there were no Raf.'

He looked at her for several moments and then shook his head. 'I have no interest in discussing hypothetical scenarios.'

'I need to hear you say it,' she murmured. 'I need you to tell me that if it weren't for Raf…'

'Why?'

'Just tell me. If there were no Raf. If I'd never got pregnant…' She stared at him, refusing to back down, even when her breath was straining in her chest.

'Fine. If it weren't for Raf then no, we wouldn't be getting married.'

Abby's heart, so fragile, so wounded already, lurched painfully. It was the confirmation she'd needed, but now that he'd said it she had no idea how to make sense of his feelings. They were so different to hers. How had she let herself fall in love with him? Or had she really had any choice in the matter?

'I don't know why you're complicating this.'

She dug her fingernails into her palms and looked past him. 'I can't marry you if I think this is just a pragmatic decision for you. If your feelings aren't engaged at all.'

'I feel many things,' he disagreed. 'I feel a desire to do what's right for my son. I feel a desire to do what's right for you.'

Abby swept her eyes shut. She'd been wrong. Some things *were* black and white, and staying here with Gabe was one end of that extreme. It was wrong, and she was crazy not to have seen that sooner. Pain warred with certainty inside her.

'I'm not your mother, and you're not your father. We were never a great love affair. I'm not begging you to do this, and you can't change history by marrying me.' She angled her face away from him, knowing she couldn't witness the cold rejection that she presumed must be on his features. She needed to say her piece and be done with it.

'I want Raf to have a family too. Neither of us knew what that was like. But this marriage would make me miserable, Gabe. And I think you'd come to resent me—even more than you do now—if we were to go through with it.'

'I don't resent you,' he said sharply.

'Yes, you do. You resent me for Calypso. You resent me for being Lionel Howard's daughter. You resent me for having your baby. I can't live with that.'

He shook his head. 'It's not that simple.'

'Shades of grey?' she prompted, her smile without humour.

He took a step towards her, his breath an impatient exhalation. 'I understand the power your father had over you and I *understand* why you did what you did that night.'

It wasn't forgiveness. She knew he'd never trust her, never love her. His words changed nothing.

'I can't marry you.' The words were loaded with all the pain in her heart, but as she said them she knew it was the right decision. Finally, amid all this confusion, she had found her way to the truth she should have discovered earlier.

He let out a sound of pure frustration. 'What the hell do you want from me? Tell me and I'll give it to you! This marriage is worth fighting for.'

'There is no marriage,' she interjected, her temper rising.

'Fine! We won't marry today. It was just an idea. Take your time, plan the wedding you want, just...'

'Time won't change the fact that you don't love me.'

The statement surprised them both. Silence fell in the room, heavy and oppressive.

Abby looked at his face and there was such confusion there that she almost pitied him. 'I'm not marrying someone who doesn't love me. You might think it's childish, but I believe in love. I want to be with someone who adores me and that's never going to be you, is it?'

For once, Gabe was the one who seemed lost for words.

'My mother loved my father,' he said finally. 'And it killed her. I swore to myself I'd never love anyone.'

'You love Raf. You love Noah.'

His lips twisted. 'Those I couldn't help.'

She turned away from him and nodded. He didn't love her; he never would. She exhaled a shaky breath, a wave of sadness threatening to drown her. She had to be courageous—if she didn't leave him now she never would, and she'd be miserable.

'You don't love me either,' he said softly. 'That's why this marriage makes such perfect sense. We get on well enough and we both adore our son. We're great in bed together and we're intellectually well-matched. You know all about my business, courtesy of your father. This marriage has everything I want.'

Abby pressed her fist against her mouth to silence a sob. 'That sounds like a perfect recipe,' she muttered.

'I'm glad you agree.'

'I don't! I was being sarcastic! I just told you I won't marry if there's no love, and you're enumerating a sensible list for a perfectly loveless marriage. It's not what I want for my life.'

Only the sound of his breathing punctuated the air. Abby kept her back to him so she didn't see the look of visceral pain that crossed his face. Being left was nothing new to Gabe—he'd been abandoned by almost everyone his whole life. He'd kept himself closed off for a reason, and Abigail was reminding him exactly why now.

Only this wasn't just about losing Abigail.

He thought of Raf leaving the castle, Raf no longer being within arm's reach, and his whole body felt as though it had caught alight.

'Our reasons for marrying haven't changed. I want to

raise my son, and I want to raise him here. If you won't stay, then we have to face the reality of a custody dispute.'

Abigail squeezed her eyes shut and when she turned to face him she was as pale as a sheet. 'Are you actually threatening to take him away from me?'

'No.' His frown deepened. 'I don't want to do that, Abigail. But he's my son and I want to be in his life.'

'You can be. That's not contingent on us marrying.'

'I want to be in his life *all the time*. I won't be a part-time father.'

'So what do you suggest?' she asked, numb all over.

'I've made my suggestion—that we get married. It seems to be the best way forward. But if you disagree, I believe it's your turn to come up with an alternative.'

She ground her teeth together. 'I won't give up my son.'

'And nor will I.' He thrust his hands on his hips. 'And when you contemplate your future, perhaps you should remember the resources I will bring to any custody battle and ask yourself whether staying here mightn't be easiest.'

She dipped her head forward, breathing in sharply, trying to inflate her lungs without success. It took several moments for the feeling of dangerous light-headedness to pass. Finally, she pinpointed him with her gaze, her eyes holding his.

'You're threatening me?'

Gabe thought about denying it, but what was the point? He was giving her an ultimatum, knowing full well what she'd choose. That knowledge sat inside him like a heavy, sharp rock, but he didn't back away. He glared at her for a long moment, ignoring the shot of pain he felt to see the hurt in her face. 'As I've said, it's your decision.'

Tears welled up in her eyes. His stomach lurched.

'I'm going to Rome for a couple of days. You can tell me what you've decided when I return.'

\* \* \*

The phone call came early the next morning. He awoke disoriented with a banging head and a throbbing low in his gut, as though the fine blade of a knife had slid along his chest all night long. He pushed up groggily, noting with a frown that he was in his Rome apartment.

But why?

He looked around, wincing when he saw a nearly empty bottle of Scotch with a solitary glass beside it.

Abby.

Memories of the day before came rushing back.

The way they'd argued; the things he'd said.

The threat he'd made.

Her face when he'd told her he would fight her for Raf. He didn't want to lose his son but, hell, he'd never planned to sue Abby for custody. He'd wanted his cake and to eat it too. Raf, Abby—it was all part of the same equation. He'd wanted to give Raf a family.

And what did he want?

Not this.

He felt the sentiment of what he'd said—he'd been honest with her but, God, he'd also been an ass. She was young and inexperienced and believed herself in love with him; instead of gently reminding her that everything was new and overwhelming, he'd thrown his lack of emotion at her like a trophy. His determination to not become a fool in love had always made sense, but now it seemed childish. Stupid. Pathetic, even.

He answered the phone in a rush, hope flaring inside him.

'Arantini.'

'Oh, Gabe?' The voice on the other end wasn't Abby's. His heart dropped.

'It's Holly Scott-Leigh. *Dr* Scott-Leigh,' she said. Gabe racked his brain and for one moment panic assailed him.

Raf? Abby? No. This was the doctor he'd convinced Noah to see, the therapist.

God, he'd let the ball drop there. His best friend was going through hell and, apart from the occasional phone call, Gabe had been so wrapped up in his own life that he hadn't bothered to so much as think of Noah.

'Yes, Holly?' He was unintentionally curt, but he could think only of Abby.

'I'm worried about Noah,' she said, her voice trembling. 'I think he needs you. Urgently.'

It was, without a doubt, the only possible thing that could momentarily push Abby from his mind.

'Why? What's happened?'

'I… I think you should come here. To London. To see him. I'm sorry, it's just… I don't know what else to do.'

Gabe was already reaching for his jacket. 'I'll come *subito.*'

# CHAPTER THIRTEEN

IT WAS ONLY right to pack the tree away.

How stupid she'd been to think she could decorate the house into a state of festive merriment and somehow make her heart whole when it had been obliterated into a thousand pieces.

Without Hughie, it would take all her efforts to get the thing down and drag it through the door, but she didn't care. She would do it because its very presence, two days after Christmas, was mocking her.

She unwrapped the lights with care, placing them on one of the chairs, and then, with a sense of satisfaction born purely of emotional need, she pushed at the tree until it collapsed with a loud, echoing thud to the ground. The scent of pine filled the air; she didn't breathe it in. She could barely breathe.

Gabe had been gone two nights.

Christmas night had been spent in a state of almost catatonic numbness, unable to comprehend what had happened. Boxing Day had been spent with Raf, and yet her ears had been listening for Gabe the whole time, for any sign of his approach.

There had been none. No helicopter to herald his return.

Was this how he expected their life to go? Would he just run away whenever she disagreed with him?

An angry sob burst from her and she stomped her foot, bending down and grabbing the tree by its narrower end, trying with all her might to drag it towards the door.

It didn't budge more than an inch.

She let out a roar, hoping that would help. It didn't.

But when she straightened, dragging a hand over her brow, she heard a noise behind her. The door slamming shut.

'What the hell are you doing?'

She whipped around, her eyes flashing to Gabe's with all the hurt and pain and accusation she felt before she sobered and tried to look cool. Hard to do while sweating and pink-faced from wrestling with an overgrown Christmas relic.

'What does it look like?' she snapped, refusing to let herself feel *anything* for the man, no matter how much she'd missed him, no matter how arrogantly handsome he looked.

'Abby...' He moved towards her and she flinched without realising it, backing away, closer to the tree. His eyes roamed her face and something passed between them, something that made her heart hurt and her chest thick with sobs she refused to give in to. Then he was Gabe Arantini, successful tycoon, tech billionaire. He stared at her for two more seconds before looking away, his eyes settling on a point past her shoulder. 'My plane is on the runway, refuelling now. When you're ready, I'll drive you to the airport.'

Abby froze, her chest cleaving, and fear had her launching at Gabe. 'Don't you dare! Don't you dare send me away!'

'What are you saying?' he asked, having to raise his voice to be heard above her.

'You don't want me, I get it. I don't care. I can't leave my son. I won't lose him. Don't you *dare* send me away from him! I'll marry you, I'll marry you. Just please let me stay with him.'

Gabe looked as though she'd stabbed him. He reached for her wrists and contained them with ease, his strong fingers wrapping around her, holding her tight. He spoke with urgency, his voice hoarse. 'I'm not sending you away from Raf.' His eyes were suspiciously moist, his voice gravelly.

'He'll go with you. You were right. This whole scheme was madness. We'll find another way to do this.'

Now Abby did sob because even though she'd told him she needed to be free of this whole marriage scenario, the reality was ripping her apart. Life without Gabe flashed before her, a barren, empty, hollow reality she didn't want to contemplate.

'I have an apartment in New York. You can have it. I'll buy somewhere else for myself. Do you have a lawyer?'

His fingers, curled around her wrists, were making her flesh warm yet her blood was ice-cold. 'No,' she whispered.

'Fine. You can use my lawyer too. I'll engage someone else.'

'Why do we need a lawyer? I have nothing to give you, and you've just said you'll let me be with Raf.'

His face tightened. 'I presume you won't want to deal directly with me,' he said matter-of-factly. 'We can arrange visitation rights through our lawyers. You keep the nannies and when I have Raf they'll come too, so at least there'll always be some kind of continuity for him.' He cleared his throat.

'Continuity,' she repeated, for no reason except that she couldn't understand what was happening and she had no idea how to make sense of it.

Gabe, as if just realising he was holding her, stepped backwards, dropping her arms swiftly and rubbing his palms on his jeans. 'Go and pack, Abigail. You've got your wish. You're going home.'

Her wish? Her wish was for Gabe to love her, for them to be a real family. He was showing her what he wanted— and it wasn't a life with her.

'Is this really what you want?' she whispered.

He stared at her, a strange mix of fear and determination in his eyes. 'I don't want to hurt you more than I have,' he muttered. 'You have to leave here. Go home.'

Tears welled in her eyes but she nodded. He was right. He'd never promised her anything like love. Her grief was all her own fault. She was the one who'd forgotten the parameters of their relationship. She was the one who'd fallen in love.

Without another word, she left the room. She moved through the house quickly, fighting an instinct, the whole time, to return to him. To beg him to reconsider. But that was a foolish impulse, one born of hope rather than reality. And so she forced herself to ignore it.

It didn't take Abby long to return their things to her suitcase. She'd brought only what she absolutely needed. There were clothes in New York. She would have a fresh start.

She lifted Raf out of the cot, her eyes brimming with tears as she carried him down the sweeping stairs. Gabe had removed the Christmas tree and the foyer was now empty, barren, like her heart and the marriage they might have had.

This was the right decision. She was numb, yet it was right.

But when Gabe approached her and his eyes dropped to the baby in her arms, she felt as if the earth was tipping on its axis. He stared at Raf and she saw his heartbreak, saw the cruelty of what she was doing, and grief throbbed hard in her veins.

'I can't take him away from you,' she said desperately. 'That's not right either.'

Gabe shifted his attention to Abby's face and then looked away again. 'I'll come to New York,' he said with an attempt at detachment. 'I'll see him often. You should be where you're happy.'

She swept her eyes shut, acknowledging that he was doing this for her. That he wanted to spare her pain, and so was sending her away. She acknowledged that even when her heart was breaking, both for herself and their son.

'If that's what you want,' she said, cuddling Raf close.

'Would you like to…?' She held their son towards Gabe and he made a guttural noise of pain before taking the boy from her and pulling him to his chest. He turned his back on Abby but she could see from the way his torso was moving that he was struggling to bring his own emotions under control.

She stood behind him, wishing more than anything on earth that she'd said nothing to him. That she'd simply married him and made the best of what they had. Sex, a baby they both loved and a future that could have been anything they chose. Maybe, just maybe, he'd been wrong. Maybe one day he would have learned to love her, despite what he thought now. And would that have been enough? Could she have spent her life waiting, hoping, wondering?

'Well,' he said finally. 'We should go.'

He didn't speak on the drive to the airport and nor did Abby. Every time she formulated what she wanted to say, she took one look at the determined set of his features and remembered that Gabe Arantini wasn't a man who did anything he didn't want. Gabe didn't want Abby's love. It had terrified him, and so he was disposing of her.

When they arrived at the airport he brought the car to a stop at a private terminal and turned to face her. 'Abby?'

She waited, her heart suspended, needing to hear what he was going to say, needing it with all of her being.

'I'm sorry for bringing you to Italy. When you told me about Raf, I reacted without thinking. I had no right to displace your life as I did. No right to manipulate you into an engagement that was so obviously wrong.'

She bit down on her lip and her huge eyes held his for several devastating moments. 'I'm sorry I fell in love with you,' she said softly.

He shook his head and reached for her cheek, cupping it with his hand. 'Don't be. I don't deserve your love—I don't want it—but that doesn't mean it's not an incredible… privilege.'

She sobbed then, because it made no sense and because she wanted him to understand something she couldn't even explain.

'Text me when you land,' he said, pulling away from her and opening his door. He came around to her side and opened it before returning to the rear of the car and removing Raf. 'And if you need anything. Anything at all.' His eyes burned her with their intensity; Abby could no longer look at Gabe.

It hurt too soul-destroyingly much.


It was her engagement ring that did it.

He found it on her side of his bed—not that she'd ever used the bed as her own. She'd come to him each night and they'd made love, but she'd acted like a guest in his room. A guest in his castle, and his life.

He lay on his back, staring at the ceiling, but it was no good. The bed smelled of her, of them. He swore sharply and sat up straight, rubbing his eyes with the palms of his hands. It hadn't even been a week—how was he meant to do this?

Every time he closed his eyes he saw her as she'd been at the airport. Her face so pale, clutching Raf. His child, and the mother of his child, boarding a flight to take them halfway across the world.

He'd sat in his car and watched the plane lift off, imagining them settling in for the flight, wondering if Abigail was nervous or relieved? Relieved to be leaving him, relieved to be free of his threats and control?

He groaned and stood, pacing out of his room towards his study. He poured himself a measure of Scotch but cradled the glass in his hand, looking at the door against which they'd made love.

A glimmer of hope flashed in his belly. She'd been worried about falling pregnant. Might she have? Might she, even now, have his baby in her belly? Would that change her mind? Surely then she'd marry him?

With rich self-disgust he threw the Scotch back, burning his mouth with the alcoholic acidity. Was he really so desperate to secure his family that he'd wish her to be pregnant when she so obviously hadn't wanted that? Was he such a despicable man?

She'd called him honourable; she'd been wrong.

He'd ruined Abigail's life. She'd given him the chance to be involved with their baby; she'd needed his help. Help he could have given to her easily. He *should* have given it to her. When he'd seen the way she was living, and comprehended how alone she was in the world, he could have made everything better. Instead, he'd strong-armed her into agreeing to marriage and moving to Italy, and all because it suited him to have her here.

And yet the thing that terrified Gabe most of all was the certainty that he would do it all again, simply because he knew that at each step of the way he'd been desperate for whatever he could get of her.

It had started as hate, hadn't it? Maybe even revenge?

No. Never revenge. Just…inexplicable, all-controlling desire. Something heavy sat low in his gut. He'd wanted her. He'd seen her in New York and after a year without women—no, not *women*—a year without *Abigail* specifically, he'd lost his mind. He'd been determined to make her his once more. So why had he treated her as he had? Why had he embarrassed her at work, and told Rémy to fire her? Why hadn't he let her explain properly—all the words he knew she needed to say, and had told her he didn't want to hear, even when he'd been aching for her to give him something that would eradicate the pain of her betrayal?

But it hadn't really been a betrayal. Oh, she'd come to

him intending to steal Calypso's secrets, but it was out of desperation and love for her father. Knowing Abigail as he did now, he didn't doubt her version of events. She would never have gone through with it.

But he would have.

He would have married her on Christmas Day knowing that it was a last resort for her. Knowing she was standing there, pledging her life and heart to him purely because he'd presented her with that sole option.

He'd been trying to prove that he was nothing like his father; instead, he was so very much worse. He'd been terrified of losing Abigail and yet he hadn't realised until now—until it was too late.

With a hoarse oath, he pitched the Scotch glass at the wall so that it cracked into several pieces and hit the ground with a splintering shriek.

He was terrified of losing Abigail and so he'd lost her.

# CHAPTER FOURTEEN

GABE STOOD OUTSIDE the door to his Manhattan penthouse for so long he wondered if, in the week since seeing Abigail, he'd become some kind of madman. It was his home—at least it had been until she'd left Italy. He felt as though a nest of snakes was writhing in his chest cavity.

He clutched the soft toy he'd bought for Raf in one hand and lifted the other to the door and knocked. Twice. Loud. Confident. Nothing that betrayed the way his stomach was twisting and his mind was spinning.

It wasn't until she pulled the door inwards that he realised how late it was. He winced at the sight of her—so beautiful, so sleepy, her long hair pulled over one shoulder, the oversized T-shirt she was sleeping in showing more leg than was helpful in that moment, for he needed to keep a clear mind.

'Gabe?' She blinked and rubbed her palms over her eyes.

'It's late, I'm sorry,' he said, shaking his head. 'Were you asleep?'

It was a stupid question—he could see quite clearly that she had been.

'What are you doing here?' She didn't invite him in. There was a wariness to her, a fear that he'd put there. At one time he might have pushed inside anyway, just as he had on the night he'd discovered Raf. But Gabe was done steamrollering Abby into submission. All along he'd been so wrong.

'Abigail.' The word came out as a hoarse plea. He cleared his throat and tried again. 'I need to speak with you.'

'Now?' She swallowed, her throat shifting, her vulnerability making him ache.

'I…can come back in the morning, if that's better?'

His contrition obviously confused her. She frowned, blinked her big eyes and then stepped backwards, gesturing for him to come inside.

He did so quickly, before she could change her mind, shrugging out of his suit jacket and discarding it carelessly over the back of a chair. 'This is for Raf,' he said needlessly, holding up the little monkey toy.

She crossed her arms over her chest. 'He's sleeping. If you wanted to see him.' She angled her face away from him and he wanted to shout, *No!,* because he needed to see her, to study her, but he didn't. Instead, he clenched his hand into a fist by his side, urging himself to be patient, to be gentle. To respect her autonomy and to respect the fact she'd probably tell him to go to hell—with good reason.

'I do, of course.' He nodded. 'But I meant what I said. I need to speak to you.'

She frowned. 'Is everything okay? Are you sick? Is it Noah?'

His chest crushed. Why hadn't he noticed the level of her compassion before? Why hadn't he understood that she was full of care for others—which in part had led to her downfall? It was compassion for Lionel that had sent her to Gabe, and compassion for Raf that had brought her to Italy.

'I'm fine.' He didn't mention Noah. It was early days there and he was keeping a close eye on the situation.

'Good.' She stepped away from him, towards the kitchen. 'Would you like anything? Coffee?'

He shook his head but followed her, watching as she poured herself water and took a small sip.

'How are you?'

'Fine,' she said, but her eyes shifted away from him and he ached for her, for the obvious hurt he'd inflicted.

'I thought that if I married you I'd be a better man than

my father. But it turns out I'm every bit as bad. Worse, actually.'

Her eyes lifted to his face and she said nothing, waiting for him to continue.

'I told myself it was right for all of us; the best thing we could do for our son. But I ignored your feelings and needs. I should have helped you to live a better life here, in New York, but I was selfish. I wanted you in Italy and so I bullied you into coming there with me. I treated you so much worse than I accused your father of doing. How you didn't scratch my eyes out is beyond me.'

She shook her head but he couldn't let her interrupt. What if she told him to leave? He needed to at least say what he'd come to tell her, and then let her decide what she wanted. And he would need to respect that decision.

'When I got back to Italy, after Christmas, I just knew I couldn't be responsible for making you miserable. All I could think about was the way you looked when we argued. The things I said. The way you stared at me as though I was…' He shook his head angrily, dragging his fingers through his hair. 'You were falling apart. You hated living with me; you hated Italy. I had to send you here because I wanted you to be happy. Are you happy, *tempesta*?'

Her eyes locked onto his for several long seconds and then she blinked, looking away hurriedly. 'I'm getting there.'

'I don't believe you.'

Her smile was miserable. 'That seems to be our problem. You never have believed me.'

His gut twisted sharply. 'No.' Regret made the word heavy. He ran his palm along the back of his neck, feeling the coarse hairs there.

'On Christmas Day you asked me if I loved you and I said no. I've never been in love. I've never been loved. But

I've been lonely and I've been alone. I've been miserable. Most of my life was that. And then I met you.'

Abby was very still, waiting, her breath held, needing to hear something that would lift the weight that had lodged permanently on her chest.

'That night, last Christmas, my God, if you knew how I felt. How I wanted you. How I fell for you.' He swore softly under his breath. 'It was my fault that the Calypso debacle cut me to the quick. For the first time in my life, I let my guard down. I let you in. I wanted every single piece of you. Not just your body—all of you. I've never felt that way before.'

'And I lied to you,' she muttered.

'You lied to me,' he confirmed grimly. 'And I couldn't forgive you for that. But nor could I forget you.'

Only the sound of Abby's laboured breath filled the room.

'I spent a year proving to myself that I was over you and then, the whole time I was in New York, I looked for you.' He grimaced. 'I don't mean I actually tried to find you. Just that my eyes were always scanning, hoping to catch a glimpse of you. Seeing you at the restaurant was an accident, but I don't think I would have left the city without you. One way or another.'

'Don't say that,' she said with a shake of her head. 'You don't need to pretend.'

'I spent a year waiting for you. I told myself I was busy, that I was angry, but I didn't so much as look at another woman.'

Abby's stomach swirled. Disbelief warred with pleasure at his admission.

'I've spent a long time pushing people away, *tempesta*. All my life. And then you came to Italy and I relaxed, because I had everything I needed. You were living with me. You were my lover, and we had a child. I had a family. But

I didn't realise how much that would hurt you. How much I was hurting you.'

'And so you let me go,' she said with a soft nod. 'I've worked that much out, Gabe. I know why you ended it. Why you sent me home. It was very *kind* of you.'

'No,' he said with a shake of his head. 'You don't understand. It wasn't because I didn't want you to stay.'

'You didn't want to hurt me,' she said, her smile one of sadness. 'You're a good person. Too good to lie to me, too good to use me.'

'I didn't want to hurt you so I sent you here, as though I could click my fingers and take us back in time. As though by sending you home I wouldn't feel like I had been hollowed out, like all of me had been dug from my body at the same time you left. I didn't want to hurt you but I didn't have any idea how much it would hurt to see you go. I've pushed people away all my life, and it comes easier to me than anything else. Even more so than admitting how I feel.'

Abby squeezed her fingernails into her palm and forced herself to face him. 'And?' she asked, the word a thin breath. 'How do you feel?'

'I feel like I have stepped into a strange world with only sharp edges and darkness. I feel like I am sinking all the time, my lungs filling with water rather than air and with no way to breathe. I wake each morning and reach for you, craving you, and then I remember. You're gone. You're here.'

'Are you saying…are you trying to say that you love me?' she demanded, hope an uncontainable beast in her breast.

'I know nothing of love,' he admitted, the words gravelly. 'What I am saying is that you are the beginning and end of my life. That without you everything is unbearable. I want to wake up and see you every morning, and hold you tight every night. I am saying that even if there were no Raf I would want you. I've spent my whole life pushing people away and I won't do it now—I can't. I want to do the opposite. I want to pull you close, to hold you near, to make you mine for the rest of my life, even when knowing how much I need you, how much power you have over me, terrifies me. *Tempesta,* you have run like a cyclone through all of me so that I'm not the same man I was the night we met. That man thought people—thought you—were disposable. I was so wrong. So very, very wrong. If you'll forgive me for being so stupid, I will make you love me too.'

And it was so ferociously determined that she laughed, a little unsteadily given that her chest was squeezing painfully.

'You're telling me you love me and still somehow doing it in a way that would control a room full of executives.'

'Apparently, I can't help doing that,' he said with a shake of his head. 'It makes what I say no less true.'

'Gabe—' she kept her distance '—I know enough of your upbringing to know how much loyalty means to you. Trust too. How will you ever trust me after what you found me doing?' Her cheeks flamed. 'You've told me again and again that you don't believe me. That you think I was unequivocally going to give those images to my father. There's no hope for us when you feel as you do. I've spent a long time coming to terms with that.'

'And so have I. I cannot live without you, and I unequivocally believe what you said.' He shook his head angrily. 'I *do* believe you. I cannot explain it. The rational part of my brain demands proof and explanations, but the part of me that knows you, that understands you, simply *believes*.' He took a step towards her and when she didn't step backwards he lifted his hands and cupped her face. 'You know almost as much about rejection and loneliness as I do.' His gaze bored into hers, seeing all the secrets of her soul. 'Your mother died and you were abandoned. Your father shut you out at every opportunity. Is it any wonder you were prepared to do anything he asked of you? In the hopes that maybe, just maybe, that might be the thing that would make him love you?'

She sobbed and shut her eyes, his interrogation, his understanding, all too much to cope with.

'He was wrong not to see your true value. But I was more so. You gave me everything—you made me feel alive and real for the first time in years. You gave me your beautiful, kind heart and I shouted at you. I practically threatened to take your son from you.' The words were loaded with anger, all directed at himself. 'Believe me, if I could take that day back, I would. With all that I am, I wish I hadn't said those things to you. I wish I hadn't given you any reason to feel pain.'

'This is about Raf,' she whispered. 'It has to be.' For she couldn't make sense of what was happening. All her dreams were coming true before her and she wasn't sure they were strong enough to hold her weight. 'You miss him.'

'*Sì*. I do miss Raf, but I'm as prepared now as I was a week ago to leave him with you, if that's what you want,' he insisted gently. 'This, right now, is about *you*. It's about the woman I fell in love with last Christmas, and somehow found my way to again. It's about the woman who gave me her innocence, who'd been waiting for me all her life, just as I had been waiting for her. It's about the woman who took a broken, angry man and made him smile once more. It's about the woman who has come to mean everything to me, who I do not wish to live without.' He ran his thumb over her lower lip and she juddered, her breath escaping her slowly, brushing over his inner wrist.

'I've trained myself not to want love. It's never been offered to me anyway.' He dropped his head so that their foreheads were touching and Abby breathed in deeply, letting his proximity chase the grief from her veins.

'I offered you love,' she whispered. 'I loved you every day we were in Italy. Even when I was so mad I could burst, I loved you… I wanted our marriage to be a real one,' she said. 'I felt so close to having everything I'd ever dreamed of. It was so magical—such a magical Christmas—with the snow, and the tree, and you and then the wedding dress…'

'From the moment we met, you have been all I've wanted. I've been stupid enough to run from that, but now I'm running right towards you. I want you, all of you, and if there were no Raf I would still be here, begging you, as a man who loves a woman more than any ever has, to marry me. To spend the rest of your life with me, letting me love you…'

Abby sobbed, a sound of pure, exquisite joy.

'You're going to marry me,' he said into her mouth and she nodded, laughing, before kissing him again.

'Can we go home now?'

He pulled away so he could study her face, see the earnestness there. 'Home? Where is our home to be?'

'The castle, obviously.'

His smile was the most beautiful thing she'd ever seen. 'Ah. And so it is, *mi amore*.'

# EPILOGUE

'RAF!' A LITTLE girl's voice squealed with delight and when Abby turned around she saw Ivy, Noah's adopted daughter, giggling in response to Raf's attempts to grab her hair. As a two-year-old, he was charming and spirited. Abby was grateful they'd retained Monique to help chase after him!

Abby walked towards the pair of children and crouched down, lifting a manicured nail to her son's nose. 'Stop that, Rafael.' She suppressed a smile when his chubby face turned towards her. 'Ivy's mommy has spent far too long braiding her hair to have it undone by the likes of you. Now, where's your bouquet, Ivy?'

'I've got it!' Holly called from the doorway, carrying three bunches of flowers and wearing a broad smile on her beautiful face. She was glowing, but Abby had known Holly almost a year and knew it had little to do with her pregnancy. Holly was one of those women who always glowed. She was warm and kind and, from the moment they'd met—the Christmas after they'd become engaged—Abby had known they would be friends.

It had proved to be so, and the proximity of Italy and England had meant that both families met quite often.

Families.

Abby turned to her reflection in the mirror, studying the bridal gown. It was the same one Gabe had chosen and given her two years earlier, a Christmas morning that was snowy and magical, just like this one. Except not like this one because she'd been so insecure then, so uncertain of her future and what her marriage would look like. Now, every day was a gift, boxed in so much security and love that she felt as though she were floating through life.

Families.

She'd been alone for so long and now she had Raf and Gabe, and Noah, Holly and Ivy, and Holly's big, chaotic extended family too.

'Your father's outside,' Holly said softly, handing a small box to Abby. 'And the groom asked me to give you this.'

Abby took the box and opened it, her fingers shaking a little at the mention of her father.

It was a big step for him to have come to Italy—and that was all down to Gabe's persistence. It was the reason they'd waited two years to marry. He'd understood, without needing to be told, how much it would mean to Abby to have her father walk her down the aisle at her wedding.

Irrespective of Lionel Howard's sins, he was the only family from her old life that she had left and she wasn't ready to shut the door on that completely. So Gabe had made it his mission to smooth the fractures of their relationship. It had been disastrous at first, but Gabe was not a man to take no for an answer, and by the following Christmas a fragile truce had been formed.

Now, a year later, it was still fragile, still young, but Abby was glad that there was the prospect of a future that included her father. If he chose not to make the most of it, then she'd accept that. She'd let him go, knowing that what she and Gabe had was special, that he could be a part of it if he wanted, but that you couldn't force love. You couldn't force someone to want you.

'What's in the box, Abby?' Ivy asked, coming to stand beside her.

'Let's find out, shall we?' She unwrapped it and lifted the lid, tears moistening her eyes when she saw the decoration inside.

'What is it?' Ivy asked again.

'It's a tradition,' Abby whispered, then smiled brightly,

lifting the decoration so Ivy and Holly could see the delicate etchings on each side. It was of the castle, she realised, a single tear running down her cheek.

'Stop that!' Holly said with a laugh, dabbing at it with a tissue. 'You'll ruin your make-up.'

'Why do we cry when we're happy?' Abby asked with a laugh. 'Because I am. Happier than I ever thought I'd be.'

'Just about as happy as you deserve, I'd say,' Holly said kindly, running a palm over her rounded tummy. 'Shall I get your father?'

Abby sucked in a deep breath and nodded. 'Yes. I'm ready.'

'Come on, you two.' Holly held her hands out to the children and guided them from the room. Abby wasn't alone for long. A moment later, Lionel walked in, his expression guarded until he looked at his daughter, properly looked at her, and then was arrested where he stood, unable to keep walking.

'You look…' He shook his head. 'You are so like her,' he said slowly.

Abby ignored the twisting of her heart, the pain that came from knowing she would always be just a reflection of her mother to him. It was enough that he was there—not because she wouldn't have been happy to marry without her father's presence, but because it was yet another proof of the myriad ways in which Gabe loved her. There had been many testaments to that fact over the two years since they'd become engaged, and each reminder of how special she was to him filled her with a rush of pleasure.

'Shall we?'

Lionel nodded, holding his arm out for Abby. She put her hand in the crook of his arm, took one last look at herself and smiled. 'Let's go then.'

They walked towards the stairs of the castle, but at the

top, before they came into view of the wedding guests, he paused, turning to face his daughter, a frown on his face.

It was natural for Abby to experience a jolt of anxiety. She didn't want her father to be there to only ruin the day. She waited, her breath held, for what he would say.

'I do love you, Abby. I know I'm not a good father. After your mother died I just couldn't be anything to anyone.' He shook his head. 'My business was everything. I look at you now and I realise I don't know anything about the young woman you've become.'

Abby expelled a sigh of relief. 'There's time to get to know me, Dad. Our door is open to you.'

And tears sparkled in his eyes as he shook his head. 'That's better than I deserve.'

Abby tilted her head. 'Yes,' she agreed with a teasing smile—the smile of a woman so completely in love and content that nothing could bring her down for long.

They began to walk once more, and halfway down the stairs the makeshift wedding venue came into sight. The foyer had been decorated with another huge tree—their third in the castle—and seats had been set to view it. She couldn't see her groom yet, though. That moment was reserved for when she and Lionel reached the ground floor and moved forward.

Then Abby's heart jolted in recognition of her mate, her partner, her purpose.

He stood, tall and handsome, in front of the tree, dressed in a jet-black tuxedo with a crisp white shirt, but it was his eyes that almost felled her. They were boring into her with the intensity that was part and parcel of his love for her.

She smiled at him, a smile of love, of understanding. As the music began to play she walked down the aisle with her father.

Noah stood beside Gabe and, as they got close, Gabe turned to his best friend and nodded at something Noah said. Noah turned to look at his own wife before patting Gabe on the back.

Later, after the ceremony, when they were dancing at the reception, their guests surrounding them with happiness and love, Abby asked her husband what Noah had said.

'He said we've done it.' Gabe grinned.

'Done what?'

'Outgrown our childhoods.' And for a second he frowned, but it was the work of an instant, then he was her Gabe once more, self-assured, arrogant, perfect.

She lifted onto tiptoe and kissed his lips softly. She would spend the rest of her life trying to erase the pain of his upbringing. Starting now.

'I sometimes find it hard to imagine Noah ever being like you described. He's so strong, like you.'

'He'd been badly hurt,' Gabe said quietly. 'And often. There aren't many people who could weather what he did...'

Gabe and Abby looked towards their friends, studying their obvious intimacy, their perfect partnership. Ivy was nearby, dancing with another friend of Gabe's, standing on the man's shoes, laughing at the jokes he was telling.

'Holly is glowing,' Abby murmured, tilting her head to look at her friend. She danced close to Noah, and she smiled at them. Noah was so like Gabe. Despite the fact they weren't biologically related, there was a similar spirit to both men. A strength and honour that ran through both. Little wonder they'd found one another and clung on in the midst of everything they'd lost.

'She is.' He nodded.

'I'm pleased for them. Another baby will certainly keep Ivy busy.'

'And save Raf from her mothering,' Gabe agreed with a laugh.

Abby grinned. He was right. Ivy adored Raf and spent most of their time together chasing after him, 'helping' him in every way.

'She'll be a great big sister,' Abby said thoughtfully.

'True.'

'And Raf? Do you think he'll make a good big brother?'

'I have no doubt he would.' He stared at her, a frown on his face as he tried to interpret her meaning. 'You'd like another baby?'

'Yes. In fact...'

He stopped dancing, holding her close. 'You're pregnant?'

'Yes.'

'You're pregnant!' His face wore a mask of such pleasure that Abby felt her eyes moisten once more. Happy tears seemed to be all she had left these days.

'I'm twelve weeks. I hope you don't mind that I didn't tell you. I wanted it to be your Christmas present.'

'Mind? It's the best Christmas gift you could have arranged.'

'Well, you helped with the arrangement,' she pointed out with a blush.

Gabe laughed, his eyes shining with passion, but then he sobered, pressing his finger to her chin and lifting her face so their eyes latched. 'I'm going to be with you this time, Abby. I'm going to be by your side for everything.'

She placed her head against his chest so she could hear the solid, reliable beating of his heart and there was truth in every drum.

'I'm going to be with you for it all, and for every day afterwards, my beautiful, irreplaceable *tempesta*. And all the Christmases of our lives.'

She smiled and swept her eyes shut, wondering if when she opened them again this would all turn out to be a dream. For how could reality be so utterly perfect? She blinked and he was there. So were their friends. Everybody as happy as before, everything as perfect as she could wish.

Outside the castle, snow began to drift downwards—the icing on the cake of their perfect Christmas miracle.

\* \* \* \* \*

# NEVER GAMBLE WITH A CAFFARELLI

## MELANIE MILBURNE

To my dear friend Heather Last, whom I met on the
first day of kindergarten a very long time ago!

Thank you for always being my friend and
for being one of the first people to say:
'You should write!'

Much love. Xx

# CHAPTER ONE

'WHAT DO YOU mean you *lost* it?' Angelique stared at her father in abject horror.

Henri Marchand gave a negligent shrug but she could see his Adam's apple moving up and down as if he'd just had to swallow something unpleasant. But then, losing her late mother's ancestral home in the highlands of Scotland in a poker game in Las Vegas was about as bitter a flavour as you could taste, Angelique supposed.

'I was doing all right until Remy Caffarelli tricked me into thinking he was on a losing streak,' he said. 'We played for hours with him losing just about every hand. I thought I'd clean him up once and for all. I put down my best hand in a winner-takes-all deal but then he went and trumped it.'

Angelique felt her spine turn to ice and her blood heat to boiling. 'Tell me you did *not* lose Tarrantloch to Remy Caffarelli.' He was her worst enemy. The one man she would do anything to avoid—to avoid even thinking about!

'I'll win it back.' Her father spouted the problem gambler's credo with arrogant confidence. 'I'll challenge him to another game. I'll up the stakes. He won't be able to resist another—'

'And lose even *more*?' She threw him an exasperated

look. 'He set you up. Can't you see that? He's always had you in his sights but you made it a hundred times worse, sabotaging his hotel development in Spain. How could you have fallen for such a trick?'

'I'll outsmart him this time. You'll see. He thinks he's so clever but I'll get him back where it *really* hurts.'

Angelique rolled her eyes and turned away. Her stomach felt as if it had been scraped out with a rusty spoon. How could her father have lost her beloved mother's ancestral home to Remy Caffarelli? Tarrantloch wasn't even his to lose! It was supposed to be held in trust for her until she turned twenty-five, less than a year from now.

Her sanctuary. Her private bolthole. The one place she could be herself without hundreds of cameras flashing in her face.

Gone. Lost. Gambled away.

Now it was in the hands of her mortal enemy.

Oh, how Remy would be gloating! She could picture him in her mind: that cocky smirk of victory on his sensual mouth; those dark espresso-brown eyes glinting.

Oh, how her blood boiled!

He would be strutting around the whole of Europe telling everyone how he had finally got the better of Henri Marchand.

The bitter rivalry between her father and the Caffarellis went back a decade. Remy's grandfather Vittorio had been best friends and business partners with her father, but something had soured the relationship and at the last minute Henri had pulled out of a major business development he had been bankrolling for Vittorio. The Caffarellis' financial empire had been severely compromised, and the two men hadn't spoken a word to each other since.

Angelique had long expected it would be Remy who would pursue her father for revenge and not one of his brothers. Of the three Caffarelli brothers, Remy had had the most to do with his grandfather, but their relationship wasn't affectionate or even close. She suspected Remy was after his grandfather's approval, to win his respect, something neither of his older brothers had been able to do in spite of creating their own massive fortunes independent of the family empire.

But Angelique had clashed with Remy even before the fallout between their families and his dealings with her father. She thought him spoilt and reckless. He thought her attention-seeking. The eight-year difference in their ages hadn't helped, although she was the first to admit she hadn't been an easy person to be around, particularly after her mother had died.

Angelique turned back to her father who was washing the bitter taste of defeat down with a generous tumbler of brandy. 'Mum's probably spinning in her grave—and her parents and grandparents along with her. How could you be so...so *stupid*?'

Henri's eyes hardened and his thin lips thinned and whitened. 'Watch your mouth, young lady. I am your father. You will not speak to me as if I am an imbecile.'

She squared her shoulders and steeled her spine. 'What are you going to do? Call me a whole lot of nasty names like you did to Mum? Verbally and emotionally abuse me until I take an overdose just to get away from you?'

The silence was thick, pulsing, almost vibrating with menace.

Angelique knew it was dangerous to upset her father.

To mention what must never be mentioned.

She had spent her childhood walking around on tiptoe to avoid triggering his ire. His temper could be vicious. As a young child she had witnessed how her mother's self-esteem had been eroded away, leaving her a wilted shadow of her former self.

But, while her father had never raised a hand either to her mother or to Angelique, the potential threat of it was there all the same. It hovered in the atmosphere. It crawled along her skin like a nasty, prickly-footed insect.

In the early years Angelique had tried hard to please him but nothing she had ever done had been good enough, or at least not good enough for his impossibly exacting standards.

In the end she had decided to do the opposite. Since the age of seventeen she had deliberately set out to embarrass him. To shock him. That was why she had pursued her career as a swimsuit model so determinedly. She knew how much it annoyed and embarrassed him that his little girl's body was displayed in magazines, catalogues and billboards all over Europe. She had even deliberately courted scandals in the press, not caring that they further cemented her reputation as a wild, spoilt little rich girl who loved nothing more than to party, and to party hard.

'If you're not careful I will disinherit you.' Her father issued the threat through clenched teeth. 'I will give every penny away to a dog's home.'

Angelique would have said, "Go on. Do it," but the fortune he threatened to give away had actually belonged to her mother. And she was going to do her darned hardest to get back what was rightfully hers.

Starting now.

The desert of Dharbiri was one of Remy's favourite places. One of his friends from his boarding-school days, Talib Firas Muhtadi, was a crown prince of the ancient province. The golden stretch of endless wind-rippled sands, the lonely sound of the whistling, pizza-oven-hot air; the vibrant colours of the sunset; the sense of isolation and the almost feudal laws and customs were such a stark change from his thoroughly modern twenty-first-century life.

No alcohol. No gambling. No unchaperoned women.

He loved his fast-paced life—there was absolutely no doubt about that—it was just that now and again he felt the need to unplug himself from it and recharge his batteries.

The hot, dry air was such a contrast to the chill of autumn that had come early back in Italy where he had spent a couple of days with his grandfather. No matter the season, Vittorio was a difficult person to be around, bitter and even at times violent. But Remy liked the sense of power it gave him to drop in without notice—which he knew annoyed the hell out of his grandfather—stay a couple of days and then breeze off without saying goodbye.

But while Remy loved Italy it was hard to decide where he felt most at home. His French-Italian heritage, on top of his English boarding-school education, had more or less made him a citizen of the world. Up until now he hadn't really had a base to call home. He'd lived in and out of suitcases and hotel suites. He liked that he didn't know where he was going to be from one week to the next. He would pick up a scent like a foxhound and go after a good deal. And nail it.

He liked to move around the globe, picking up business here and there, wheeling and dealing, winning the unwinnable.

He grinned.

Like winning that winner-takes-all hand with Henri Marchand in Vegas. It had been a masterstroke of genius on his part. He didn't like to be *too* smug about it but, truth be told, he did actually feel a little bit proud of himself.

He'd hit Henri Marchand where it hurt: he had taken that double-crossing cheat's Scottish castle off him.

Victory was more than sweet—it was ambrosial.

Remy had come out to Dharbiri so he could reflect on his prize. Tarrantloch was one of the most beautiful and prestigious estates in Scotland. It was isolated and private. It would make a fabulous base for him—a place he could call home. It would be the perfect haven to hunt, shoot, fish and hang out with his friends during his infamous week-long parties. He could have gone straight there to take ownership but he didn't want to appear *too* eager to take possession.

No, it was better to let Henri Marchand—and his spoilt little brattish daughter Angelique—think this was just like any other deal done and dusted.

There would be plenty of time to rub her retroussé little nose in it.

He couldn't wait.

Getting a flight to Dharbiri was hard enough. Getting access to where Remy Caffarelli was staying was like trying to get through an airport security check-in with a fistful of grenades or an AK47 in her hand luggage.

Angelique ground her teeth for the tenth time. Did she *look* like a security threat?

'I need to speak to Monsieur Caffarelli. It's a matter of great urgency. A family...er, crisis.'

*Her* family crisis.

The attendant on the reception desk was cool and disbelieving. Angelique could only suppose he was used to fielding off droves of female wannabes who would give an arm or a leg—or both—to have a few minutes with the staggeringly rich, heart-stoppingly gorgeous Remy Caffarelli.

As if *she* would ever sink so low.

'Monsieur Caffarelli is not available right now.' The attendant gave her a look that immediately categorised her as just another hopeful, starry-eyed wannabe. 'He is dining with the Crown Prince and his wife, and according to royal protocol he cannot be interrupted unless it is a matter of utmost political urgency.'

Angelique mentally rolled her eyes. It looked like she would have to try another tactic; find some other way of getting under the radar. But she was good at that sort of thing.

Outsmarting. Outmanoeuvring. Outwitting.

She smiled to herself.

That was her speciality.

It didn't take long to bribe a junior housemaid who recognised Angelique from a magazine shoot she'd done a couple of months ago. All it took was an autograph to get access to Remy's suite.

The young housemaid had mentioned how important it was Angelique wasn't seen in Remy's room other than by Remy himself. Apparently there were strict protocols on women and men socialising without appropriate supervision. As much as it annoyed her to have to hide until she knew for sure it was Remy entering the suite, Angelique decided to play things safe.

She scanned the room for a suitable hiding place.

Behind the curtains? No; she would be seen from outside.

The bathroom? No; a housemaid might come in to clean up the appalling mess Remy had left there.

Angelique looked at the wall-to-ceiling wardrobe running along one wall.

A little clichéd perhaps…

But perfect!

# CHAPTER TWO

REMY FELT A strange sense of disquiet as soon as he entered his suite; unease; a sense that the place was not quite the way he had left it. He had cancelled the evening housekeeping visit because he hated people fussing around him all the time. Surely they hadn't gone against his wishes?

He closed the door and stilled.

Waited.

Listened.

His gaze scanned the luxuriously appointed suite for any signs of a disturbance. His laptop was still open on the desk and the screensaver was the same as when he'd left to have dinner. The can of soda he had half-drunk was still sitting where he'd left it, and a ring of moisture from the condensation had pooled around the bottom.

His gaze went further, to the open door of the palatial bedroom. The bed cover was slightly crumpled from where he had sat while he'd taken a call from one of his office staff in Monte Carlo. One of the towels he'd used when he'd showered was still lying on the floor. The clothes he'd worn earlier were in a messy pile nearby.

It was jet lag, that was all. He gave himself a mental shake, shrugged off his dinner jacket and threw it over the arm of the nearest sofa. He reached up and loosened his tie. It had been feeling a little tight all evening, but rules were rules, and he was happy to go along with them because out here he could forget he was the youngest son of the Caffarelli dynasty.

Here there was no one measuring him up against his older brothers or his impossible-to-please grandfather.

Out here he was as free as a desert falcon. He had the next few days to kick back and chill out in one of the hottest places on earth. Life could be pretty good when *he* was in the driving seat.

Angelique held her breath for so long she thought she would faint. But she knew she had to wait until Remy was well and truly inside the suite and in a relaxed mood before she came out of the closet—so to speak.

Not that there were too many of his clothes *in* the closet.

Most of them seemed to be on the floor of the bedroom or spilling haphazardly out of his lightweight travel bag. The en suite bathroom she'd scoped out earlier was just as bad. He'd left a dark ring of stubble in the marble basin when he'd shaved and there had been yet another wet towel on the floor.

It confirmed what she already knew: Remy Caffarelli was a spoilt playboy with more money than sense who had grown up with servants dancing around to satisfy his every whim.

It was a tiny bit ironic of her to point the finger at such a shiny black kettle as Remy when she too had grown up surrounded by wealth. But at least she knew how to pick up after herself and she could cook a three-course gourmet meal with one arm and her appetite tied behind her back.

Remy had never even boiled an egg.

He had probably never even boiled a kettle!

Angelique clenched her fists and her jaw.

*He just boiled her blood.*

She heard him moving about the suite. She heard the ring pull of a can being opened. It couldn't be alcohol, as this was a totally dry province. There were stiff penalties for bringing in or consuming contraband liquor.

She heard the click of his laptop being activated and then the sound of his fingers typing on the keyboard. She heard him a give a deep, throaty chuckle as if something he'd just read online or in an email had amused him.

Her belly gave a little flip-flop movement.

He had a *very* nice laugh. He had a *very* nice smile. He had a *very* nice mouth. She had spent most of her teenage years fantasising about that mouth.

*Stop it right now, you silly little fool!*

*You are not going to think about his mouth, or any other part of his totally hot, totally amazing body.*

Just as Angelique was about to step out of the wardrobe, she heard a sharp, businesslike knock at the door of the suite. Her heart gave a jerky kick against her breastbone.

Was he expecting someone?

One of his star-struck wannabes, perhaps? Oh God! If she had to listen to him having bed-wrecking sex with some bimbo who had been smuggled into his room…

'Monsieur Caffarelli?' an official-sounding voice called out. 'We wish to have a word with you.'

She heard Remy's footsteps as he moved across to open the door. 'Yes?' he said in that charming, 'I'm happy to help you' way he had down to a science.

The official cleared his throat as if he found what he was about to say quite difficult. 'We have received some information that you have a young woman in your room.'

*'Pardon?'* Remy's predominantly French accent made Angelique's belly do another little tumble.

'As you are well aware, Monsieur Caffarelli, the dictates of our province state that no single woman must be unchaperoned with a man unless she is his sister or his wife. We have reason to believe you have someone in your room who does not fit either of those categories.'

'Are you out of your mind?' Remy sounded incredulous. 'I know the rules. I've been coming here long enough. I would never do anything to insult Sheikh Muhtadi. Surely his officials—including you—know that?'

'A junior member of our housekeeping staff has tearfully confessed to allowing a young woman access to your room,' the official said. 'We wish to check on whether this is true or not.'

'Go on. Check.' Remy sounded supremely, arrogantly confident. 'You won't find anyone in here but me.'

Angelique heard the door of the suite being flung open and her breath screeched to a skidding halt in her throat. Her heart was pounding like a sledgehammer on a rocky surface. It actually felt like it was going to leap out of her chest. She shrank back inside the closet, hoping the shadows of the space would conceal her. She even closed her eyes, just like a little child playing hide and seek, thinking that if she couldn't see them, they couldn't see her.

She heard firm footsteps moving about the suite, doors being opened and closed. The curtains were swished back. Even the drawers of Remy's desk were opened and then shut.

A drawer? They thought she could fit in a *drawer*?

'See?' Remy's tone had a touch of irritability to it now. 'There's no one here but me.'

'The closet.' The more senior of the two officials spoke. Angelique could almost picture him giving a brisk nod towards her hidey-hole. 'Check the bedroom closet.'

'Are you joking?' Remy coughed out a laugh. 'Do you *really* think I would do something as clichéd as that?'

The mirrored door slid back on its tracks. Angelique raised her right hand and gave a little fingertip wave. 'Surprise!'

Remy could not believe his eyes. He blinked to make sure he wasn't imagining things. That could *not* be Angelique Marchand in his closet.

He opened his eyes and looked again.

*It was.*

'What the hell are you doing?' He glared at her so fiercely his eyes ached. 'What are the hell are you doing in my room? In my closet?'

She stepped out of the closet as if she was stepping out on to one of the catwalks she frequented all over Europe. She moved like a sinuous cat, all legs, arms, high, pert breasts and pouting full-lipped mouth. Her distinctive grey-blue eyes gave him a reproving look. 'That's not a very nice welcome, Remy. I thought you had better manners than that.'

Remy had never thought he had a temper until he'd had to deal with Angelique. He could feel his rage building up inside him like a cauldron on the boil. No one made him angrier than she did. She was willful, spoilt and a little too determined to get her own way. Did she

have no sense of protocol or politeness? What the hell
was she doing here? And in his room?

Did she have any idea of the trouble she could get
him into?

She had made him look like a liar. Trust was everything in a place like Dharbiri. He might be a friend of
the Crown Prince but flouting the rules out here was a
definite no-no, friend or foe.

He could be deported.

Charged.

The blood suddenly ran ice-cold in his veins.

*Flogged.*

'You had better have a very good explanation for
why you're in my room,' he said through gritted teeth.

She swept her thick, wavy, glossy black mane of hair
over one slim shoulder. 'I came to see you about my
house. You *have* to give it back.' She nailed him with
a look that was diamond-hard. 'I'm not leaving your
side until you sign me over the deeds to Tarrantloch.'

'Monsieur Caffarelli,' the older official spoke in a
stern 'don't mess with me' tone. 'Would you please ver-
ify if this young woman is personally known or related
to you? If not we will have her immediately evicted and
the authorities will deal with her accordingly.'

*Deal with her?* Remy didn't like the sound of that.
As much as he hated Angelique, he could not stand by
and see her come to any harm. He took a deep breath
and put on his best 'let's be cool about this' smile. 'I'm
afraid there's been a little mix-up. I had no idea my fiancée was going to surprise me by turn—'

'Your fiancée?' Angelique and the senior official
spoke in unison.

Remy gave the official a conciliatory smile. 'We've
been trying to keep our engagement a secret. The press

make such of fuss of this stuff at home.' He gave a Gallic shrug. 'You know how it is.'

The official straightened his shoulders, his expression as formal as a drill sergeant. 'This young woman may well be your fiancée, but it is against the laws of our land for her to be alone with you without a chaperone.'

'So, we'll get a chaperone,' Remy said. 'She won't be with me long in any case, will you, *ma chérie*?'

Angelique's eyes narrowed to hairpin slits but her voice had a false sort of sing-song quality to it that grated on Remy's already overstretched nerves. 'Only for as long as it takes, *mon trésor.*'

The official puffed himself up to his not considerable height. 'Due to the circumstances of your fiancée's… ahem…surprise visit, neither of you will be permitted to leave the province until you are legally married.'

*'Married?'* Angelique had joined Remy in a choked gasp of horror.

'You're joking?' Angelique gaped at the official with wide shocked eyes. 'You *have* to be joking!'

'He's not joking,' Remy muttered just low enough for her to hear it. 'Go along with it. Try and keep cool.'

*Keep cool? Who was he kidding?* He didn't feel cool. He'd never had to think so fast on his feet in his life. Pretending she was his fiancée had just popped into his head. And it still might not be enough to get them over the line.

'I'm not marrying you!' She flashed him a livid, blue-lightning look. 'I'd rather die!'

'Yes, well, you just might get that choice,' he said. 'We're not in France, Italy or England right now. Didn't you check out the Smart Traveller website before you came?'

Her throat rose and fell. 'I didn't think. I just...'

'Not thinking is something you do remarkably well.' Remy gave her a dressing-down look. 'You've made a lifetime's work of it.'

Her small hands clenched into tight fists and her eyes gave him another deadly glare. 'I thought you were best friends with the Crown Prince. Can't *he* do something?'

'Afraid not.' Remy had already had this debate with his friend during university. 'The royal family have a lot of power but not enough to overrule laws of the elder tribesmen of the province.'

'But that's ridiculous!'

Remy gave her a cautionary look. 'If you're going to stand there spluttering insults like a Roman candle firecracker, I'm not going to lay down my life for you.'

She opened and closed her mouth, seemingly lost for words. Not that it would last. He knew how quick and sharp her tongue could be. She always tried to get the last word.

He was the only person in her life who wouldn't let her have it.

'Monsieur Caffarelli?' The official stepped forward. 'We must leave now to make the necessary arrangements to conduct the ceremony first thing in the morning. We will arrange alternative accommodation for your fiancée. You will understand that she is not permitted to spend the night in your room.'

'But of course.' Remy gave him another charming smile. *I don't want her here in any case.* 'I understand completely. I sincerely apologise for my fiancée's impulsive behaviour. She is a little wilful and headstrong at times, but once we are married she will soon learn to toe the line. I'll make absolutely sure of it.'

Remy smiled to himself when he saw the two red-hot spots of colour pooling in Angelique's cheeks. She was standing rock-steady but he knew her well enough to know she was beyond livid with him. He could see it in her stormy eyes and in the clenched posture of her jaw. Too bad they had to have a chaperone. He would have quite liked to see what that anger looked like when it was finally unleashed.

Angelique turned to look at the senior official, her expression now meek and demure, those thick, impossibly long eyelashes batting up and down for good measure. 'Please may I have a private word with my, er, fiancé? Perhaps you could chaperone us from the lounge. We'll leave the door open here. Would that be acceptable?'

The official gave a formal nod and indicated with a jerk of his head for his sidekick to follow him out to the lounge area.

Remy got the full, fiery force of Angelique's gaze as she swung around to face him once the officials had gone. 'There's no point glaring at me like that,' he said before she could let fly. 'You're the one who brought this about.'

She visibly shook with rage. It reminded him of the shuddering of a small two-stroke engine on the back of a dingy.

'Fiancée?' She sounded like she was choking on the word. 'Why couldn't you have said I was your sister or...or even your cousin?'

'Because the whole world knows I'm one of three brothers who were orphaned when we were young. And since both of my parents were only children, I don't have any cousins.'

Her eyes fired another round of hatred at him. 'Did you have to make that comment about controlling me as if I'm some sort of waspish virago? You did it deliberately, didn't you? You just can't help yourself. Any chance you get, you like to thrust home the chauvinist dagger.'

Right now that wasn't the only thing Remy wanted to thrust home. He had always tried to ignore the sexual attraction he felt for her. In the past she had always been banned by his family or too involved with someone else. But it was hard to ignore the tingling that was stirring in his loins right now.

And if they had been in any other place he might well have done something about it.

'Got under your skin, did it, *ma petite*?'

'You set my father up, didn't you?' Her expression was tight with barely compressed rage. 'I know how your mind works. You wanted to hit him where it hurt most because of that stupid deal in Ibiza. But I'm not letting you get away with it. I'll fight you tooth and nail until you give me back my house.'

Remy gave her a cool and totally unaffected look because he knew how much it would annoy her. 'Fight me all you like. There's no way I'm giving it back. I won it fair and square. Your father knew what he was getting into—he knew the risks he was taking. But I must say, I think it's pretty pathetic of him to send you out here to try and butter me up.'

Her head jerked back. 'You think *that's* why I'm here? As if I would ever sink so low as that. You're the last man on earth I would ever consider seducing.'

'Likewise, *ma coeur*; you don't float my boat, either.'

A flicker of uncertainty came and went in her gaze and her perfectly aligned, beautiful white teeth sank into her bottom lip.

But just for a nanosecond.

She suddenly pulled herself upright, like an abandoned hand puppet that had just been reconnected with a firm hand. 'And as for marriage... Well, that's just totally ridiculous. It's out of the question. I *won't* do it.'

'It'll just be a formality,' Remy said. 'We don't have to take this seriously. It probably won't even be recognised as legal back home. We'll just do what they require and then we'll leave. Simple.'

*'Simple?'* Her eyes shot their fury at him again. 'Tell me what about this is simple. We'll be married—' she gave a little shudder as if the word was anathema to her '—or at least, we will be on paper. I don't care if it's legal or not. I don't want to be married to you. I can't think of anything worse.'

He gave her a smile. 'We'll get it annulled as soon as we get back to Europe.'

'This is outrageous! This is a...a *disaster*!'

'Of your own making.' He used his 'too cool for school' tone again. He loved the way it triggered something feral in her. She went off like a bomb every time.

She flattened her mouth into a thin white line, her eyes looking murderous. 'This is *no*t my fault. This is *your* fault for being so determined to score points. You don't need Tarrantloch; your family have properties bigger and better than that all over the world. Why did you have to take the one thing I love more than anything else?'

Remy felt a little niggle of guilt. Just a niggle; nothing major. Nothing he couldn't ignore.

He'd set himself a goal and he'd achieved it.

That was the Caffarelli credo—goal; focus; win.

Remy could have taken any one of the businesses in the Marchand Holdings portfolio if he'd been so inclined, but Tarrantloch was the one thing he knew Henri

Marchand would regret losing the most. He had a score to settle with Henri that had nothing to do with his grandfather's dealings with him.

It was far more personal.

Remy had just about got the Ibiza development in the bag when an anonymous email had spooked the vendor. It hadn't been too hard to find out who had sent it. Henri Marchand was devious but not particularly smart at covering his tracks. Remy had sworn he would get revenge, no matter how long it took.

Tarrantloch was Henri Marchand's most valued, prized possession. It was his ultimate status symbol. Henri liked to play Laird of the Highlands with a coterie of his overfed, overindulged, overweight corporate cronies by his side.

The fact that his daughter—his only child and heir—fancied herself in love with the place didn't come into it at all.

Not even a niggly bit.

Remy was running a business, not a charity, and the one person in the world he felt the least charitable towards was Angelique Marchand.

'It's mine now. Get over it.' He refused to allow sentimentality to mess with his head. 'It's not like you'll be homeless. You live in Paris most of the year, don't you?'

Her expression was so rigid with anger he could see a muscle moving in and out in her cheek. 'I planned to live at Tarrantloch after my retirement.'

He whistled through his teeth. 'That's some seriously long-term planning. You're what, twenty-five?'

Her teeth made a grinding noise. 'Twenty-four. I'll be twenty-five next year in May.'

'So, what age do swimsuit models retire?' He couldn't

stop his gaze sweeping over her body. To say she had a knockout figure was a bit of an understatement.

More than a bit, actually.

He could not think of a body he found more delightful to look at. Distracting. He had been distracted by it for the last few years, and so too had just about everyone throughout Europe. He still remembered the first time he had driven past a billboard with the then-nineteen-year-old Angelique on it. She had been draped along the edge of an infinity pool in some exotic tropical location, wearing a couple of miniscule triangles of fabric that left just enough to the imagination to cause serious discomfort in his nether regions.

To say she had a traffic-stopping figure was putting it rather mildly.

'I want to branch out into other areas of the business,' she said.

'Such as?'

She glowered at him. 'I'm not going to discuss my career plans with you. You'll just rubbish them. You'll tell me I'm wasting my time or to go and get a real job or something.'

Remy felt that little niggle of guilt again. He hadn't been exactly encouraging of her plans to pursue a modelling career. When he'd first heard she was going to quit school to sign up with a modelling agency, he'd put aside his grandfather's ban on contact with her and had called and told her to reconsider.

But listening to advice was not something Angelique was particularly good at doing.

'Monsieur Caffarelli?' The official spoke from the open doorway. 'The room is now ready for your fiancée.' He turned to Angelique. 'If you will come this

way, *mademoiselle*? We have two chaperones to accompany you.'

Angelique glared at Remy as she stalked past him.
He caught a whiff of her signature fragrance as she went
by. It hovered about his nostrils, enticing him to breathe
in deep. He had always associated the smell of sweet-
peas with her—strong, heady and colourful.

His brain snapped back to attention like an elastic
band being flicked by a finger.

Within hours they would be man and wife.

Usually whenever the 'M' word was mentioned to
him he had a standard, stock phrase: *over my dead body*.

But somehow—right here and now—it didn't have
quite the same ring to it.

# CHAPTER THREE

ANGELIQUE COULD NOT even close her eyes, let alone get to sleep. She spent most of the night pacing the floor, cursing Remy, *hating* him. How could he have done this to her? He couldn't have thought of a worse punishment.

*Married.*

*To him of all people!*

It didn't matter if it was legal or not. She had sworn she would *never* marry. She would never allow someone else to have that sort of control over her, to have that sort of *commitment* from her.

She had seen first-hand her mother's commitment. Kate Tarrant had taken her marriage vows way too seriously. She had been browbeaten and submissive from day one. She had toed the line. She had obeyed. She had given up her freedom and her sense of self.

Angelique would *never* do that.

Marriage and all it represented nauseated her. Unlike most girls her age, she couldn't even bear the thought of wedding finery. Who wanted to dress up like a meringue, be smothered in a veil and be given away like a parcel to some man who would spend the next fifty years treating her like a household slave?

There was a knock on the door and when she opened it she found a maid holding a tray with fresh fruit, rolls and steaming hot, rather unusually fragrant coffee. 'Your breakfast, *mademoiselle*.'

Was this the time to announce that—despite her half-French bloodline—she actually loathed coffee and could only ever face tea first thing in the morning?

Probably not.

Not long after that maid left, another one much older one arrived, carrying a massive armful of wedding finery which she informed Angelique she would help her get into in preparation for the ceremony at ten.

'I'm not wearing that!' Angelique said as the maid laid out an outfit that looked more like a circus tent. A particularly beautiful circus tent, however. On closer inspection she saw there were fine threads of gold delicately woven into the fabric and hundreds of diamonds were stitched across the bodice.

'These are the official bridal robes of the province,' the maid said. 'The Princess Royal was married in them in July. It is a great honour that you have been given permission to wear them.'

*I can't believe I'm doing this*, Angelique thought as she stood and was wrapped in the voluminous folds. The irony wasn't lost on her. She made a living out of wearing the minimum of fabric. Now she was being wrapped in metres of it like some sort of glittering present.

Her blood simmered.

*It boiled.*

How could it be possible that within a less than an hour she would be married to Remy Caffarelli?

'Are we done?'

'Just about.' The maid came at her with a denser than normal veil dripping with even more diamonds and a train that was at least five metres long.

'Oh no.' Angelique shied away. 'Not that.'

The maid gave her a pragmatic look. 'Do you want to get out of here or don't you?'

'Are you OK with this?' Crown Prince Talib Firas Muhtadi said to Remy as he finished his second cup of thick, rich, aromatic cardamom-scented coffee. 'Things are really unstable right now in our province. The tribal elders are notoriously difficult to negotiate with and highly unpredictable. It's best to do things their way just to be on the safe side. We don't want a major uprising over an incident like this. Best to nip it in the bud and keep everyone happy.'

Remy mentally rolled his eyes as he put his cup back down on the saucer. 'No big deal. It's just a formality, right? It's not like this marriage—' he made the quotation marks with his fingers '—will be recognised at home.'

Talib looked at him for a long moment without speaking.

'You're joking, right?' Remy said, feeling a chill roll down his spine like an ice cube. *Please be joking.*

'Marriage is a very sacred institution in our culture,' Talib said. 'We don't enter into it lightly, nor do we leave it unless there are very good reasons for it.'

*What about total unsuitability?*

*Being polar opposites?*

*Hating each other?*

'I fought it too, Remy,' Talib added. 'But it's only since I met and married Abby that I realised what I've been missing out on. Oh, and yes, the marriage will be considered legal in your country.'

*Damn.*

*Double damn.*

* * *

The first thought Remy had was it could be anyone under that traditional wedding dress and long veil and he would not be any the wiser. But he instantly knew it was Angelique because of the way the robes were shaking, as if her rage was barely contained within the diamond-encrusted tent of the fabric that surrounded her slim body.

And her eyes.

How could he not recognise those stormy grey-blue eyes? They flashed with undiluted loathing through the gauze of the veil as she came to stand beside him.

He suddenly had a vision of his oldest brother Rafe's wedding day only a few weeks ago. The ceremony had been very traditional, and his bride, Poppy Silverton, had been quite stunningly beautiful and unmistakably in love. So too had Rafe, which had come as a bit of a surprise to Remy. He'd always thought Rafe was the show-no-emotion, feel-no-emotion type, but he'd actually seen moisture in Rafe's eyes as he'd slipped the wedding band on Poppy's finger, and his face had been a picture of devotion and pride.

His other brother Raoul was heading down the altar too, apparently just before Christmas. His bride-to-be, Lily Archer, had been employed to help rehabilitate Raoul after a water-skiing accident which had left him in a wheelchair. Remy had never seen Raoul happier since he'd announced his engagement to Lily, which was another big surprise, given how physically active Raoul had always been. But apparently love made up for all of that.

Not that Remy would know or ever wanted to know about love. He'd had his fair share of crushes, but as to falling in love…

Well, that was something he stayed well clear of and he intended to keep doing so.

Loving someone meant you could lose them. They could be there one minute and gone the next.

*Like his parents.*

Remy sometimes found it hard even to remember what his mother and father had looked like unless he jogged his memory with a photo or a home video. He had been seven years old when they had died, and as each year passed his memories of them faded even further. Listening to their voices and seeing them moving about on those home videos still seemed a little weird, as if a tiny part of his brain recognised them as people he had once known intimately but who were now little more than strangers.

He had completely forgotten their touch.

But there was one touch he was not going to forget in a hurry.

As soon as the cleric asked Remy to join hands with Angelique, he felt a lightning zap shoot up his from his hand, travel from the length of his arm and straight to his groin as if she had touched him there with her bare hands. He hadn't touched her even when her father had brought her with him when he had socialised with Remy's grandfather in the years before their fall out. Being eight years older than her, Remy had occasionally been left with the task of entertaining her during one of his grandfather's soirées. Even as a young teenager she had shown the promise of great beauty. That raven-black hair, those bewitching eyes, those lissom limbs and budding breasts had been a potent but forbidden temptation.

He had always made a point of *not* touching her.

Would the cleric expect him to kiss her? Not that

the idea didn't hold a certain appeal, but Remy would rather kiss her in private than in front of a small group of conservative tribesmen.

After all, he didn't want to offend them.

Angelique's hand was tiny. His hand almost swallowed it whole. But then the whole of her was tiny. Dainty. He felt a primal stirring in his loins when he thought of what it might be like to enter her. To possess her. To feel her sexy little body grip him tightly…

*Whoa, keep it in your trousers. Remember, this is just an on-paper marriage.*

The cleric went through the vows and Remy recited his lines as if he were an actor reading them from a script. No big deal. They were just words. Meaningless words.

When Angelique came to her lines she coughed them out like a cat with fur balls. She almost choked on the promise to obey him.

'I now pronounce you man and wife.' The cleric gave Remy a man-to-man smile. 'You may lift the veil and kiss your bride.'

Angelique's eyes flickered with something that looked like panic. 'I'd really rather not.'

Remy didn't give her time to finish her sentence in case she blew their cover. Besides, he'd kissed dozens of women. All he had to do was plant a perfunctory kiss on her lips and step back. Everyone would be happy.

*Easy.*

He lifted the heavy veil from her face and planted his mouth on hers.

Angelique had spent years during her teens imagining this very moment—the first time Remy kissed her. She had imagined it when other dates were kissing her, closing her eyes and dreaming it was actually Remy's mouth moving on hers, his hands touching her, his body wanting her. Quite frankly, those mind-wanderings of hers had made some of those kisses—not to mention some of her sexual encounters—a little more bearable.

But not one of her imaginings came anywhere near to the real deal.

Remy didn't kiss sloppily or wetly or inexpertly.

He kissed with purpose and potency.

The firm warmth of his lips, the taste of him, the feel of him was so…so *intensely* male, so addictive, she couldn't stop herself from pushing up on tiptoe to keep the connection going. His mouth hardened and then she felt his tongue push against her lips just as she opened them.

His tongue slid into her mouth and found hers.

She heard him smother a groan as her tongue tangled with his.

She felt his body stir against her as he gripped her by the hips and pulled her flush against him.

She heard the cleric clear his throat. 'Ahem…'

Remy dropped his hands. He looked slightly stunned for a moment, but then he seemed to give himself a mental shake before he grinned charmingly and rather cheekily at the cleric. 'Almost forgot where I was for a moment.'

The cleric gave him an understanding smile. 'It is very good to see an enthusiastic couple. It bodes well for a happy and fulfilling marriage.'

Angelique ground her teeth. Remy was enjoying this much more than he should. She could see the glint in his eyes as they reconnected with hers. She gave him an 'I'll get you for this later' look but he just grinned even wider and gave her a wink.

'The Crown Prince and his wife have a put on a special banquet in honour of your marriage,' the cleric said.

*Oh no! Don't tell me there's going to be a reception with speeches.*

But as it turned out it was more like a party. A dry party. Which was a crying shame, as right now Angelique needed a glass of something alcoholic—make that two glasses and to hell with the calories—because she was now officially *a married woman*.

*Arrrggh!*

The reception room was as big as a football field, or so it appeared to Angelique. How many friends did Remy have out here, or had someone rented a crowd? There were at least a thousand people. Who had a wedding that big? It was ridiculous! It was like a wedding extravaganza, a showpiece of what a celebrity wedding reception should be. The room was decked out in the most amazing array of satin ribbons, balloons and sparkly lights that hung from the high ceiling like diamonds. They probably *were* diamonds, she thought as she glanced up at the chandelier above her head. *Yep, diamonds.*

They were led to the top table where Angelique was finally introduced to the Crown Prince's wife, Abby, a fellow Englishwoman who had met and fallen in love with Talib earlier that year. A royal baby was due in a few months, which Abby explained had given an extra boost to the celebrations. It seemed Dharbiri was in party mode and an event like this could on for days. *Great.*

Remy took her hand and led her out to the dance floor for the bridal waltz. 'Loosen up, Angelique. You feel like a shop-window mannequin in my arms.'

Angelique suppressed a glare. 'Get your hands off my butt.'

He smoothed his hand over her hip and then tugged her against him. 'That better?'

She looked at him with slitted eyes. 'We're supposed to be dancing, not making out.'

'I thought you'd be great at dancing.'

'I *am* great at dancing.'

'Then show me your footwork.'

Angelique moved in against him and let him take the lead. The music was romantic with a flowing rhythm so she let her body move in time with it. She started to feel like a princess at a ball, or a star contestant on one of those reality dance shows. They moved in perfect unison around the dance floor. The other couples—and there were hundreds—swarmed backwards to give them more room.

'Nice work,' Remy said once it was over. 'Maybe we should do that again some time.'

'You trod on my toe.'

'Did not.'

'Did so.'

He gave her a grin as he pinched her cheek. 'Smile, *ma chérie.*'

She smiled through clenched teeth. 'I want to scratch your eyes out.'

'Did I tell you how beautiful you looked?'

'I can't breathe in this dress. And I have no idea how I'm going to fit in the bathroom. They'll have to take the door off or something.'

He grinned again and tapped her gently on the end of the nose. 'You'll find a way.'

Angelique let out a breath as she watched him turn

to speak to another guest. There were times when Remy took his charm into very dangerous territory...

'You have to try this,' Remy said as he came over with a loaded plate from the banquet a little while later.

Angelique breathed in the delicious smell of lamb with herbs and garlic. She couldn't stop her gaze from devouring everything on his plate. Along with the juicy lamb pieces, there was a couscous salad and some sort of potato dish and flatbread. The carbs would be astronomical. 'No.' She gave him a tight smile for the sake of anyone watching. 'I'm not hungry.'

'Here.' He forked a piece of lamb and held it in front of her mouth. 'You have to try this. It's amazing.'

'I don't want it.'

His eyes locked on hers, hard, determined. Implacable. 'Open your mouth.'

Angelique's belly shifted at his commanding tone but she was not going to let him win this. This was *her* battle, not his. She was the one who had to keep her body in top shape for her career. She had been counting calories and carbs since she had landed her first contract. Since before that, actually. It was the only thing she could control. She knew what she had to do to keep her body perfect. She was not going to allow anyone, and in particular Remy Caffarelli, to sabotage her efforts.

She gave him a flinty look. 'I said I'm not hungry.'

'You're lying.'

She felt the penetrating probe of his dark-brown eyes as they tussled with hers. Heat came up from deep inside her, a liquid molten heat that had nothing to do with food but everything to with hunger.

*Sexual hunger.*

Angelique knew one taste would not be enough. She

would end up bingeing on him and then where would that get her?

*His kiss had already done enough damage.*

*And that dirty dance routine...*

She could not afford to let herself be that vulnerable again. She was in control of her passions. She did not slavishly follow her desires. She had self-control and discipline.

She did *not* want him or his food or his fancy footwork.

Angelique pulled out an old excuse but a good one; she was nothing if not a great actress when the need arose. She put a hand to her temple and gave him a part-sheepish, part-apologetic look. 'I'm sorry, Remy, it's just I've been fighting a tension headache ever since I got up. Well, actually, I didn't get up, because I didn't go to bed in the first place. I couldn't sleep a wink.'

He studied her for a moment as if weighing up whether to believe her or not. 'Maybe you're dehydrated. Have you had enough to drink?'

'I could kill for a glass of wine.'

He gave her a wry look. 'You could get killed for having it.'

Angelique felt a cold hand of panic clutch at her insides. 'We *are* safe now, aren't we? I mean now we're—' she gave a mental gulp '—married?'

Remy's expression sobered for a moment, which made that fist of panic grip a little tighter. 'We're safe as long as we act as if this is a real marriage. It would be foolish to let our guard down until we're on the plane home.'

Angelique swallowed as she cast a nervous eye over the crowd of people who had joined in the wedding celebration. They looked friendly and innocuous enough, but how could she be sure one or more of them weren't waiting for her to make a slip up?

Her stomach pitched with dread.

Never in her wildest dreams had she ever thought something like this would happen. She had wanted a face-to-face with Remy. She hadn't given a thought to where he was or whom he was with or whether it would be convenient or politic *or safe*. She had focused solely on her goal to get him to hand back the deeds to Tarrantloch.

Now she was pretending to be married to him.

*Not pretending*, a little voice reminded her. *You* are *married to him*.

Angelique turned back to look up at Remy. 'Why do you come out here? It's not the sort of place I thought you would be drawn to. It doesn't really suit your party-boy image.'

He gave a shrug of one broad shoulder. 'The Crown Prince is a friend of mine. We went to university together. I like to visit him now and again.'

'Do you come here often?' Angelique gave herself a mental kick for not rephrasing that a little less suggestively.

He gave her a wicked look. 'No single, unchaperoned women in my room, remember?'

She compressed her lips. 'I'm being serious. How many times do you, er, visit?'

He put his plate down on a nearby table. 'Not as often as I'd like. I only get out here once a year. Two, if I'm lucky, like this year when I came out for Talib and Abby's wedding.'

Angelique's eyes widened to the size of the plate he'd just put down. 'But…but *why*? What's so great about it?

I don't see anything that's relaxing or beautiful about it. It's just a bunch of boring old sand dunes.'

He put his hand on her elbow and led her away to a quieter area. 'Will you please keep your opinions to yourself until we're out of danger?' he hissed out of the corner of his mouth.

Angelique wriggled out of his hold, not because she found it unpleasant, but because she found she rather liked it. *A lot*. She hadn't realised until now how much she had come to rely on him protecting her. To come to her rescue. She had blundered into a minefield and yet he had remained calm and steady throughout. Even cracking jokes about it.

Was *he* scared?

If so, he had shown little sign of it until now.

'I'm sorry, but I'm not used to this,' she said. 'You've been coming here for ages. This is my first time. I'm what you would call a desert virgin.'

'What about that bikini shot of you I saw in New York a couple of years back? You were draped over a sand dune with a couple of camels in the background.'

Angelique mentally raised her brows. So he'd seen that, had he? And taken note of it. 'It was staged. The sand dunes were in Mexico and the camels were cranky and smelly. One of them even tried to bite me. It was a horrible shoot. The designer was impossible to please and I ended up with a massive migraine from sunstroke.'

A frown appeared between his eyes. 'Why do you do it?'

She felt her back come up. She'd heard this lecture before, too many times to count. The most memorable one had been from him. 'Why do I do what?'

'Model. Put yourself out there in nothing but a couple of scraps of fabric.' His tone sounded starchy and disapproving. Old-fashioned. *Conservative*. 'You're capable of so much more than being some gorgeous too-perfect-to-believe image young guys jerk off to when they're in the shower.'

Angelique gave him an arch look. 'Is that what *you* do?'

His eyes hardened. His mouth flattened. A muscle ticked in his jaw. On-off. On-off. 'No.' His tone was clipped. *Too* clipped. 'I don't think of you like that.'

*He was lying.*

Just like she had been lying about her hunger.

How...*interesting*.

The thought of him being turned on by *her*, orgasming because of *her*, was deliciously shocking. It made her flesh tingle. It made her juices run. It made her need pulse and ache to feel him come to completion with her, *the real her*, not some airbrushed image that didn't even come close.

*Are you out of your mind?* The sensible part of her brain kicked in again.

*You are* not *going to sleep with Remy. Whether he wants to or you want to.*

Angelique looked up at him, noting the dull flush that had flagged both of his aristocratic cheekbones. 'So, when do we get to step out of this charade? We can leave for the airport once this is over, can't we? I've got my bag packed all ready to go. All you have to do is say the word and I'm out of here with bells on. Not the wedding variety, of course.'

His dark-brown eyes seemed to go a shade darker as they held hers. 'We're not leaving tonight.'

Angelique felt that fist of panic come back, but now it was two fists.

Two very big, very *strong* fists.

'But why not? You have a private jet, don't you? You can leave whenever you want.' She swallowed and looked up at him hopefully. Desperately. 'C-can't you?'

Remy turned his back so anyone nearby couldn't see his expression, his voice sounding low and deep, like a rumble of an imminent earthquake under the ocean floor. 'There is a tradition we have to uphold. We can't leave until we officially consummate the marriage.'

Angelique jerked back from him. 'You're joking. You *have* to be joking! There's no way we have to do *that*! How would anyone know if we, um, did it or not?'

He gave her a levelling look. 'We'd have to prove it.'

Her brows went up. Her eyes went wide. Her heart started to gallop. Her inner core got hot. *Very hot.* 'You mean like witnesses or something? Oh my God, I can't believe this! I'm so not a threesome person. I'm not even a twosome person. I—' She clamped her mouth shut. She had given away too much as it was.

'We'll need evidence that you're a virgin.'

Angelique blinked. *'Pardon?'*

'Blood.' He had his poker face on. 'On the sheets. We have to display them the next morning.'

She gave him a narrowed look. 'Whose blood?'

His mouth cracked in a half-smile. 'Yours.'

Angelique sent him a fulminating glare. 'I just *knew* you were going to say that. The only blood I want to see spilled right now is yours.'

'You're really hating this, aren't you?' His expression was amused.

Her eyes went to slits again. 'By "this" I suppose you mean this ridiculous subservience.'

He gave one of his loose, get-over-it shrugs. 'It's the way things are done here.'

She shook with outrage. 'But it's the wrong way!'

'The women here are happy.' His voice was calm, measured. 'They don't have to do anything but be who they are. They don't have to primp and preen. They don't have to have a spray tan every week or put on false nails or colour their hair. They don't have to pretend they're not hungry when they're starving, because they're not going to be judged solely on their appearance. It is who they are on the inside that matters.'

He was describing a paradise...or was he?

She set her mouth. 'That's only because they probably don't know what they're missing. If just one woman gets a glimpse of what she could have, you could have total anarchy out here.'

An amused quirk tilted his mouth. 'And I suppose you'd be out front and leading the charge of that particular riot?'

She gave him a beady look. 'You'd better believe it.'

# CHAPTER FOUR

REMY WAS ENJOYING every minute of his 'marriage' so far. It was so amusing to press all of Angelique's hot buttons. He knew exactly what to say and how to say it—even the way to look at her to get a rise out of her. The reason he knew was because deep down he felt exactly the same.

Marriage was a trap.

It was stultifying. Restraining. A freedom-taking institution that worked better for some than for others.

And he was one of the others.

He didn't like answering to anyone. He had spent too much of his life living under the shadow of his brothers and his grandfather. He wanted to make his own way, to be his own person. To be known as something more than a Caffarelli brother or grandson.

He didn't want to be someone's husband.

And as for being someone's father... Well, he was leaving that to his two older brothers, who seemed pretty keen on the idea of procreating.

Remy was not interested in babies with scrunched-up faces and dirty nappies; sleepless nights, running noses, temper tantrums. Not for him. *No way.*

He was interested in having a good time. Playing

the field. Working the turf. Sowing his oats—the wild variety, that was.

And at times his life could get pretty wild.

He loved the element of risk in what he did—scoping out failing businesses, taking chances, rolling the dice. Chasing success, running it down, holding it in his hands and relishing the victory of yet another deal signed and delivered.

He was a gambler at heart, but not an irresponsible one. He knew where to draw the line, how to measure the stakes and to raise or lower them when he needed to.

And he was a firm believer in the golden rule of gambling: he only ever lost what he could afford to lose.

Besides, he'd already suffered the worst loss of all. Losing his parents so suddenly had been shattering. He still remembered the crushing sense of loss when Rafe had told him about their parents' accident: the panic; the fear; the terror. It had made Remy feel that life was little more than a roll of a dice. Fate was a cruel mistress. Your life could be perfect and full one day, and terrifyingly empty the next.

Remy looked down at Angelique who was trying to disguise her fury at the little 'proof of virginity' story he'd spun her. He wondered how long he could spin it out. She looked so infuriated he thought she was going to explode. She probably had no idea how gorgeous she looked when she was spitting at him like a wild cat. He wouldn't mind having those sharp little claws digging into his back as he rocked them both to paradise.

*Are you out of your mind?*

*If you sleep with her you won't be able to annul the marriage as soon as you get home.*

Right. They would have to share a room—there

would be no avoiding that—but he could always sleep on the sofa.

*There had better be a sofa or you're toast.*

'Right.'

Angelique looked up at him and Remy realised he'd spoken aloud. 'Pardon?' she said.

'How's your headache?'

She looked at him blankly for a moment. 'My...? Oh yes; terrible. Absolutely excruciating.' She put a hand to her temple again. 'I'm getting blurred vision and I think I'm seeing an aura.'

'We'd better get you to bed, then.'

The words dropped into the silence, suspended there, echoing with erotic undercurrents that were impossible to ignore.

'To sleep,' Remy said. 'Just in case you were getting the wrong idea.' Like his body had. It was already hard. Getting harder. *Deep breath.*

She angled her head at him suspiciously. 'Why do I get the feeling you're playing with me?'

He wanted to play with her all right. His body said yes but his mind kept saying no, or at least it was saying no so far. But how long would he be able to keep his hands off her? Theoretically she was the last woman in the world he wanted anything to do with. She was too high-maintenance. Too wild.

But, theory aside, when it came down to practice, well, he was only human. And she *was* hot. He normally preferred blondes but there was something about Angelique's raven hair and creamy skin that had a touch of old-world Hollywood glamour about it. She walked into a room like a movie star. He didn't think it was put on or something she'd learned on the catwalk. He'd seen her do it since she was a kid. *She made an entrance.* It was like she was making a statement: *I'm here. What are you going to do about it?*

She was here all right.

She was right, smack bang in the middle of his life and he couldn't wait to get her out of it.

'You take life too seriously, Angelique.'

'That stuff about the sheets...' She chewed her bottom lip for a moment. 'That's not really true, is it?'

Remy felt a sudden urge to ruffle her hair or pinch her cheeks like he would a little kid. She was so cute when she let her guard down. He couldn't remember ever seeing her look that vulnerable and uncertain before. Angry, annoyed, irritated, yes—but vulnerable? No. If she felt it, she covered it well, but then who was he to talk?

'Why?' He kept his face deadpan. 'Aren't you still a virgin?'

She gave him a pert look. 'Aren't you?'

He laughed. 'An emotional one, maybe, in that I've never been in love. But I've been around a few times.'

She gave her eyes a little roll. 'I can just imagine.'

'How many?'

'How many...what?'

'Lovers.'

She stilled, every muscle on her face seeming to momentarily freeze. But then she gave a little toss of her head and sent him haughty look. 'I fail to see why that should be of any interest to you.'

'I'm your husband.'

One.

Two.

Three.

*Blast off.*

Remy could time her down to a nanosecond. Her face

went rigid again, her teeth clenching together, her eyes flashing at him like a turbulent gun-metal-grey ocean. 'You're enjoying every minute of this, aren't you?' she hissed at him. 'I bet you can't wait to get back to Italy or France, or wherever it is you live these days, to tell everyone how you tricked me into marrying you. You'll be dining out on this and how you got Tarrantloch off my father for decades, won't you?'

'Calm down.' Remy held up a hand like a stop sign. 'I'm not the one who brought about this marriage. You're the last person I would consider marrying if I was considering marriage, which I'm not, nor ever will be.'

'Ditto.'

'Fine. Then at least we're square on that.' He pushed his sleeve back and glanced impatiently at his watch. 'I think it's time this party was over. Come on. Let's get out of here.'

Angelique followed him with feigned meekness as they said their goodnights to the other guests and officials. Her little white lie about her headache was now lamentably and rather painfully true. Her temples were pounding by the time she got to the suite with Remy. She felt nauseous and lightheaded and her heart began to pound once he closed the door and they were finally alone.

Alone.

In the bridal suite.

She affected a light and breezy tone. 'Do you want to toss a coin for the bed?'

His dark-brown eyes looked darker than they had during the reception. She couldn't make out the shape of his irises at all. He took a coin out of his pocket without breaking his gaze from hers and laid it on the back of his left hand, covered by his right. 'Heads or tails?'

'Heads.'

He flipped the coin high in the air and deftly caught it as it came back down, his gaze still locked on hers. 'Want to change your mind?'

Angelique raised her chin. 'Once my mind is made up I *never* change it.'

His mouth kicked up a little on one side, those dark-chocolate eyes gleaming. 'Ditto.'

She leaned forward to see how the coin had fallen but he hadn't uncovered it. He held it in his closed palm in the space between them. 'Go on. Show me.' Her voice sounded huskier than normal but she put that down to the fact he was in her personal body space. She could smell his citrus, wood and male smell. She could see the rise of fresh dark stubble on his jaw.

*She could feel his desire.*

It was pulsing in the air like sound waves. There was an answering throb in her body like an echo. Her inner core shifted. Tensed. Clenched. *Hungered.*

She suddenly became aware of her breasts inside the lacy cage of her bra. She became aware of her tongue as it moved out over her lips, depositing moisture to their surface. She saw his hooded gaze follow its passage and something in her stomach unfurled, as if a satin ribbon was being pulled out of its centre.

She took a little swallow. 'Um…the coin?'

His gaze was still fixated on her mouth as if it were the most fascinating mouth in the whole wide world. 'What about it?' His voice sounded deep and rough around the edges.

'I want to know who won.'

'I did.'

Angelique frowned at his confident tone. 'You can't possibly know that without looking.'

His mouth went up at the corners again. 'I have a sixth sense about this sort of stuff. I won. You lost.'

She coughed out a little sound of scorn. 'You think I'm going to fall for that without seeing the evidence? Open your palm.'

His eyes locked back on hers; they seemed to be glinting at the challenge she had laid down. 'Want to make me?' he said.

The floor of her belly shivered. He was near to impossible to resist in this mood. Was that how he bedded so many women? No wonder they fell like ninepins around him. He was just simply irresistible in this playful mood.

But Angelique didn't do alpha males and Remy was very definitely an alpha male. It was in his blood. Had been born and bred to rule, to take charge, to take control and hold onto it no matter what. To lead, not to follow. He was too commanding, too sure of himself, too ruthless and way too sexy.

Too much a Caffarelli.

Too much of an enemy.

Too much of everything.

She hitched up her chin and squared her shoulders. 'Thanks but no.'

His eyes glinted some more, moving slowly between her mouth and her gaze, burning, searing all the way. 'Shame. I was looking forward to a little tussle for possession. It could've been fun.'

Angelique knew he wasn't talking about the coin. She blew out an uneven breath. 'You have the bed. You're much taller than me.' That was an understatement. He'd had to stoop through every door they'd been through so far. 'I can curl up on the sofa.'

'What sofa?'

She chewed her lip as she glanced around the suite. It had everything *but* a sofa. 'Oh... Well, then...'

'The bed is big enough for both of us. You stick to your side. I'll stick to mine. It's only for one night.'

Angelique tried to read his expression but he had his poker face back on. 'I hope you don't snore or talk in your sleep.'

'If I do just give me a shove in the ribs.'

She gave him a frosty look. 'I'm not going to go anywhere near you.'

A sexy smile tilted his mouth. 'Then you'd be the first woman I've shared a bed with who hasn't.'

Angelique spent an inordinate amount of time in the *en suite* cleansing her face and brushing her teeth. She even brushed her hair for a hundred strokes to delay going back into the bedroom. But when she came out of the bathroom there was no sign of Remy. He hadn't even bothered to leave her a note to tell her where he had gone or when he would be back... Or whom he was with.

*Careful; you're starting to sound like a wife.*

She shook off the thought and pulled back the covers on the massive bed. The tension of the last twenty-four hours—seventy-two if she counted the time since she'd found out Tarrantloch had been lost—had finally caught up with her. As soon as her limbs felt the smooth, cool embrace of the impossibly fine linen she felt every muscle in her body let go. She melted into the mattress, even though it was far too firm for her, and closed her eyes on an exhausted sigh...

* * *

Remy came back to the suite at three in the morning to find Angelique fast asleep.

Right in the middle of the bed.

Her mane of glossy black hair surrounded her head like a cloud. Her blood-red lips were soft and slightly parted, her skin now without its armour of artfully applied make-up. Now she had lost the layer of worldly sophistication she looked young and tiny, almost fragile. There were dark shadows underneath her eyes that her make-up must have hidden earlier. Her slim body— personally he thought she was *too* slim—was curled up like a comma, the sharpness of her hipbone jutting out from beneath the covering of the bed linen.

He could see the spaghetti-thin straps of her nightie, an ivory white that was a perfect foil for the creamy tone of her skin. The upper curves of her breasts were showing just above the sheet. He'd always thought of them as Goldilocks breasts—not too big, not too small, but just right.

He gave himself a mental shake and turned away from the sight of the temptation lying there.

*Hands off, remember?*

He rubbed a tired hand over the back of his head and down to the knotted muscles in his neck. He'd had to pull some strings to get out of Dharbiri by first light. He didn't want to spend any more time than he had to 'married' to her. If the press got wind of this back home, it would go viral in no time. He didn't want to be made into a laughing stock. He could just imagine the headlines: *World's biggest playboy gets hitched. The last of the Caffarelli rakes bites the dust.*

He wanted to erase it from the record. Wipe it from his memory. Get back to normal.

Get her out of his life.

Remy looked at her again. She murmured something in her sleep and stretched out her arms and legs like a cat—and not just any old moggy—a beautiful, exotic cat that was begging to be stroked.

He wondered who her latest lover was. He hadn't read anything just lately in the press about her, which was surprising, as hardly a month or two went by without some mention of her caught up in some scandal or other. He often wondered how much of it was true. He knew from his own experience that not everything that was reported was accurate. But how she was keeping her head below the parapet was a mystery if not a miracle. It was not an easy feat to stay under the radar when around every corner was a camera phone. You didn't have to be a member of the paparazzi to get a shot of a celebrity or any other high profile person these days.

He'd had a few candid camera shots he'd rather weren't out in the public domain. The press always made it look far worse than it was. He wasn't a heavy drinker, and he had never and would never touch party drugs. But somehow he had been portrayed as a hard-partying, hard-drinking playboy.

The playboy bit was true.

He wasn't going to deny the fact he'd bedded a lot of women. And he wasn't going to stop any time soon. Which was why he had to get this marriage annulled as soon as possible. Call him old-fashioned but, on-paper marriage or no, he was not going to betray those promises he'd made. As far as he was concerned, infidelity was a deal breaker even in his most casual relationships. Sleeping around on a partner was not what a real man would do.

Talking of sleeping… He smothered a yawn as he

heeled off his shoes and unbuttoned his shirt. He tossed it in the vague direction of a chair and put his hands on the waistband of his trousers.

*Nah, better keep them on.*

He could do with a few more barriers between him and Sleeping Beauty right now. He just hoped two layers—three, if you counted hers—would be enough to keep him out of danger.

# CHAPTER FIVE

ANGELIQUE ROLLED OVER and breathed in the scent of lavender-scented sheets, citrus and wood and…warm, sleepy male.

Her heart gave a little flip-flop as she looked at the tanned arm lying across her stomach. It looked so dark, hairy and foreign against the ivory white of her satin nightie. It felt like an iron bar was holding her in place.

His strongly muscled legs were entangled with hers, just loosely, but they felt rough and strong. Powerful.

*Had they…?* She gulped. *Had sex?*

No.

*No!*

*Hang on a minute…* Her body didn't feel any different. She knew without a doubt she would feel *very* different if Remy had made love to her.

She would feel…*satisfied.*

Because she couldn't imagine him not doing the job properly. There would be no half-measures with him. He would know his way around a woman's body like a curator knew their way around a museum. Interesting—some might say Freudian—choice of metaphor, as it felt like an aeon since she'd been intimate with anyone; but still.

Sex had always been a bit of a disappointment to her.

She tried to enjoy it but she had never felt truly comfortable with any of her partners. Not that she'd had as many as the press liked to make out.

Her first experience of sex had been when she had gone to New York to sign with the agency. A photographer had hooked up with her for a couple of months but she hadn't really felt valued as a person; rather, she'd felt more of a commodity, a bit of arm candy to be paraded around to gain Brownie points with his colleagues. That relationship, as well as one or two others, had made her come to the conclusion that sex was something men *did* to her, rather than something she experienced *with* them. She had always been able to separate herself from the act, to keep her mind to one side, to be the impartial observer.

She had talked to girlfriends about it and they had assured her she just hadn't met the right partner. That it was all a matter of chemistry and timing. Animal attraction.

It was ironic that Angelique had one of the most looked-at bodies in the world, yet she felt a stranger to it in terms of passion. She knew how to pleasure herself but it wasn't something she did with any regularity. She didn't have the inclination or the desire. She wondered if she was just one of those people with little or no sex drive.

Remy's arm tightened across her middle and he nuzzled against the sensitive skin of her neck. 'Mmm...' he murmured sleepily.

The sex drive Angelique thought was non-existent suddenly made an appearance. It was centre-stage and wanted to be noticed. She felt it stir within her core, a tugging sensation, a needy little ache that wouldn't go away. Her breasts tingled from the brush of his arm as he shifted position again. His legs were entwined with hers and his erection—*his rock-hard erection*—was pressing against her thigh.

Was he even awake?

Maybe he was so practised at this he could do it in his sleep. She mentally rolled her eyes. It wouldn't surprise her.

One of his hands moved up and gently cupped the globe of her breast. Even through the satin of her nightie she felt his warmth and the electricity of his touch. It made her hungry for more, to feel that large, firm hand on her, skin to skin.

He rolled his thumb back and forth over her nipple, making it ache and tingle with pleasure.

OK, so he *had* to be awake.

The sensible part of Angelique knew this was the time to step in and remind him of the hands-off nature of their relationship, but the newly awakened *sensual* part of her was saying the opposite.

She wanted hands-on.

His mouth found the super-sensitive area just behind her earlobe. Angelique shivered as his tongue moved over the area in slow, lazy strokes. His hand moved up from her knee to the top of her thigh in one smooth caress that made her inner core clench tight with longing, triggering a rush of dewy moisture between her thighs.

He shifted position again, rolling her further on to her back as his body moved over hers.

*You really should stop him.*

*Not yet! Not yet!*

His hooded eyes slowly opened and then he flinched back from her as he let out a rather appropriate profanity. 'What the hell do you think you're doing?'

Angelique gave him a pointed look. 'What am *I* doing? You're the one with my breast in your hand.'

He frowned and looked down at his hand as if he had only just realised it was attached to his body and that he was the one with control over it. He dropped it from her and moved away and up off the bed.

He scraped the same hand through the thick black tousle of his hair and turned to glare at her. 'You should've woken me.'

She arched a brow. 'So you really *can* do it in your sleep.'

He gave her an irritated frown. 'Looks like you were running on automatic pilot as well. When were you going to call a halt?'

Some little demon inside Angelique decided it was time to rattle *his* cage for a change. She gave him a sultry look from beneath her lashes, her 1950s Hollywood movie-star look. 'Maybe I wasn't.'

A cynical look came into his eyes and his mouth hardened. 'It won't work, Angelique. I'm not staying married to you for a minute longer than I have to, so you can forget about your plans to snare yourself a rich husband. I'm not playing ball.'

She decided to press him a little further. *This was so much fun!* She had never seen him look quite so furious. His jaw was clenched and his hands were fisted. Where was his puerile sense of humour now? 'But you want me. You can hardly deny that.' She glanced at the tented fabric of his boxer shorts before giving him another smouldering smile.

His brows snapped together. 'You are *such* a piece of work. Is this how you hook your claws into every man who crosses your path?'

Angelique slowly stroked her right foot down over

her left ankle, her chest arched back as she rested on her elbows. 'You're hardly one to talk. Women run each other down to get into your bed. I didn't run to get here. I didn't even walk. I got here by default.'

'And now you're getting out of it.' He stepped forward and ripped the bed linen off her like a magician pulling a cloth from a table.

Angelique gave a startled squeal as he grabbed one of her ankles and tugged her towards him. 'Get your hands off me!'

'That's not what you were saying a minute ago.' He pulled her upright but she stumbled and would have fallen except for his arms coming around her to steady her.

She thought he would let her go but he didn't. If anything his firm grip on her hips tightened. She felt every imprint of his fingers pressing into her skin; she even wondered if they would leave marks.

She looked at his mouth, always a big mistake, but there you go. She couldn't seem to help herself. Her gaze was drawn like a tiny piece of metal to a powerful magnet.

Their bodies were touching, feeling, *discovering* each other's contours.

Angelique felt the heft, weight and heat of his erection pressing against her belly. It stirred her senses into a madcap frenzy of longing that took over her whole body. She felt the rush of heat from her core, the liquid of lust that was outside of her control.

'This is not what I want,' he ground out but still he didn't let her go.

'I don't want it either.' *You liar. You do want it. You want him.*

He suddenly put her from him, stepping back and

raking a hand through his hair again. 'OK… Let's get some time out here.'

*Time out?*

*I want time in!*

Angelique's little demon wasn't quite ready to back down. 'You're scared. You're worried you might get to like having me around, aren't you, Remy? You're not used to that feeling. You're the one who hires and fires your bedmates week by week. You don't form lasting attachments. You form convenient, casual alliances that temporarily scratch your itch.'

He glowered at her again. 'I do *not* want you around. You're nothing but trouble. You attract it and you revel in it. I don't want it.'

'Then give me back Tarrantloch and I'll be out of your life as soon as you can say blackjack.'

The silence vibrated with palpable tension.

'No.' His one-word answer was clipped and determined. *Very* determined. *Caffarelli* determined.

Angelique hitched up her chin. 'Then you're stuck with me. I'm not leaving your side until you give me what I want.'

'You don't want Tarrantloch.' His lip curled mockingly. 'What you want is a pat on the back from your father.'

'Ha ha,' she scoffed. 'And what *you* want is a big tick of approval from your grandfather. You think by taking possession of Tarrantloch that it will somehow win favour with him.'

He gave a harsh bark of laughter. 'I do not need my aging grandfather's approval to get on in life. I've made my own way. I don't need anyone's tick of approval to be happy.'

'You're not happy. That's why you're so restless. You

can't settle because you're not happy with who you are on the inside.' *Just like I'm not happy.*

His eyes flashed with ire. 'Oh, and you're an expert on that, are you? The woman who doesn't eat in case she puts on a gram of flesh. Don't make me laugh.'

Angelique hated that he knew so much about her, about her insecurities. How did he *do* that? They had barely seen each other for years, yet within such a short time he had summed her up in a sentence. 'I have a contract—'

'That insists you parade yourself in front of people who don't give a damn about you, to make millions of dollars for *them*. *You're* not important to them, only your body is. They don't want what's inside you, they're only interested in what they can get out of you.'

It was true.

It was painfully, agonizingly true.

It was a blunt truth she had come to acknowledge only very recently, which was why she was so keen to get out of the industry, to come at it from a different angle—the design and marketing angle.

But her confidence had always been the kicker and now it was even more so. She hadn't gone to university. She had no business degree or diploma. She hadn't even finished school. She had no official qualifications. What sort of ability did she have to run her own business?

She would be such a babe in the woods. It was cut-throat and dog-eat-dog out there. She had seen it first-hand. People with good intentions, with good skills and awesome talent were pushed aside by the power brokers, the money men who were only interested in the profit line.

'I'm not planning on modelling for too much longer.'

His gaze hardened. 'So am I part of the back-up

plan? The rich husband to bankroll your—' he made quotation marks with his fingers '—retirement plan?'

'I have my own designs.'

He looked at her for a moment in silence, a frown deepening across his forehead.

'Designs?'

Angelique let out a little breath. She had told no one about her plans. It seemed strange, almost ironic, she would be telling *him*. 'Not every woman is a size zero. There are women out there with post-baby bodies, with scars, who've had mastectomies, or with the track marks of age. None of us are perfect.'

'I can't believe you just said that.'

Her shoulders went down on a sigh. 'I'm tired of being the poster girl for perfection. It takes a lot of hard work to look this good.'

'You look pretty damn good.'

Angelique felt a frisson of delight at his comment. He *liked* the way she looked?

*But it's not real.*

If she ate properly she would be a size—maybe even two sizes—bigger. Would he—and the rest of the world—find her so attractive then?

She was a physical fraud.

And an even bigger emotional one.

Angelique hadn't been in touch with her emotions since the day she had stumbled across her mother's unconscious body when she was ten years old. She could still see the glass of water with the faint trace of her mother's lipstick around the rim.

The pill bottle that had been empty.

The silence.

Not even a heartbeat.

No pulse.

*No mother.*

Angelique had locked down her emotions and acted like a puppet ever since.

'I want to launch my own swim and leisurewear label. I've wanted to do it for a while. I want more control over my life and my career.'

'You'll need money to do that.'

'I know. I have some savings put aside, but it's not quite enough. I have do it properly or it will fold before it gets off the ground.'

'Is anyone offering to back you?'

'I've approached a couple of people but they were a little gun-shy.' She let out a little sigh. 'I think my reputation as a bit of a hell-raiser put them off.'

'How much of it is true?'

Angelique looked at him. 'The gun-shy people?'

'The hell-raising.'

Her shoulders went down in a little slump. 'I'm no angel...I've never tried to be. It's just the press make it out to be a hundred times worse than it is. I only have to be standing next to someone at a party or a nightclub or social gathering to be linked to them in some sort of salacious scandal.'

'You never defend yourself.' His expression was inscrutable, as if he was still making up his mind about her, whether to believe her or not. 'You've never asked for a retraction of any of the statements made about you.'

'What would be the point? Defensiveness only makes it worse.' She let out another sign. 'Anyway, to begin with I welcomed the gossip. I figured any publicity is good publicity. Some of the most famous models in the world are known for their behaviour as much as their looks.'

He rubbed a hand over his jaw. The raspy sound was loud in the silence. 'I have a couple of contacts who might be able to help you with launching your designs. I'd have to look at what you've got on the table first. I'm not going to recommend anything that hasn't got a chance of flying. I prefer to back winners, not losers.'

Angelique felt a little piqued that he didn't instantly believe in her. She hadn't realised until now how much she wanted him to have faith in her ability. To believe that she wasn't just another pretty face without any substance behind it. 'I wouldn't dream of putting your precious money at risk.' Her words were sharp, clipped with resentment.

He gave her a levelling look. 'I might love a gamble, Angelique, but at the end of the day I'm a businessman. I can't allow emotions to get in the way of a good business decision.'

She sent him a chilly glare. 'You didn't worry too much about your emotions when you tricked my father out of Tarrantloch. That wasn't a business decision. It was a personal vendetta and I'll never forgive you for it.'

'I admit I wanted to pay him back for what he did to my grandfather. We almost lost everything because of what he did.' His look was darkly scathing. 'But it wasn't just about that. I bet he didn't tell you the details of his underhand behaviour over the Ibiza account I was about to close? He would have put a completely different spin on it for his precious little girl.'

*His precious little girl.*

Angelique had to choke back a laugh. If only Remy knew how much her father despised her. He never showed it in public. He couldn't afford to tarnish his reputation as a devoted father. He put on a good show when the need arose but as soon as the doors were closed Henri would revert back to his autocratic, boorish, hyper-critical ways. She had always known her father had wanted a son as his firstborn but her mother had failed to deliver one.

Angelique was a living, daily reminder of that failure.

'I know my father isn't a plaster saint but neither is your grandfather,' she tossed back.

'I never said he was. I know how difficult he can be.'

She folded her arms across her chest. 'I don't want your money, Remy. I want you to give me back what is mine. That's all I want from you.'

'Not going to happen, *ma chérie*.' He gave her an intractable look. 'And, just for the record, I haven't finished with your father. Tarrantloch is nothing compared to what he did to me in all but defaming me online. I'm not stopping until I get the justice I want.'

Angelique curled her lip. 'Is that why you jumped at the fiancée charade that led to this ridiculous marriage? You saw a perfect opportunity for revenge. For rough justice. Forcing my hand in a marriage neither of us wants in order to score points. That's so...*pathetic* I want to throw up. '

His brows jammed together. 'Do you really think I'd go that far? Come on, Angelique, you're not thinking straight. I don't want to be married to anyone, let alone you. If by any remote chance I choose to settle down with someone it won't be with someone like you.'

She gave him a huffy scowl. '*Like me?* What does that mean? What's wrong with me?'

He let out a breath as he pushed a hand through his hair. 'Nothing's wrong with you... It's just, I don't see you as wife material.'

'Because?'

'Because you're not the "marriage and babies" type.'

Angelique raised her brows. 'You want...*babies*?'

He reared back from her as if she'd asked him if he wanted a deadly disease. 'No! God, no. I'm just saying...'

She gave him another scowl. 'I'm not sure what you're saying. Maybe you could elaborate a bit. Fill in the blanks for me.'

He looked about as flustered as she'd ever seen him. It was a rare sight. He was normally so in control—joking around. Having a laugh at everyone else's expense. Now he seemed to be back-pedalling as if he had stepped on a land mine and wasn't quite sure how to step off it without an explosion. 'It's not that I don't think you'd be a great mother.'

'But you think I'd be rubbish at being a wife.'

'I think you'd find it hard to compromise.'

Angelique blurted out a laugh. 'And *you* don't? Oh, for God's sake, Remy. You really are unbelievable. You're the least compromising person I've ever met. If I'd make a rotten wife, then you'd make an even worse husband.'

'Then thank God we'll be able to stop being a husband and wife as soon as we get back to England.'

'You really think it will be *that* simple?' Angelique asked. 'What if someone hears about this? A journalist or someone with contacts in the media? Did you see how many people were at our wedding? What if someone took a photo? What if *everyone* took a photo?'

His expression locked down, leaving just one muscle moving in and out on the left side of his jaw. 'No one is going to find out. We can annul this as soon as we land. I've already spoken to my lawyer in London. We can go straight to his office from the airport. It will be over and we can both move on with our lives as if it never happened.'

*Good luck with that*, Angelique thought. She'd been lucky lately in keeping her face out of the gossip pages but she knew it wouldn't last. If a journalist got a whiff of what had happened in Dharbiri she and Remy would be besieged by the media as soon as they landed. But then, anyone with a camera phone could snap a picture of them together and email or text it to a newspaper.

Even arriving at Heathrow together was going to cause a stir because there were always people coming back from holidays from tropical locations where her body had been on yet another billboard.

*Oh joy...*

# CHAPTER SIX

REMY COULD NOT believe the sort of attention Angelique attracted. Even before they had cleared Customs people were nudging each other and pointing. Several came up and asked for autographs. Some took photos, even though the signs in the customs area strictly forbade the use of phones or cameras.

'Do you have to be so damn nice to everybody?' he said in a low, gruff tone as he ushered her through to where a driver was waiting to collect them. 'Can't you pretend you're not you? Let them think they've got the wrong person or something. I've done that heaps of times. It works like a charm.'

'*You've* got the wrong person if you think I'd be rude to someone who paid a lot of money for a swimsuit I've modelled.' She smiled at another fan who came over with a pen and a boarding pass for her to sign.

Remy could feel his blood pressure rising. Was she doing this on purpose? People were looking at *him* now, trying to figure out who he was and how he fitted into her life. How long before they recognised him and put two and two together?

He took her firmly by the elbow. 'We have to go. *Now.*'

'Hold your horses.' She winked up at him cheekily. 'Or your camels.'

She smiled again as yet another person came over and told her how much they admired her, and that they didn't believe for a second all that rubbish about her and the English banker who was married, and how it wasn't her fault the marriage had broken up because it was obviously doomed from the outset, blah, blah, blah.

Remy had to wait until they were in the car before he asked, 'Did you know the banker was married when you hooked up with him?'

'I didn't hook up with him.' She flicked some imaginary lint off her clothing. 'I was photographed next to him in a hotel lobby. I was waiting for the porter to bring out my luggage.'

He frowned at her. 'Are you seriously telling me you didn't have anything to do with him? That you didn't have a secret love tryst with him in that hotel?'

She gave him a bored look. 'Does every woman you speak to end up sharing your bed?' She held up her hand and gave her eyes a little roll. 'No, don't answer that. I already know. If they're under the age of thirty, they probably do.'

'I don't do married women. I might be a playboy but I do have *some* standards.'

'Good to know.' There was something about her tone and the exaggerated way she inspected her perfectly manicured nails that irked him.

'What do you mean?'

'It's very reassuring, that's all.'

He frowned again. He could sense she was up to something. 'What is?'

'That you don't *do* married women.'

'Why's that?'

Her look was arch when she turned to look at him. 'Because I'm married.'

A surge of hot, unbridled lust rose in his loins. He could not think of a woman he wanted more than her right now. It was pounding through him like an unstoppable tide. It tapped into every thread of desire he had ever felt for her, thickening it, swelling it, *reinforcing* it.

He covered it with a laugh. 'But not for much longer.'

She put her chin in the air and inspected her nails again. 'That annulment can't happen soon enough.' She lowered her hand back down to her lap and studied it for a moment. 'I can't think of a worse forty-eight hours in my life.'

'Hell of a short marriage,' he said after a little pause. 'Do you think that's some sort of record?'

She shrugged one of her slim shoulders a little without looking at him. 'Maybe.'

Another silence.

'Are you heading back to Paris after this?' Remy asked. 'This' being the sign-off of their brief marriage. He didn't want to admit it but he would miss her. A bit. A niggly bit. She was incredibly annoying but vastly entertaining. He could think of worse things to do with his time than spar with her. She stimulated him physically and intellectually. Not many women did that.

In fact, he couldn't think of the last one that had...

'I have a shoot in Barbados.' Her shoulders went down dejectedly. 'I have to lose at least three pounds before then.'

'You're joking, surely?'

She gave him a resigned look. 'No one wants to see a bloated belly in a bikini they're going to pay a hundred and fifty pounds for, are they?'

'But you've got an amazing belly.' He'd been having

shower fantasies about it for years. He compared other women to her. He knew it was wrong but he couldn't help it. She was his benchmark. That billboard in New York all those years ago had nailed it for him. No one even came close.

He suddenly found himself imagining her belly swelling...growing larger with the bloom of a child... *his* child...

*Whoa! What are you thinking?*

She pressed her lips together. 'I've got a belly like every other woman. It has its good days and its bad days.'

Remy studied her for a moment. 'Is that why you don't eat?'

She visibly bristled. 'I *do* eat.'

He gave a disparaging grunt. 'Not enough to keep a gnat alive.'

She sent him a flinty glare. 'So you keep a catalogue of all your lovers' food intakes, do you?'

'You're not my lover.' A fact his body was reminding him of virtually non-stop. Why wasn't it letting up?

'No.' Her chin hitched up until she was eyeball to eyeball with him. 'I'm just your wife.'

Remy felt his back come up at the way she said the word. It was like she was spitting out a nasty object, something foul and distasteful. 'Why are you so against being a wife? Your parents were happily married, weren't they? Everyone said how devastated your father was when your mother died. He was inconsolable.'

'Yes, he was...' Her expression clouded and her teeth nipped into her bottom lip.

He wondered if he should have mentioned her mother's death. Suicide was a touchy subject. Kate March-and had taken an overdose after a bout of depression, which had supposedly been accidental, and rumour had it Angelique had found her body.

She had been ten years old.

The same age his brother Rafe had been when their parents had been killed.

Remy had seen first-hand what a child with an over-blown sense of responsibility went through. It had only been since Rafe had met Poppy that he had let that sense of responsibility ease. Rafe had taken stock of his life and was a better and happier man for it.

Raoul had done much the same, recognising his life would not be complete without Lily Archer, the woman who had shown him that physical wholeness was not as important as emotional wholeness.

But what could Angelique teach Remy other than patience and self-control?

Remy wondered if finding her mother like that was why she was such a tearaway. Losing her mother in such a way must have hit her hard. Had she blamed herself?

He looked at her sitting with her arms folded across her middle, her gaze focused on the tote bag on her lap. A frown was pulling on her forehead and her teeth were savaging her lower lip. She looked far younger than her years. Vulnerable.

'Did you blame yourself for your mother's death?'

'A bit, I suppose. What child wouldn't?' She started plucking at the stitches in the leather of her bag strap, tugging at the tiny threads as if to unpick them one by one. 'If I'd got home earlier I might've been able to save her. But I'd stopped at a friend's house on the way home from school. I'd never done that before.' She stopped picking to look at him. 'Needless to say, I never did it again.'

There was a lot of pain in her eyes. She covered it

well but it was there lurking in the depths. Remy saw it in the way she held herself, a braced posture, guarded, prepared. Vigilant. There was so much about her that annoyed him, yet how much of that was a ruse to cover her true nature? Her brash wilfulness, her impulsiveness, her refusal to obey instructions could well be a shield to hide how vulnerable and alone she felt.

'Monsieur Caffarelli?'

Remy had almost forgotten they were still in the car until it came to a halt and the driver opened the partition that separated the driver from the passengers.

'There are paparazzi outside,' his driver said. 'Do you want me to drive another block or two?'

'Yes, do that.' Remy took out his phone. 'I'll give my lawyer a call to see if he can meet us somewhere else.'

'How did they know we were going to your lawyer's office?' Angelique asked.

'God knows.' He put his phone to his ear. 'Brad. You looked out of your window lately?'

'I was just about to call you,' Brad said. 'I've just had Robert Mappleton on the line. He heard a rumour you're married to Henri Marchand's daughter and—'

'Where the hell did he hear that?' Remy barked.

'Not sure,' Brad said. 'Maybe someone in Dharbiri spoke to the press. All I know is this is like winning the lottery for you right now.'

'What are you talking about?' Remy said.

'Have you forgotten? You've been trying to win this guy over for months. *The* Bob Mappleton of Mappleton Hotels?'

'That crusty old bastard who refused to even discuss a takeover bid, even though the shareholders are threatening to call in the administrators?' Remy curled his lip. *All because of that inflammatory email Henri March-*

*and had circulated.* 'Yeah, how could I forget? He'd rather face total bankruptcy than strike a deal with me.'

'Well, here's the thing,' Brad said. 'He just called and said he's changed his mind. He wasn't prepared to do business with a hard-partying playboy, but now you're married to Henri Marchand's daughter he figures that stuff Marchand said about you last year can't have been true. He wants to set up a meeting. He's as old-school and conservative as they come but this marriage of yours couldn't have come at a better time.'

Remy felt his scalp start to tingle. The biggest take-over bid of his career: a chain of run-down hotels he knew he could make into the most luxurious and pop-ular in the world. The Ibiza development was child's play compared to this.

The catch?

He had to stay married in order to nail it.

He looked at Angelique who was giving him the evil eye. He could see the storm brewing in her grey-blue eyes. He could feel the air tightening along with her body. Every muscle in her face had turned to stone. 'Call him and set up a meeting for the end of next week,' he said to Brad.

'Why next week? Why not this week? Why not today?' Brad asked.

Remy grinned. 'Because I'm going on my honey-moon.' And then he closed his phone and started count-ing.

One.

Two...

*'What?'* Angelique spluttered. 'I'm not staying mar-ried to you!'

'Has anyone ever told you how cute you look when you're angry?'

Her eyes iced and narrowed, her voice coming out through clenched teeth. 'Don't try your charm on me, Remy Caffarelli. It won't work. I'm not staying married to you, so you can just call your lawyer right back and tell him we'll be up there in a less than a minute to sign on the dotted—'

'What if you were to get something out of it?'

Her head slanted at a suspicious angle. 'Such as?'

'I'll back your label,' Remy said. 'With my connections and guaranteed finance you could really take your designs places. You'll become a global brand overnight.'

She wavered like a wary dog being offered a treat from someone it didn't quite trust. 'How long would we have to stay married?'

He gave a shrug. 'A couple of months tops. We can get the wheels rolling on our business ventures and then call it quits. Easy.'

'It's still going to be a paper marriage, right?'

Remy found himself wondering if he could tweak the rules a tad. Just a tad, mind. A couple of months with Angelique in his bed could certainly make the temporary sacrifice of his freedom worthwhile.

Besides, it wasn't as if he could sleep with anyone else while he was officially married to her. It went against everything he believed in.

'That would depend.'

'On what?'

'On whether you wanted to be celibate for two months or whether you wanted a paper marriage with benefits,' he said.

An insolent spark lit her gaze. 'Is that the only choice I have? Celibacy or you?'

Remy gave her a winning smile. 'I know; it's a tough one. But wait. There's more. I'll set up a business plan and employ accounting staff to see to the details while you get on with designing and sourcing fabrics.' It was like reeling a fish on the line. He could practically see her mouth watering. *He was going to win this.*

'It's not enough.'

He frowned. 'What do you mean, it's not enough? I'm the one taking a risk here. I haven't even seen one of your designs. You could be rubbish at designing for all I know.'

Her small chin came up. 'I want more.'

More what? Money? Sex? He could tick both those boxes several times over. 'I won't sleep around on you, if that's what's worrying you,' Remy said. 'I'm a one-at-a-time man and I'd expect the same commitment from you. I won't settle for anything else.'

Her eyes held his a challenging little lockdown that made the base of his spine shift like sand moving in an hourglass. 'I'm not going to sleep with you, Remy.'

*Sure you're not*, Remy thought. He could feel her attraction for him ringing in the air like a high-pitched radio frequency. She wanted him but she didn't want to be the first one to give in to it.

He saw it in those looks she gave him when she thought he wasn't looking: hungry, yearning, lustful. She was proud and defiant, determined to withstand the temptation he was dangling before her.

He was used to women caving in to his first smile. Angelique's resistance to his charm was doing the opposite of what she probably intended. Instead of making him want her less, it made him want her more. She was a challenge. A goal to score. A prize to claim.

*A bet to win.*

'Do you want to put money on that?' he asked.

She gave him a mordant look. 'Thanks, but no.'

'You're definitely not your father's daughter.'

'Ah, but that's where you're wrong,' she said, still eyeballing him with those stormcloud eyes.

Remy could feel his desire for her thundering through his blood. How he loved a woman with spirit, and they didn't come much more spirited than Angelique. He would relish every single moment of having her finally succumb to him. The chase would be fun but the catch would be magnificent. He could already taste the victory. He could feel it in his blood and in his bones.

He would have her.

He would have her right where he had always secretly wanted her.

*In his bed.*

Her beautiful face was held at a regal height, her eyes glittering with an implacable purpose. 'I think you'll find I'm very much my father's daughter.'

'Because you don't know when to quit when failure is staring you in the face?' He gave an amused chuckle. 'That would certainly be a case of the apple not falling far from the tree.'

Her chin stayed at that haughty level, her mouth set in a tight line. 'I'll stay married to you on one condition and one condition only.'

Remy felt a warning tingle course through his blood; even the back of his neck started to prickle. 'Go on.'

The corner of her mouth lifted as if she knew she had this in the bag. 'I want Tarrantloch at the end of it.'

# CHAPTER SEVEN

REMY DREW IN a breath. Why couldn't she want a life-long stipend or a bank vault of diamonds? But no, not Angelique; instead she had insisted on the one thing he didn't want to relinquish. Would *never* relinquish.

Tarrantloch was a trophy. He wasn't prepared to hand it over before he'd enjoyed everything it represented: *success. Revenge. Justice.*

He leaned forward to give the driver instructions to take him to his regular hotel in Paddington. He wanted time to plan a counter-move. He wasn't going to let her manipulate him. His mind shuffled through the ways he could turn this to his advantage. She didn't want the property half as much as she wanted to beat him at his own game. This was another one of her power plays.

'You drive a hard bargain,' he said when he sat back again.

She acknowledged that with an aristocratic tilt of her head. 'You want me to be your wife? That's the price you have to pay.'

Remy knew he could turn this around. Easily. Besides, she had got under his skin with her haughty airs and don't-touch-me looks.

He knew she wanted him.

It was in the air between them every time they were

alone. It had been there for years, truth be told. Now he
could act on the desire he had always suppressed for her.
He could finally indulge his senses, binge on her body
until she was out of his system and out of his head. It
would not be much of a hardship spending a month or
two with her in a red-hot affair. He would be the envy
of every man with a pulse.

Remy smiled a secret smile. He would be the one
to finally tame the temptress, the wild and sultry Angelique Marchand.

'I don't know…' He rubbed at his jaw as if thinking
it over. 'Tarrantloch for a couple of months of pretence?
Doesn't seem fair to me.'

*'Fair?'* she shot back incredulously. 'Of course it's
fair. I never wanted to be anyone's wife either, for real or
pretend. It will just about kill me to spend two months
acting like I feel something for you other than loathing.'

Remy had never wanted to make her eat those words
more than at that moment. She didn't hate him as much
as she made out. She hated that he saw through her
game-playing and manipulative attempts to outsmart
him.

But he would *always* win.

Losing was not an option for him.

'Like you, I want more.'

Her eyes suddenly flared. 'How much more?'

He gave her a smouldering look. 'I think you know
how much more.'

She tried to disguise a swallow. 'You're joking.'

'It's a big house,' he said. 'I put a lot at risk to acquire
it. I'm not going to relinquish it unless I think it's well
and truly worth it.'

She gave him a gimlet glare. 'I think I should've
faced the gallows or the firing squad or a public flog-

ging back in that godforsaken place we just left. It would've been preferable to this…this *outrageous* proposition of yours.'

Remy laid his arm along the back of her seat, his fingers close enough to touch the nape of her neck. 'What's so outrageous about making love with someone you've desired for years?'

'I don't desire you. I've *never* desired you.' Her eyes flashed pure venom at him. 'I detest you.'

He caught a coil of her hair and tethered her to him. He watched as her grey-blue eyes flared and her tongue swept over her lips again. 'I could make you eat those words, *ma belle.*'

Her mouth was pinched tight. 'You can't make me eat anything.'

There was something incredibly arousing about her defiant stance. She pulled against his push. She had always stood up to him. Challenged him. Annoyed him. Goaded him. 'I'll have you eating out of my hand soon enough.' He gave her a confident smile. 'You won't be able to resist.'

She grabbed her hair and tugged it out of his hold even though it must have hurt. 'I hate you for this.'

He gave a negligent shrug. 'So what's new?'

Her eyes narrowed to slits. 'I mean I'll *really* hate you.'

'So.' He curled his lip mockingly. 'You've only been pretending up until now?'

'I can't believe you're being so ruthless about this.' She continued to glare at him. 'You don't want me at all. You just want to win the upper hand.'

He caught her hand and brought it to his groin, holding it against his throbbing heat. 'Oh, I want you all right, princess,' he drawled. 'Make no mistake about that. And what I want, I get. Every. Single. Time.'

She snatched her hand back and glowered at him. 'Then you've met your match, Remy Caffarelli, because I bend my will to no man. If you want to sleep with me, then you'll have to tie me to the bed first.'

Remy smiled a sinful smile. 'I can hardly wait.'

Angelique seethed as she waited for him to come round to open her door when they arrived at his hotel. The press must have been given a tip-off as they surged towards him, but he just gave them one of his butter-wouldn't-melt smiles.

'Mr Caffarelli, the news of your marriage to Angelique Marchand has surprised everyone. Have you any comment to make on your whirlwind relationship?'

'No comment other than to say I haven't even told my family about it yet.' Remy grinned at the television camera. 'Rafe, Raoul, if you're watching this—sorry I didn't tell you guys first. You too, *Nonno*. Bet you didn't see that coming. But I wanted to surprise you all. Who would have thought it? Me, head over heels in love.'

Angelique mentally rolled her eyes as Remy helped her out of the car. 'Do you have to be so…?'

'Smile for the cameras, *ma chérie*,' he said as he took her by the hand in a firm, almost crushing grip.

'But I—'

'Miss Marchand.' A journalist thrust a recording device at her. 'Your marriage to Remy Caffarelli is the biggest scoop our network has had in decades. There are photos going viral with you in that gorgeous, ancient wedding dress. Can you tell us about your secret wedding?'

'It was very romantic,' Remy said before Angelique

could answer. 'Very traditional too, wasn't it, *mon amour*?'

'Very.' Angelique stretched her mouth into a smile. 'In fact, you would not believe quite *how* traditional it—'

Remy pulled her tightly against his shoulder. 'Right, show's over, folks. We've got things to do.'

'Miss Marchand, there's been some speculation going around on whether or not Remy has followed the example of his older brothers in not making his bride sign a pre-nuptial agreement. That's surprising, given the Caffarellis' wealth. Is that true in your case?'

Angelique felt Remy's hold on her tighten to the point of pain. But then he seemed to force himself to relax, although she could still feel the tension in him as he stood with his arm loosely around her shoulders. 'Yes, that's true,' she said in dulcet tones. Two could play at this game. 'It just goes to show how much he loves and trusts me.'

'Will you show us your rings?' a female journalist said.

'No rings as yet,' Remy said. 'We're still waiting for them to be finished. I'm afraid I didn't give the designer enough notice.'

Angelique looked up at him with feigned affection. 'It was an impulsive, spur-of-the-moment proposal, wasn't it, *mon cher*? You just couldn't hold it in any longer, could you?'

His dark-brown eyes warned her she would be paying for this later but right now Angelique didn't care. 'That's right,' he said. 'I couldn't wait to make her my wife. Now, if you'll excuse us...'

'One last question, Miss Marchand,' the female journalist said. 'Does your marriage to Remy Caffarelli mean there is now an end to the bitter feud between your father and Remy's grandfather, or are you star-crossed lovers?'

'Um...'

'I'm sure Henri Marchand will be thrilled to know his daughter has married a man who worships the ground she walks on,' Remy said smoothly.

'So you didn't ask his permission, then?' the female journalist asked with a cheeky smile.

Remy gave the journalist a level look. 'I did not believe that was necessary. Angelique is an adult and does not need her father's permission to do anything, much less marry the man she has loved since she was a teenager.'

'Is that true, Miss Marchand?' The journalist swung the recording device back to Angelique. 'Have you been in love with Remy since you were a girl?'

Angelique felt her teeth grind together behind her smile. 'Absolutely. Head over heels. Besotted. Totally, utterly smitten.'

Remy held up a hand to field off further questions. 'That's all, folks. No further comment.'

He practically dragged her into the building with him. 'Hey, not so fast,' Angelique said, almost stumbling over the pavement. 'I'm wearing heels.'

He slowed his pace but his grip on her hand didn't loosen. 'Behave yourself, Angelique, or you might find your time with me unnecessarily unpleasant.'

She threw him a caustic look. 'More than it is already?'

His expression was deceptively cool and composed but she knew she had riled him to the edge of his control. She felt it in the tense grip of his fingers. 'If you want to get your way at the end of this then you'll have to play the part of the happy bride, especially in public. Do you understand?'

'So, you agree to give me Tarrantloch?'

A steely glint came into his eyes. 'We'll see.'

Angelique narrowed her gaze in anger. 'If you don't give me a straight yes or no then I'm going to walk back out there and tell those journalists this is nothing but a sham.'

His hold on her wrist tightened like a vice. 'You're not going anywhere, young lady. For once in your life, you're going to do as you're told. That will make a refreshing change for you, *n'est-ce pas*?'

'Welcome back, Mr Caffarelli,' the hotel manager said as he came over to shake Remy's hand. 'A little bird tells me congratulations are in order. On behalf of all of us here, may I wish you both a very happy future together.'

*'Merci,'* Remy said with a polished smile.

Angelique had to bite her tongue not to blurt out the truth but she knew in the end she would be the one to look foolish. Remy had a knack for turning things to his advantage. Didn't the last twenty-four hours prove it? He was going to make the most of being married to her.

*Damn him!*

'How long are you staying with us?' the manager asked.

'Just tonight,' Remy said. 'We'll be moving on first thing in the morning. If you could keep the press away from us, I would greatly appreciate it, Thomas.'

'Will do, sir.' Thomas beamed. 'We took the liberty of preparing the bridal suite for you.'

*Not another one!*

'That was indeed very kind of you,' Remy said with a glinting smile. 'I'll make sure we do it justice.'

Angelique had to wait until they were in the lift and alone before she could give him a piece of her mind. 'I can't believe you said that. Now they'll be sniggering down there imagining us up here doing…it.'

He hooked a dark brow upwards. 'It?'

She folded her arms and glowered at him. 'I bet it's a pretty regular occurrence, you bringing scores of women upstairs to have sex with them.'

'Never in the bridal suite, however, and only one at a time.'

She flickered her eyelids in disgust. 'You're unbelievable.'

The lift doors pinged open and he waved for her to go ahead of him. 'Jealous, *ma belle*?'

Angelique made a rude vomiting noise as she breezed past him. 'You have *got* to be joking.'

He opened the suite door but blocked the entrance with his body. 'This is the fun part.'

'Pardon?'

He held out his arms. 'I get to carry you over the threshold.'

Angelique backed away. 'Oh, no you don't. You're not putting your hands anywhere on me—

'*Hey!* What are you doing? *Put me down this instant!*'

Remy's arms were like steel cables around her as they carried her into the suite. Angelique kicked her legs and pummelled his chest with her fists but it was like a goldfish trying to fight off a tiger shark. 'Is that the best you can do?' he taunted as he kicked the door shut with his foot.

Angelique grabbed a fistful of his hair and pulled. *Hard*. 'I'm just starting, so don't say I didn't warn you.'

He slid her down the entire length of his rock-hard

body, leaving her in no doubt of his red-hot desire for her. 'So am I,' he drawled and covered her mouth with the blistering heat of his.

It was a hard kiss, an almost crushing one, but it stirred an ember inside Angelique into a suddenly combustible flame. It didn't matter that she was supposed to be fighting him off for the sake of her pride. All that was important now was keeping his mouth locked on hers as her senses spun, twirled and reeled in delight.

His hands were rough as they gripped her by the hips, his erection heavy and urgent against her feminine mound. She felt the tug and drag of desire deep and low in her belly, that restless urge to be closer to him, to be possessed by his thick, hot length, was almost unbearable.

Every lustful thought or dream she'd had about him was making her giddy with the anticipation of finally experiencing his possession. Was that why she had continued to niggle and goad him—to push his buttons? To make him lose control and do what they had always wanted to do to each other even though, if asked, both would have flatly denied it?

She kissed him back with primal heat, using her teeth and her tongue, her hands still tightly fisted in his hair, her breasts jammed up against his chest, making her nipples ache and tingle as they were abraded by the fabric of his shirt.

His tongue duelled with hers until she was making needy, hungry little whimpering noises in the back of her throat. One of his hands went to the zip at the back of her dress and lowered it in one swift but smooth slide, his warm hand cupping her bottom through the cobweb lace of her knickers as he pulled her even closer to his turgid length.

An inferno seemed to be raging inside her body. It was lighting spot fires all over her flesh, burning her, searing her with the need to feel him skin on skin.

'Damn you,' he growled against her lips, making them vibrate with lust.

She tugged at his lower lip with her teeth, tasting blood but not sure if it was hers or his. 'Damn you right back.'

He sucked in a breath and crushed his mouth to hers again, harder this time, going deeper with his tongue until no corner of her mouth was undiscovered. He was consuming her like a hungry man does a feast and she was doing exactly the same. He was a sensual banquet she couldn't resist. Would she ever have enough of his mouth, of his electrifying touch?

His hands shoved her dress away from her shoulders, letting it puddle at her feet. He unhooked her bra and cupped her right breast in his hand as his other kept her locked against his pulsing heat. His thumb moved over her tight nipple in a mesmerising back-and-forth motion that made her spine loosen like oil poured into a rusty lock.

Angelique slid a hand between their bodies so she could unzip him. Ever since that shocking moment in the car when he'd pushed her hand against him, her palm had been tingling to feel him without the barrier of clothes.

He groaned with approval against her mouth as she freed him from his underwear. She shaped him with her fingers first, getting to know the feel, length and weight of him. Then she started rubbing up and down his silky shaft, registering every guttural sound he made, delighting in every flinch or movement of pleasure he made. She felt the beading of his pre-ejaculatory moisture and rolled it around the head of his penis, inciting him, urging him on. Daring him. Wanting him. Aching for him.

He was on his own sensual mission to get her naked. Her knickers were soon dispensed with and she had barely stepped away from the tiny circle of them when his fingers found her hot wetness. She gasped as he slipped them inside her; it was the sweetest torture to have him but not have him quite the way she wanted him. She moved against the blissful friction, making throaty little pleas against his plundering mouth.

'Condom.' The word sounded like it was wrung out of him.

'Have you got one?' *Dumb question.* He probably had hundreds on him. Maybe even thousands. He probably had his own insignia on them.

'In my back pocket.' He walked her backwards further into the suite, his mouth still fused to hers as his hand searched for the protection in the pocket of his jeans.

Angelique took the foil packet off him and saw to the business end of things. She tried not to fumble in her haste but her hands were shaking in anticipation. For most of her adult life she had dreamed and fantasised about feeling this level of lust.

It was overpowering.

Totally consuming.

Unstoppable.

It was as if every nerve in her body was standing up on its tiptoes and screaming out for release. *Now! Now! Now!*

It made every single encounter she had had—not that there had been many—pale in comparison.

'You are so damn hot and wet and ready for me,' he

said as he tumbled with her onto the king-sized bed in a sexy tangle of limbs.

'Yes.' One word was all she could manage. Her heart was racing, her blood pumping and her flesh tingling as he came over her with his weight.

He hitched up one of her legs over his hip and entered her so deeply she cried out as his thickened flesh stretched hers to capacity. He immediately stilled and looked down at her with a frown knitting his brows together. 'Am I rushing you?'

Angelique let out a little breath. 'No… Sorry, I'm a bit out of practice. It's been a while.'

His dark eyes searched hers. 'How long?'

'A few weeks… Months…'

His gaze was still locked on hers. 'Months?'

'OK, a year…and a bit. Two, actually…'

'But the press…'

'Get it wrong occasionally.'

His frown was still tugging at his forehead like stitches being pulled beneath the skin. 'Why do you let people say all that stuff about you when it isn't true?'

Angelique stroked a finger down his sternum, focusing on its journey rather than staying connected with his gaze. 'I don't care what people think. I know what's true. That's all that matters to me.'

'Stop distracting me.' He captured her hand and held it firmly in the cage of his. 'I want to talk to you.'

She couldn't help an exaggerated little eye-roll. 'I bet that's what you say to all the girls.'

His frown deepened. 'Will you stop it, for God's sake? I'm trying to have a sensible conversation with you.'

'While your body is doing what it's doing to mine?' Angelique writhed beneath him. 'Can't you feel that?'

He bit back a curse and moved within her. Deeply. Roughly. Urgently. 'I can't stop myself from wanting you. I hate myself for it.'

She grabbed at his buttocks and dug her fingers in to hold him in place. 'I hate myself for it too. I hate *you* for it. For how you make me feel.'

His mouth curved in an indolent smile. 'How do I make you feel?'

She tried to glare at him but it didn't quite work with his body still intimately connected with hers. Instead, she pushed out her bottom lip in a pout. 'Mad.'

'I like it when you're mad at me.' He gave one slow, deep thrust. 'It turns me on.'

Angelique felt her belly do a funny little shuffle like the pages of a book being thumbed. Her body was fully aware of him. Excruciatingly so. Every nerve ending was primed for his next thrust. She felt the tension building in her flesh with every erotic movement of his body in hers. He increased the pace and her pleasure rapidly climbed with the pulsating throb of her swollen, sensitised tissues as they each clamoured for release.

He hitched her leg higher over his hip and drove even deeper.

It was like detonating an explosive device.

Angelique felt the explosion deep in her body, radiating out in pulsing waves that ricocheted through her. She shuddered and screamed, a raw, primal-sounding scream that was unlike any other sound she had ever made before. But then she had never felt anything like this before either. She bucked beneath his rocking body to keep the exquisite sensations going for as long as she could. Finally they faded and she was left in a blissful state of lassitude.

But he wasn't finished with her yet.

He shifted position slightly, slowing his pace until her body was crawling with need once more. She felt the tingling start all over again, the tightening of muscles, the pulse of longing and the steady climb to the summit that was tantalisingly just out of reach.

He slipped a hand underneath her buttocks and raised her as he thrust deeper and faster. She looked at his face, at the taut set to his features as he fought for control. His eyes were hooded, his jaw like honed steel, his breathing sounding harsh and laboured. She had never seen a more erotic sight. A beautifully cut and carved man in full arousal, poised to explode, waiting for that final trigger.

Angelique lifted and then rolled her hips. He grimaced as he tried to hold back but then she rolled her pelvis again. She felt the exact moment when his control slipped. He stiffened and then let out a shout, the pumping action of his body triggering another wave of pleasure through her body that travelled all the way to her fingertips and toes.

He slumped over her, burying his head to the side of her neck, his warm breath and stubbly skin a deliciously sensual caress against hers.

Angelique was so used to sparring with him that this new connectedness was faintly disturbing. If he could read her body so well, how well could he read her mind?

She wasn't used to feeling such powerful sensations during sex. She had never felt that level of desire or need before. She had never orgasmed with a partner before. She'd always pretended and got away with it.

This was so new and exciting. Breathtaking. Tantalising. Addictive.

*Dangerous.*

Remy finally lifted his head and looked at her. 'Was that good for you?'

His arrogant confidence made her retort 'Average.'

His brown eyes glinted as if he knew she was lying. 'Then maybe I should try and improve my rating.' He stroked a lazy finger down between her breasts where a tiny slick of sweat had pooled. 'You're incredibly beautiful.'

She gave him one of her bored looks. 'Do you know how many times I've heard that?'

His eyes tethered hers; dark, probing, penetrating. 'Ah, but do you believe it?'

Angelique felt as if he had already cracked open a corner of her mind and was examining the contents with a high-beam searchlight. She put her hands on his chest and pushed him away. 'I have to get up. I don't want the condom to leak.'

He got up and dealt with the disposal of the condom while she went in search of her clothes. She felt foolish and somehow sordid, scrabbling about the room, picking up her underwear and redressing while all he had to do was straighten his clothes and zip up his trousers.

Was it somehow indicative of the imbalance of their relationship? She would always be the one who felt naked and exposed while he would only reveal what he wanted her to see.

He was in control.

She wasn't.

'Is this yours?' Remy asked, holding up a diamond pendant swinging on a fine gold chain.

Angelique went to take it off him but he held it just out of her reach. 'Give it to me.'

His mouth was curved in a sarcastic smile. 'Where are your manners, *mon amour*?'

She ground her teeth and flashed him a resentful look. 'Please.'

'Not good enough.' He held the pendant higher as she took another swipe at it. 'I want to hear you ask nicely.'

She felt a ripple of annoyance course through her, tightening every muscle to snapping point. 'Give it to me, *please.*'

His chocolate-brown eyes contained a goading glint. 'You can do better than that, *ma belle*. I want to hear you beg.'

Angelique felt the sudden rush of her fury as it unleashed itself from the tight restraints she had spent a lifetime keeping in place.

She would *not* beg.

She would *not* plead.

She would *not* give in to his command like a servant who had no rights. She would scratch his eyes out before she did that.

She flew at him like a dervish, calling him every foul name she could think of. It all came bubbling out like poison—the rage, the hatred, the feeling of impotence, the shame at being under his control when she had worked so hard not be under any man's control.

He had subdued her sensually.

He had ambushed her.

*Disarmed her.*

Now he wanted to break her spirit just like her father had done to her mother.

Of course, she was no match for him. He took control of her flailing fists before they could even land a punch. 'What the hell is wrong with you?' he asked, frowning at her.

Angelique pulled against his iron-like hold. 'Let go of me, you...you *bastard*!'

'Not until you simmer down.' His tone was calm but implacable. 'You're going to hurt yourself carrying on like that. What's got into you?'

Tears started and burned in her eyes. It was the greatest shame of all to be snivelling like a child in front of him but there was nothing she could do to stop the flow once it had started. She choked back a sob but another one soon followed, and then another, and another until she finally bowed her head and gave in to the storm of weeping. It was lowering to find herself in such a vulnerable state. How could she have let this happen? What was wrong with her? Where was her pride and determination? Had his powerful love-making undone her completely? How would she get herself together again?

Remy released her wrists but he gathered her to him, putting his arms around her so the wall of his body supported her. One of his hands went to the back of her head and gently stroked her hair as she shook with sobs against him. 'I've upset you.' His voice was very deep and sounded surprised. Perhaps even a little shocked.

Angelique gave an almighty sniff, and as if by magic a neatly folded white handkerchief with an embroidered black *C* on it was handed to her. 'Thanks.'

'Don't mention it.'

She blew her nose and scrunched the handkerchief into a ball inside her hand. 'I'm fine now.' She took a ragged breath and glanced up at him with an attempt at wryness. 'Bet you don't think I'm so beautiful now.'

His expression was clouded with concern as he looked down at her. 'I was only teasing. You do know that, don't you, *ma petite*?'

Why did he have to keep calling her those wonderful endearments in that sexy accent of his? It made it so much harder to hate him.

*You don't hate him.*

Angelique skirted around the thought and gave him a small self-deprecating smile. 'It's a bit of a hot button for me. A red rag, if you like. I don't beg. Ever. For anything.'

'I'll make a note of it.'

The silence thrummed for a moment.

She tucked a tendril of hair back behind her ear. 'Um…I guess I should go and clean up.'

He handed her the pendant, his expression now inscrutable. 'It's very nice. Was it a gift from one of your lovers?'

The fine chain tickled Angelique's palm as it coiled there. 'It was my mother's.' She raised her chin a fraction. 'Just for the record, I don't accept gifts from my lovers. Ever.'

He held her gaze for a beat or two, his still dark and unfathomable. 'Apart from Scottish mansions, of course.'

She pursed her lips at his counter-move. Would he end up giving her back Tarrantloch? He hadn't made any promises. Nothing was written down or signed. They had consummated their relationship, but did that mean anything to him other than yet another sexual conquest?

Angelique gave a little shrug of her shoulder as if it didn't matter to her either way. 'I'm sure you'll do the right thing when it comes to the end of our relationship.' She met his gaze again with a bold look. 'Have you got a date in mind or are we just going to wing it?'

The screen was still down over his eyes but a tiny muscle tightened near his mouth. 'Don't worry. I'll give you plenty of notice.'

She smiled a saccharine-sweet smile. 'Big of you.'

He let out an audible breath. 'You have first shower. I have some things to see to. We'll eat out at nine.'

'But I—'

The door clipped shut and after a moment Angelique dropped her shoulders on a sigh. He had a nasty habit of getting in the last word.

She would have to break him of it.

# CHAPTER EIGHT

REMY HAD BARELY stepped out of the hotel when his mobile buzzed. He looked at the screen and winced. 'Rafe, I was just about to call you and—'

'Tell me I did not just see you telling the press you've married the devil's spawn, Angelique Marchand,' Rafe said.

Remy glanced around to see if anyone was close enough to listen in. 'That's not a very nice way to speak of your brand new sister-in-law, bro.'

Rafe let out a curse. 'Are you out of your mind? What the hell are you playing at?'

'Hey, it's not Angelique's fault her old man is a double-crossing tool.' Remy couldn't help thinking how ironic it was to find himself defending her when normally he was finding any excuse to criticise her.

'Don't tell me you're in love with her, because I don't believe it for a second. The only person you love is yourself.'

'That's a bit harsh. I love lots of people. Even you.'

'Come on, Remy, this is me—Rafe. I know you. You would never fall in love with Angelique. She's as far away from your ideal woman as she could be. You've always said what a little slutty shrew she is. What's going on? Has Henri Marchand done the dirty on you? Forced you to marry her? Set up some sort of dodgy deal?'

'None of the above,' Remy said. 'Angelique followed me to Dharbiri and, to cut a long story short, she was found in my room and I had to marry her to keep from causing a public riot which might have ended up in one or both of us losing the skin off our backs. I decided not the take the chance.'

'Are you kidding me?' Rafe asked.

'Not at all,' Remy said.

'You said she followed you to Dharbiri. Why didn't you say something earlier if you were involved with her? Why let us find out like this?'

'I wasn't involved with her. Before this I hadn't seen or even spoken to her in years. She came to see me about her father's house. Remember Tarrantloch in Scotland? I won it off Henri Marchand in a bet.'

Rafe swore again but this time it was more a sound of admiration. 'So, it's just a marriage on paper, right?'

Another little silence, while Remy thought of how to answer. He didn't want to lie to his brother but neither did he want to discuss what had happened not ten minutes ago. His body was still singing from what was one of the most—if not *the* most—exciting sexual encounter of his life.

'You haven't,' Rafe said, sounding stern and incredulous at the same time.

'Hey, what *is* this?' Remy said. 'I don't ask you about your sex life with Poppy. Back off. I know what I'm doing.' *Sort of.* 'It's cool. Everything's cool.'

'You married our family's worst enemy's daughter without a pre-nup,' Rafe said. 'I don't think that's cool; I think that's outright stupidity. You're jeopardising everything we've worked for, just like *Nonno* did. Have you learned nothing in your thirty-two years on this planet?'

'What was I supposed to do?' Remy felt his hackles come up. 'Let her take the rap for being discovered in my room? I had to think, and think fast. There wasn't time to draw up a pre-nup. I did what I thought was the best and safest thing.'

'Being legally tied to Angelique Marchand is *not* safe,' Rafe said.

*Tell me about it.* 'I won't stay married to her for any longer than I have to,' Remy said. 'I'm working it to my advantage. Remember the Mappleton hotel chain I've been trying to buy for months? Henri Marchand's rumours about me turned old man Mappleton off, but now I'm married to Angelique he wants to play ball. I'm meeting with him next week. If I nail that deal, it will be worth any minor inconvenience of being married.'

'I can't help thinking this could blow up in your face.'

'You always think that about me,' Remy said. 'I like taking chances. Going with the gut. I always land on my feet. Always. Goal. Focus. Win. Remember?'

Rafe let out a long breath. 'Watch your back, Remy. Keeping your enemies close is wise, but sleeping with them is not.'

*Sleeping with them is the fun part*, Remy thought as he ended the call.

In fact, he couldn't wait to do it again.

Angelique was putting the finishing touches to her make-up when her mobile phone rang. She glanced at the screen to see it was her manager, Mackenzie Hillstrom, from her New York modelling agency. 'Hi, Mac, I was going to call you but—'

'Darling girl, I should hate you for not inviting me to your totally awesome desert wedding, and for not even telling me you were dating one of the most eligible and gorgeous men on this planet, but I forgive you, because you've just landed yourself the biggest contract of all time,' Mackenzie said.

'I…I have?'

'Forget Barbados and bikinis and bum-biting camels in Mexico. You are now the new poster girl for designer bridal wear. Every top designer wants you on his or her books! There's a bidding war going on as we speak. You looked absolutely amazing in that traditional garb. No one but you could pull that exotic look off. You've created the biggest sensation in bridal wear since the royal wedding.'

*Bridal wear?*

*Was this fate's idea of a twisted joke?* 'Um… Wow, that's great.' Should she tell her manager her marriage to Remy was only temporary, a charade unlikely to last longer than it took him to nail the Mappleton account?

'This is the big break you've been waiting for,' Mackenzie went on in her fast-paced New York accent. 'You're our golden girl now. You'll earn millions out of this. It will set you up for life—me too, when it comes to that. I'll email you the contract. Get it back to me as soon as you can. Take the next couple of weeks off while I sort the spring schedule out. Shanae will fill in for you on the Barbados shoot. Any questions?'

'No…that sounds wonderful.' *I think.*

Angelique put the phone down on the dressing table. She looked at it for a long moment, wondering if she should call her manager straight back and tell her she didn't want to take up the offer. Her life seemed to be spinning out of control in an alarming manner. A part of her wanted the money that was being put on the table, but the fame and constant exposure that would go with it gave her a troubling sense of unease. She had planned for months to get out of modelling. She was tired of living in the false world of perfection.

*Her body was tired.*

She had notebooks and slips of paper with designs doodled all over them. When would she have time to pursue her dream if she was caught up in a hectic shooting schedule? She didn't believe in doing things in half-measures. If they wanted her to be the next it girl in bridal wear, then her designs would have to wait...

Angelique was made up, coiffed and poised when Remy came back to the suite. She felt much more in charge when she had her professional armour on. It seemed important to give Remy the impression their love-making had made little or no impact on her. But it was hard to ignore the way her senses jumped to attention as soon as he came in the door, even harder to ignore the way her skin tightened all over and the way her inner core contracted. 'Nice walk?' she said.

His espresso gaze moved over her in a lazy sweep that tightened her skin and her inner core another notch. 'I wonder how long it would take me to get you out of that dress?'

She squared her shoulders even as her belly flipped over. 'What happened before was a mistake. I'd rather not repeat it.'

A hint of a smile lifted the corner of his mouth. 'You're not a very good liar, *ma chérie*. What happened before is going to happen again. And soon and often.'

Angelique felt a shiver course down her spine at the dark glitter of unbridled lust in his eyes. 'I think it would be foolish to complicate things with that level of involvement. We don't even like each other. It's rather unseemly to be going at each other like wild animals.'

His smile tilted a little further. 'Unseemly?'

She willed herself to hold his gaze for as long as she could. 'Primitive.'

He closed the distance between them in an easy stride or two. She knew she should have stepped back but her feet seemed to be bolted to the floor. She drew in a sharp breath when he put a hand to the nape of her neck. His warm palm was slightly rough against her soft skin and a shower of sensations spiralled through her at the delicious contact.

His eyes were so dark they looked like bottomless black pools. His mouth was so sexy, so sensually contoured, her insides shifted restlessly and her own mouth started to tingle.

'The thing is, *ma belle*, I feel very primitive when I'm around you.' His hand cupped her left cheek, his thumb pad giving one stroke over her lips that sent every nerve into a frantic dance.

Angelique's heart skipped a beat as his thighs brushed against hers. She felt the bulge of his erection. It spoke to everything that was female in her. Her senses were not sleeping or dormant now; they were wide awake and hungry for his touch. Ravenous. 'Find yourself another plaything.' She was really rather proud of how curt and cold she sounded. 'I will not be used by you.'

His thumb pad moved back over her lips, his eyes still locked on hers. 'Is that really what you want? To go back to a hands-off arrangement?'

*No!* 'Yes.' Angelique moistened her lips and tasted salty male. It was like tasting a powerfully addictive drug. She wanted more. Now. *Right now.*

His gaze searched hers for a pulsing moment. 'Fine.' He dropped his hand from her face and moved away.

Fine? She looked at him in numb shock. *Fine?* Why wasn't he challenging her? Why wasn't he making her eat her words? Damn it! She wanted him to make her eat her words!

He glanced at his designer watch. 'We should get going. I don't want to lose our booking; I had to pull some strings to get a table at such short notice.'

'I find that very hard to believe.' Angelique curled her lip as she picked up her purse. 'The Caffarelli name can get you a table just about anywhere, I would've thought.' *Let's see if I can push a few more of those buttons of his.* 'Maybe I'll change mine and see if I can cash in on some of the benefits.'

His expression hardened to stone. 'Don't get ahead of yourself, Angelique. This is not permanent. Don't kid yourself that it will be anything but what it is right now.'

'A war zone?' she quipped.

'Temporary.' He held the door open with a pointed look. 'Shall we?'

It was a popular restaurant owned and operated by one of Britain's celebrity chefs, which meant it was a famous-person hot spot, so the paparazzi were nearly always on hand.

Angelique quailed at the thought of fending off another round of intrusive questions. She was a pretty good actor but any body-language expert worth his or her credentials would be able to see Remy was still angry with her. He hadn't spoken a word to her during the short trip to the restaurant. He had spent the entire time tapping emails into his phone.

'Couldn't we have stayed and dined in the hotel?' she asked as he helped her from the limousine.

'No.' His hand was firm as it took hers.

'But surely we should be avoiding all this attention as much as possible?' She gave him a pouty glance. 'Anyway, what will people think? We're supposed to be on our honeymoon. Eating's supposed to be the last thing on our minds.'

'Yes, well, it's probably the last thing on *your* mind, but I'm starving. I need food and I need it now.'

Angelique rolled one shoulder haughtily. 'Why are men at the mercy of their basest desires?'

He gave her a glinting look. 'Why do women deny their needs as if it's something to be ashamed of? It's not wrong to feel hungry or horny. It's completely natural.'

'You know something?' She frowned at him. 'I've always really hated that word.'

'What, hungry?'

'Horny. It's sounds…I don't know. Coarse.'

A mocking smile angled his mouth. 'So underneath that brash, streetwise exterior is a sweet old-fashioned girl? Don't make me laugh.'

Angelique glared at him. 'You don't know me. Not the real me.' *No one knows the real me.*

He tucked her arm through one of his as he led her into the restaurant. 'Maybe now's a good time to start.'

Dining out for Angelique was like sharing a room with Remy—full of wicked temptation. Being tired and emotionally out of sorts made it much harder for her to rely on her steely resolve to keep to her strict diet. Just like kissing or touching Remy, one taste was enough to throw caution to the wind. Making love with him had changed everything. It was like trying to eat one peanut or one French fry: it was impossible; she would always want more. More of him. *All* of him. But how could she have him when he didn't want this arrangement to last any longer than it took to seal his latest business coup?

The Caffarelli brothers—before Rafe had married and Raoul had become engaged—had written the rule-book for rakes. Of the three of them, Remy had the worst reputation for the rate of turnover of partners. He had never had a relationship last more than a week or two.

But then, why would he?

He was spoilt for choice. Women adored him and flocked about him like bees around blossom. He was never in one place longer than a week at a time, which of course made it easy for him to be casual about his hook-ups.

Did he ever want more than just sex? Did he ever think about the companionship and loyalty his brothers were now experiencing? Did he think about the promise of stability and a love that would last through good times and bad? To have someone to share the bond of children with, to watch as they grew from babies to children to adulthood? To love and protect them, nurture them and teach them how to be good, trustworthy citizens?

Angelique's brow furrowed as she looked down at the menu. Instead of the words printed there, she started to picture a tiny baby with a shock of jet-black hair and big brown eyes fringed with dark lashes.

Remy said he didn't want children.

She had said the same. Many times.

*But it wasn't quite true...*

'By the way.' Remy looked up from the menu he was perusing. 'We are not leaving this restaurant until I've seen you eat something. Understood?'

Angelique's back prickled. 'I have to think of my figure, especially now.'

'Why especially now?'

She gave him an imperious look. 'You're not the only one getting a ratings boost from our marriage.'

He cocked his head in interest. 'Oh, really?'

'My manager is firming up a new contract for me to consider. Once I sign it, I'm going to be booked up for months and months.'

'Tell them to wait. Tell them you're not available until after Christmas. I want you with me for the next month or two at the very least.'

Angelique felt her heart give a little skip at the thought of him wanting her with him but then she remembered his precious business deal. He wanted her for show, not for her.

It was an act.

A game of charades.

Even though technically she was free to be with him while her manager negotiated the schedule, she resented him arrogantly assuming she would drop everything just because he told her to.

She was *not* going to be ordered about by him.

'Do you really think you can just march into my life and take control as if I have no mind or will of my own?'

He gave her a knowing look. 'I didn't come marching into your life. You came blundering into mine. Now it's time for you to take responsibility for it.'

'By following you around like a stupid little lapdog?' She gave an exaggerated shudder of distaste before curling her lip at him. 'I don't think so.'

His mouth flattened and his eyes flashed her a warning. 'You will do as I say or I'll take everything off your father. Do you hear me? Everything. There won't be a penny left for you to inherit once I'm done with him. Don't say I didn't warn you.'

Angelique pressed her spine back against the supports of her chair. 'Do you really think I will respond to threats?'

'You will if you know what's good for you.'

*What would be good for me would be to put as much distance between you and me as is globally possible.*

It was too dangerous being with him. How soon before she caved in and fell into his arms again? She had to get away. She had to think. Clear her head.

*Protect her heart.*

Angelique put her napkin down on the table and pushed back her chair. 'Will you excuse me?'

His brows snapped together. 'Where are you going?'

'I'm going to the powder room.' She gave him a lofty look. She didn't have to tell him *which* powder room. *Like one several thousand kilometres away.* 'Do I need to ask your permission first?'

His dark, unreadable eyes measured hers for a moment. 'Fine. Go and powder your nose. But if you're not back here in two minutes I'll come and find you.'

*I'll be miles away by then.*

Angelique only got as far as the street when she was stopped, not by Remy but by her father. He came striding towards her from the cab he had just vacated. His cheeks were puce and his brows were joined over his formidable nose.

'Is it true?' he asked. 'Have you married Remy Caffarelli?'

It was probably perverse of her, but she felt a strange sense of satisfaction at having done something so shocking and outrageously disappointing to her father. He looked like he was having a conniption. 'News certainly travels fast in this city,' she said lightly. 'How did you find out?'

He gave her a poisonous glare. 'Do you have any idea of the utter fool you've made of me? I was at my club when one of my colleagues informed me. He read a tweet about it. There was a photo of you in a wedding outfit that looked like something out of *The Arabian Nights*. How could you do this to me? You couldn't have thought of a worse punishment, you silly little cow. Have you no brain in that stupid, big, fat ugly head of yours?'

'Apologise to my wife or I'll flatten you.'

Angelique spun around to see Remy standing there. He had a grim look on his face and his fists were clenching as if he was already rehearsing his first punch. 'Don't.' She put her hand on his arm. 'It's not worth it.'

He gently but firmly unpeeled her fingers from his wrist and faced her father. He spoke in French and it wasn't pretty. Angelique watched as her father's face went from puce to bright crimson and then back to puce. Even the tips of his ears were bright red, as if he was going to explode on the spot.

'She is my daughter,' Henri said through tight lips. 'I'll speak to her any way I like.'

Remy suddenly seemed so incredibly tall as he stared down her father. 'She is my wife and no one gets to speak to her like that.' His tone was commanding, authoritative. Intractable. 'Apologise now or suffer the consequences.'

Her father huffed and puffed but finally he muttered what one could only very loosely describe as an apology before he sloped off back into his cab like a chastened dog being sent to its kennel.

Remy put a protective arm around Angelique's waist. 'Does he normally speak to you like that?'

She pressed her lips together as she watched the lights of the cab fade into the distance. She felt a sudden desire to cry and had to blink a few times to get control. No one had ever come to her defence before. Her mother had been too weak; the household staff too scared of losing their jobs.

*'Ma petite?'*

Angelique looked up at him. Had he ever looked more handsome, more dashing and gorgeous than right now? How could she ever have thought she hated him? She quickly shielded her gaze. 'We don't have the best relationship. His short fuse and my smart mouth aren't a good combination for familial harmony.'

He brushed her cheek with a light-as-air glide of his finger. 'Has he ever laid a hand on you?'

'No. But he uses words just as lethally. He did it to my mother. I'm sure it caused her breakdown. She just couldn't take it any more.'

His expression flashed with disgust. 'Why didn't you say something earlier? I would have sorted him out years ago.'

Angelique gave a weary sigh. 'I wanted to plenty of times but who would've believed me? It would blot his copybook too much to be seen as anything but a devoted father. The fact that he bawled me out like that in such a public place is a testament to how much he hates you. He would normally never speak to me like that if there was an audience.'

Remy took her hands and gave them a light squeeze. 'Promise me something.'

'What?'

'Don't ever be alone with him. Ever. Do you understand? Never.'

Right at this very moment, Angelique would have promised him anything. 'I promise.'

'Good girl.' He brought her hands up to his mouth and kissed both of them in turn, his eyes still holding hers. 'So, tell me about this new contract. You didn't get round to telling what it was about.'

She gave her eyes a little roll. 'You're not going to believe what they want me to do.'

His brows snapped together. 'Not a naked shoot?'

Angelique laughed at his fierce expression. 'No, nothing like that. I'm to be the new poster girl for designer bridal wear.'

'Bridal wear?'

'Yes. How ironic is that? I never even wanted to be a bride and now I'm going to be wearing frothy wedding dresses and voluminous veils every day of the week, and earning millions for the privilege.'

His dark gaze searched hers for a moment. 'And you're pleased?'

Angelique pasted on her brightest smile. 'But of course. For one thing, I won't have to diet so stringently. Just think of the multitude of sins I can hide under a hoop skirt.'

A smile kicked up the corners of his mouth. 'This calls for a celebration. Want to go back to the hotel and order in room service?'

'But what about the table you had to work so hard to secure?'

He gave a shrug. 'Personally, I think the place is overrated. My brother Rafe's wife, Poppy, would probably agree with me. Did I tell you she's a cook?'

'I think I read that somewhere.' She fell into step

beside him as they walked along the footpath. 'What's she like?'

'Gorgeous.' He gave her a sudden grin. 'I mean that in a brother-in-law kind of way, of course. She reminds me of my mother. So does Raoul's fiancée, Lily. They're both really lovely girls. A bit too homespun for me, but still, each to his own.'

'Careful, Remy, you're starting to sound envious.'

He shook his head, his smile fading away. 'I'm not cut out for that domestic scene. I'm like you; I like my freedom too much. Babies seem such smelly, noisy things. And then they grow up and become annoying smart-mouthed tearaways who keep their parents up all night worrying about them. No. Not for me. Definitely not.'

Angelique gave him a playful little shoulder-bump. 'I'm sure not all children turn out horribly spoilt, obnoxious brats like you and me.'

He gave her a crooked grin as he gently shoulder-bumped her back. 'God forbid.'

# CHAPTER NINE

REMY WATCHED an hour later in their suite as Angelique nibbled at an undressed green salad and took occasional sips from a glass of Chianti. When she wasn't acting tough and being lippy, she was surprisingly good company. Quirky. Funny. Engaging.

Something had shifted in their relationship outside the restaurant.

He had been brought up to defend and protect women. Not by his grandfather, who exploited them any chance he could, but by his father before he had died and his two older brothers. Remy didn't mind the occasional verbal brawl, but insulting a woman and calling her names was not something he could ever tolerate.

He had never liked Angelique's father, even when Henri had been a regular visitor at his grandfather's villa in Rome, well before he had come across him in business. Remy had always found him two-faced, sly and conniving. The fact that Henri had been verbally abusing his wife and daughter disgusted Remy but it didn't surprise him. Men like Henri Marchand used power in dishonourable ways. They snatched at it whenever they could and gave little thought to the harm they were causing others.

Remy wondered if Angelique's wilful and at times

reckless behaviour was a reaction to the tyranny she had lived under for so long. While she didn't live with her father, and hadn't for a long time, he still seemed to have power to hurt her. He'd seen the way she'd flinched at Henri's horrible words. It was no wonder she was so adamantly opposed to marriage since the example set for her had been so appalling.

Protecting her had been an automatic reaction for Remy. He had been prepared to use force if he'd had to, although generally he didn't condone physical violence. His anger at her escaping from the restaurant had turned so quickly into something else.

He still wasn't quite sure exactly what it was…

'Do you want some more wine?'

Angelique shook her head. 'No, one is enough. I'm not a big drinker. Too many calories.'

Remy frowned as he looked at her barely touched meal. 'This new contract… How does that fit in with your plans to focus on designing?'

She put her glass back down and met his gaze. 'It'll take ages, possibly months or even up to a year, to get to the manufacturing and selling stage. I'll need an income in the meantime. I can't live on air.'

He gave her a dry look. 'You're doing a pretty fine job of it so far. You've only taken a couple of nibbles of that piece of lettuce.'

'I don't need a lot of food.' She gave his empty plate a baleful glance. 'Unlike some people, who have disgustingly voracious appetites and seemingly hollow legs.'

'I'm not a glutton. I just love food.'

She arched a neatly groomed eyebrow in a worldly manner. 'And sex.'

He gave her a glinting smile. 'That too.'

There was a little silence.

She passed the tip of her tongue over her lush lips and an arrow of lust speared Remy in the groin. Was she thinking of their passionate union earlier?

He hadn't *stopped* thinking about it.

He hadn't stopped feeling it tingling in his flesh like aftershocks in the wake of an earthquake. He could still taste her sweet vanilla and milk taste. He could still feel the softness of her lips, the boldness of her clever little tongue, the smooth glide of her hands and fingers.

He suppressed a shudder as he thought of what that mouth and those hands could do to him. What that gorgeously tight, feminine body *had* done to him.

*Made him lose control.*

'We're going to have to share that bed,' Remy said. 'Maybe we should put down some ground rules first.'

'What do you suggest?' Her expression was pert. 'A chalk line down the middle?'

'I was thinking more of a roll of pillows or a bolster.'

'How about a barbed wire fence?'

Remy felt another arrow hit bull's-eye. 'I wouldn't want you to get hurt when you head over to my side.'

She gave him an arch look. 'What makes you think I would come over to your side?'

'You think we can keep this thing between us on ice? Seriously, how long do you think that's going to last? You're hot for me. You can deny it all you like, but I know you want me. You've always wanted me.' *Like I've always wanted you.*

She flickered her eyes upwards. 'I can't believe the size of your ego. I might have wanted you, but I've *had* you, and quite frankly once is more than enough.'

Remy felt the rush of a fresh challenge fire through his blood. She was playing hard to get. It was another point-scoring game to her. She had sensed his weakness and was going in for the kill.

Did she want him to beg?

He would *never* do that.

He could live without sex—for a while. Sure he could. Monks did it all the time. It was supposed to be good for the mind. It was supposed to be mentally cleansing...or something.

'So, what are you saying? I didn't float your boat or something?'

'The sails gave a little flutter but that was about it.'

She was lying. He had felt her spasms and he had heard her cries. Unless she was a very good actress, she'd had the orgasm of her life. Why then was she so keen not to repeat it? 'If you change your mind then just lean over and tap me on the shoulder,' he said. 'I'll be happy to get your motor started.'

She gave him a withering look. 'Don't hold your breath.'

Angelique came out of the bathroom half an hour later to find Remy lying on his back with an e-reader flopped down on his chest. His eyes were closed, his breathing was steady and even, his body naked from the waist up. She wasn't sure if he was naked below the waist, because the sheet was covering him, but she had a feeling he wasn't the type of guy to wear pyjamas to bed.

She let her eyes feast on his naked chest and broad shoulders. Each muscle was so perfectly contoured, toned and taut with not an ounce of excess flesh on him anywhere. His hair was tousled, as if he had not long ago run his fingers through it, and his face was shadowed with evening stubble.

All of the Caffarelli brothers were staggeringly gorgeous but Angelique had always found Remy's dark features particularly so. It was something about his chocolate-brown eyes, the way they glinted with amusement or mockery even when he was doing his deadpan thing. It was the way his mouth was fashioned, the lower lip fuller than the top one. The chiselled leanness of his jaw; the way he always looked like he hadn't shaved closely enough. It was something about his hands with their long, tanned fingers that felt like a Taser zap when they touched her.

Angelique carefully approached his side of the bed and lifted the e-reader off his chest. He made a low murmur and she paused before she put the e-reader on the bedside table. She tiptoed round to her side of the bed, gently peeled back the covers, slipped in and huddled right on the edge so no part of her body was anywhere near his. She closed her eyes and willed herself to sleep but the citrus scent of his aftershave stirred her senses. She could feel the warmth of his body; it seemed to be reaching out to her, enveloping her...*tempting her.*

She jammed her eyes even tighter together and brought the covers right up to her chin.

*She would not touch him!*

Angelique must have drifted off eventually because she when she opened her eyes it was light and Remy was already up, showered and dressed. He'd dropped the towel he'd used over the back of the velvet covered chair he was now sitting on as he typed something into his phone, a heavy frown between his brows.

'Don't you *ever* pick up after yourself?'

'Hmm?' His tone was absent and he didn't even look her way as he kept typing.

Angelique swung her legs over the side of the bed,

slipped her arms through her wrap and tied it around her body. She came over to where he was sitting, picked up the damp towel and held it between two fingers. 'Do you ever spare a thought for the person who has to come in and service your room?'

'What?' He glanced at her then, his expression still dark with a frown.

'You leave stuff everywhere. The least you could do is hang your towel up or leave it in the tub or the shower cubicle if you're not going to use it again.' She put her hands on her hips and glowered at him. 'Stop typing when I'm talking to you!'

'You're not talking to me, you're nagging me.'

'Yes, well, that's what wives are forced to do, because their lazy husbands don't see the hours of invisible work that goes on behind the scenes to keep a house running smoothly.'

He rose to his feet and Angelique took a little step back. Without her heels he towered over her and she had to crick her neck to keep eye contact. His expression was mocking as he looked down at her. 'And just how many houses have you run, *ma chérie*?'

She pursed her lips. 'I'm just saying...'

He held her gaze for a long moment. He seemed to be thinking about something. She could see his mouth shifting from side to side in a contemplative manner. 'Can you cook?'

'Yes. I've been to cookery schools in France, Italy and Thailand. Why?'

'Would you cook a dinner for me?'

Angelique frowned. 'What, you mean every day, like in a traditional marriage?'

'No, nothing like that. I want to entertain Robert Mappleton—you know, the guy I've been trying to win over? He's ultra-conservative and traditional. He's been wined and dined thousands of times in the best restaurants across the globe. What I think would really impress him is a home-cooked dinner in a private setting. Will you do it?'

She caught her lower lip between her teeth. The sooner she helped Remy nail his deal, the sooner they could go their separate ways. That certainly wasn't half as attractive as it had been a day or so ago. She had her own contract to consider now. Would the top-end designers currently courting her still want her if she was divorced?

*Probably not.*

'Which private setting did you have in mind?'

'Tarrantloch.'

Angelique glared at him. 'You insensitive bastard!'

'What?'

She narrowed her gaze to slits. 'You really are the most unfeeling jerk I've ever come across. How much more do you want to rub my nose in it? You stole my house and now you want me to play the 1950s housewife in it? Arrggh!'

'I guess that's a no?'

Angelique glowered at him. 'You're damn right it's a no. How could you be so cruel?'

'I was actually thinking of you,' he said. 'I thought you'd be more comfortable cooking in a familiar kitchen.'

'I'd be more comfortable if the deeds to my home were back in my hands where they belong.'

He gave her a dry look. 'Then perhaps you need to work on charming me into changing my mind, *ma petite*, hmm?'

Angelique felt a traitorous spurt of longing assail her.

How did he do that to her with just one look? Those dark eyes smouldered and she was instantly aflame. How was she going to resist him when all she wanted was to be back in his arms?

*But she wasn't going to let him know that.*

She narrowed her eyes even further. 'Are you black-mailing me?'

'I prefer to call it negotiating.'

'Negotiating my foot! You want me to sleep with you. Why don't you come right out and say it?'

His eyes scorched hers. 'I want to sleep with you.'

Angelique's inner core contracted. Her breasts tingled. Her heart skipped and then raced. She ran her tongue over her suddenly dry mouth. She saw the raw, naked lust in his dark eyes. She felt it in the crackling air she was trying to drag into her lungs. She felt it in the firm grip of his steely hands as they captured her by the hips and pulled her against him.

Heat against heat.

His mouth came down, hovering just above hers. 'This is what I want.' He toyed with her lips in a tanta-lising little tug-and-release game that made her spine turn to liquid.

*I want it too. So, so much!*

'And this…' He stroked the seam of her mouth with his tongue, teasing the sensitive flesh, taking posses-sion as soon as she opened to him.

She tried to smother a whimper but her bones were melting like an ice sculpture in the Dharbiri desert sun as he explored every corner in intimate detail. One of his hands went to the small of her back, pushing her closer to his hot, hard heat, the other deftly untying the ties of her wrap and unpeeling it from her body.

He pushed aside the satin straps of her nightgown

and it slipped off her body and pooled at her feet. His hand cupped her breast, her nipple brushing against his palm, making her senses hum with delight. Need unfurled in her body, stretching like a sun-warmed cat, reaching into all of her limbs, making them soft and pliant as he crushed her to him.

Angelique tugged his shirt out of his trousers and blindly undid the buttons as her mouth fed off his. She unhitched his belt, undid his waistband, rolled down his zipper and then boldly took possession of him. He groaned into her mouth as he kicked off his shoes and stepped out of his trousers.

They stumbled back towards the bed, knocking one of the table lamps over in the process. He came down over her, his thighs trapping hers, his mouth still working its heady magic on hers.

Angelique arched her back as he left her mouth to concentrate on her breasts. The feel of his tongue and teeth on her flesh was a blissful torture. She writhed and gasped and clutched at his head.

He didn't stop at her breasts. He went lower to the cave of her belly button, dipping in and out with his moist tongue, laving her flesh, trailing even lower.

She automatically tensed. This was so personal. So very intimate.

He calmed her with a gentle hand on her thigh. 'Not comfortable with this?'

Angelique felt a blush crawl into her cheeks. He thought she was so hip and worldly but this was the one thing she had never felt comfortable sharing with any partner. It was all very well, pretending to have an orgasm when someone was rocking and humping above her, but *this* was something else. 'Um...'

'It's fine, *ma petite*. You don't have to do anything you're not comfortable with.'

Was it the fact he had given her the freedom to say no that made her now want to say yes? She slowly met his dark gaze. 'I've never done this with a partner...'

Something moved in his eyes. A flicker of surprise? Delight? 'Do you trust me to make it good for you?'

Angelique suddenly realised she did. Hadn't he already shown her what her body was capable of in terms of pleasure? She had never experienced anything like the supremely passionate response she had felt in his arms with anyone else. She wanted to experience *this* with him; this incredible intimacy would leave her with something precious and unique to remember when their marriage was over. 'Yes...'

He gently caressed her thighs, waiting until she was open and relaxed before he traced her folds with his tongue. All of her nerves writhed and danced, twirled and fretted for more. He did it again, separating her this time, tasting her, briefly touching her clitoris to give it time to get accustomed to the sensation. He slowly built the movements of his tongue against her swollen flesh, making her shiver all over as tiny ripples began to course through her. He was patient and gentle. Experimental. Gauging her response, learning her body's secrets and indulging her senses until she was suspended on a precipice, hovering, wanting, aching, but not quite able to take that final plunge.

'Come for me, *ma petite*,' he coaxed her softly. 'Don't hold back.'

'I want to but I can't.'

'Yes you can.' He stroked her tensed up thighs until they released. 'You can do it. Just stop thinking and let go.'

Angelique felt the flickering of his tongue against her and a wave of pleasure came rolling up from deep inside her. She felt every muscle in her body tighten before the final lift off. She went careening into oblivion, shuddering and shaking as the tide of release passed through her like a powerful relaxant.

Remy came back over her and pushed her wild hair back off her face. 'Average?'

Angelique couldn't stop a coy smile. 'How do I know, since I don't have anything to compare it to?'

His gave her one of his smouldering looks. 'I can soon fix that.'

'Wait.' She put a hand on his chest, her gaze sultry. 'There's something I have to see to first.'

He drew in an audible breath as her hand moved down his body. But she wasn't content with just stroking and caressing him. She wanted to taste him as he had tasted her. This was another act she had shied away from in the past, but right now it seemed perfectly natural to pleasure him with her lips and tongue.

She pressed a pathway of kisses down his chest, swirling her tongue into his belly button before going inexorably lower. She felt his abdominal muscles contract the closer she got to her target. She breathed over his erection at first, letting him feel the dance of her breath, letting him experience the anticipation of her imminent possession.

'I usually put a condom on at this point.' His voice sounded rough. Gravelly.

Angelique gave him a seductive look from beneath her lashes. 'There isn't time.'

'But I— *Oh God.*' He sucked in another breath as she set to work on him.

It was thrilling to have him so in her power. She

had never realised how arousing it was to feel him and hear him struggle for control. She was ruthless as she drew on him, not giving him a chance to pull away. She tasted the hot essence of him against her tongue, felt the tension in him against her lips as she moved them up and down his shaft.

He grabbed at her head with both of his hands, presumably to push her away, but she refused to budge. She hummed against his swollen flesh and he gave a quickly muttered curse and then spilled.

After it was over he fell on the bed on his back, his chest rising and falling as he tried to get his breathing under control.

Angelique trailed a light fingertip up and down his chest. 'Better than average?'

He turned his head and gave her a sinfully erotic look. 'The best.'

'Are you just saying that?'

'No.'

*Wow. Oh wow.* Her fingertip came back up and circled one of his flat, dark nipples. 'How soon before you can go again?'

'Why do you ask?'

She gave a casual little shrug. 'Just wondering.'

He rolled her back over and trapped her within the cage of his arms. 'You still want to play, *mon trésor*?'

She traced his lower lip with her fingertip. 'Might as well make the most of our time together.'

He stopped the pathway of her finger by holding her hand in his. 'Just so we're clear on this—I'm not making any promises about Tarrantloch. I won it fair and square. I don't do sentimentality or guilt trips. You need to understand and accept that.'

'But I thought you said—'

'If we continue to sleep together, it's because we want to satisfy the mutual attraction we feel. It's not about and should not be about anything else.'

Angelique knew how determined he could be, but then so could she. Clearly locking horns with him wasn't going to work. It had never worked before. She would be better served in finding another way to appeal to his sense of fairness—assuming he had one, of course. Charm him. Woo him. Beguile him. *Outsmart him.*

She tiptoed a fingertip down his sternum again. 'Do you ever *not* get your way?'

He gave her a lazy smile. 'Giving in is about as much in my nature as submission and demureness is in yours.'

'I don't know about that.' Angelique gave a little sinuous movement beneath him. 'I'm feeling pretty submissive right now.'

His eyes glinted as his hands pinned her arms either side of her head, his strong thighs trapping hers with erotic intent. 'Then I'd better make the most of it.'

And he did.

# CHAPTER TEN

ANGELIQUE BREATHED IN the sharp, clean air of the high-lands as Remy helped her out of the car the following day. Tarrantloch in autumn was bleak and cold but that was part of the raw beauty of it. The turreted grey stone mansion had been in her mother's family for over three-hundred years. It was set in a large verdant clearing in the middle of a forest and had its own lake and a burn that ran with ice-cold water full of salmon and trout.

She had spent some of her happiest times here as a child before her mother had turned into a browbeaten shadow of her former self. Coming here had been some-thing Angelique and her mother had done together in the early days to spend time with her maternal grand-parents while Henri had been busy with his business affairs in Europe.

But, once her grandparents had passed away within a year of each other, Tarrantloch had been left idle with just a handful of servants, as her father had insisted on living in his homeland of France so he could commute more easily to Italy, where he had his major business interests, including those with Vittorio Caffarelli.

Over the last couple of years, however, he had come back and taken up residence, strutting around like a proud peacock as he conducted various house parties with his business cronies. It disgusted Angelique to see her mother's home exploited by her father and she had mostly kept well away unless she knew he was abroad on business.

Angelique hadn't been to Tarrantloch since the summer when she'd had a ten-day break from her schedule. It seemed surreal to be here now, officially married to Remy, knowing the house was no longer hers.

*Might never be hers again.*

Remy had decided he wanted it as a trophy. What else could it be to him other than a prize to gloat over? He had luxury homes all over Europe and the Mediterranean. Besides, if he wanted to see snow he could go to his chalet in the Swiss Alps.

No, Tarrantloch was his way of publicly claiming victory over her father. What pained her the most was Remy could so easily turn around and sell it once it had served its purpose. And, one thing she knew for certain, he wouldn't be offering it to her for mate's rates. He was a ruthless, hard-nosed businessman. He wouldn't allow sentimentality or emotions to influence him.

*But she was not going to give up until she had exhausted every possible avenue to get it back.*

Angelique walked with Remy over the pebbled driveway to the front door. 'Have you kept on any of my father's staff?' she asked.

'None, apart from the gardener, and he's on notice.'

She raised a brow. 'Why not?'

'Because not one of them was doing a proper day's work.' He took out the keys he had in his pocket and unlocked the heavy door. 'I'm going to conduct some interviews while we're here. I want to employ locals, people who know the house and want it to be preserved. Your father surrounded himself with a motley crew of sycophants who didn't do much more than take up space.'

Angelique was inclined to agree with him. More than inclined. She had never liked the obsequious butler and housekeeper her father had hired. The devoted staff her grandparents had employed had left in dribs and drabs over the years, either through retirement, death or disenchantment. 'So who's here now?'

'Just us.'

She blinked. 'What? No one at all? Just us?' *Alone?*

He gave her a wickedly sexy smile. 'It's our honeymoon, *ma chérie*. We're not supposed to have people with us.'

Her belly gave a little quivery swoop. 'But what about the dinner with Robert Mappleton? After all, isn't that why we're here?'

'That's not until the end of next week.'

'Why not get it over with this week?'

'Ah, but that would appear too eager, *n'est-ce pas*? Better to let him think I'm in no great hurry to play ball.'

Angelique sent him a wry look. 'I can see why you've accumulated the wealth you have at such a young age: you're as cunning as a fox.'

He grinned as he held the door open for her. 'No point in being too predictable. Where's the fun in that? No, my philosophy is to keep them guessing for as long as you can and then reel them in when they least expect it.'

*Is that what you're doing with me?* Angelique wondered as she followed him inside. Hadn't she already been reeled in? She had been so determined to keep out of his bed, to keep immune to his potent charm, but as soon as he'd kissed her at the wedding ceremony in

Dharbiri her fate had been sealed. What hope did she have resisting him when his passionate possession made her feel so alive and vital as a woman?

Coming here with him for a two-week 'honeymoon' was only going to make her need of him all the more entrenched. She knew that, but had come anyway, even though she could have made up some excuse to do with her new contract. She had signed and emailed it earlier that day. Her manager had already lined up a shoot with three of the biggest names in haute couture in Paris.

Angelique rubbed her hands up and down her arms as the chilly air of the old house goose-bumped her skin. 'Right now I'm kind of wishing I had gone to Barbados.'

Remy flashed her a quick grin. 'Where's your sense of adventure, *ma petite*? It won't take long to lay a fire.'

'There's central heating. The main switch is over there.'

'I'll see to it and the luggage while you have a wander around. Make yourself at home.'

She gave him a flinty look. 'Excuse me, but up until a few days ago this *was* my home.'

'Then you won't need me to take you on a guided tour, will you?'

Angelique glowered at him. 'Why are you doing this? Why are you rubbing my nose in it like this? I realise you have issues with my father over what happened between him and your grandfather but that's nothing to do with me. I didn't do any dodgy deals. Why am I the scapegoat?'

His look was brooding and intractable. 'This isn't about you, Angelique. Last year your father circulated rumours about me that cost me millions. I don't take that sort of stuff lying down. I wanted revenge, not just for myself but also for what happened to my family. My grandfather almost lost everything when your father pulled the rug from under him.'

'You don't even like your grandfather!' Angelique threw back. 'Why are you so keen to get justice for him?'

'I'm not getting it for him,' Remy said. 'I'm getting it for Rafe. He worked harder than any of us to rebuild our assets. Rafe has always shouldered the responsibility of looking after Raoul and me. I wanted to do my bit to show him his sacrifice hadn't gone unnoticed or been taken for granted.'

'Don't you care that you're hurting me in the process?'

'How am I hurting you?' His expression turned mocking. 'You're the one who just landed a multimillion-dollar contract simply because you're married to me. I have yet to reap any benefits, especially if this Mappleton deal falls through.'

*But I don't even want that contract. I shouldn't have signed it. I wish I hadn't.*

Angelique pushed the errant thoughts back and planted her hands on her hips. 'I seem to recollect you got some fringe benefits last night.'

His eyes started to smoulder as he closed the distance between them in a couple of lazy strides. 'I didn't hear you complaining.'

She pushed her bottom lip out in a pout. 'I have bruises.'

A frown flickered across his forehead. 'Where?'

Angelique turned over her wrists to show him where his fingers had faintly marked her skin when he'd held her down the night before. Every time she saw the tiny marks she felt a shudder of remembered pleasure go through her. It had been like being branded by him.

Owned by him. Controlled by him. She had been more than willing, which somehow made it worse. She didn't want to need him in such an intensely physical way. She had always been the one in control with men in the past. Being dominated by Remy, even playfully during sex, made her feel as if she was relinquishing all power to him, especially when he still hadn't told her if he was going to give her back her home.

He took her left wrist, brought it up to his mouth and gently brushed his lips against the almost imperceptible mark. 'I'm sorry. I didn't realise I'd hurt you.'

She felt a traitorous ribbon of desire unfurl inside her. 'You didn't hurt me. I just have a tendency to bruise easily.'

His thumb moved over her pulse point. 'Maybe you should be the one who does the tying up next time.'

Angelique arched a brow. 'You'd let me do that?'

His eyes smouldered some more. 'Only if I knew I could get out of it.'

*Like our marriage.*

It wasn't for ever. He wanted to be free as soon as his business deal was signed and secured. The bitter irony was *she* was going to help him achieve it. She would be breaking her own heart. Trashing her dreams. Ruining her hopes.

There would be no happy-ever-after with Remy.

It was foolish to dream of black-haired babies with chocolate-brown eyes. It was crazy to think Remy would ever utter an endearment he actually meant. It was madness to want him to fall in love with her.

*It was madness to have fallen in love with him.*

She would have to fall out of love with him. Quick smart. It would be the ultimate in humiliation to have him find out how she felt. It sounded so pathetic, being hopelessly in love with someone since you were sixteen.

Unrequited love.

Obsessive love.

That was all it was—a fantasy. A teenage infatuation that had grown into an adult fixation.

The sooner she got over it the better.

Angelique stepped back from him with a casual air. 'What plans have you made about food and so on? I'm pretty sure my father wouldn't have left anything healthy and nutritious in the pantry.'

'I've organised a food parcel from our hotel in London. It's in the car with our luggage. I'll do some more shopping tomorrow.'

She widened her eyes in mock surprise. 'You actually *know* how to shop for food?'

'I do occasionally pick up the odd item or two. I quite enjoy it.' He turned to the thermostat on the wall and began adjusting the temperature settings. 'My mother used to take us shopping with her. She was keen for us to experience as normal a life as possible because she hadn't been born to money or privilege. If we behaved well, she'd buy us a *gelato* at the end.' His hand dropped from the panel and he turned. He had a wistful expression on his face. 'Rafe would always have chocolate, Raoul would always have lemon, but I used to have a different flavour each time...'

Angelique studied him for a moment. He looked like he was mentally recalling each and every one of those outings with his mother. The boating accident on the French Riviera that had killed his parents had occurred the year before she had been born. She had only ever known the Caffarelli brothers as orphans. From her youthful perspective they had always seemed terribly sophisticated and racy, with their eye-popping good looks and wealthy lifestyle. But behind the trappings of wealth and privilege was a tragedy that had robbed three little boys of their loving parents.

Angelique remembered too well the shock of feeling alone. The utter desperation she had felt at seeing her mother's body lowered into the ground on the dismally wet and grey morning of the funeral was something she would never forget. The build-up of emotion inside her chest had felt like a tsunami about to break. But somehow she had kept it in because she hadn't wanted to disappoint her father. He had said she must be brave and so she was. But inside a part of her had died and gone with her mother into that cold, black hole in the ground.

Angelique blinked away the memory and said, 'It must have been devastating for you when your parents were killed.'

A screen came down over his face. 'I got over it.' He moved past her to go back outside to get their bags. 'Stay inside out of the cold. I won't be long.'

Had he really got over it? He had only been seven years old. It was young for any child to lose a parent, yet he had not lost one but both. Angelique suspected that, like her, his restlessness and wild, partying lifestyle had come out of that deep pain of being abandoned so suddenly and so young. He was anchorless and yet shied away from anything that would tie him down.

His grandfather Vittorio could not be described as a nurturer. He was a cold, hard, bitter man with a tendency to lose his temper at the least provocation. She hadn't seen Vittorio for a number of years, but in the old days when she and her father had been regular visitors to the Caffarelli villa in Rome she had given him a wide berth.

Of the three boys Remy seemed the most willing to deal with his grandfather. He visited him more often than his brothers and seemed to have a better relationship with him than either Rafe or Raoul, possibly because Remy had always relied on his natural charm to win people over.

Angelique wondered if Vittorio had found out about their marriage yet. It had been three days and as far as she knew Remy hadn't called or spoken to him other than what he'd said on camera when the press had stormed them.

What did his brothers think? Had they contacted him and told him what a fool he was for marrying someone like her? She had always been a bit frightened of Rafe, who was so much older, but Raoul had always been nice to her.

Would he too think it was the worst disaster in the world for Remy to be locked in a marriage with her?

Remy was dusting the snow off his shoulders as he came inside when his phone rang. He knew it was his grandfather because he had set a particular ringtone to Vittorio's number. He deliberately hadn't called Vittorio before now to talk about his marriage to Angelique because that was what his grandfather would have expected, and Remy had learned over time that it was more tactical to do what he *didn't* expect. It gave him more leverage with the old man and, he liked to think, a measure of respect. '*Nonno*, nice of you to call. What's new?'

'I have a newspaper in front of me that says you've married Angelique Marchand.' His grandfather's voice had that thread of steel in it that used to terrify Remy as a young child. 'There's also a photo of you together outside some hotel in London.'

'Is it a nice photo?' Remy asked. 'She'll be hell to live with if it isn't.'

He heard Vittorio's intake of breath. 'Is this a set-up? One of your pranks to gain publicity or something?'

'It's no prank. We're married and we're staying married.' *Until I have that Mappleton deal in the bag.* Not that he could tell his grandfather that. If old man Mappleton got a hint that Remy's marriage to Angelique wasn't authentic, he would pull the plug on any negotiations.

'You always did have a thing for that girl,' Vittorio said.

Remy hadn't realised he'd been so transparent about lusting over her in the past. He'd thought he'd done a pretty good job of disguising it. 'Yes, well, you've seen what she looks like. I'm only human.'

'Why didn't you just screw her and get her out of your system?' Vittorio continued. 'Why on earth did you marry her? Have you got her pregnant or something?'

Remy gave himself a mental shake when an image of Angelique with a baby bump came to mind. 'No, I did not get her pregnant. I'm in love with her.' *Ouch. That hurt. Not sure I want to say that again. It might make it happen.*

*Perish the thought!*

Vittorio gave a disdainful laugh. 'The day you fall in love is the day hell freezes over or I get accepted into heaven. Take your pick; neither of them is going to happen. You don't have the capacity to love. You're exactly like me in that regard. Love is for emotionally weak people who can't survive without being propped up by someone else.'

Remy knew his grandfather was scathing about his brothers for falling in love. He mocked them any chance he could, picking Poppy and Lily to pieces as if they were not real people with feelings but department-store items Rafe and Raoul had picked up that, in Vittorio's opinion, were somehow faulty.

Remy didn't like admitting it but deep down he was starting to feel a little envious of how happy his brothers were. How settled; secure; anchored. His life of flying in and flying out of cities and relationships had always seemed so exciting and satisfying up until now.

He shook off the thought like the snow he'd just brushed off his shoulders. 'Be that as it may, you have to admit she's great to look at. What more could a man ask for than a stunningly beautiful wife who loves him?'

'She's stunning but she's Henri Marchand's daughter. Do you really want to mix your blood with the likes of him?'

*What was his grandfather's obsession about babies?* It was making Remy distinctly uneasy. 'We're leaving the breeding to Rafe and Raoul. Angelique wants to keep her figure.'

Vittorio grunted. 'She won't stay with you. You mark my words. Next thing you know, she'll slap divorce papers on you and take half your assets. You're a fool to enter a marriage without a pre-nuptial agreement. I thought you had more sense than your brothers. Seems I was wrong.'

It did worry Remy about the lack of a pre-nup but he wasn't going to dwell on it while he had other more pressing matters to deal with. Besides, Angelique had her own reasons for wanting the marriage to continue.

The bridal-wear gig was huge. He'd already seen hundreds of tweets about it. It was amusingly ironic to think of her modelling the one type of outfit she loathed more than any other.

'How's that new housemaid working out?' Remy asked.

'She's got a face like a monkey.'

Remy rolled his eyes. Some things never changed. 'I might pop over in a couple of weeks to see you once I've sorted out a few business issues. I'll bring Angelique with me.'

Vittorio gave another cynical grunt. 'That's if she's still with you by then.'

# CHAPTER ELEVEN

ANGELIQUE CAME DOWN to the large sitting room where Remy was stoking a roaring fire. Warmth was spreading throughout the house now the heating was on but the sound of the flames crackling and spitting in the fireplace reminded her of cosy times with her grandparents when she was young.

The removals company had obviously come and taken away her father's personal belongings, leaving just the original furniture. Without Henri's things here it was like stepping back in time to a happier period in her life.

But it still annoyed her that Remy had possession of her family home and was so determined to keep it. It was all very well sleeping with him and fancying herself in love with him, but at the end of the day she had to get her home back.

Her goal was to get the deeds to Tarrantloch back where they belonged. Nothing else was supposed to distract her from that.

Not Remy with his smouldering looks, spine-loosening smile, his magical touch and mind-blowing love-making. She could indulge in an affair with him for the period of their marriage but it had to end with her achieving her mission.

Tarrantloch was meant to be hers and she would not be satisfied until she had it back in her possession.

Remy stood up and glanced at her over his shoulder. 'Warming up?'

'You certainly move fast.' Angelique walked further into the room. 'You've had every trace of my father's occupation of the place removed.'

He kicked a piece of charcoal back into the fire with the side of his shoe before he looked at her again. 'That's normally what a new owner does, is it not?'

Angelique set her jaw. Did he have to rub it in every chance he got? 'What do you plan to do with it?'

'I want to base myself here.' He dusted off his hands from having placed another log on the fire. 'It's private and far enough away from a major city to put off the paparazzi.'

She frowned at him. 'But you're a big city man. You spend most of your time in casinos and clubs. You'd be bored out of your mind up here in the highlands with nothing but the wind and the rain and the snow for company.'

'I don't know about that...' He nudged absently at the fire with the poker. 'Rafe's been raving about the mansion he bought in Oxfordshire—the one that Poppy's grandmother used to work in when she was growing up.' He put the poker back in its holder and faced her again. 'He originally planned to turn it into a luxury hotel for the rich and famous but now he's living there with Poppy. It's home to them now, it's where they plan to bring up a family.'

'That's all very well and good, but you're not a family man,' Angelique pointed out. 'You're going to get lonely up here unless you regularly fly in some party girls to while away the long winter nights.'

He shrugged a shoulder and kicked at another piece of charcoal that had fallen out of the fire. 'It may surprise you, but I don't spend all of my time partying and gambling. That's one of the reasons I love Dharbiri so much. It's so different from the life I live in the city.'

'It's certainly different.' Her tone was wry. 'It's not a place I'm going to forget in a hurry.'

He met her gaze across the glow of the firelight. 'Apart from the sand and the heat it's much the same as here. It has a bleak sort of raw beauty about it. You can hear the silence.'

She gave him a knowing look. 'It might be isolated and a little bleak up here but no one's going to come barging in threatening to flay you alive if you have an unchaperoned woman in your room.'

He acknowledged that with little incline of his head. 'Perhaps not, but I bet there are quaint old ways and customs up here in the highlands and on some of the west coast islands.'

'I still don't think you'll last a winter up here.' Angelique sat down on the sofa and curled her legs underneath her body. 'It can get snowbound for weeks and the wind can bore ice-pick holes in your chest. And don't get me started about the rain in summer. It goes on for weeks at a time. Quite frankly, I don't even know why they bother calling it summer. It should be called the wet season, like in the tropics.' She flicked her hair back behind her shoulders. 'Oh, and did I mention the midges and mosquitoes? They're as big as Clydesdales.'

He crossed one ankle over the other as he leaned against the mantelpiece, a lazy smile curving his lips. 'If it's as bad as you say then why do you love it up here so much?'

She looked at the flickering flames before she answered. 'I spent some of the happiest days of my life up here when I was a child.'

'You came here with your parents?'

'My mother,' Angelique said. 'It was her parents', my grandparents', home. My father never used to come because he was always too busy with work. I think the truth was he didn't get on with my grandparents. They didn't like him. I was too young to remember specific conversations but I got the impression they thought he was two-faced.' She looked back at the fire again. 'They were right. Everything changed when my nanna died. The grief hit my mother hard and then my granddad died less than a year later. It was devastating for my mother. That's when things started to get a little crazy at home.'

Remy was frowning when she looked at him again. 'That's when she became depressed?'

Angelique nodded. 'She must have felt so lonely once her parents were gone. She was shy and lacked confidence, which was probably why my father was attracted to her in the first place. He saw her as someone he could control.'

Remy's frown was more of anger than anything. 'I wish I'd flattened him when I had the chance. What a cowardly son of a bitch.'

'You hurt him far more by taking Tarrantloch off him,' Angelique said. 'And of course by marrying me. That really stung. He won't get over that in a hurry.'

His expression turned rueful. 'Yes, well, my grandfather isn't too happy about it either.'

'You've spoken to him?'

'He called when I was bringing in the bags. And it wasn't to congratulate me.'

'No, I expect not.' She hooked her hands around her

knees. 'I guess the congratulations will come in thick and fast once we divorce.'

The silence was broken only by the hiss and crackle of the flames in the fireplace.

Angelique chanced a glance at him but he was staring into the fire as if it were the most befuddling thing he'd ever seen. Was he worried about their lack of a pre-nup? It was certainly a worrying thing for a man with wealth—or a woman, for that matter—to be exposed to the possibility of a financial carve-up in the event of a divorce.

The only way to avoid it would be to *stay* married.

Which was not something Remy would be likely to suggest, even to keep control of his fortune. He didn't do love and commitment. He was the epitome of the freedom-loving playboy. Tying him down would be like trying to tame a lion with a toothpick.

It wasn't going to happen.

Remy turned from the fire. 'I don't suppose there's any point in asking if you're hungry?'

Angelique unhooked her hands from around her legs. 'I am, actually. It must be the cold wintry air. I used to eat heaps when I came here as a kid. My nanna was a fabulous cook.'

'Your grandparents didn't have a housekeeper?'

'Yes, but nanna still did most of the cooking. I used to help her. I can still make a mean batch of oat cakes and flapjacks.'

He smiled a sexy smile as he held out his hand to her. 'I'm told it can sometimes get very hot in the kitchen.'

Angelique felt a tingle in her core as his strong fingers wrapped around hers. She gave him a sultry look. 'If you think it's going to be too hot for you, then you should stay out of there.'

He brought her up against his body, his *aroused* body. Another tingle coursed through her, making her nipples stand to attention. His gaze zeroed in on her mouth for a pulsing beat. 'I'm pretty sure I can handle it.'

She moved against him, just the once, but it made his eyes go almost black with desire. 'You think?'

He swept her up in his arms and carried her towards the door. 'Let's go and find out.'

Remy slid her down his body once they got to the kitchen. Her body inflamed his; he had been burning for her ever since they'd arrived. It seemed years since he'd last made love with her but it had only been last night. And what a night that had been.

He craved her.

Ached for her.

His groin was tight with longing; he wanted to sink into her and lose himself. Block his thoughts—the rational, sensible ones, that was. He wanted to feel the magic of her touch, the way her body clenched so tightly around him as if she never wanted to let him go. He could not remember a more passionate, exciting lover. It felt different somehow...more intense; as if his skin had developed a new, overly sensitive layer that only responded to her touch.

Remy started playing with her lower lip in little tug-and-release bites. 'How's the heat so far?'

She snaked her arms up around his neck and threaded her fingers through his hair. 'Not hot enough.' She slid her tongue into his mouth and he nearly disgraced himself then and there.

He took control of the kiss, deepening the thrusts of his tongue as it chased and subdued hers. She gave little gasps and encouraging groans, her body pressing as close as she physically could. He felt her mound rubbing against his erection, a tantalising tease of the delights to come.

He lifted her up on to the kitchen bench and stood between her spread thighs. 'You're wearing too many clothes,' he growled against her mouth.

She nibbled at his lips. 'That would be because it's below freezing outside.'

He grabbed at the back of his cashmere sweater and tugged it over his head. Next came his shirt, which lost a button or two in the process. 'Now let's start on you.'

She gave him a seductive look as she undid the tiny pearl buttons of her designer cardigan. She was wearing a black lacy camisole underneath that showed the shadow of her cleavage and the perfect globes of her breasts. 'I'm not wearing a bra.'

His groin tightened another notch. 'I can see that.'

She peeled the shoestring straps over her shoulders, one by one, lowering the lacy garment slowly, like a high-class stripper. 'You want to touch me, don't you?'

*I want to do more than touch you.* 'What gives you that idea?' Remy did his deadpan face.

Her lips curved upwards in a siren's smile. 'I'm not going to let you touch me until I'm good and ready. You have to be a good boy and wait.' She lowered her camisole a little further, revealing a tightly budded pink nipple. 'Do you think you can do that?'

Remy had to count backwards to stop himself from jumping the gun. His need was pulsating with such relentless force it was painful. 'I'll wait, but you do realise at some point in the future you're going to pay for this, don't you?'

She gave a little mock shiver. 'Ooh! Is that supposed to scare me?'

'Be scared,' he growled. 'Be very scared.'

She exposed her other breast, all the while holding his gaze with the dancing, mischievous heat of hers. She glided her hand down over her belly to the waistband of her pencil-thin designer jeans. 'I'm wet. I bet you want to feel how wet, don't you?'

Remy had never been so turned on. He was fighting to keep his hands off her. He couldn't think about anything but the need to thrust into her to the hilt and explode. 'I'm hard. I bet you want to feel how hard, huh?'

Her eyes sparkled as she traced a fingertip down the ridge of his erection through the fabric of his trousers. 'Mmm; impressive.' She took the same fingertip and traced it down the denim-covered seam of her body. 'I guess I should get out of my jeans. Would you like that?'

*I would love that.* 'Take your time.'

She slithered down off the bench, pushing him back with a fingertip. 'Not so close, big boy. You don't get to touch until I give the go ahead.'

Remy mentally gulped. This was going to end badly if she didn't speed things up a bit. He could feel his erection straining against his jeans. He just hoped the fabric was strong enough to hold him in.

She was definitely going to pay for this.

And it would involve a leather whip and handcuffs.

Angelique locked gazes with him and slowly undid her zipper. The sound of it going down was magnified in the throbbing silence. She stepped out of her heels and then she peeled the jeans off her legs. Once they were off she stepped back into her heels, leaving just the black lace of her knickers on. 'So...' She ran the tip of her tongue over her lower lip leaving it wet and glistening. 'Are you getting excited?'

*Way, way beyond that.* 'What do you think?'

She traced his erection again, her eyes still holding his in a sexy little lock that made his blood heat to boiling. 'How badly do you want me?'

*Off the scale.* 'Let's put it this way. Right now I could do you in five seconds flat.'

Her eyes flared and then her lips pushed forwards in a pout. 'That sounds like I would be left high and dry.'

'Don't worry. I'd take you along for the ride.'

She put that teasing fingertip to work again. 'What if I was to strike up a little deal with you?'

Remy marvelled at her self-control. He'd always thought he was a master at keeping his desire under his command but she had pushed him to the very limit. His body was a mass of twitching nerve endings and primal urgings. But he was still in enough control— only just—to recognise manipulation when he saw it. 'What sort of deal?'

She slowly lowered his zipper. 'A deal where we both get what we want.'

He sucked in a breath as her fingers tugged his underwear aside. It was hard to think straight when she was touching him, stroking him to the very edge, but he was not going to be tricked or manoeuvred into giving away what he had spent years fighting to gain.

Besides, he hadn't just done it for himself: he had done it for his brothers. It wasn't his prize to give away. It represented far more than a victory over a double-crossing enemy. Taking ownership of Tarrantloch was finally setting right the wrongs of the past. Handing it over to the sole heir of the man who had almost destroyed his family's fortune was the very last thing he would consider doing, no matter what his relationship with Angelique was. Or wasn't.

He pushed her hand away and stepped back from her.

'Game over, *ma belle*. I'm not giving you Tarrantloch in exchange for a quick screw up against the kitchen bench. I'm not *that* desperate.'

Her expression switched from sexy siren to outraged virago within a heartbeat. 'You bastard.'

'*Orphan* is the correct term.'

She came at him then like a spitting cat, all claws, snarls and scratches. 'I hate you!'

Remy restrained her by holding both of her flailing arms behind her back, which rather delightfully pushed her pelvis into blistering contact with his. 'You don't hate me. You want me.'

Her grey-blue eyes flashed venom at him. 'Why won't you give me what I want?'

He ripped her knickers down with a ruthless jerk of his hand. 'What do you want the most?' He probed her folds with his painfully erect penis. 'Tell me. Right now, what do you want the most?'

He heard her swallow as he made contact with her slippery moistness. 'I want what's rightfully mine.'

'Then at least we're on the same page,' he said and then he sealed her mouth roughly with his.

Angelique lost herself in his kiss. To be truthful she had lost herself the day she had flown to Dharbiri. Remy had taken control of not just the situation, but also her life and perhaps even her destiny. He had introduced passion and excitement to her and now there was no going back. She didn't want to go back.

How was she going to live without this rush of excitement every time his mouth met with hers?

She had thought she would play him at his own game: up the stakes, tantalise him, tease him until he gave in, but he had turned her efforts around to his advantage.

He was not going to be hoodwinked out of relinquishing Tarrantloch. Nothing she did or offered was going to change his mind.

Tarrantloch was his talisman of success.

His only weakness that she could see was that he wanted her. But even that need was under his tight control. She had ramped up his desire to the point where she thought he would agree to anything.

But it seemed she was the one who was the more desperate.

His mouth was hard against hers but she worked at softening it with little pull-backs and strokes of her tongue. Once he'd eased off a bit she nipped at his lower lip with her teeth, and then laved it with the glide of her tongue.

She felt him rummaging around for a condom, his hands leaving her in order to apply it, but his mouth didn't budge from plundering hers.

He was at her entrance and nudging to possess her. She opened her legs and stood up on tiptoe to welcome him. He surged so thickly and so forcefully she felt her back bump the bench behind. He set a furious pace but her body was so wet, and aching so much, it was a blessed and welcome assault of her senses to feel him pumping so hard. She came almost immediately, not even needing the coaxing stroke of his fingers. All it took was a little roll and tilt of her pelvis and she was flying off into the stratosphere, screaming and sobbing all the way.

He didn't waste time waiting for her to come back to earth. He rocketed after her with a deep, primal grunt as he unloaded. She felt the rise of goose bumps over his back as she held him against her, his hectic breathing a harsh sound in the silence.

Angelique wanted to hate him for turning the tables on her but somehow she couldn't access that emotion right now. So instead she held him and stroked her hands over his back and shoulders, planting soft little teasing kisses to his neck and behind his earlobes.

He eased back from her but only so he could rest his forehead against hers. Their breaths mingled intimately in the space between their mouths. 'I wasn't too rough, was I?' His voice sounded gruff, almost apologetic.

Angelique trailed a fingertip over his bottom lip. 'I wanted you any way I could have you.'

His dark gaze meshed with hers. 'You really turn me on like no other woman I've ever been with, but I have a feeling but you already know that.'

She smiled a little smile and did another circuit with her finger, this time pushing it into his mouth so he could suck on it. It sent a shudder down her spine when he did. His mouth was hot and moist, and his tongue a sexy rasp against her soft skin. When she pulled it out she said in a voice that wasn't quite even. 'You do a pretty fine job of lighting my fire too.'

He held her gaze for an interminable moment. 'We should do something about a meal. I don't want you fading away on me. I have plans for you and, believe me, you're going to need your stamina.'

She traced each of his eyebrows in turn, a playful smile pushing up the corners of her mouth. 'When you look at me like that, I get a wobbly feeling in my girly bits.'

His eyes glinted dangerously as he tugged her back against him. 'And so you damn well should,' he said and brought his mouth down to hers.

# CHAPTER TWELVE

REMY WATCHED AS Angelique slept in the tumble of sheets, pillows and bedcoverings that had become their love-making nest over the last three weeks. He had extended their stay because a sudden snowfall had made it impossible for Robert Mappleton to get to their meeting so Remy had to postpone it until the roads cleared.

And what a time it had been.

He and Angelique had made love not just in the bedroom but the bathroom and the sofa in the sitting room; the morning room; the linen room; the utilities room and the kitchen four or five times over. Angelique had delighted him, shocked him, teased and tantalised him until he only had to look at her and his body would swell with lust.

He had lit a fire in the master bedroom. The flickering flames were casting their usual golden glow over the room. There was another fluttering of snow outside; he could see it falling silently past the windows in ghostly handfuls. It had been snowing on and off for a couple of days now but the roads were open again. He felt a niggling sense of disappointment as he had secretly harboured a fantasy of being snowed in with her for weeks on end. Maybe right up to and including Christmas.

Every couple of days they had driven to the village

to buy supplies at the local store. He liked the normality of it, the hunting and gathering that was an everyday occurrence for most people. Angelique knew a few of the locals and had stopped and chatted to them, introducing him as her husband with a naturalness that made him feel like a fraud. If she felt the same way, she showed no sign of it.

Robert Mappleton had left by helicopter that afternoon after an overnight stay. Angelique had shown the class and grace he had come to expect from her. It seemed she could be whatever he wanted or needed her to be: a playful, adventurous lover; an intrepid hiker across the moors or through the forest; a gourmet cook in the kitchen and an engaging, convivial hostess. She had made the old man feel at home, plying him with fabulous home-cooked food and old-fashioned highland hospitality. Mappleton had been charmed—besotted would have been closer to the mark. He had spent most of the time chatting to Angelique and had only given Remy his attention—and cursorily, at that—to sign the papers to hand over the Mappleton chain for a princely sum.

Remy knew he should be feeling happy. Proud. Satisfied. Victorious.

But his mind was restless.

It was time to put an end to this madness but Angelique had a photo shoot lined up in Paris the following day to kick-start her new modelling career. He could hardly walk out on her when so much was at stake for her. As least modelling bridal wear would be better for her than swimwear. There would be less pressure on her to be rail-thin all the time. Over the last few days he had noticed her eating a little more than usual. It had delighted him to see her enjoy her food instead of seeing it as an enemy.

*Talking of enemies...*

He was having more and more trouble thinking of her as an opponent. He looked at her lying next to him; at the way the light fell on her cheekbone as she was lying with her head resting on one of her hands. She looked so peaceful. Relaxed and sated.

He felt a little free-fall inside his stomach as he recalled the way she had crawled all over him earlier that night. His body was still humming with the aftershocks of having her ride him.

Was there no end to this driving lust he felt for her? He kept waiting to feel that flat feeling of boredom, the tinge of irritation that nearly always occurred about now in his relationships. He would look at the woman in his bed and wonder: *what was I thinking?*

But when he looked at Angelique in his bed, he thought: *how can I keep her there?*

Angelique made a sleepy sound from the tangle of sheets and then opened her eyes. 'What time is it?'

'Late. Or early. I guess it depends on whether you're a night owl or a lark.'

She sat up and pushed her dark hair back over her naked shoulders. 'I'm not sure what I am any more. I think I've crossed too many time zones or something.'

Remy pushed himself away from the mantelpiece. 'I'm cooking breakfast this morning. I think it's time you had a break from the kitchen.'

Her brows lifted. 'Wonders will never cease. I never thought I'd see the day when you put on an apron.'

He grinned at her. 'Not only that, I actually picked up a towel and hung it back on the rack. How's that for becoming domesticated?'

She gave him a beady look. 'Toilet seat?'

'Down.'

She gave a slow smile. 'Wow. That's pretty impressive. Maybe there's hope for you as a husband after all. Some girl in the future is really going to thank me for training you.' She tapped her finger against her lips musingly. 'Maybe I should think about opening a school for future husbands. There could be a big market for that: *give me your man and I'll whip him into shape.* What do you think?'

'Did you say *whip*?'

'I meant that metaphorically.'

'Pity.'

Her eyes danced with mischief and his blood raced. 'You don't really want me to beat you, do you?' she asked.

He came over to the bed and tipped up her chin with the end of his finger. 'I sometimes wonder if I'll ever know the real you. You're full of surprises.'

Her look was all sexy siren. 'Who do you want me to be?'

He dropped his hand from her chin. He felt strangely dissatisfied by her answer. He was all for playing games when it suited him, but he wanted to *know* her: the *real* Angelique Marchand. What she felt and thought and believed in. What she valued.

*Who she loved.*

It was ironic but in many ways she reminded him of himself. She had forged a reputation for herself as scatty and irresponsible, as a wild tearaway who had no intention of putting down roots. She had shied away from commitment like he did. She had hated the thought of the formality and entrapment of marriage. She was a free spirit who wanted to live and enjoy life on her terms.

But was that who she really was? Or was it what she thought people expected her to be?

Remy tried to think of another girl who would be in his bed in the flickering firelight some time in the future and couldn't quite do it. He kept seeing Angelique with her fragrant cloud of dark hair, her arresting grey-blue eyes and her bee-stung mouth with its lush, kiss-me ripeness...

He gave himself a mental shake.

He wasn't interested in a future with her. He wasn't interested in a future with anyone.

He was interested in the here and now.

Today and tomorrow were his only focus.

He didn't want to think any further ahead.

Angelique swung her legs over the edge of the bed, but as she stood up she tottered for a moment and went a ghastly shade of white. He put out a hand to steady her. 'Are you all right?'

She looked a little dazed for a moment or two but then her colour slowly returned. 'Whoa, that was strange. I thought I was going to faint. It's not like I've not been eating enough. I still feel full from all that chocolate pudding I had last night.'

He pushed a tiny tendril of hair back from her face. 'Maybe I've been keeping you up too late.'

She smiled cheekily as she danced her fingertips down his bare forearm. He felt the electric shock of her touch all the way to his groin. 'I'm the one who's been keeping you up.'

He was up right now—painfully so. But she was still looking peaky even if she was putting on a brave front. He knew that about her if nothing else. She was excellent at hiding behind various masks. He gently patted her on the behind. 'Have your shower while I rustle up some breakfast. How does bacon and eggs sound?'

The colour drained from her face again and she quickly thrust a hand to her mouth and bolted for the *en suite*. Remy followed her to find her hunched over the toilet seat, retching without actually bringing anything up. 'Oh, *ma petite*, why didn't you say you were feeling sick?' he said.

She wiped her mouth on the face cloth he handed her. 'I didn't feel sick until you mentioned… Urgh.' She gave a little shudder. 'I'm not even going to say the words.'

'Shall I call a doctor?'

'What on earth for?' She got to her feet and grabbed her hair and, using its length, tied it in a loose knot behind her head. 'It's just a stomach bug. I've had them before. It'll pass in twenty-four hours or so.'

He reached for her forehead but it was clammy rather than hot. 'Do you want to go back to bed?'

She pushed his hand away, a little frown creasing her forehead. 'Stop fussing, Remy. I'm fine.'

'You look pale.'

'I haven't got my make-up on.'

'Personally, I prefer you without it.' He followed her back into the bedroom. 'Are you sure you don't want me to call a doctor?'

'And make me look like a drama queen for dragging him or her out here to diagnose a virus? No thanks.'

Remy pulled back the covers on the bed. 'In. Rest for an hour and see how you feel.'

She rolled her eyes and flopped back down on the bed. 'You should keep well away from me. It might be catching.'

'I'll risk it.'

'I should probably warn you, I'm not a very good nurse. I have no patience or compassion.'

He smiled as he touched her cheek with a lazy finger. 'I think you'd make a very good nurse. You'd look hot in a uniform too.'

She cranked one eye open. 'I thought you preferred me without clothes?'

He gave her hand a gentle squeeze. 'Right now I'd prefer you to rest up. We have to get you to Paris in tip-top shape.'

'And after Paris?'

'We have Raoul and Lily's wedding.'

A little frown pulled at her brow. 'Are you sure I should go to that?'

'I want you there.' He meant it, which was a little surprising. Worrying, actually. He had to let her go at some point; no point dragging this on too long.

'But I thought once your business deal with Robert Mappleton was done we were going to go our separate ways.'

Remy searched her gaze but he wasn't sure what he was looking for. 'It would look a bit suspicious if we parted within a day or two of the contract being signed. And your manager is going to be pretty pissed with you if you suddenly announce you're getting a divorce. I think we should leave things as they are until after Raoul and Lily's wedding. It's only a matter of weeks. We can reassess things in the New Year.'

'What have you told your brothers about us? Surely they know the truth?'

'Yes, but that's not the point. I don't want a big press fest on our break-up occurring right in the middle of Raoul and Lily's wedding.'

Remy had spoken to Raoul not long after Rafe had

called. But, rather than berate him for marrying Angelique, he had said what his grandfather had said—that he'd always sensed Remy had a thing for her and that his little spin about her being hell on heels didn't ring true with him. It had annoyed Remy to think he hadn't disguised his feelings as well as he'd thought. What would Raoul make of his feelings now?

Angelique's gaze narrowed. 'You're not falling in love with me, are you?'

He coughed out a laugh. 'Are you joking? I've never fallen in love in my life.'

'Good.' She closed her eyes again. 'I don't want any hearts broken when this is over.'

Remy got up from the bed. 'I'll come and check on you in an hour.'

'I'll be back in the ring and punching by then.'

'I'll look forward to it.'

He walked to the door but when he turned back to look at her she had turned her back and was huddled into a tight ball.

Something shifted in his chest: a slippage; a gear not quite meshing with its cogs.

He shook off the feeling and walked out, closing the door softly behind him.

Angelique rolled over to her back, pressing a hand to her churning stomach. She was due for a period. She had taken herself off the pill months ago because she felt the brand she'd been on was making her put on weight. She hadn't bothered renewing her prescription because she hadn't been dating anyone. But she didn't feel period pain, just this wretched, churning nausea. That near-faint had happened a few times before when she hadn't eaten enough. But she could hardly use the lack of food as an excuse because she had been eating normally over the last couple of weeks. The thought of not having to bare her body all the time in a bikini was like being let out of prison. She was almost getting excited about the Paris shoot. Almost.

She swung her legs over the edge of the bed again and tested her balance. So far so good. Her stomach was uneasy but her head was more or less clear. She padded back to the bathroom and stepped into the shower. She closed her eyes as the water cascaded down and mentally calculated when her last period had been—was it four weeks or five?

She was occasionally overdue; disruptions came with the stress of dieting and travelling.

Anyway, they'd used condoms. The failure rate was miniscule...but enough to be slightly worrying. Terrifyingly worrying.

Angelique put a hand to her concave belly. It wasn't possible. She wasn't the type of girl to get herself pregnant. It just couldn't happen.

She thought of the first time when Remy had taken for ever to withdraw. Had some of his Olympic-strong swimmers sneaked out past the barrier of the condom and gone in search of one of her desperate little eggs?

*Oh, traitorous body and even more traitorous hormones!*

Panic set in. She felt it clutch at her insides. She felt it move over her skin like a clammy shiver. She felt it hammering in her chest.

She couldn't be pregnant. *She couldn't be.*

Buying a pregnancy test in a village this small was out of the question. She would have to wait until she got to Paris. And then after Paris, baby or no baby, she would have to attend Raoul and Lily's wedding and pretend everything was normal in front of their family and friends. It seemed so tacky to be attending a romantic wedding when theirs had been so extravagant yet so meaningless.

Angelique felt a pang of envy for Raoul's bride-to-be, Lily. How excited she must be getting prepared for her wedding. Doing all the girly things to make her day so special. Angelique cringed when she thought of her wedding to Remy. The whole thing had been nothing but a big, overblown sham. She was a fraud. A fake bride. A fake wife. And this was a fake honeymoon.

If she was pregnant would Remy insist on her staying with him for the sake of the child? He would end up hating her for tying him down. He might even end up hating the child.

Angelique bit her lip as she looked in the mirror at her body. For years she had denied her body, punished her body, controlled her body, but now it would not just be hers but the shelter in which her baby—hers and Remy's baby—would grow and develop.

She could not think of getting rid of it. It was certainly an option and one she felt other women were entitled to make. But it wasn't for her.

She put a hand to her flat belly. How could it be possible that she and Remy had made a baby? He didn't even like her.

Well, maybe that wasn't quite true. He certainly didn't hate her any more. She had seen him looking at her with lust, longing, amusement, and even annoyance when she got in the last word, but not hatred.

Their relationship had changed over the last three weeks. They still bickered occasionally but it was a sort of foreplay. They were both strong-willed and determined and didn't like losing an argument or debate.

It was foolish of her to have fallen in love with him

but it had happened so long ago it was pointless flagellating herself about it now. She had fallen in love with him at the age of fifteen.

She still remembered the day it had happened. She had gone with her father to Vittorio's villa for a function. Remy had been home for a visit and he'd been assigned the task of keeping her entertained while her father and Vittorio had a business meeting before dinner. She had been waiting in the home entertainment room, idly leafing through one of her fashion magazines, when Remy had come in. She hadn't seen him in a year or two. Her heart had quite literally stopped when he had come in. He had been so tall and so staggeringly handsome, with that lazy smile that had travelled all the way to his eyes.

But as soon as she had stood up his smile had disappeared. He'd seemed a little taken aback seeing her dressed in a short denim skirt and a clinging top that revealed a generous amount of cleavage due to the brand-new push-up bra she'd bought.

He had cleared his throat, walked briskly over to the television, selected a movie and set it running. 'There, that should keep you happy for a while.'

'I'm not twelve,' she'd said with a pout.

He'd pushed a hand through his thick overly long hair. 'It's a good movie. It won two Oscar nomination and three Golden Globes.'

She had put on her beseeching face. 'Will you watch it with me?'

He had muttered something that sounded very much like an English swear word before he had sat down on the sofa furthest away from her. But he had stayed and watched it with her. He'd even laughed at the funny bits, and at one point paused the movie to go and get some popcorn he'd charmed one of the housemaids to make.

Yes, falling in love with him had been the easy bit.

*Falling out of love was going to be the kicker.*

# CHAPTER THIRTEEN

'ARE YOU SURE you're all right?' Remy asked Angelique when they landed in Paris. 'You've been so quiet and you still look a little pale.'

'I'm fine.' She gave him a tight smile. 'I'm just nervous. The thought of all those wedding dresses is enough to make my insides churn.'

He put an arm around her waist as they walked out to the waiting car. 'You'll blow everyone away as soon as you walk up that aisle.'

Angelique hadn't been sick for the last couple of days but she still felt queasy in the stomach. She had managed to keep it from Remy but then saw a pharmacy ahead and wondered how she could sneak in and get a testing kit without him noticing. But just then his phone rang and she seized the opportunity. She pointed to the ladies' room and mouthed the words to him about needing to take a pit stop. He nodded and turned away, plugging one ear so he could hear the conversation without all the noise of the busy airport terminal.

Angelique walked briskly into the shop and bought tampons—that was her positive thinking working overtime—and a pregnancy kit. She put both items in her tote bag and came out with her heart thumping so loudly she could feel it in her throat.

Remy was still talking on the phone and only turned around when she appeared by his side. He ended the call and slipped his arm back around her waist. 'That was Robert Mappleton. He said to say hi.'

'He's a very nice man,' Angelique said, falling in step beside him as they made their way out to the waiting car. 'He really misses his wife. She died eight years ago after a long struggle with breast cancer. They'd been married for forty-nine years. She used to do a lot of the background work in the business. I think that's why it went downhill so badly. He's been grieving all this time.'

Remy glanced down at her. 'He told you all that?'

She nodded. 'We talked about the grieving process—the denial, the anger, the bargaining, transition and then acceptance. I told him how lost I'd felt when my mother died. He was very understanding. He and his wife couldn't have children.' She gave a little sigh. 'Wouldn't it be cool if we could choose our parents? I would've loved a father like Robert Mappleton instead of my own.'

Remy's arm tightened protectively. 'I wish I could have mine back, just for a day, to tell him how much he meant to me. And my mother.'

Angelique leaned against his shoulder. 'They'd be very proud of you and your brothers.'

His expression clouded and he looked away. 'Of Rafe and Raoul maybe, but me? I'm not so sure.'

'But why? You've just nailed the biggest deal of your career. It's bigger than anything your brothers have done.'

He looked at her again. It was a hard look: cynical; jaded. 'It's just another deal.' He dropped his arm from her waist and took her hand instead. 'Come on. We'd better get you to the church on time.'

Remy stood at the back of the photo shoot in one of Paris's gothic cathedrals as Angelique was photographed in a variety of bridal outfits. She looked stunning in every one of them. It made him think of their wedding back in Dharbiri. She had looked fabulous then too, but nothing about that day had been real.

He couldn't help imagining her as a real bride, walking down the aisle not to a crowd of photographers but to him.

He blinked and shook his head. It was definitely too hot and stuffy in here or something.

He looked back at the action playing out in front of him. The photographers, all six of them, issued commands and directions, which Angelique followed tirelessly like the consummate professional she was. Her manager had come over and introduced herself earlier, telling him how Angelique's star was set to shine brighter than any model she had represented before.

Remy felt proud of Angelique in a way he had never quite expected to feel. He had always thought her spoilt and wilful, yet seeing how she treated the more junior staff on the shoot with respect and kindness made him realise he had seriously misjudged her.

*You're falling for her.*

*No, I'm not.*

*Yes, you are. Big time.*

Remy's phone vibrated in his pocket but instead of ignoring it he welcomed the distraction. He didn't even check the screen to see who was calling as he stepped outside the cathedral to answer it. 'Remy Caffarelli.'

'I want you and your brothers here tomorrow for a family meeting,' Vittorio said.

*Typical*. His grandfather always expected everyone to dance around him at a moment's notice. Remy would go when he was good and ready and not before. 'I can't drop everything just because you fancy a family get-together.'

'Where are you?'

'In Paris with Angelique. She's working.'

'She wouldn't know how to work unless it was flat on her back.'

Anger tightened every muscle in Remy's spine. 'That's my wife you're insulting. I won't have you or anyone speak about her like that.'

'If you don't come here tomorrow I'll tell the press your marriage to that little black-haired slut is nothing but a sham.'

Remy felt a cold hand of dread grab at his guts. It wasn't the deal with Robert Mappleton he was most worried about. What would happen to Angelique's new-found career if that sort of leak got out before her first shoot was even over?

How on earth had Vittorio found out? His brothers would never have betrayed him. He had sworn them to secrecy.

There could only be one person who would want to do the dirty on him even if it hurt his only daughter in the process.

Henri Marchand.

Angelique came over to where Remy was standing at the back of the church once her shoot was over for the day. 'I didn't expect you to stay the whole time. You must be bored out of your brain. There's nothing more tediously boring than watching mascara dry— Hey, is something wrong? Why are you frowning like that? Are you cross with me?'

Remy forcibly relaxed his frown. 'Sorry, *ma petite*. It's not you. It's my grandfather. He's insisting on a family meeting tomorrow. He won't take no for an answer. Can you ask for a day off? I know it's short notice.'

She frowned at him. 'He wants *me* there? But why?'

'I'll explain it later. I don't want anyone listening in. Do you think you can get tomorrow off?'

'I'm sure it'll be fine. There's been a delay on the next collection. Mackenzie just told me about it. We're shooting at a private château in Vichy the day after tomorrow so I'm all yours till then.'

Remy put his arm around her shoulders and hugged her close. 'Best news I've had all day.'

Angelique didn't have time to do anything about the pregnancy test because Remy had organised a flight straight to Rome. She tried to put her worries to the back of her mind. She was probably imagining her symptoms anyway. Stress always made her stomach churn. And being late with a period was certainly not unusual; it came with the territory of dieting and travelling across time zones.

And, to be fair, Remy had been keeping her up late at night, not that she was complaining. The nights in his arms were the highlight of her day. Not that he had restricted their passionate interludes to the evenings: mornings, mid-morning, lunchtimes, afternoons and evenings had been spent in a variety of activities that had made every cell in her body shudder with delight.

It worried her that it might soon be over. His deal was done and dusted. The only thing keeping them together was her modelling contract—a contract she didn't even want.

Rafe and Poppy arrived just as they were getting out of the car at Vittorio's villa, so there was no chance of slipping away and finding out one way or the other about the result.

Rafe was distinctly cool with Angelique but Poppy was anything but. She wrapped her arms around Angelique and gave her a warm hug. 'It's so lovely to meet you.' She pulled back to look at her. 'Oh. My. God. You're *so* beautiful! I'm having such a fan moment. I feel I should be asking for your autograph or something.'

Angelique loved her already. 'Congratulations on your marriage.' It was the first thing she thought of to say.

Poppy's toffee-brown eyes twinkled. 'Congratulations on yours.' She leaned in close so the boys couldn't hear. 'And all that rubbish about it being a sham just to save your necks doesn't fool me for a second.'

Angelique quickly schooled her features. She wasn't ready to play confidante just yet, even if Poppy was the sort of girl she longed to have as a best friend. 'Sorry to burst your bubble, but I'm not in love with him. We're just making the most of being stuck together. I've always fancied him, but then what girl with a pulse wouldn't?'

'Oh, well…sorry. I just thought… Never mind.' Poppy's flustered look was replaced with a smile. 'Just wait until you meet Lily, Raoul's fiancée. She's a darling. She's quite shy but once you get to know her I'm sure you'll adore her.'

'I'm not worried about Lily or Raoul,' Angelique

said. 'It's Vittorio I'm concerned with. I've always been a little terrified of him.'

Poppy rolled her eyes. 'Tell me about it. I avoid him as much as possible. So do Rafe and Raoul. I think Remy is the only one who can crack a smile out of him. But you know him, don't you? Rafe told me you used to come here a lot when your father and Vittorio were business partners.'

'Yes, but it was a long time ago, and there's been a lot of dirty water under the bridge since then.'

Poppy gave her a friendly smile. 'Maybe, but you weren't the one to put it there. Now, let's go and meet Lily and Raoul. That's their car arriving. See?'

Angelique watched as a slim ash-brown-haired young woman stepped out of the car to go around to the driver's side with a pair of crutches. 'I thought Raoul couldn't walk any more?'

'He can take a few steps now,' Poppy said. 'Lily's been amazing for him. They're just the most adorable couple. Check out the way he looks at her. It just makes me melt.'

Angelique felt an ache around her heart when she saw Raoul take the crutches from Lily. He smiled a smile that was so much more than a smile. It was the smile of a man hopelessly in love. But when she looked at Lily she saw the same thing: Lily was besotted with Raoul and was not one bit ashamed about showing it.

They came over to where the rest of them were standing. Raoul leaned heavily on his crutches to offer a hand to Angelique. 'Welcome to the family, Angelique. It's good to have you here again. It's been a long time. Too long.'

Angelique felt a sudden rush of emotion. Raoul had

always been the nicest to her. '*Merci.* I'm sorry about your accident. I sent a card. Did you get it?'

He gave her a warm smile. 'It meant a lot to me. It made me smile, which I wasn't doing a lot of back then.' He rebalanced on his crutches so he could get Lily to step forward. '*Ma chérie*, this is Angelique, an old family friend and now Remy's wife. Angelique, this is my fiancée, Lily Archer.'

Angelique took Lily's hand. 'I'm very pleased to meet you.'

'And you,' Lily said with a shy smile. 'Wow, you really are as stunning as you are on those billboards and in those magazines.'

'You should see me before breakfast,' Angelique said. 'I spend a fortune on cover-up and I'm on a constant diet. How I look is totally fake.' *I'm a fake.*

Lily's smile said she didn't believe it for a second. 'Maybe you could give me some make-up tips for my wedding. I'm not very good at that stuff.'

'I would be happy to. You have amazing blue eyes. They're so incredibly dark. Has anyone ever told you that?'

Lily smiled and glanced at Raoul who was looking at her with such a tender look it made Angelique's heart suddenly contract. 'Yes; yes, they have. Many times.'

There was a rumble from inside the villa like a dragon emerging from his cave. Vittorio suddenly appeared at the front door with a savage frown between his brows as his gaze fell on Angelique. 'I always knew you'd be trouble. You're just like your two-faced father.'

Angelique stepped forward with her shoulders back and her chin at a combative height. 'I don't think it's fair that I should be judged for the wrongs my father did to you and your family. I had nothing to do with it. I'm an innocent party.'

Vittorio glared at her. 'There's not too much about you that's innocent.'

Angelique stared him down. 'Yes, well, perhaps there's some truth in that, given what your grandson has been doing with me over the last three or four weeks.'

'You shameless hussy!' Vittorio spat at her. 'I bet your double-dealing father put you up to this. No wonder he couldn't wait to crow about it when he called me the other day. You tricked Remy into marrying you so you could carve up his assets when you bail out of it.'

Remy stepped up and put an arm around Angelique's waist. 'I've already warned you about speaking about or to Angelique in a disrespectful manner. She is my wife, and you will treat her with the respect accorded to that position.'

Vittorio curled his top lip. 'How long are you going to keep her? She's not going to stay with you. She'll do the dirty on you first chance she gets. You've left yourself wide open. She's a witch. A Jezebel. You're crazy to think she's going to stick by you. She'll take half of what you own because you've been thinking with your—'

'I'm not taking anything that isn't rightly mine,' Angelique said.

Vittorio laughed. 'Do you think my grandson will hand that castle over just because you opened your legs for him? He's not that much of a fool. His winning that property off your father was the one time I felt proud to call him my grandson. He won't relinquish a prize like that. He's too much like me to give in just because a beautiful woman bats her eyelashes at him.'

'That's enough!' Remy barked. 'Stop it right there.'

Poppy came to the rescue. 'I think it's time for us

girls to get to know one another over some devil's food cake, which strangely enough seems rather appropriate just now. You boys can have your family meeting. We want no part of it.'

Lily touched Angelique's hand. 'Maybe this would be a good time to swap make-up tips.'

'You could be right,' Angelique said.

Rafe took Remy aside after Vittorio had stormed off in a temper. 'You OK?'

Remy clenched and unclenched his fists. 'I swear to God I could have punched him for that.'

'Yes, well, maybe you're feeling hot under the collar because there's a bit of truth in what he said.'

Remy glared at his brother. 'Don't you start. I'm nothing like him.'

Rafe gave him his 'older and wiser' look. 'We're all a bit like him, Remy. There's no point trying to hide from it. It's best to face it and deal with it. We've all used people to get what we want. We've learned it off him. But it doesn't mean we have to go on being like that. I know I've always taught you and Raoul to set goals and to focus, but I've come to realise that winning at any cost is not always the right or the wisest thing to do.'

'I know what I'm doing.' Remy tightened his jaw. 'I don't need your advice or guidance any more.'

Rafe gave his shoulder a squeeze. 'Sorry. I have this lifetime habit of feeling responsible for you. You're old enough to make your own decisions.'

*And take full responsibility for them*, Remy thought.

'Is Angelique all right?' Raoul asked as he came over once Rafe had left to join Poppy and the girls. 'She looked really pale and fragile. You haven't been giving her a hard time, have you?'

Remy slid his brother a look. 'Trust you to be the softie. She's fine. She's had a stomach bug and the shoot she was on yesterday was long and tiring.'

'What's going on with you two? Is it true what she said to *Nonno*?'

'You know what Angelique's like,' Remy said. 'She likes centre stage. The bigger the scene she makes, the better.'

Raoul's mouth tightened in reproach. 'She's a nice kid, Remy. I've always thought so. A bit messed up because of her mother dying so young and all, but she's a got a good heart. Just because she's got an asshole for a father isn't her fault. She didn't screw us over. Henri did.'

'And I got him back,' Remy said through tight lips.

'Yes, by taking the one thing Angelique loves above everything else.' Raoul readjusted his crutches under his arms. 'You should give Tarrantloch back to her. It doesn't belong to you, bet or no bet. It belongs to her.'

'How do you know I wasn't planning to do that once our marriage comes to an end?'

Raoul gave him a levelling look. 'That's some parting gift, bro. But have you considered she might not want it to end?'

Remy gave a short bark of cynical laughter. 'Can't see that happening. She hates being married to me. She's only sticking with it while she gets her new modelling gig off the ground. She thinks marriage is an outdated institution that serves the interests of men rather than women.'

'Yes, well, it's certainly served your interests,' Raoul said.

'What's that supposed to mean?'

'You didn't have to sleep with her. You could have

got her out of Dharbiri and annulled the marriage once you got home.'

Remy flashed a glare his middle brother's way. 'Since when is who I sleep with your business?'

Raoul held his glare. 'If you divorce her, all hell could break loose. She could take half of your assets.'

'I thought you said she was a nice kid?'

'She is, but that's not to say she wouldn't want to get back at you for breaking her heart.'

'I'm not breaking her heart, OK?' Remy said in an exasperated tone. 'What is it with you and Rafe? You fall in love and expect everyone else to do the same. She doesn't even like me. I can't help thinking she's biding her time to turn things on their head. She's smart that way. She likes having the last word and she'll do anything to get it.'

'Have you really got so cynical you can't see what's right in front of your nose?'

'What? You think she loves me or something?' Remy said. 'Sorry to disappoint you, but Angelique's a great actress. She's no more in love with me than I am with her.'

Raoul gave him a look.

'What?' Remy gave another bark of a laugh but even to his ears it sounded hollow. 'You think *I'm* in love with *her*? Come on. No offence to you and Rafe, but falling in love is not on my list of things to do. I don't have that particular gene.'

'It's not a matter of genetics,' Raoul said. 'It's a matter of choice. If you're open to it, that is.'

'Well, I choose not to be open to it. I don't want that sort of complication in my life. I'm fine just the way I am.'

'You'll end up like *Nonno*,' Raoul said. 'Stuck with a

houseful of obsequious servants who pretend they like him when all they do is laugh and snigger about him behind his back.'

'I know what I'm doing, Raoul.'

'Yeah, and you're doing a damn fine job of it too. But, if you're so sure of Angelique's motives, why don't you give her Tarrantloch now and see if she still wants to stay with you? Take a gamble, Remy—or are you too scared of losing where it matters most?'

Remy let out a tight breath as his brother limped away to join Lily, who was looking at them with a worried frown.

Poppy came over with a cup of coffee and a slice cake for Remy. 'Have you seen Angelique?' she asked. 'She said she was going to the bathroom but she's been ages. Is she OK?'

'She's fine. She had a stomach bug a couple of days ago.' *How many times do I have to say this?* 'She's still getting over it.'

Poppy's expression flickered with something. 'Oh. I just wondered...'

'What?'

'Nothing.' She pinched her lips together as if afraid of speaking out of turn. She put a protective hand over her belly as a rosy blush spread over her cheeks.

Remy felt like someone had just slammed him in the solar plexus. It was a moment before he could get his breath back. His mind was reeling.

'Excuse me...' He almost pushed Poppy out of the way as he moved past.

# CHAPTER FOURTEEN

ANGELIQUE LOOKED AT the dipstick.

*Negative.*

Why was she feeling so disappointed? It was ridiculous of her to feel so deflated. Why was she thinking about little dark-haired babies when she stood to gain squillions from parading around in bridal wear on every catwalk in Europe?

Because she didn't want to be a pretend bride.

Not on the catwalk. Not in a photo shoot. Not in magazines and billboards.

She wanted to be a real bride, a real wife and a real mother.

'Angelique?' There was a sharp rap at the door.

She quickly stuffed the packaging and results in the nearest drawer underneath the basin. ' Just a second...'

She checked her appearance in the mirror. She looked like she'd just auditioned for a walk-on part as a ghost in a horror movie.

The door handled rattled. 'Open this door,' Remy commanded. 'I want to talk to you.'

Angelique stalked over, snipped the lock back and opened the door. 'Do you mind? What does a girl have to do to get some privacy around here?'

He glanced to either side of her. 'What are you doing in there?'

She gave him a look. 'What do you think I was doing? What do you do when you go to the bathroom? No, on second thought, don't answer that.' She brushed past him. 'I know what you guys do.'

He captured her arm and turned her to face him. 'Are you pregnant?'

Angelique blinked at him in shock. 'What?'

His mouth was set in a grim line. 'I asked you a simple question. Are you pregnant?'

'No.'

'But you thought you were?'

She waited a beat before answering. 'Yes...'

He frowned so heavily his eyebrows met. 'And you didn't think to mention it to me?'

'I wanted to make sure first.'

'So you could do what? Announce it to the press? Post a tweet about it? Drop it on me to force me to keep our marriage going indefinitely?'

Angelique pushed past him. 'That's just so damn typical of you. You think everyone is going to do the dirty on you.'

'Do you realise how insulting this is?' He swung around to follow her. 'Don't you think I had the right to know you suspected you were carrying my child? This is something we should've been facing together. You had no right to keep that information to yourself.'

'You seem pretty certain it's your child,' Angelique said. ' How do you know I wasn't trying to foist another man's baby on you? You should watch your back, Remy. You think you're so smart, but I could have tricked you and you wouldn't have suspected a thing.'

'I don't believe you would sink to that level. You like

to act streetwise and tough but that's not who you really are. Your father might be a double-crossing cheat but you're not cut from the same cloth.'

'You don't know me.'

'I know you can't wait to get out of this marriage.' His jaw was locked tight with tension. 'Well, guess what? You got your wish. I'm releasing you. You're free to go as of now. I won't have anyone tell me I'm exploiting you by sleeping with you or getting you pregnant against your will, or keeping your precious castle just for kicks. Just go. Leave. Tarrantloch is yours. I'll send you the deeds.'

Angelique had dreamed of this moment, the moment when she would have Tarrantloch back in her possession. Why then did she feel like she was losing something even more valuable? 'You want me to leave?'

'That's what *you* want, isn't it?'

*Here is your chance.*

*Tell him what you want.*

But the words were stuck behind a wall of pride. What if she told him she loved him and wanted to stay with him for ever? He had never given any sign of being in love with her. Lust was his language. She had made it her own. If he loved her, wouldn't he have said so?

'Yes.' The word felt like a dry stone in her mouth. 'That's what I want.'

'Fine.' He let out a breath that sounded horribly, *distressingly* like relief. 'I won't make any announcements to the press until after Christmas. I don't want to compromise your modelling contract.'

That was the least of Angelique's worries. She was already trying to think of a way out of it. 'Thank you.' She pressed her lips together as she gathered up her bag.

She would not cry. She would not beg him to let her

stay. She would not tell him she loved him only to have him mock her. 'Will you say goodbye to the others for me? I don't want to create a scene.'

He gave a rough-sounding laugh. 'What? No big dramatic exit? You surprise me. That's not the Angelique Marchand I know.'

Angelique turned at the door and gave him a glacial look. 'Then perhaps you don't know me as well as you thought.'

As exit lines went, it was a good one. The only trouble was she could barely see where she was going for the tears that blurred her vision.

But she resolutely blinked them back and walked out of the villa and out of Remy's life without anyone stopping her.

And she wouldn't be coming back.

# CHAPTER FIFTEEN

'BUT YOU CAN'T possibly spend Christmas on your own!' Poppy said. 'Rafe, darling, will you tell your impossibly stubborn brother he's got to be with us? He won't listen to me.' Her bottom lip quivered as tears shimmered in her eyes. 'I can't bear the thought of anyone spending Christmas all alone.'

'It's nothing to get upset about,' Remy said, feeling like a heel for triggering Poppy's meltdown. 'I just don't feel like socialising, that's all.'

Rafe put his arm around Poppy and drew her close. 'Poppy's feeling a bit emotional just now, aren't you, *ma petite*?'

'I think we should tell him,' Poppy said with a little sniff.

'Tell me what?' Remy said, looking between the two of them.

'We're having a baby,' Rafe said with a proud smile. 'We found out a few weeks ago but didn't want to overshadow Raoul and Lily's wedding. We were going to wait until they got back from their honeymoon to announce it at Christmas.'

Remy's smile pulled on the tight ache in his chest that had been there since he had set Angelique free. 'Congratulations. I'm happy for you. That's great news.'

He even managed a short laugh. 'How about that? I'm going to be an uncle.'

'Will you *please* come to us for Christmas?' Poppy pleaded. 'I know you don't want to be anywhere near your grandfather just now, but we're supposed to be a family. It won't be the same without you there.'

*It won't be the same without Angelique there.*

Remy thought of the cosy family scene Poppy was so keen to orchestrate: wonderful cooking smells and warm fires in every room. A fresh pine-scented Christmas tree decorated with colourful bells and tinsel with thoughtfully chosen and artfully wrapped presents for everyone beneath it. His brothers and their wives would be talking non-stop about brides and honeymoons and babies. The photos from Raoul and Lily's wedding—where Angelique's absence in them would cause him even more pain—would be pored over and he would sit there being the odd one out—along with his grandfather, of course.

He'd rather be on his own than suffer that.

'Sorry, but I have other plans.'

'I wonder what Angelique has planned,' Poppy said as she handed back Rafe's handkerchief. 'Maybe I'll invite her. Do you think she'd come now that you're not going to be there?'

Remy frowned. 'Why would you invite her?'

'Why shouldn't I invite her?' Poppy gave him a haughty look. 'I loved her the minute I met her. So did Lily.'

'You spent all of five minutes with her!'

'Maybe, but it was enough to know she's a lovely person.'

'I never said she wasn't.' Remy caught his brother's look. 'Lately, I mean.'

'Did you know she's cancelled the bridal wear contract?' Rafe said. 'It will cost her a fortune to get out of. One of the designers is threatening to sue.'

Remy felt his stomach drop. 'Where did you hear that?'

'Social media,' Rafe said. 'Where else?'

Angelique stood back and inspected the tree she had set up in the sitting room of Tarrantloch. The scent of pine filled the air with a pleasantly sharp, clean tang. It brought back wonderful memories of Christmas with her grandparents all those years ago. She had even found in the attic the decorations they had used back then—miraculously overlooked by the ruthlessly efficient removal men—including the angel she had loved so much as a child. The angel was looking a little the worse for wear with her yellowed robes and moth-eaten wings but Angelique didn't have the heart to replace her.

The festive season was the worst time to be alone. She had spent far too many of them in hotel rooms or with people she didn't particularly know or like to do it again this year.

Poppy had invited her to spend it with her and Rafe in Oxfordshire, with Lily, Raoul and Vittorio, but she'd politely declined, even when Poppy had assured her Remy wasn't going to be there. Angelique hadn't asked where he would be spending Christmas or who he'd be spending it with.

She didn't want to know.

The sound of helicopter blades outside gave her a little start. Robert Mappleton wasn't due to arrive until tomorrow, on Christmas Eve. She had invited him because she'd found out he had spent every Christmas alone since his wife had died.

Angelique peered out of the window, but it wasn't Robert who got out of the helicopter. Her heart banged against her chest as Remy came through the icy wind towards the house. She dusted off the tinsel sparkles clinging to her yoga pants before opening the front door. 'What are you doing here?'

'I want to talk to you.'

She folded her arms. 'So talk.'

'Aren't you going to invite me in?'

She put her chin up. 'I'm expecting company.'

He flinched as if she'd just struck him. 'Who?'

Angelique saw his throat move up and down. His eyes looked tired. He needed a shave more than usual. 'Robert Mappleton.'

His expression turned to stone. Unreadable stone. 'I guess I should've guessed that.'

Angelique unfolded her arms. 'Why aren't you spending Christmas with your family?'

He gave her a brooding look. 'I don't trust myself in the same room as my grandfather. Every time I see him I want to punch him.'

'I told my father I *would* punch him if he came anywhere near me.'

Remy stood looking at her for a beat of silence. 'So…I guess I should leave you to it…' He raked a hand through his windblown hair. He was too late. He'd left it too late. His gamble hadn't paid off. She had moved on with her life. Robert Mappleton was far too old for her but she was probably searching for a father figure, given hers was so appalling.

*He was too late.*

'Why are you here?' Angelique asked.

Remy was sick of all the game playing, the pretence

and subterfuge. He decided to take one last gamble. His pride was on the table but it was a small price to pay.

*It was the price he was prepared to pay.*

'I wanted to tell you I love you.'

Her eyelids flickered. 'You...*love* me?'

Remy gave her a self-deprecating look. 'You looked shocked.'

'But you never said a word... You sent me away.' She narrowed her gaze at him, her cheeks firing up with red-hot anger. 'How could you *do* that to me?'

Remy took umbrage at her cutting tone. 'I thought that's what you wanted. For God's sake, I asked you straight out what you wanted. You said you only wanted Tarrantloch.'

'I was pretending!' Angelique said. 'How could you think I would want a big old, draughty castle instead of love?'

Now it was his turn to look shocked. 'You want love?'

Angelique felt tears prickling at the back of her throat. 'I want love and marriage and...and a baby.'

Remy blinked. 'You want a baby?'

She brushed at her eyes with the back of her hand. 'I know you're going to think this is utterly ridiculous, but I was bitterly disappointed when that pregnancy test was negative.'

'Why?'

'Because without it I had no reason to stay with you.'

'But what about your modelling contract?'

'You just don't get it, do you?' Angelique said. 'You don't get me at all. I *hate* being a model. I hate having to look perfect all the time. I only ever got into it because I knew it would annoy my father. I want to design clothes, not parade around in them.'

Remy took her by the shoulders. 'You want to stay with me? Is that what you're saying?'

Angelique looked up into his dark brown eyes. 'I've wanted to stay with you since the night you put on *The Lion King* when I was fifteen and watched it with me.'

Remy's fingers tightened. He was frightened to let go of her in case this was all a dream. 'You love me?'

'Desperately.'

'Then why the hell didn't you say so?' He glared at her. 'Do you realise the torture you've put me through? I could put you over my knee and spank you.'

Angelique gave him a cheeky smile. 'Is that a promise?'

He clutched her to his chest, almost crushing her in the process. 'I thought I'd lost you. I thought it was too late. I thought *I* was too late. When Rafe told me he'd heard a rumour you were trying to get out of your contract I started to think...*to hope*...it was because you weren't happy with your life.' He pulled back to look at her. 'Tell me I'm not dreaming this.'

She smoothed away the frown between his brows with her fingertip. 'Do you think we're always going to fight?'

He captured her finger and kissed its tip. 'I hope so. It's so much fun making up.'

Angelique's eyes sparkled. 'Do you think Robert Mappleton would mind if we have a slight change of venue for Christmas?'

'What did you have in mind?'

She toyed with his shirt collar. 'Well...it sounds like Poppy's gone to a lot of trouble and it would be really nice to have a proper family Christmas for once. And I really want to see Raoul and Lily's wedding photos and hear all about their honeymoon.' She lifted her gaze to his. 'Would you mind?'

'For you, *mon amour*, I would agree to anything. But first I have something to give you.' He took out a box from his anorak pocket and handed it to her.

Angelique opened the box to find an engagement and wedding ring ensemble that was so exquisitely and yet so simply crafted it took her breath away. She blinked away a sudden rush of tears and looked up into his gaze. 'It's perfect! It's absolutely gorgeous! How did you know I would love this so much?'

He gave her a twinkling smile as he scooped her up into his arms. 'I took a gamble.'

# EPILOGUE

REMY LOOKED AROUND the sitting room of Dalrymple House where his family was gathered for Christmas. His grandfather was sitting grumbling about the stock market fluctuations with a very patient Robert Mappleton. Raoul was sitting on the sofa with his legs up on an ottoman. Lily was tucked in close to his side, looking up at him with such rapt attention it made Remy's chest feel warm. Rafe was helping Poppy carry in egg nog and nibbles but stopped in the doorway to give her a lingering kiss under the mistletoe.

Remy looked across at Angelique who was on the floor in front of the Christmas tree cuddling all three of Poppy's cute little dogs. Chutney, Pickles and Relish were instantly besotted with her and had no shame about showing it. Pickles—who according to Rafe was a hard nut to crack—had even snuck in an extra couple of licks.

Angelique laughed as she got off the floor to come over to Remy. 'Did you see that, darling? I won Pickles over straight away. He couldn't resist me.'

'I saw you sneak him a treat,' Remy said. 'In my book, that's cheating.'

She gave him a grin as she wound her arms around

his middle. 'You're just jealous because you didn't think of it first.'

'I'm not jealous.'

'Yes you are.'

'Am not.'

'Will someone tell those two to stop bickering?' Rafe said from over by the mistletoe.

'They're not bickering,' Raoul said from the sofa. 'They're just warming up for a kiss. See, what did I tell you? Any second now. *Bingo*.'

* * * * *

# A PRIVATE AFFAIR

**A.C. ARTHUR**

# CHAPTER ONE

*Milan, Italy*

RILEY GOLD DIDN'T give a damn. She walked into the hotel ballroom knowing she was the best-dressed woman in the room.

Her dress was an RGold exclusive—black sheath, skew neck, half sleeve, back slit. The shoes were Louboutin crisscross pumps. Her shoulder-length honey-bronze highlighted hair was pulled up in a slick bun that had taken thirty minutes to perfect. Her makeup was simple, with dark eyes and matte berry-toned lips.

She was ready for the New Year's Eve party sponsored by *Design International*—a global magazine that routinely featured the hottest designers worldwide. As the chief executive of market research and product development at Ronald Gold Fashions, Riley was representing the company at this party, even though she was on her annual vacation.

RGF was on top of the domestic fashion market

and holding strong at the top five in the global market. The company her grandfather had built and her father now ran was everything to Riley. It was her life, as the tabloids never failed to remind everyone.

RGF's Ice Princess Still as Frigid as Ever

That was the latest headline. A picture of her walking into RGF's Manhattan headquarters beneath it. Riley could still see the bold-print letters splashed across the front of the magazine as if they'd been emblazoned on the insides of her eyelids. Despite the headline and the article she refused to read, Riley had taken extreme pride in the classy dove-gray pantsuit she'd been wearing in the picture. She'd learned a long time ago that appearances were everything. It didn't matter if she felt like crap, as long as she was flawless on the outside.

Flawless and brilliant.

Riley crossed the room, smiling and waving at industry people she knew. She stopped for a quick double-cheek air kiss with an international textile associate and provided vague answers to a fashion blogger's questions about what RGF had in store for New York Fashion Week. Her target was in sight and she was steadily making her way toward him— without looking as if she'd only come to this party to see him. Admittedly, he was a big part of the reason, but she didn't have to act like it.

There had to be at least three hundred people in

the hotel's massive ballroom. A band played while staff weaved in and out of the guests with trays of hors d'oeuvres and flutes filled with champagne. Glitz and glamour were the theme on this New Year's Eve, with some of the top names in fashion wearing signature gowns and tuxedos. The air buzzed with excitement—for the New Year as well as the upcoming fashion season.

Riley was excited about the latter, as well. A lot was riding on the top-secret Golden Bride couture collection. This was the first major project Riley had worked on in the three years after the colossal mess she'd made of an international distribution deal that should have been a slam dunk.

Her assistant, Korey, had learned that up-and-coming designer Perry Reddleson would be attending this party. Ron Gold, Jr., CEO and lead designer at RGF, wanted Perry on his team. Riley had vowed to make her father proud by convincing Perry to work for the company. She'd practiced her pitch at least a hundred times during the flight here and again in her suite as she'd dressed for tonight. Now was the moment of truth.

"Perry Reddleson, I didn't expect to see you here," she said, coming to a stop in front of him.

He was a slim man with a head of sandy-brown curls that fell to his shoulders. His signature black frame glasses and dimples were on full display as he grinned back at her.

"The impeccable Riley, so very lovely to see you here in the city of fashion," he replied. He snagged two glasses from the tray that was being carried past and offered her one.

Riley accepted the glass and launched into her pitch. Twenty minutes and another glass of champagne later, Perry was grinning as he said, "All you had to do was ask. I'd be honored to talk about the possibility of joining the RGF empire."

He had a nice smile, Riley supposed. She was more concerned with the answer he'd just given her. It earned him a genuine smile from her, even as she began thinking of how fast she could head back to her room. The job she'd come to do was done, and more than anything else, she was ready for some time alone. To unwind and just be herself. Something, she thought as her fingers moved over the stem of the empty glass she held, that she never had enough time to do.

"You won't regret it," Riley told him. "RGF is more than its reputation. We pride ourselves on keeping a family-oriented work environment. If you were to officially join us, you wouldn't be just another designer—you'd be family."

He chuckled. "You don't have to continue to sell me on the offer, Riley. I've been following RGF's success for a long time. And I'm honored that the Ice Princess herself came all this way just to speak to me. There's no way I would turn down this opportunity."

Riley hated being called the Ice Princess. The tabloids had given her that nickname after the Walter Stone fiasco. And while she wasn't about to give Perry a tongue-lashing for using the stupid name, she did raise a brow as she stared at him. The act had Perry laughing loudly as if she'd just told a fabulous joke.

"Just kidding, Riley. Come on, let's dance," Perry said.

He plucked the glass from her fingers and placed it, with his own, on the next tray to pass them. He was taking her hand before Riley could cordially turn down his offer and in seconds she found herself on the dance floor.

The song wasn't a slow tune, which meant he really didn't need to hold her so closely. Yet Riley didn't pull away. She was certain any one of the media staff that were present would snap a picture on their phone and immediately text it to their editor. The picture of her dancing with Perry would no doubt grace the cover of at least one tabloid first thing tomorrow morning. Any other fashion house looking to snag Perry's talent would see that RGF had beaten them to the punch. With that thought, Riley moved easily to the rhythm of the music. She smiled and eased out of Perry's embrace so she could spin around before coming back to join Perry. The

move gave anyone aiming for a photo op an unfettered view of her smiling…and wearing an RGold
original dress.

Another minute and the song was over. The band
would probably continue to play until midnight when
the DJ, who was set up in the far corner of the ballroom, would take over. Riley still hoped to be upstairs in bed by that time. Now she decided it was
time to conclude this meeting.

"Well, I certainly don't wish to stop your celebrating," she said and dropped her hands from his shoulders. "I appreciate you taking the time to speak to me."

Perry let his hands slip from her waist. "Surely
you're not leaving the party. We still have an hour to
go until midnight. There's champagne to drink and
more dancing to be done!"

Riley smiled at the joy in his sea green eyes. "Oh
no, I think I've had enough partying for one evening," she told him.

"Nonsense," a deep voice said from behind her.
"You have to make time for just one more dance."

Riley's shoulders instantly stiffened at the familiar voice.

"You don't mind, do you, Perry?" he asked as he
shook Perry's hand.

"Of course not," Perry replied. "As long as she
continues to have a good time. We should all be on
the dance floor at midnight. I'll be talking to you
soon, Riley."

She managed a quiet good-night to Perry, her genuine smile already shifting to the cool, aloof one she'd grown famous for.

This time, the band did begin playing a slower tune, and to her dismay, Chadwick Warren stepped closer and asked, "Shall we dance?"

Riley didn't like how close he was.

Nor did she like how well he wore that single-button charcoal-gray tuxedo. Chaz, as everybody called him, was too tall, standing beyond even her older brother RJ's six feet two inches. His face was too chiseled, eyebrows too thick and beard cut too precisely. There were waves in his close-cropped ebony hair, too many of them, and he smelled… Well, the cologne he wore smelled too damn good.

There was no way Riley would ever let on that she was bothered by any of the above. She nodded and took the final step to close the distance between them.

"You look stunning tonight," he said the moment his arms slipped around her waist, his hands flattening at the small of her back.

For the second time tonight, Riley lifted her arms to let her hands rest on a man's shoulders. The first time had been for business. This time, she prayed, would not overshadow the work she'd just completed.

"Thank you," she replied. "You're wearing the Crew, from King Designs's winter collection. It's an excellent cut that wears well, even if a modern cut would have worked better."

The color of the tux also added to the intense look in his deep brown eyes.

He chuckled. "I'll take that as a compliment."

For a split second Riley thought she could become lost in his soulful eyes. She wondered how it would feel to run her fingers over his rich mocha-hued skin. That was ridiculous. She didn't shake her head to clear the thoughts and remind herself of who and what he was, but she did shift her gaze to a woman across the room wearing a blue sequin gown. Again, they were most certainly surrounded by reporters, bloggers and photographers, so Riley's smile stayed in place as she concentrated on moving with the music, instead of the fact that she was dancing with the enemy.

"Seeing you like this is a pleasant surprise," Chaz said after a few moments of silence.

"I've spent every New Year's Eve in Milan for the last three years," she responded before snapping her lips shut. He did not need to know anything that personal about her.

Chaz looked down at her seriously.

"You don't usually dance at parties was what I meant," he said.

He was right. She did not dance at parties. Whatever events Riley attended were carefully selected and always related to RGF business in some way. She would not admit that the last thing she'd wanted to do tonight was attend this party. If she'd been able to do exactly as she'd wanted, Riley would be upstairs in her room with a cup of hot chocolate and a tray of Oreo cookies—her favorite guilty pleasure. She would be in bed wearing her pajamas and watching some old holiday movie. That would have been the perfect way to bring in the New Year.

And if she'd been able to do that, instead of attending this party, she would have missed seeing him. Riley was definitely okay with that. She'd first met Chaz when she was seventeen at a fashion show in Miami. Years went by where she only caught stories about him either via office gossip or the media. And then last year he moved back to New York.

"I had a meeting with Perry," she told him, and took a step back, letting her hands slide down his chest and torso until they were once again at her sides.

He looked at her quizzically this time. "The song's not over."

"But I'm done," she replied.

He released his hold on her and gave a slight nod. "Like Cinderella running from the ball before the stroke of midnight."

Riley lifted her chin. "I don't believe in fairy tales."

# CHAPTER TWO

DAMN.

That woman could wear a bedsheet and she'd still be the sexiest lady he'd ever set eyes on. Too bad she was public enemy number one. Or rather, her family—the Golds—were the archenemy of Chaz's uncle, Tobias King. Chaz had been inducted into the feud via his parents' deaths when he was nine years old. And again a year ago when family loyalty insisted he take a leave of absence from his thriving social media consultation business to help rebrand and boost sales for the men's line at King Designs.

All of that came second to the fact that each time he'd been in the company of Riley Gold this past year, she'd treated him like he was part of the Republic and she was a high-ranking official with the Resistance. The thought made Chaz smile, even when his body had already begun to react to seeing her in that tight black dress.

She looked dangerous, desirable and just a little bit frightening. Like a badass goddess in five-inch heels.

Chaz brought the glass to his lips and took a sip of aged whiskey while keeping his gaze leveled on her. She stood across the room, near a highboy table decorated to match the room's gold-and-black decor. Her hair, which Chaz preferred loose and dancing over her shoulders, was pulled up so that the slender line of her neck was visible. Diamonds sparkled at her ears and matched the triple-tier bracelet on her left wrist. The skewed-neck design of the dress left one delectable tawny-hued shoulder bared, its tight fit outlining the perfection of her curves. Chaz took another swallow from his glass and convinced himself that the fixation he'd had on Riley Gold, for longer than he cared to admit, wasn't at all foolish or immature.

The man she was speaking to offered her a drink and she accepted, but she would not sip from that glass. If he was correct, and Chaz was ninety-eight percent certain he was, the glass was filled with scotch. Riley did not drink hard liquor. Champagne and red wine were her preference, as were desserts over any other portion of a meal. The fact that he knew those things and too many more to count was probably a little obsessive, but nobody had to know that but him.

"See something you like?"

Chaz didn't blink at the heavily Italian-accented voice. He did spare a glance to his right, where Franco Vitali now stood.

"I see several things of interest," Chaz replied.

Franco chuckled. "Even if you were not their biggest competitor in the US, she would not give you the time of day. Her heart has been frozen since the scandal years ago."

"Not my concern," Chaz told him. "I like variety."

He did—normally. Chaz had a general affection for women and gave them his time as the need arose. Which, for the last ten years, seemed to be quite often. Starting with a simple bachelor blog, Chaz had quickly built a social media following that consisted mainly of women trying their best to end his lone-star status. He'd parlayed that success into Conversation Media, a multimillion-dollar social media consulting firm that Chaz was extremely proud to own. Riley, on the other hand, occupied another space in his mind. One he had yet to figure out.

"Me, too," Franco continued. "Listen, there are dozens of models in my suite. They could not come down as they were not invited. You, my friend, are invited to join me upstairs to bring in the New Year properly."

Chaz managed a bland grin in Franco's direction. He'd known the guy for years, as he was one of Italy's most talented designers. And he had an eye for good art, just like Chaz. But Chaz had never partied with Franco.

"I think I'm good with my own celebration," Chaz said.

Franco shrugged his slim shoulders. "Suit yourself, *compagno*."

Alone once again, Chaz looked across the room only to be disappointed. Riley was gone. It was just as well. At least he'd had a partial dance with her. There could never be anything between them, anyway. His uncle, the feud, his new position at King Designs and the pending success of Chaz's new venture—ChatMe, a social media platform designed for on-the-go millennials enjoying the single life—stood in the way.

That meant Chaz had better things to do than to nurse thoughts about Riley Gold. He could save those for when he was alone in bed, as he'd been far too often to admit. Finishing his drink, Chaz decided he had time for one more business connection before the New Year rolled in. He was heading toward a well-known fashion magazine editor when he caught a glimpse of that infamous black dress and those long, sexy legs.

Chaz knew he shouldn't do it. He should continue his trek toward the editor, share a drink and small talk with her while dropping subtle hints about the new men's collection being debuted at Fashion Week. He should ignore Riley Gold the same way she always tried to ignore him.

But he didn't.

He couldn't. Which made no sense at all. Chaz never chased a woman.

To be fair, he wasn't actually doing so now. He was just walking toward the balcony. There was no rule against a man deciding to get some air…in the place that a beautiful woman was doing the same. And it wasn't because each time he'd seen her tonight she'd been with another man—two other men—who had been standing very close to her. That definitely wasn't the reason he stepped onto the balcony, because Chaz was not inclined to be jealous of anyone.

She was on the phone with her back to him.

He should walk away now. Just let her do what she did best: freeze people—or rather, him—out for no reason. It was tempting as he stood there and thrust his hands into the front pockets of his pants. There were still plenty of women in the ballroom who he could dance with, have drinks with while the New Year rolled in and maybe even take upstairs to his room for the night. He also hadn't forgotten Franco's offer to attend his private party. Again, plenty of willing women. Chaz did not have to stand here and deal with Riley Gold.

But the moment he heard the small hitch in her voice as she'd yelled at whoever she was speaking to, he knew he wasn't going up to any private party. And he wasn't going to snag some other woman from the ballroom. He was going to stay right here until he knew Riley was okay.

"Yes," she continued. "I told him that."

She was nodding while holding the cell phone to

her ear, as if the person she was speaking to could somehow see her.

"I said that, too. Look, RJ, you really didn't have to call. You should be getting ready for Uncle Harry's New Year's Eve party, and not worrying about whether or not I could close the deal. Which, as a matter of fact, I did. Perry will be in New York on January 5 to meet with you and Dad."

So this was about business. She was speaking to Ronald Gold III, better known as RJ, next in line to sit on the throne at RGF. Chaz almost turned back at that point. Riley's business was RGF's business and that did not involve him. He should have known the only thing causing any type of emotional reaction in her would have to do with her family company. All she ever did was work.

"Yes. Thank you. Happy New Year to you, too," she finished before pulling the phone away from her ear and disconnecting the call.

The wish she'd offered her brother was filled with frustration, and Chaz watched as she leaned over, resting her elbows on the railing. Straight ahead were the Duomo cathedral and glittering lights of the Milanese skyline. A gorgeous sight to behold. But Riley lowered her head and sighed.

Chaz had never seen her this way. Riley Gold was a fierce, intelligent woman who had proved herself as one of the most talented and shrewd businesswomen he'd ever met. If she had a weakness, no one would ever know what it was. If she faltered, nobody would ever witness it. She was gorgeous and on point every second of every day. Until now.

His first instinct was to walk right up, wrap his arms around her waist and revel in the feel of her back pressed against him. He would remind her that there was a time for business and a time for pleasure. Then he would drop a soft kiss on her temple and continue to hold her until she cuddled into his embrace. Then he would...

Chaz cleared his throat and pushed those ridiculous thoughts out of his mind. "Working on New Year's Eve?" he asked, still standing a short distance away from her.

She jumped, her elbows slipping on the railing so that it appeared she might fall. Chaz didn't hesitate. He hurried over, wrapping his arm around her waist in the same way he'd just been contemplating, and pulled her back against him.

"It's okay," he whispered against her temple. "I've got you now."

For a split second Riley enjoyed the comfortable warmth that engulfed her. But when his breath whispered over her skin and the reality of who he was and where they were hit her, she quickly moved out of his grasp.

"What are you doing?" she asked as she spun

around to face him. "Were you eavesdropping on my conversation? Is that why you were sent to this party?"

While her father liked to entertain conspiracy theories about company espionage, Riley prided herself on being a bit more levelheaded. Besides, Chaz had only worked in brand management for King Designs for the past year. It wouldn't be his job to hire a new designer, if he even knew enough about the industry to do so. But he had followed her out here for a reason.

"I was concerned when you left the party and I wanted to make sure you were all right," he said and casually folded his arms across his chest.

His legs were slightly spread, so that he looked formidable and enticing all at once. It appeared to be a practiced move—no doubt it was intended to make women swoon because it had a Morris Chestnut feel to it. The fact that Morris was one of Riley's favorite actors had to be the reason she thought Chaz looked so good standing there.

Riley cleared her throat.

"I'm fine," she said evenly. "Thank you for your concern, but you can leave now."

He smiled. A slow and potent action that had her clenching the phone and her purse just a little tighter.

Riley had no idea why this was always her reaction to him. He was just a man, after all. She interacted with a lot of men on a daily basis. There was nothing about Chaz Warren that made him any different from the others. Except maybe the fact that his family was her family's longest and most detested rival. Still, that never stopped her from reacting to his presence, no matter how hard she tried not to. Even now, the heat that always suffused every part of her when he was around was creeping to the surface. She felt it in her cheeks, in the way her breasts grew fuller and her center began that slow, needy pulsating.

"Not until I'm satisfied you're not going to jump over the railing because you don't like your family checking up on your work," he replied.

"What? Oh, so you *were* eavesdropping," she said and frowned.

"You weren't exactly whispering."

"It was nothing. And as I stated before, I'm fine," she said evenly.

Riley took another step back, but not in retreat. She told herself it was self-preservation, something she was very good at.

"Are you afraid of me, Riley?"

Her response was an immediate chuckle. "Don't be ridiculous," she replied and attempted to walk around him.

He blocked her path. He didn't touch her but stood directly in front of her. His gaze was dark and intense, deep brown eyes and thick neat brows staring down at her. Riley didn't look away.

"You've no place to run this time," he said, his voice going lower. Sexier.

She remained unfazed, at least on the outside. "I don't run from anything," she told him. "And I'm not easily intimidated."

He tilted his head curiously and arched a brow. "Good. Now we can finally get this out of the way."

He took another step and leaned in before pausing to look down at her hands. Riley had not moved a muscle. She held eye contact with him. A part of her wanted to take another step around him, while another part—the stubborn and inquisitive part—stood still and waited. For what, she wasn't quite sure. All she knew for certain was that she wanted to know what he was going to do next—almost as much as she wanted Perry Reddleston to come work for RGF.

"Is that a yes?" he asked.

"I didn't say anything," she replied.

"Exactly," he said. "You didn't tell me to get the hell away from you, nor did you mention calling security. So I'm asking, is your silence a yes?"

Riley licked her now-dry lips. "My silence? What exactly should I respond 'yes' or 'no' to?"

He didn't actually need to say it. Riley knew what he was asking. She recalled having a similar conversation with him six months ago.

"This isn't new, Riley. It's been brewing between us for years. How long do you plan to keep brushing it off?"

Was that what she'd been doing? Her previous answer to Chaz had been an unequivocal "no." There was nothing between them and to solidify that fact she'd made a point to stay away from him. Which was probably the reason he presumed she'd been running. But tonight, as he'd just stated, she was standing still…and very close to him.

"One night, Riley," he said, his voice going lower.

His face was just inches from hers as he stood in what should have been an uncomfortable stance. But he wasn't trying to move. He just stayed there waiting…for her.

"Give this thing between us one night," he continued.

"There is no 'thing' between us," she whispered.

He eased closer, brushing his lips lightly against hers before pulling back. "Are you sure?"

"Yes."

Chaz stood up straight.

"You're sure there's no 'thing' between us? Or you're sure you won't give us one night?"

"I'm sure you're trying to push my buttons and I'm not in the mood," she replied.

"And yet, you're still standing right here."

"You're in my way," she countered.

Chaz stepped to the side.

"Now I'm not," he said. "And you're still here contemplating whether or not you're up for one night with me. You won't do it. You'll continue to run because that's what suits you."

No. He did not just make this a dare. But as Riley

continued to stare at him, she knew that was exactly what he was doing. Her brothers had done this to her so many times while they were growing up and Riley had never backed down.

But Chaz Warren was not her brother. He was a very attractive man who made her body respond every time she saw him, regardless of what her brain warned. He was the man who had just teased the hell out of her with that chaste kiss. Riley wanted more. She hadn't realized how much until this very moment, but she wanted Chaz Warren in her bed.

"Yes," she said without another thought.

Chaz shook his head and grinned. "You're killing me here, Riley. What exactly are you saying yes to?" he asked.

Tired of this verbal sparring, Riley closed the space between them. She reached up to cup the back of Chaz's head and brought his mouth down to hers for a searing kiss.

# CHAPTER THREE

CHAZ HAD NO IDEA. There was no way he could have prepared for how potent the kiss would be. No way in hell.

She looked like any other beautiful woman with hazel eyes and intriguing high cheekbones. Her body was what a teenage boy's wet dreams were made of and she smelled like sin walking. But he'd been around the fashion industry for more than half his life, so none of that was abnormal to him.

Still, the punch in his gut the moment his lips touched hers was nothing to ignore. The warmth that spread slowly to every corner of his body as his tongue brushed against hers and her body pressed closer to his was way beyond what one simple little kiss should have caused.

He'd kissed women before. And had done a whole lot more. But nothing, none of those times, had left him feeling as off balance as he did at this very moment.

With heroic strength Chaz pulled his mouth away from hers. But he did not let her go. He couldn't.

"One night," she said before Chaz had even caught his breath. "In my room. You'll be gone first thing in the morning. And we will never…ever speak of this again."

She was giving him the rules. Chaz was never good at following rules, especially not ones that he hadn't come up with. However, he knew exactly who he was dealing with and what was at stake for both of them if they proceeded.

"I'd rather twenty-four hours, but we can play that by ear. When the time comes, if you still want me to, I'll leave when the sun comes up, but it starts right here, right now," he said before taking her mouth again.

This time it was his tongue pushing her lips apart as he sought the warmth inside. She seemed surprised at first but was clearly ready for their go-round within seconds. Her hands—pressing against the back of his neck as if she thought she was guiding this kiss—felt too good to focus on. There was so much more Chaz wanted to explore with Riley and he only had one night to get it all in.

Her tongue joined his, stroking in a rhythm that seemed practiced and new at the same time. His hands moved down to the dip in her back just before the curve of her ass. Chaz pressed her close to him as he took the kiss deeper. She was tall, probably about five feet seven or eight without the heels she was wearing, so she fit against him perfectly. And with the feel of her body against his, Chaz couldn't wait to get her naked.

Riley moved her hands, slipping them past his shoulders to press firmly against his chest. Chaz immediately pulled back.

"Not here, not like this," she said and looked around as if she thought someone might see them.

They were alone on the balcony, the party inside going full swing without a care for the two people who'd slipped out. But Chaz understood. It was no secret that Riley did not like the press. She did the required press releases and interviews, but she tried to stay out of the spotlight. It didn't matter—her family's company was one of the most talked about in the industry. There was no way the press would stop doing stories on her; even though Riley and Walter Stone hadn't married and the phenomenal partnering of RGold Fashions and Stonemill Apparel, a renowned global distributor, was off, they still covered her and they weren't always kind.

Chaz didn't answer immediately. He kept his arms around her and walked them back until they were standing on the other side of a decorated and lit Christmas tree at the far end of the balcony.

With her back pressed against the wall of the building, Riley still looked up at him with concern.

Chaz touched a finger to her cheek and let it slide slowly down to the line of her jaw.

"I'll protect you, Riley," he said softly. "You don't ever have to worry about that."

"I don't need your protection," she said.

Chaz smiled. "I know," he told her. "But I'll do it, anyway."

He kissed her again, his hands moving down her sides. She wrapped her arms around his neck, holding him tightly against her. Chaz groaned at the spurt of possession and need. He grabbed the hem of her dress, pushing it up her legs so he could feel more of her skin, get even closer to her. Riley dragged one leg up, wrapping it around his waist until he was delightfully trapped in her grasp.

He couldn't believe he was here, with Riley Gold, touching her and kissing her. His erection pulsed and pressed eagerly against his zipper. He wanted to be inside her now, but he couldn't pull himself away from her to get them to the elevators and eventually to her room. He needed something first. He needed to give her something, just this little bit to relax her and to promise himself what was to come.

Chaz moved his hand until he felt the silky skin of her inner thigh. She bucked instantly and tilted her head back to arch into him. He cursed, his mouth sliding over her bared shoulder.

Heat greeted his fingers before he even slipped the thin piece of silk covering her mound to the side. She'd eased her hands inside his jacket and now her nails dug into his chest. He slid two fingers inside her and she gasped. She jerked at the contact, groaning as he pressed deeper and shifted her hips until she could move in rhythm with his thrusts. He gritted his teeth at the delicious feel of her moist heat and the tightness that circled him. Closing his eyes, he clenched his teeth at how good this felt even though it wasn't his hard dick easing in and out of her.

She gripped his shirt in her fists as her body tensed. The sound of his fingers moving in and out of her echoed in his ears and had his dick jumping. She gasped and stilled, her heated walls gripping him tighter before her release came, her body trembled and she moaned in his arms.

Seconds later, fireworks popped off, and the sound of people cheering and singing filtered out from the ballroom onto the balcony.

It had taken them exactly sixteen minutes to weave through the celebrating crowd in the ballroom and head toward the elevators. When they finally arrived at the door to her suite, Riley unlocked it and led Chaz inside. She dropped her purse and the key card on the sofa table and kept moving through the lavishly decorated space. Chaz stopped at the fully stocked bar tucked in a corner of the living room and asked Riley if she wanted champagne. She opted for wine and Chaz selected water. Now they were sitting on the terrace, finishing their drinks and watching the last of the fireworks show.

It didn't take a genius to see that her nerves were more than a little frayed. Probably a combination of the crowd they'd encountered in the hallway and the fact that he was actually in her room. So they would slow down a bit until she was certain of herself and what she wanted from him once more.

"Why are you here alone?" she asked after a few minutes of silence.

Chaz sat back on the lounge chair, his legs spread in front of him.

"I always travel alone."

"Yet you always find someone to spend your time with," she countered.

Chaz looked over to her.

"What?" she asked as he continued to stare. "You're in the papers a lot. With this woman and that woman. Between you, Maurice and Major, I don't know who the true Fashion House Playboy is."

Considering she'd lumped him into a category with two of her brothers, Chaz figured the comment wasn't a total insult.

"For a person burned by the lies in tabloids, you should know better than to believe anything they print," he replied, anyway, but then wondered if he'd gone too far. The last thing he wanted was to irritate her.

"You're right," she countered, quicker than he expected.

"But if you want to know if I have a girlfriend, the answer is no."

Her fingers moved on her thigh, but she didn't speak. They'd slowed down, Chaz thought. From the time they'd first come up here, until now, her fingers had gone from clenching together, to rubbing along the stem of the wineglass, to resting on her thigh. Chaz had never seen Riley nervous. He doubted she felt that way often and he almost smiled with the realization that she must be relaxing with him.

"Do you have a boyfriend?"

Chaz was almost positive she was single, but he didn't want her to think he was presumptuous.

"No," she replied. "I'm not in the market for a boyfriend, fiancé or husband. I'm fine being single."

Because the other way hadn't worked for her. Chaz knew and had no desire to rehash any of that for her.

"So am I," he said.

"Why? Your uncle definitely believes in the institution of marriage. I'm surprised he's not pressuring you to settle down."

"That's precisely why I'm still single," Chaz admitted. "Uncle Tobias was on his fourth wife when he took me in after my parents' deaths. Twenty-four years later and he's on wife number eight. He averages around three to four years with each one, before he decides to trade for a newer model."

"Wow, that's a little harsh. You don't think he's really falling in love with them?"

"Only if he can fall out of love with them just as often. It seems like a vicious cycle to me."

"A cycle indeed," she added. "My parents may be the exception to the rule. They've been married for thirty-eight years this coming June. I think theirs is a real, true love."

"But you're not looking for that yourself?"

She shook her head. "Absolutely not. My focus right now is on RGF. That's all."

"Yes, it's about to get busy on the work front for both of us. But you should always have a balance between work and play," he said and then stood. "Do you want another glass of wine?"

Another drink, more small talk, whatever it took to make Riley feel comfortable with the deal they'd made. He could still smell her sweet and intoxicating scent on his fingers and his erection hadn't abated, but there was no rush. They had all night.

Then what?

Then nothing. They'd get up in the morning and go home. Done.

When she nodded, Chaz took their glasses inside. He poured them both some wine and returned to the terrace. Riley was standing now, too, leaning a hip against the railing as she watched him walk toward her. Chaz handed her the glass.

"Do you have a New Year's resolution?" she asked.

He shrugged. "Never make them. My professional goals are the same each year."

Chaz watched as one of her elegantly arched brows lifted.

"What about your personal goals? Balance of work and play, remember?"

She smiled and Chaz felt the air leave his lungs. Straight white teeth and plump lips. The memory of their scorching kisses would forever be emblazoned on his mind. But it wasn't her mouth that had physically assaulted Chaz in that moment, it was the light he saw flash in her eyes. The little bit of laughter that had joined her smile.

"I want to take more time to paint," he admitted. Something he'd never told anyone else.

"You're an artist?"

"Something like that," he said before downing the contents of his glass. He was suddenly very thirsty.

And very ready to take her. Chaz looked at the empty glass momentarily and then walked over to a table and set it down.

When he returned to stand in front of Riley, he asked, "What's your New Year's resolution?"

She tilted her head as she contemplated a response.

"To have a kick-ass launch at every event this year," she replied without hesitation.

Chaz stepped closer, lifting a hand to cup her cheek. "Then let's not think about work tonight. If this is the only time you'll have for play this year, let's make it count."

He'd been rubbing his thumb over the smooth skin of her cheek when it brushed past her lip. In seconds she was licking the same spot. His cock jumped.

"I agree. We'll make tonight count," she whispered.

Chaz took her glass and set it on the table next to his before pulling her into his arms, taking her mouth into a hot kiss. She returned his kiss with fervor, twining her arms around his neck and pulling him closer.

There wasn't any part of her that he didn't want to touch, kiss, lick and thoroughly enjoy. He couldn't thank her enough for agreeing to this, for wanting this as much as he did. Dragging his mouth from her lips, he suckled her neck, his hands going flat on her back before he unzipped her dress.

"Happy New Year, Riley," he whispered the moment his fingers moved along her bare skin.

She shocked and pleased him immensely by pressing a hand between their bodies and finding his rigid erection before unzipping his pants. "Happy New Year, Chaz."

# CHAPTER FOUR

HE WAS HARD and hot in her hands. When her slim fingers wrapped around his thick cock, Riley sighed with pleasure, while the persistent hum of arousal grew in the pit of her stomach. After unzipping his pants and freeing his erection, she'd closed her eyes to savor the feel of him and the wonder of this moment. She was actually doing this, and she was enjoying it.

Opening her eyes, Riley glanced down to see her hands on him. Their skin tones were different, hers lighter, his darker. Her fingers seemed too small against his length and width, yet she jerked him slowly, sliding her fingers from the base of his cock until her thumb brushed over the tip.

Chaz sucked in a breath and groaned, "Do that again."

She did, but not because he said so, because she liked it, too. His skin felt silky and the sound of his groan rubbed along the most primal part of her. The part that enjoyed the power she had at this moment.

"I thought about…this." She'd almost admitted that she'd thought about him specifically instead of simply fantasizing about the physical that was now happening. For Riley there was a distinct difference—thinking about him on a personal level could include wondering what his hobbies were, his favorite meal or movie, while considering how it would feel to kiss him or have sex with him was physical, pure and simple.

"You thought about jerking me off until I came in your hands." His voice was low but deep.

Her fingers stilled over his tip, feeling the first drops of warm moisture.

"I thought about you, too, Riley. I thought about taking your mouth in a hot-as-hell kiss." As if to punctuate that statement he cupped her cheeks and pressed his lips to hers. The kiss was chaste for only a second, before his tongue pushed through the barrier of her lips, tangling instantly with hers until she was breathless.

"I thought about getting my hands on you," he continued when his mouth was moving over the soft skin of her jaw.

Riley continued stroking him while tilting her neck back so he could have better access. Just a few minutes ago they'd toasted the New Year, now Riley felt as if she needed another drink. Anything to cool the heat that was soaring through her at this moment.

"Harder, Riley, honey. Stroke me harder."

He was pumping into her hand as his tongue trailed a hot path down her skin.

"Yeah, like that," he groaned and nipped the skin of her collarbone with his teeth.

Riley shivered and clenched her teeth as she fought to hold in the moan of pleasure that soared through her body. This was just sex. It wasn't some epiphany that would change the way she viewed relationships or even how she felt about Chaz and his family.

She needed his clothes off and moved her hands from his rigid length up to his chest, where she was about to push his jacket over his shoulders. A loud sound stopped her and Riley realized it was more fireworks popping off. She looked around them quickly and felt a cool breeze over her bare skin.

Damn! They were still outside on the balcony. Riley backed away from him, praying no one had seen them. Chaz's gaze found hers, and before she could speak he scooped her up, carrying her through the glass doors and into the bedroom.

While he took his time laying her down on the bed, his hands moved furiously to remove her dress. Riley was just about to lift her leg to remove her shoe when he said, "Leave them."

She shivered, this time from a chill and the way he was staring at her with such raw hunger. For a moment Riley thought she might have gone too far. Was she really going to do this? It had been so long... too long.

"Everybody thinks you're perfect. They have no idea." He sounded as if he were in awe, his voice running like warm oil along every nerve in her body.

She propped herself up on her elbows and dragged her legs onto the bed slowly until the spiked heel of her shoe dug into the cream-colored silk duvet. With her eyes locked on his, Riley let her knees fall apart and reveled in the quick hiss of breath he expelled before the guttural curse that followed.

If nothing else, Chaz Warren was damn good for her ego.

He looked at her as if she were the only woman in the world—no, as if she were the only woman in the world *he* wanted. That want was apparent in his eyes, which had grown darker than their usual russet-brown color. His lips thinned as his tongue snaked out to ease over them. He looked hungry and she felt as if she were sitting on a sterling-silver tray, offering herself to him.

Chaz snatched his jacket off. His fingers moved lightning fast over the bow tie and buttons of his shirt, until his chest was bare and it was Riley's turn to lick her lips at the delectable specimen standing before her.

"I've watched you for so long, wondering what this moment would finally feel like."

Why did his voice arouse her this way? He was just a man talking as men sometimes did during sex. It should not have sent shivers down her spine or caused her thighs to tremble. But it did.

She'd already undone the buckle of his pants so all he had to do was push them and his boxers down his toned legs. He paused to remove his wallet from his back pocket.

He pulled out a strip of condoms and tossed them onto the bed beside her. "I don't know if this is gonna be enough for twenty-four hours."

"I have some," she told him before reaching for the plastic and ripping one packet from the others.

While he finished removing his pants, boxers and shoes, Riley tore open the condom packet and tossed the plastic to the side. She was just about to sit up so that she could put the condom on him, when Chaz stood at the end of the bed. Her fingers paused over the latex while she soaked in every gorgeous inch of his body. In the dimness of the room—there was only light from the small lamp near the window she'd forgotten to turn off when she left—he looked like a chocolate Adonis. Every part of his body was perfectly sculpted, from the bulging biceps and pectoral muscles to his tapered waist and beautiful erection, which jutted forward as if it, too, were glad this moment had finally arrived. But even with all that, Riley's eyes went right back to his shoulders. She definitely had a thing for good strong shoulders on a man.

"Tonight, you can have whatever you want, Riley."

Like he could read her mind, Chaz reached out to take one of her ankles in his hand. She had no idea what he was about to do but didn't really give a damn as long as he buried his long cock deep inside her as soon as humanly possible.

Chaz lifted that leg until it was extended straight into the air. He kissed her ankle and rubbed his hand up her bare calf. The closer his fingers came to her inner thigh, Riley's fingers trembled and she almost dropped the condom she'd forgotten she was holding. He inched higher until his fingers touched the tender folds of her pussy, easing through them to find that she was already slick with need.

"Is this for me?" he asked, and Riley had to gulp hard before she could form a coherent response.

"Tonight," she whispered.

For a moment Chaz looked as if he wanted to say something else, but he nodded instead. He dragged two fingers down her slit, back and forth until the sound of her arousal mixing with the motion echoed in the room. She gasped because a single touch had never made her this edgy and needy before. Riley wanted to jump up and wrap her legs around him. She wanted him inside her. Now!

With that thought, she rose and reached for him. Chaz was faster. He grasped her wrists, stopping her from touching him.

"We don't have to rush," he said. "I want to take my time with you, Riley. I want you to remember every second of this night."

Riley shook her head. "I want it now. Hot and fast."

He did not immediately respond and in those quiet seconds Riley realized she ached enough to beg. But, oh, how she prayed she wouldn't have to. Every higher deity in the universe must have heard her prayer because in the next seconds Chaz slipped the condom from her fingers and sheathed his thick length. He pushed her back onto the bed and lifted both her ankles to rest on his shoulders.

"This time," he said, his brow furrowed as he eased onto the bed. "Just this one time we'll go fast."

Riley didn't know if she should thank him or not, but the thought died when Chaz planted his hands under her ass cheeks and spread her enough so that his dick could slide into her with one slow and viciously erotic thrust.

Chaz knew exactly what was happening here. He should have guessed it would go this way. Riley would fight to control every situation. She would hold on to that control like a safety net and the only way beneath the shields she'd erected around not just her heart, but her entire life, was through pleasure. It was the one thing she couldn't fight, because she hadn't received enough of it in her life. She hungered for it even though she would never allow herself to admit that. But Chaz knew and he'd waited long enough for the moment where he could start to push past her barriers.

He'd eased into her until his heavy sac touched the

warm wetness of her folds. She'd stretched for him so beautifully, her walls opening and then gripping him so tight he'd had to close his eyes to the staggering bliss. His entire body had gone still as his mind wrapped itself around the feel of her.

Now Chaz pulled out until only the tip remained sheathed by her heat. He watched her arms slam down onto the bed, fingers gathering the duvet as she squeezed, and shook her head. "Don't," she whimpered.

"Shh. I got you," he promised and slammed into her again.

She wanted fast and hot. Chaz would oblige.

His knees were on the bed now and he grasped her ankles again, spreading her legs this time until they were in a wide V. He thrust into her in quick succession, watching as every emotion from surprise to fulfillment flitted across her face. Her hair had been so neat he'd been afraid to touch it while in the ballroom, but now strands had broken free of the smooth knot, falling around her face in an angelic fashion.

"Yes!" Her teeth were clenched as the word fell from her lips. Her eyes were closed, full breasts moving with each thrust.

Chaz moved a hand down until his thumb covered her clit. She gasped and he smiled on the inside.

"This hot enough for you?" He circled her clit with the gentlest touch.

She panted and nodded.

"Look at me, Riley." Chaz didn't want her to just remember every second of this night. He wanted her to remember everything he did to her. Every touch, kiss and spark of pleasure he elicited from her.

Her eyes opened slowly as if she were waking from a deep slumber—lovely cognac-brown eyes with just a hint of red along the edges. How many times had Chaz awakened in the middle of the night, dick hard and on the brink of embarrassing the hell out of himself, because those eyes had taunted him in his dreams? Too damn many.

He pulled his hand back and slipped a finger slowly into his mouth, his dick throbbing inside her as her intent gaze followed that finger from his lips and back down. He touched her clit again and she closed her eyes.

"No, Riley. Open those pretty eyes, baby. I want you to see everything I do to you."

Her eyes popped open quickly and Chaz circled her clit with his damp finger while only marginally slowing his thrusts into her. She yanked a hand away from the blanket to reach up and cup her breast. Squeezing so her pebble-hard nipple peeked between her fingers. Chaz clenched his teeth at the sexy sight.

"Tell me you want it faster, Riley. Tell me now!"

She was moaning and stroking her breast. "Faster!" It was an emphatic whimper and Chaz loved the sound.

He pounded into her, continuing to work her clit until she was gasping and moaning. He wanted to hear her say his name but knew she wouldn't. Not without him prompting her. And Chaz wasn't going to prompt her. Not for everything. There were pieces of Riley he wanted, but only if she gave them freely. And right now, all she was about to give him was her release.

"Fast and hot," he groaned. "You're so fuckin' hot, Riley! I don't care what anybody else says, you're scorching hot, baby!"

She arched off the bed, her thighs trembling as her release stormed through her body.

"Yes! Give it all to me, Riley! Give me what's mine."

Chaz lost himself in the moment. Glorious sensations rippling over every muscle in his body as he continued moving in and out of her. There'd never been a place that felt like this. The perfect fit, the deep thrusts, the mind-boggling feeling that pulsed through him as he gritted his teeth and held on tightly to her ankles when his own release filled the condom.

When he could take a breath without feeling as if he were going to pass out, Chaz kissed both her ankles and smiled at those sexy-as-hell heels she was still wearing. He was just about to ease her legs down to the bed, pull out of her and lie beside her, when Riley moved first.

She lowered her legs, ignoring his grip that instantly loosened. She was away from him and off the bed in seconds. Chaz was still on his knees blinking as she grabbed a black silk robe from a chair and carried it into the bathroom, where she immediately closed and locked the door.

# CHAPTER FIVE

OKAY, THAT WAS DONE.

It was good. Damn good.

But it was done.

So why were her thighs still trembling and her body already missing the warmth of his?

Riley kicked off her shoes, dropped her robe onto the closed toilet and rested her palms on the cool marble top of the sink. She lowered her head and took a deep breath. When she looked up, the woman staring back at her through the mirror was only slightly foreign. Her eyes were bright with remnants of desire. Her cheeks were flushed, lips plump from his kisses. Delicious kisses that had served as the appetizer to a greater entrée she couldn't have imagined if she'd tried.

She wanted him again. *Dammit!*

Riley turned on the water, hoping the noise would take the foolish thoughts from her mind, but then realized they'd agreed to twenty-four hours or at the very least sunrise tomorrow. He'd only been there an hour and a half, which meant she still had plenty of time to indulge in Chaz's scrumptious body. She leaned forward and splashed water on her face. It was cool and her body shivered with the contact. She pulled her hair free from the pins that still partially held it back and took the next few minutes to wash up.

She'd intended to take some time to clean up and then return to the bedroom, to face the music so to speak. Instead Riley pushed her arms into the sleeves of her robe and tied it tightly around her waist before moving to sit on the lip of the soaker tub, and closed her eyes.

She'd had sex with Chaz Warren.

And not one time had he complained about her not making enough noise, or not praising every move he made. There'd been no requests for her to do anything he'd read about online or saw in some movie. She wasn't given instructions on how to please him and she'd never once had to wonder if he would please her. Riley's orgasm had come like a full-blown explosion of sensation that still had her body quaking.

Walt had always complained. Nothing Riley did was ever right for him, and to be honest, she'd stopped trying long before she'd caught her ex with another woman.

*I won't go into specifics but things could get pretty frigid in Riley's bedroom.*

Riley closed her eyes as she recalled the quote she'd read in the newspaper the day after she'd walked calmly out of Walt's condo, leaving him and a model she'd seen before—but would love to never see again—naked in bed. She hated that she remembered those words and hated more how they still made her angry. She wouldn't allow them to make her self-conscious. Riley knew how to bring herself pleasure and she'd had a few experiences with other men besides Walt, so she knew his words had been laced with vindictiveness. If their sex life wasn't what it should have been, Riley wasn't solely to blame. But she'd wanted to spare her family and the reputation of their company so no rebuttal to Walt's inappropriate declaration was made.

Which was why this fling between her and Chaz would definitely end in twenty-four hours. There was no doubt in her mind about that.

With her shoes in hand, Riley walked out of the bathroom and into the empty bedroom. Chaz was gone, and a quick punch of disappointment landed in the pit of her stomach. She walked to the closet and placed her shoes inside before turning slowly to look around once more, confirming that the room was empty.

"I thought you might be thirsty."

She startled at the sound of his voice and glanced in the direction of the door to see Chaz standing there with two glasses of champagne. He was wearing his boxers and nothing else and her body instantly responded with disappointment shifting to the slow burn of arousal.

"Yes. Thank you." For lack of anything better to say, Riley met him as he came into the room and accepted a glass. Her bare feet moved across the plush beige carpet until she could sit on the side of the bed.

"You don't have to be nervous," he said.

She finished the sip of champagne and looked toward the end of the bed where Chaz now sat.

"Why would you think I'm nervous?"

"You're not talking."

"I was drinking."

He shrugged and took a gulp of champagne. "Guess what I mean is that this doesn't have to be uncomfortable. We can just take things as they come."

"Right. For the next twenty-four hours." Riley glanced at the clock. It was almost two in the morning. "I've had a really long day."

"Me, too." Chaz finished his champagne and walked around to the other side of the bed. "I was hoping you weren't going to expect sex all night long. I mean, not that I wouldn't be glad to oblige. I'm pretty sure I wouldn't fall asleep on you. But it might be a good idea to get some rest."

She hadn't meant to, but Riley smiled. "I wasn't expecting sex all night long."

"Great. We agree." He proceeded to arrange the pillows before pulling back the duvet and sheet.

Riley had been watching over her shoulder and set her glass on the nightstand before easing off the bed to pull the bedcovers down on her side. She normally slept in a nightgown but she wasn't about to walk across the room to the bureau where she'd put her clothes to retrieve one. The robe would do just fine for tonight. Her pillows didn't require a lot of adjustment and she lay easily on her side of the bed.

Chaz lay on his side. He pulled the covers midway up his chest. The chest that was still bare and undeniably enticing. There was a scar beneath his left pectoral. She'd seen it when he was standing in the doorway. She wondered how he'd gotten it.

"This is the only time I'm a fan of lights-out in the bedroom." It was an easy comment made seconds before he leaned over and hit the button that turned off both bedside lamps simultaneously.

The room went dark and Riley's heart began to pound a different rhythm. It wasn't a totally unfamiliar feeling but one that she didn't welcome now. She pulled the covers up, tucking them tight beneath her armpits, and closed her eyes. She could do this. She could sleep in the same bed with a guy. Although she'd never done it before.

Riley Eliza Gold was twenty-nine years old, one of the youngest woman executives at RGold Fashions. She'd graduated summa cum laude with a degree in statistics from Columbia and went on to hone her skills at the Parsons School in New York. She was in charge of a multimillion-dollar line within her family's company, their legacy. There was nothing she couldn't do.

Except, at the moment, she was having a hard time regulating her breathing knowing that if she just extended her arm she would touch a man. Chaz Warren, the renowned brand manager for King Designs, her family's biggest rival, to be exact.

That last thought probably wasn't the smartest one she'd had tonight since it only increased her breathing and had her clenching the sheets.

Riley was counting down from one hundred when something moved beneath the sheet. It could have been her imagination since her mind was going at a rapid pace, but no, it wasn't. His foot touched hers and she jumped.

"Shh. It's just me."

Well, of course it was him, who else would be in her bed?

Riley's eyes were wide-open and staring into the darkness. And this was the second time he'd *shh'd* her. She wasn't a child and she didn't like it.

"I figured you weren't the cuddling type, but I wanted to reassure you that you weren't alone." Did his voice sound richer, huskier in the dark?

"I'm definitely not the cuddling type." It was an honest reply even if she didn't exactly like how it sounded. "And I know I'm not alone." Because when she was alone at night she could breathe. She could also fret that she might well be alone forever, but at least she could breathe easily while doing so.

"Do you normally cuddle the women you sleep with?"

"Whoa, I have a strict rule about no discussion of prior lovers while in bed with the current lover."

"We're not lovers." Her response was quick.

He moved over, not close enough to touch her, but close enough that she no longer had to stretch out her arm to touch him.

"For the next twenty-four hours we are."

His feet brushed against hers again, but she didn't jump this time.

"I've cuddled before. I can see the appeal, but it's not high on my list of things to do after sex." He paused. "What about you?"

Riley had already realized the folly in asking that question and she'd hoped he would stick to his rule about not discussing former lovers.

"I don't see the appeal, either." There, she didn't have to admit that Walt was always in a hurry to leave the bed when they were finished, and that with the couple of men she'd slept with in the three years since her very public breakup, she'd been the one to get up and leave first. Just as she'd done with Chaz.

"So we won't cuddle," he said. "We'll just lie here and go to sleep."

"And play footsie?" Riley added.

"Well, since you asked." Chaz turned on his side

and extended his legs so that both of his feet tangled between hers.

They were warm, and focusing so much on this simple yet very different touch had managed to calm the anxiety that was steadily building inside of her. She smiled into the darkness.

Chaz listened as Riley's breathing steadied and she finally fell asleep. He couldn't see the clock but he'd guess maybe a half hour to forty minutes had passed since they'd first climbed into bed. Riley Gold wasn't used to sleeping with men. The assessment kind of went with the tabloid's perception of her, but a part of Chaz had always envisioned her as the intelligent businesswoman who shed that shield in the privacy of her own home, opening up to the man in her life. However, instinct had told him cuddling wasn't on her agenda. That and the fact that she'd gotten into bed and lain so close to the edge he was afraid she might fall off. Still, just as pleasure was the key to tearing down her defenses, touch was one of the first steps to that pleasure.

Their feet were still entwined as she lay on her back and he on his side. She hadn't made any move to get closer to him, but she hadn't ordered him back to his side of the bed, either. That was progress.

Why he was even the least bit concerned about that progress, Chaz had no idea.

This was just sex. Long overdue and really good

sex, but just sex nonetheless. He wasn't in the market for anything else. And neither was she. They were the perfect couple, or noncouple, as their business lives came first.

Except for tonight. Chaz wasn't going to think about his business or the work he was doing for his uncle and he didn't want Riley thinking about her job, either. These moments were reserved for them. While this hadn't been the way Chaz thought he would end his evening, he was glad things had turned in his favor.

He'd had sex with the infamous Riley Gold. A triumphant smile touched his lips but fell away the moment he recalled how quickly she'd jumped up from the bed and run into the bathroom. For a few startled seconds he'd wondered what that was about, but realized he already knew. While the fashion industry might look at Riley like some worldly princess trying to make a name for herself, Chaz had always felt he knew her better. It was strange, this insight into a woman who'd done nothing but brush him off since the first day they'd met.

Chaz wasn't Riley's type—he was too outgoing, had too many women and was too public with his social media background in comparison to the privacy she fought like hell to maintain. And yet, they'd been drawn to each other from the start. So much so that he was barely restraining himself from touching her again. Sure, his feet were on hers and for the last little while he'd been content with that. Now, not so much.

He eased over slightly until the warmth from her body beneath the covers reached out to him. With the lightest touch imaginable, Chaz let his fingers trace a line from her wrist up her bare arm. To do this he'd had to push up the sleeve of her robe. Her skin was so soft and warm he ached to kiss her right there, in the spot where her elbow bent and around to her shoulder, over her back, down to her... She stirred and in the next seconds Chaz knew she was wide-awake. But she'd made no move to push him away.

Chaz eased his hand around her waist and untied the belt of her robe. He pushed the silky material off her arm and pressed his lips lightly to her shoulder. She didn't move or speak but he felt her body relax. He kissed her there again and moved closer to her, so close the hard length of his cock now rubbed against her upper thigh. If she had a reaction to feeling him so hot and ready for her, she wasn't showing it. Despite that little chink in his ego, Chaz continued.

He ran his hand over the parts of her skin he'd just kissed, easing her onto her side so his lips could glide over the skin of her back. Untangling the lower part of his legs from hers allowed Chaz more range to continue tasting her golden skin. The faint hint of her floral perfume lingered and he wondered if she'd rubbed the fragrance over every part of her body. He kissed down the path of her spine, his fingers moving over her skin softly. The small of her back was a delectable little spot where Chaz couldn't help but plant openmouthed kisses, circling his tongue from one side to the other, as if the very act was somehow branding her as his.

She sighed, a quiet little whoosh of breath that encouraged and further aroused him. He planted his palms on the smooth globes of her ass and closed his eyes to sensations rippling through his body at that simple touch. Riley Gold had a great ass. Plump enough to make his dick hard just from watching her walk across the room and delicious enough naked to make him grit his teeth and pray for patience. He'd already given her hot and fast at her request, now Chaz was aiming for nice and slow.

He kissed one rounded half and then the other before touching his tongue lightly to the top of her crease. Her breath quickened but she did not speak. Her body felt relaxed and compliant while the thought of her waiting for what he planned to do next had to be one of the most erotic moments he'd ever experienced.

Chaz didn't keep her guessing. He followed the line with his tongue, gripping her cheeks in his hands until they were overflowing his fingers. When he was down far enough, he extended his tongue until he could touch the warm lips of her pussy. She was already wet for him. He groaned and took another lick.

"I love that you're already bare for me." He murmured the words and didn't know if she heard them or not before his tongue was on her heated flesh once more.

He slid his hand from her bottom to her thigh and lifted her top leg higher, giving himself greater access. His mouth was fully open now and all over her with slow but hungry strokes of his tongue. It was a cliché but Chaz didn't give a damn, she tasted so irresistibly sweet. He never wanted to stop tasting her. But her thighs had already begun to shake and his dick was painfully hard, poking through the slit in his boxers. He was going to pull away and grab a condom, in just a second, after he licked her right there…

Riley hissed loudly and arched her back the second his tongue inched inside her warm entrance. She shattered in his hands, her moans echoing in the room while her climax shook her body.

Chaz moved the moment she was still again. He rolled over to the side of the bed where he'd left his empty champagne glass and the strip of condoms. He pulled one free, tore open the packet and sheathed his bobbing length. When he eased onto the bed again, he reached around to touch Riley's chin, turning her face toward his.

"Tonight, it's only about pleasure, Riley. Yours. Mine. Nothing or nobody else. Understand?"

He could feel that she was nodding but Chaz needed to hear the words. He wanted to hear her voice.

"Say it. Tell me you want this. That you want me. Say it, Riley."

He hadn't realized how desperately he needed to hear those words. The feeling was urgent and deeply seated inside him, just as the need to break down her barriers was. Chaz couldn't explain either circumstance. He wasn't in the market for a girlfriend or any type of commitment. Sure, he'd wanted Riley in his bed for a long time, but this was different. He knew it even though he couldn't explain it.

"I want you." Her voice was husky and sexier than any other sound he'd ever heard. "I want this." She reached up to flatten her palms on his chest and moved them slowly down until she could wrap her fingers around his thick length. "I want it all right now, Chaz. Right. Now."

She was still lying on her side but had turned slightly to touch him. Chaz touched her hip and then reluctantly eased her hand away from his length. It was a necessary bit of torture so that he could completely remove her robe. When that was done, he returned her to the position on her side, with her plump ass facing him.

"You can have it now," he whispered and lifted her top leg so that he could slide between her thighs. "You can have anything, Riley. Any damn thing you want." He clenched his teeth as he slid deep into her with one long stroke. He was buried inside, and still, Chaz felt the burning desire for more. He began stroking in and out, loving the feel of her heated moisture gliding seamlessly along his rigid dick. He closed his eyes and let the pleasure overtake him while one word echoed in his mind repeatedly: *damn*.

In one night, Riley Gold might have completely damned him.

# CHAPTER SIX

"LET'S GO SIGHTSEEING," Chaz suggested the next morning. "Isn't that what people do in Milan?"

They were sitting across from each other at a round table positioned close to a window.

"Unless you're in the industry and then Milan's mostly about work." Her response was a bit curt as she stared down at her tablet. She moved a finger over the screen, going from one email message to another, reading and scribbling notes in the stripe-covered notebook beside the tablet. To the other side was a small plate with an untouched croissant and a half-full cup of coffee that was undoubtedly cold by now.

"You do know what a vacation is, don't you, Riley?" He didn't wait for her to respond. "It's when you leave work at the office and just relax. Lie in bed all day or go see places you normally don't get a chance to see when you're so busy working."

She didn't move her head but raised her eyes to stare at him. It was one of the sexiest things he'd ever seen.

"I know what a vacation is. I also know that Fashion Week is right around the corner—"

"And it'll still be around the corner when we return to New York tomorrow."

She shook her head and returned to her emails. "I'm not surprised you don't understand."

"What's that supposed to mean?" Chaz was sitting back in the chair, his tuxedo pants on but not buttoned, his feet and chest bare.

Riley sighed and crossed one leg over the other. "You're not as invested in this business as I am. Sure, you're at King Designs now, rebranding all of Tobias's lines that are flailing, but everybody knows your real love is your social media chain."

She knew more about him than Chaz had presumed. He'd process how he felt about that later. Right now, Ms. Gold needed to be corrected.

"I don't do anything half-assed," he countered.

"That's not what I meant."

"But it's how you presented it. And yeah, I came back to New York to help my uncle rebrand some of the lines that had taken a backseat to the expensive couture designs. I'm rebuilding areas that needed more attention not because they're flailing, but because King Designs needs to remain a full-service fashion house. And thankfully, Conversation Media, my Fortune 500 company, is doing well enough that I could afford to step away for a while to do what I can for family. That's called loyalty."

She tilted her head and folded her arms over her chest. She'd gotten out of the bed before him, and when he woke, she was wearing fuchsia satin pajama pants and top. Her hair had been smoothed back and hung in a long tail down her back. She wasn't wearing any makeup and was still stunning.

"Again, I didn't mean to offend you. I was just saying that you may not have as much at stake since King is your secondary job."

He wondered if she realized she'd just offended him again. Luckily, Chaz had a thick skin and was more amused than offended. Riley honestly thought she was stating a fact and nothing else.

"My family is important to me. Just as yours is to you. But putting that aside, this is still a vacation. So, let's get dressed and head out for a fun-filled day like other coup—ah, other tourists."

With any other woman Chaz might have been lucky enough to avoid the mistake he'd just made. Not with Riley.

"We are not a couple. And for that reason, plus a half dozen others, we cannot go traipsing around Milan seeing the sights and soaking up the local flavor."

"The couple thing is just a title. Tell me the real reason you don't want to go out." Because she was being way too adamant about this.

"That's the reason. We're not a couple. In fact, for all intents and purposes, we're enemies. The press would have a ball writing headlines about us being together in Milan and my father would freak when he saw them. Your uncle probably would, too."

"That feud is theirs not ours." He knew that wasn't going to be enough so he held up a hand to stop her rebuttal. "But I get it. Why add fuel to the flame? Fine. Then we'll have to figure out something fun we can do in this room."

Riley arched one elegant brow and Chaz's dick jumped on command.

"Man, Riley, you are killing me!" he groaned and shook his head. "But I'd rather not spend my one and only day with *the* Riley Gold in bed. And if you ever repeat that I'll have to kill you."

She laughed.

It was a quick burst that sounded so pure and so infectious that Chaz found himself smiling, too.

"So tell me, if I wasn't here right now and you weren't working, what would you do today?"

She was still smiling when she shrugged. "Probably lie on the couch and watch movies."

"Okay." He shook his head. "We can do that. What type of movies do you like?"

He almost said he didn't want to watch any romantic comedies or movies where women got even by killing their spouses or whoever wronged them, but he refrained. If she named a movie like that Chaz would have to suck it up and watch, just for the sake of being with her.

"You sure you want me to pick the movie?"

No. He wasn't.

"Yeah, I'm sure."

"Okay, but don't forget this was your idea."

It *wasn't* cozy sitting on the hotel couch with her legs stretched over Chaz's lap. And she *hadn't* enjoyed the risotto alla Milanese much more than she had ever before because he'd been laughing at her for eating what was essentially a bowl of rice while he savored his so-called heartier dish of osso buco.

Similarly, the movie they were watching was one of her favorites. She'd seen it so many times that she'd saved it on her tablet, which they'd hooked up to the television. So the reason she was laughing and seeing Joe and Kathleen fall in love differently had nothing to do with Chaz's lively commentary throughout the film. Nothing at all.

And she absolutely was not turned on by the fact that he'd watched not only one of her favorite romantic comedies, but three. They were on their fourth one. They'd been on this couch all day, getting up only to use the bathroom and answer the door for room service. Riley couldn't recall when she'd spent such a relaxing and entertaining day. But she wasn't going to give Chaz all the credit. He just happened to be here with her. All day long.

With that thought Riley pulled her legs away from

his lap, bringing them up to her chest, and wrapped her arms around them.

"We can turn this off now. It's almost over, anyway," she told him.

He'd watched her legs as they moved and now dragged those sinfully dark brown eyes up to meet hers.

"When it's over, we can pick the next one or go sit on the balcony for a while if you need to get some air."

Riley needed more than air to understand why she'd put herself in this position in the first place. It was foolish to believe she could spend one full day with this man, or any man for that matter. Why bother kidding herself about ever having a fulfilling relationship? That wasn't in the plans.

"I think I've watched enough movies for today."

Riley stared at the television. She'd seen enough women find their perfect guys and keep them. Yes, watching romantic comedies with him was an even bigger mistake than agreeing to this twenty-four-hour tryst.

"Is that really what's going on, Riley?"

Her head snapped back so she could look at him. "I know when I've had enough of watching movies, Chaz."

This was the second time today she'd snapped at him. The first had been during breakfast when he'd done exactly what he was doing now—looking at her as if he knew something she was too daft or too stubborn to admit.

"Or have you had enough of this?"

*This?*

It was nothing. That was what she'd been telling herself for the past few hours when her mind drifted to how their current situation resembled so many of the movies they'd been watching. A man and a woman getting to know each other, feeling the attraction between them brewing and deciding how best to proceed to get what they wanted most—happy-ever-after.

"I agreed to one night and then went along with a full twenty-four hours," she said because that was the best excuse she had for getting herself into this predicament. Riley did not go back on her word, no matter how uncomfortable she might feel.

"And you were fine with that twenty-four hours being just about sex."

"That's all there is," she replied and turned on the couch to drop her legs to the floor. The former position made her feel too vulnerable, to unsure of herself.

"That's cool, Riley. If you can't take anything else, we can do what we agreed."

Chaz got up from the couch and came to stand in front of her.

"Here or in the bedroom?"

After breakfast he'd gone down to his room. When he returned, he was wearing sweatpants, pristine white tennis shoes and a white T-shirt that molded to every indentation of his chest. All of that gorgeousness was standing in front of her now, offering her everything she'd dreamed of sexually. Riley swallowed. Hard.

From this position it was just a matter of reaching out, pushing the pants down past his hips and freeing his cock. She could have him in her mouth in seconds. She'd thought about that very act all night long.

"I wouldn't have guessed this arrangement would irritate you so much. After all, it was your suggestion." Her words were a stall tactic, which Riley hated having to use.

"Not irritated, Riley, baby. Aroused."

He licked his lips and lifted a hand to his chest, letting it glide slowly down until it grazed the very noticeable and very hard bulge of his dick through the sweatpants.

She resisted the urge to lick her lips, too.

"I know the difference, Chaz. And regardless of our agreement, I'm not going to have angry sex with you."

He tossed his head back and laughed.

"You're not going to watch movies with me all day long and you're not going to have sex with me. So, tell me, Riley, what are we going to do?"

This was ridiculous. It was frustrating and embarrassing. All the things she'd felt anytime she was with Walt.

"Fine," she snapped.

Her fingers shook only slightly as she grabbed the waist of his sweatpants. He took another step closer and Riley pushed the pants down past his hips. She didn't bother pushing the boxers down, but instead reached her hand inside the opening and grabbed his dick.

"That's it, baby. Take what you want."

His words were raspy and sounded dirty.

She liked them.

Riley scooted her butt to the edge of the couch, spreading her legs so that Chaz was now standing between them. She jerked her hand from the base of his length to the tip, watching hungrily as her fingers moved over the silky dark skin. Her mouth watered and she dipped her head, extended her tongue and took her first taste.

She owned a penthouse in Manhattan, a Lamborghini, had a trust fund she hadn't touched a penny of yet and, thanks to her budding career and smart investments, became a millionaire years ago at the age of twenty-five. But nothing she'd accomplished up to this point in her life had given Riley the surge of power she felt with Chaz's dick in her mouth.

With her throat muscles relaxed, she took in his full length. Hollowing her cheeks, she sucked while her tongue licked the bottom of his shaft. One hand was still at the base of his dick, holding him in place while the other fondled his heavy sac. Her eyes were closed as she worked her mouth over him while the sound of his guttural moans and the feel of his fingers raking over her scalp, pushing away the band that held her hair, rang like music to her ears.

He pulled back and pumped into her mouth with slow movements that almost seemed painful if the sound of his grunts were any indication. But the way he held her head so tight to him and the slight tremble in his thighs when she held him deep in her throat made Riley feel as if she were flying. Soaring actually, over the entire world that had read Walt's stupid article and believed every word about her being frigid and inexperienced in the bedroom.

"Damn! Your freakin' mouth!" His words were punctuated with deep breaths and loud exhales. "Your sweet, hot little mouth."

Riley let her lips slide over his dick as she pulled back slowly. He wrapped her hair around his fingers and gripped tighter, trying to keep her from releasing him completely. That wasn't her plan. Instead she flicked her tongue over the crest of his cock, easing into the slit that dripped sugared drops of his precum. He hissed, sucking air through clenched teeth as his head fell back on his shoulders. Riley had looked up just in time to see the moment of surrender in this infamous sophisticated billionaire. Triumph was like a nightcap and they hadn't even experienced the full meal yet.

She knew the moment Chaz had reached his breaking point when just as she sucked him in deep again and tightened her mouth around him, he released her head and stepped back from her hastily.

"Take off your clothes," he grumbled as he pulled his shirt up and over his head in a matter of seconds.

Riley didn't bother being offended by his command. She could still be in control of this interlude. When she was naked, she stood. Chaz had just finished removing his shoes and was taking a condom out of his wallet before tossing the wallet onto the table and pushing his pants and boxers down and off. He must have replenished his condom stash when he went to his room because the two leftover from last night were still on the nightstand in the bedroom. This one Chaz held between his teeth while he removed the rest of his clothes. Riley stepped forward, snapping the packet away from him. She tore it open and removed the latex so that when he stood gloriously naked in front of her she quickly sheathed him.

"This is what you want?" It was a question he didn't give her a chance to answer because before Riley could speak Chaz wrapped an arm around her waist and pulled her against his chest.

She tilted her head to stare up at him and he bent down to meet her, crashing his lips over hers and taking a brutally hot kiss. Tongues, teeth and moans mixed and mingled while naked bodies pressed together in the middle of the living room in a luxury Milan hotel. This could have been a scene in a movie—a tawdry sex flick, not the romantic comedies they'd been watching all day.

He lifted her off the floor, wrapping her legs around his waist while his mouth still worked over hers. Riley wrapped her arms tightly around his neck as Chaz moved them back to the couch. She wasn't thinking of anything now besides how good his kisses were and how the taste of him would forever be emblazoned in her mind when he sat on the couch, holding her close on his lap. Riley eagerly pulled away from his mouth. She dropped her hands between their bodies and grabbed his cock while lifting her body to position herself over him.

"Now." She breathed the single word just as the tip of his dick touched her wet opening.

"Whatever you want," he replied before taking her nipple between his teeth for a quick tug.

Riley gasped and slammed down onto him. He filled her completely, snugly but comfortably. It took her a couple seconds to let the pleasure of his presence inside ripple up her spine and spread throughout her body. Then she was riding, coming up on her knees and rotating her hips in a rhythm that once again had Chaz gasping and murmuring something about her lips, her tightness and how much he enjoyed all of the above. She marveled in the words, let them wash over her along with the unmitigated pleasure sex with him was bringing her. He matched her rhythm, cupping her butt tightly and licking her breasts as she arched over him.

Riley was definitely soaring now, but this time it was over puffy white clouds that lulled her into a place where only pleasure existed. She bounced over him knowing that it could only get better from this point.

"Yes, Riley! Take everything you want. Let go and take it all."

He gave her permission. She took it and more until her release crashed over her, splintering her into a million pieces that scattered over sweet blissful clouds.

# CHAPTER SEVEN

*Manhattan, New York*
*One week later*

RILEY WAS IN her element. She walked around her desk, flipping through the report that Korey, her assistant, had just handed her.

"These projections are off." She glanced across the page to the end of each row, then down to the bottom to get the totals. Numbers were Riley's nirvana. She'd always been able to gather and analyze data fast and accurately. A talent that had guided her decision to focus on market research within the company.

"Which is probably why Sigmund has been calling every day since he sent them over. I don't know how many times I had to tell him that you were on vacation."

Korey was a recent college graduate with an eye for detail and excellent fashion sense. Today he wore black slacks, suede shoes and a black button-front dress shirt with the sleeves rolled up to his elbows. Normally that look proved too casual and just slightly messy for Riley, but Korey made it appear classic.

"Get him on the phone. He has to do better. We're paying him too much money and we've got way too much riding on this for him to flake on us now."

"No problem. Let's see, it's about seven in the morning his time, but he should be up."

Riley flipped back to the first page and paused when her stomach made an unruly sound.

"Or should I wait until after you've ordered some dinner?"

Korey also thought he was a comedian.

Riley turned to him ready to frown, but her stomach made the sound again and she felt the beginnings of a headache. Crap!

She turned her wrist and looked at her watch. It was almost seven. She'd been in the office since six this morning and her last meal had been at noon.

*You need to make time to take care of yourself. Eat. Rest. Live outside this office.*

The words rolled through her mind as if her mother were standing right in front of her. Marva Gold was a stern but loving mother. She'd had to be to raise four children—three boys and one girl—in the shadows of the glitz and glamorous world of fashion. She was also the commanding force behind the Gold Foundation, which provided scholarships and other programs for marginalized youth through-out the US.

"Schedule a call for first thing tomorrow morning. I want to speak with him before my meeting with RJ. We have huge orders for this collection and if he hears Sigmund isn't sure how many of those orders he can fill on time, he's gonna flip."

Riley circled back to her desk and sat in her custom-made ergonomic chair. Two years ago during an annual physical, her doctor mentioned how much she worked, and when she hadn't been able to promise to cut down, he'd suggested she make work as comfortable as possible. A chair that didn't have her back and neck aching every day was an improvement. Not a big enough one, but at least she was trying.

"Does that mean we're getting out of here before nine tonight?"

"Is that a complaint I hear?" Riley didn't bother to look up. She'd dropped the report on her desk and immediately started looking at the sketches that had been scanned into the presentation for tomorrow's meeting. These were the designs that would be fea-tured in her segment of their first show of Fashion Week. RJ and the rest of the production team would be studying them for the umpteenth time tomorrow. Then they'd look at the models wearing the gowns and make the final decision for which ones would be in the show. Nervous didn't quite explain how she was feeling right now.

"Not a one," Korey continued. He held his tablet in one hand and typed as he sat in the chair across from her desk. Probably sending Sigmund an email about tomorrow's phone conference.

"But I was thinking I could probably make it to at least drinks for the dinner party I'd planned to attend."

She did look up at him then.

"Why didn't you say something? You didn't have to stay here with me tonight. I could have managed without you." Despite her reputation, Riley was not coldhearted and she didn't treat people like they were trash or beneath her.

She was friendly and easy to work with. At least, that was what Korey said after being here almost six months. The two of them had hit it off during the interview, on a day that had begun horribly for Riley. The fact that Korey had been able to make her laugh and focus on something else besides whatever headline had been floating around at that time sealed his fate as her new assistant.

He was essentially the closest thing she had to a friend.

"Nope, my job is to be here when you're here and it pays me well." Korey finished the email and looked up at her with a pointed smile.

Riley grinned but then sighed as her temples throbbed. "I need an aspirin."

"Maybe you need to have dinner and go to bed. We've been in the office past nine every night since you came back from Milan."

"It's crunch time." That was the excuse she'd been giving herself these past seven days each time thoughts of that night in Milan crossed her mind.

"True."

She'd expected him to say more, but instead he continued to stare at her.

"What?"

He shrugged. "I'm just debating where the line is at this moment."

Because she knew what he was referring to, Riley gave him a reassuring look. "You're safe."

Korey looked relieved as he leaned forward, resting an elbow on his knee. "What happened in Milan? You left focused and intent but came back a little... off."

"What?" Panic sliced through her with a sharp edge. "I'm the exact same."

Korey's hands were up immediately, waving back and forth. "No. No. Not in a bad way. Absolutely not, you're always on point. Always. There's just a little difference. Like how quickly you were able to admit you've been here too long tonight. If this were last month you would have been determined to push through."

Milan hadn't changed her.

One night did not make a difference to her life.

"I can admit when I'm tired." It was the safe reply. "That's all it is, Korey. So you can go get your drinks. And I don't care how drunk you get, I want you here tomorrow at six. Not a second later."

"Now, that's the prevacation Riley talking." Korey chuckled and jumped up from his chair because prevacation or not, he knew it was only safe to cross the line temporarily.

"See you in the morning. Have a fun evening."

Fifteen minutes later she was still sitting in the same spot.

Had she changed because of the night she'd spent with Chaz? Because that was the only thing that had been different about this year's vacation. After thinking on it another few seconds Riley slammed her palm on the desk and shook her head. It was just sex, damn!

She shut down her computer and grabbed her bag and purse before leaving the office. She wasn't different. Korey was overreacting, something he did frequently. He was lucky she liked him like a little brother and that he was so organized and knew a great pair of thigh-high boots when he saw them or she would have definitely fired him a thousand times by now.

Minutes later Riley stood at the elevator feeling smug because that last thought sounded much more like her. If she *were* acting any different, that was. But she wasn't. Everything was the same as it had been before she'd gone to Milan. All she had to do was keep telling herself that and it would be true.

By the time she made it to the garage Riley was shaking her head. She was pitiful and she hated to admit it. She wasn't the same since Milan because now she couldn't get Chaz and the feel of his hands on her body out of her mind. And as if her thoughts weren't traitorous enough, her phone dinged with a text message notification. When she read the text, saw who it was from, her heartbeat quickened and butterflies danced a happy little jig in her stomach.

Chaz hadn't been his usual self today.

Or the day before, or even the day before that. In fact, he could admit that he'd been thinking about Milan—or rather a very enjoyable twenty-four hours in Milan—much more than he'd assumed he would.

It wasn't like he didn't have anything else to do. Chaz just couldn't get Riley out of his mind. But when he looked up to see his uncle walking into his office unannounced, he hoped there was some business issue the man needed to discuss that would help Chaz focus on other things.

His uncle began as soon as he sat down. "I heard Ron sent his little girl to Milan to snatch Perry off the market."

Well, this wasn't going to go the way Chaz thought it might.

Tobias King was a big man, six feet three-and-a-half inches—two inches taller than Chaz—two hundred and eighty-something pounds. Chaz was only partially guessing. He'd gone to Tobias's last doctor's appointment to make sure his uncle's blood pressure was in check. High blood pressure was a silent killer and with the stress of the company and seven ex-wives, Tobias was always borderline and terribly neglectful when it came to his health.

Now that Chaz was in New York for a while, he would make sure his uncle took better care of himself, even if it meant treating Tobias like he was a child.

"It's not a big deal," Chaz replied. "You've got a good design team and they're coming up with fresh and innovative ideas. This men's collection is going to speak directly to professional millennials and they're gonna love it."

Chaz was certain of that fact because he'd spent hundreds of hours researching this demographic and studying the look, price and packaging of their clothes. He'd kept a few employees that were in the branding department when he came, but he'd hired half a dozen more to create a team that would produce quickly and efficiently.

"But she's a slick one, that Riley. Polished and primped all the time and smart as a whip. I've heard her talk at conventions and the rare times she speaks to the press. She's got her father's attitude but her mother's look. A dangerous combination."

Tobias was going bald but wasn't quite ready to shave his head, so he kept the remaining hair cut very low. He'd even taken to wearing fitted hats and had designed a collection of them with matching casual jackets. His low-cut beard was white, giving him a distinguished older-gentleman appeal, while his steely deep brown eyes remained as astute as they'd been when he was in his twenties.

"She's not that bad." The moment he said those words, Chaz regretted them.

Not actually *regret*—that was a word Chaz didn't allow himself to associate with. He believed everything happened for a reason and that when things didn't go the way he planned, he just had to reconcile himself with that reason. Still, those weren't the words he'd meant to say and now he'd have to deal with the backlash, which he had no doubt was coming swiftly.

"How do you know how bad she is? Did you run into her while you were in Milan? I hoped you wouldn't when I found out she was down there."

"I've known Riley for a few years now, Unc." Chaz had always called him "Unc" instead of Uncle Tobias. It was shorter, and to the nine-year-old who had been grieving his parents when he first came to New York, the less he had to say, the better.

"Yeah, well, this was the first time she's been direct competition to you."

Chaz shrugged. "I didn't go to Milan just to meet up with Perry. And we actually did get a chance to talk. He was meeting with RGF this week but that doesn't mean he's officially working for them."

"Oh, he is. Look at this." Tobias slammed the fashion magazine onto Chaz's desk.

It was open to an article naming Perry this year's hottest and most desired designer. And first on the list of fashion houses Perry wanted to work for was RGF.

"We're fine. PR's getting the buzz out about the lines we're pushing this season and the sales projections are seventy-six percent higher than this time last year."

Tobias grabbed the brim of his red hat and pulled it off. "It's gotta work. We've gotta get back on top."

"We will. Don't worry," Chaz told him.

Tobias shook his head and walked toward the door. When he turned back, he extended his arm and was waving his hat at Chaz as he talked. "Keep an eye on her. She's planning something big."

Chaz didn't hesitate. "You didn't bring me here to watch what anybody else is doing. King Designs is in a class by itself and I'm going to make sure nobody forgets that."

Tobias drew his lips into a tight line and gave a curt nod before leaving Chaz alone. Twenty minutes later when he'd deemed work impossible, Chaz drove his Mercedes GLS back to his apartment. Once he'd showered and changed he sent the text that had been on his mind all damn day.

Have dinner with me.

# CHAPTER EIGHT

CHAZ WAS WAITING for Riley. He sat at the table near the window and stared out at the unfettered view of Manhattan. There was a chill in the air and they were calling for snow, but from sixty-two stories up, the city looked perfect.

The white tablecloth, two long white candles, sparkling crystal and silverware and the small glass vase with two red roses were perfectly arranged on the table. He'd rented the entire upper level of the LeGrange restaurant to preserve their privacy. The lights had been dimmed and in the far corner near the bar a man played jazz on the piano.

Chaz was hungry, but he wasn't worried. If Riley hadn't accepted his dinner invitation, she would have returned his text message telling him so. Standing him up would have been too normal and Riley was anything but that. In fact, Chaz was almost certain she would have taken pleasure from personally declining his offer. The thought made him smile. Riley was competitive and proud and she did not like a dare. Even a subtle one such as having dinner with him. The whole suggestion was taking her out of her comfort zone, something Riley would not like but would be unable to resist for fear of being thought of as less than.

The latter part was what Chaz hated. The moments when he knew Riley was doubting herself despite the confidence that wrapped around her like a winter blanket.

A new text message from Chaz's driver told him that Riley was on her way up. Chaz motioned for the server to pour the wine.

Because the room was empty Chaz could see straight across to where the elevator doors opened. When she stepped off, he stood.

Another server had been waiting at the elevator and he accepted Riley's long black coat and ivory scarf. She kept her cream-colored purse with its gold chain strap and gold RG emblem on the front. Riley wore a long chocolate-brown pencil skirt with a matching jacket that was belted at the waist and fastened with a large button at her left shoulder. Her pumps were four-inch heels, increasing her five-foot-seven-inch height until she would be almost nose to nose with him.

She stopped in front of him, piercing him with her steady gaze. Chaz smiled and offered her a glass of wine. "Good evening."

Riley accepted the glass but did not smile in return. "Good evening."

"You look stunning as usual."

She sipped from the glass. "Thank you. What are you trying to do?"

Candid. No-nonsense. Sexy.

"I'm trying to eat. Haven't had anything since lunch so I'm starving. Here, take a seat so we can order our food." He pulled out her chair and waited the few seconds while she contemplated if she were, in fact, going to have this meal with him, or if she'd just shown up to tell him his "date" was not acceptable and how far she planned to go, before she finally sat.

Chaz went to his side of the table and sat across from her. He took the black napkin from the plate and spread it over his lap.

"You know that's not what I meant."

He handed her a menu. "I'm aware. But I figure we can talk while we eat. I'll answer all your questions and then you can tell me how your day went. Or I can start and tell you I'm thoroughly tired of meetings."

The server arrived, and Riley gave him her order without looking at the menu. Impressed, Chaz followed her lead but ordered a bigger steak and a baked potato instead of asparagus. He was just finishing a sip of his wine when the server left them alone and Riley's question came firing back.

"We said twenty-four hours. That was it. You were not supposed to contact me again."

She sat with her back straight, shoulders squared, and her tone hadn't gone a notch above casual. He almost smiled because there were so many things about this woman who captivated him.

"I was still at work and I had a feeling you were, too. We both need to eat." He let his hands fall to his lap instead of shrugging.

"Before Milan we ate separately. I expected we would continue to do so."

Chaz had expected he'd get back to work at King and take care of a few things regarding the launch of his new app. He hadn't thought he'd want to see her as badly as he did.

"Relax. We're having a meal. There's nobody here to see us and run back to tell the world. It's just you, me and the steak I can't wait to taste." It really was that simple. Chaz frowned as he thought about how many times he'd wanted to pick up the phone and call her or even send an email or text in the last week but hadn't done so because he'd known she would have this exact reaction.

They were consenting adults keeping in touch with each other—that should not have been a problem.

"You know what the tabloids would say. Not to mention our family."

"Stop."

The single word came out much stronger than he anticipated, but the quick close of her lips and the second of shock that flashed in her eyes was exactly the response he wanted.

"I've said this before and I'd really like not to repeat it again. That feud is between my uncle and your father. It's ridiculous that you and I, or your brothers and I, or any of us for that matter, would carry it on like a torch to be passed through the generations."

She opened her mouth to speak but Chaz held up a hand, stopping her. "I wanted to see you, Riley. I wanted to talk to you again. To spend some quiet time with you after a really long week. That's all."

Instead of replying she removed her napkin from the plate, opened it and placed it on her lap. Neither of them spoke for a few moments. Chaz figured she needed the time to gather her thoughts. She had two choices: get up and leave, or sit here and deal with the dinner and conversation. He was positive she would opt for the latter since he knew she'd had his driver take her home to change clothes before coming. No way would she have gone through all that if she didn't want to see him, too.

As the music played in the background Chaz thought he saw her moving her head to a familiar song.

"You know Nancy Wilson?" It wasn't like the musician was playing popular music. Chaz had requested jazz because it soothed him.

"My mother has all her albums in plastic on a shelf in her sitting room. Just a few years ago she finally agreed to stop playing them and let Major have the songs digitally remastered and added to a playlist for her. Now if she's not working, she has her headphones in while she sings along to Sister Nancy. That's what she's called her since I can remember, as if they were long-lost friends."

A soft smile covered her face and the leeriness Chaz had about her not relaxing enough to enjoy this dinner dissipated. It was obvious she loved her mother dearly. Just speaking about her had brought an air of contentment around her that Chaz didn't see often enough.

"Both my parents liked jazz. I remember it playing in our house all the time. When I came to live with my uncle, I didn't hear it as much. He was more of an R & B kind of guy. But when I got my first MP3 player, I downloaded every jazz song I could find." He still remembered how excited he'd been to see the songs on his playlist. For days that was all he'd done—lie in his bed and listen to the music because it made him feel closer to his parents even though he knew they were never coming back.

"Your parents died when you were young, right?"

"Nine." He'd been young and scared to death of what would happen after the social worker and the police officer arrived at his house to tell him and his babysitter that his parents' car was hit head-on by a drunk driver.

"I'm sure that was tough. But your uncle took you in and you seem to have turned out well."

He chuckled. "Gee, thanks."

She waved a hand. "You know what I mean."

"Yeah, my uncle and his wife, Arlene—she was number four—they came to pick me up from the neighbor who had let me stay there temporarily so I wouldn't have to go into foster care." Saying those words after twenty-four years seemed odd.

"Wait, his wife's name is…Veronica. Right? She loves fur." She reached for her glass and Chaz watched her slim fingers grip the stem.

"Veronica is number eight, and yes, she loves fur. It's all over the house." He had to shake his head because the memory of Veronica's redecoration of King Towers, as it would always be known to Chaz, was almost horrific.

"For the record, I'm not totally against fur," she said after a quick drink.

"I'm not, either. But she definitely missed the 'less is more' lesson."

*Ahh, there was that smile.*

"You are not wrong about that," she replied with a chuckle.

The server brought their food and conversation died for a few minutes. The steak was phenomenal, and when he looked up in between bites, he realized the company was exactly what he needed.

"I've been inundated with meetings," he said between bites. "Juggling the design work with the new app I'm launching is more tiring than I thought it would be."

She dabbed the napkin to her lips. "An app? I thought you owned a social network site."

"That's where I started but Conversation Media's sort of morphed into a few other directions. ChatMe is our new subscription-based platform and it's launching in three weeks."

"Is this one for singles, too? How many dating sites does the world need?"

Chaz could have taken offense but he was growing accustomed to Riley's biting candor. There seemed to be absolutely no animosity in her words, just simple statements that meant what they meant.

"This project is geared toward millennials, and no, it's not specifically for dating. But let's not talk about that." He knew the moment the words were out she detested them.

"Let's not." She picked up her knife and fork, cut a piece of steak and slowly put it into her mouth.

He watched her lips moving and instantly thought of when they'd been wrapped around his dick. He dropped his hands to his lap and kept his gaze focused on her.

"What?" she asked when she finished chewing.

He shrugged. "Never thought the sight of a woman eating could be so sexy until now."

She looked like she was going to discontinue the meal but then shrugged just as he had, before cutting another piece of steak and putting it into her mouth. She liked him watching her. Her fingers shook slightly as she held the fork and guided it to her mouth. At the same time, color darker than the blush she wore fused her cheeks. He hadn't planned on this but he couldn't help it—his dick had grown so hard in the last few seconds, pressing firmly against his zipper, Chaz had no choice but to move his hand to cup the bulge.

She finished that bite and licked her lips. He resisted the urge to groan. He desperately wanted to release his painfully hard erection and beckon her to wrap her mouth around him one more time.

"Your food is going to get cold." She lifted her glass to her lips and treated him to another peek of her tongue just before the deep red wine slid smoothly into her mouth.

"I'm no longer hungry for food." It was an honest reply, one that was hitting him with more force than he'd considered. Each time he'd thought of her this past week he'd recalled their time together in Milan, the sex and the talking. Tonight he'd craved both but had no idea the physical could be so jolting or encompassing.

"But wasn't that what this was about?" She cut a

strip of asparagus into three pieces and speared one piece with her fork.

Chaz's gaze had gone to her plate, anticipation beating with his heart as he waited to watch the food go into the warm cavern he wanted so desperately to slip his dick inside.

"This is about so much more," he admitted.

This was insane.

And empowering.

Riley walked into her penthouse with Chaz a few steps behind. She dropped her keys and purse on the table a couple feet inside the foyer and reached for the buttons of her coat. His hands were there immediately, coming around her to pull the coat from her shoulders.

"The closet is over there," she said with a nod to the left.

She moved deeper into the apartment, hearing him opening the closet door and envisioning him hanging her coat and then his own. Her heels clicked on the glossed wood floors and she went to her pale gray sectional to take a seat at the far end. She picked up the remote from the glass end table beside the couch and touched the button that would activate the window blinds. A low hum echoed off the twenty-foot ceilings as black custom-fit blinds came down over the floor-to-ceiling windows.

"You buy the penthouse with the best view of the

city but use blinds to close it out," he said as he sat on
the other end of the couch. He was across the room
from her now and the sight of him relaxing in her
apartment gave her pause because she'd never had
guests, other than family, here before.

During the ride from the restaurant to her place
Riley had resigned herself to the fact that they would
have sex one more time. It might be smarter, but it
was definitely futile to ignore the attraction between
them. Besides, from the moment she saw him standing beside the table in the dining room of a restaurant
he'd rented solely for their privacy, she'd known she
wanted to be in bed with him again.

"I've seen this view all my life." It was an even
reply that she did not believe required more conversation.

"And the blinds keep the outside from coming in."

He didn't bother to phrase that as a question. He
probably knew she wouldn't answer if he did.

"It's a great space. I can see touches of you all
around."

So they were going to have chitchat first. She
could do that. Although she'd wanted to straddle him
when he'd cupped his erection in the restaurant, and
when they'd rode in silence, she'd wondered what it
would feel like if he slid across the seat and slipped
his hand up her skirt.

"I hired a decorator."

He nodded. "Who knew you well."

He stood then and walked around. Her style was contemporary, the colors in this area of her home were soft gray, crisp black and cool white. There was glass, sterling silver, light-colored wood flooring covered in the center by a plush gray rug.

Chaz was in her space. His tall, broad form seeming to dominate the area. He wore a black suit, slim-fit pants and a jacket, stark white shirt that added casual to the professional, shined Tom Ford loafers and a stainless steel Tag Heuer watch on his left arm. She was more than intrigued by the deep hue of his skin, the strong edge of his jaw and the shadow of a mustache and beard he wore.

"This is an interesting piece."

Riley was not pleased by the instant pang of awareness she felt when he turned to face her, holding the phallus-shaped rose quartz in his hand. The soft warm color of the crystal against Chaz's dark clothing was a jolting contrast that put Riley on edge.

"I liked the color." That wasn't what she wanted to say. It wasn't how she wanted to say it. She sounded like an idiot.

Chaz looked down at it, holding it in his hands in the same way he'd held his erection.

"A paperweight?"

There was amusement in his tone.

Riley jumped from the couch and crossed to stand near him by the mantel where the piece—the Heart, as she'd called it—had been placed.

"A decoration," she said and reached for it.

He moved his hand just out of her reach.

"A decoration that sparks something in your eyes."

She looked away from him but that made her feel like a coward, so she returned her gaze to meet his. "I use it when I meditate. The healing properties of the crystal assist in seeking calm and restoring energy." She left out self-confidence and contentment because he didn't need to know that she fought hard to maintain those things. And he definitely did not need to know that the idea of meditation had come from the therapist she'd been seeing for the past three years.

"Does it work?"

His fingers were still wrapped around the crystal, palm toward the wider base, thumb rubbing over the smooth tip. Her pussy throbbed and her heart rate increased.

"How frequently do you meditate with it?"

She swallowed when she finally looked up from his fingers to meet Chaz's gaze. His eyes had grown darker, his voice deeper.

"That's private," she said in a tone that also seemed huskier.

"There's no one here but me and you. Show me, Riley."

No. She couldn't. It was a ritual she'd developed for herself. A safe space that refilled her when she struggled, empowered her when she felt weak and comforted her when the privacy she craved began to strangle her.

He stepped closer and took Riley's hand. He kept his eyes locked on hers while wrapping her fingers around the crystal. It was warm from his touch and the intense sexual energy he exuded seeped into her palm. He was silently daring her to share this very intimate part of herself with him. She shouldn't, but she wanted to.

Snatching it from his hand, Riley walked away. When she realized he was still standing in the same spot, she looked over her shoulder and asked, "Are you coming?"

# CHAPTER NINE

SECONDS AFTER ENTERING her bedroom, Riley lowered the blinds. She placed the crystal on her bed and turned on the lamp on the nightstand. After moving to the stand on the other side of the bed she turned on the second lamp, and the room was cast in a warm glow.

Chaz stood in the doorway. Riley pointed toward the beige couch adorned with pillows near the window.

"The best view is from over there," she told him.

He moved in silence over the beige carpet.

Once he was seated, Riley stepped out of her shoes. She placed them neatly at the end of her bed instead of going into her closet as she normally did. There was nothing normal about this night. She unzipped her skirt and pushed it down her legs, noting the soft scrape of material over her nylon-covered legs. The jacket came next and she folded the garments, draping them over the end of the bed. When she chanced a look at Chaz, his gaze was riveted on her. A warm tendril of desire slipped slowly down her spine. Her bra, nylons, the thin wisp of lace panties were all removed and Riley climbed onto her bed.

Her meditation routine usually included candles and the tracks of crashing waves and trickling springs she had programmed to a special playlist. Tonight there was only Chaz.

Her heart thumped so loud she thought for sure he could hear it from where he sat about twelve feet from the bed. She lay back against the pillows, closing her eyes briefly and then opening them to stare up at the ceiling.

She could do this.

More important, she wanted to do this.

Extending her arm, Riley grabbed the crystal. She closed her eyes and focused on everything from the feel of it against her palms, to its shape and its purpose. Surprisingly, the desired calm came over her even though she was not alone. She could hear the waves in her mind and feel the warmth of the sun against her bare skin. And the crystal began to warm. It started to feel familiar in her hand, but not only because she'd used it so much in the past year. It felt like another phallus she'd held just a week ago.

She needed to clear her mind of everything but her happy place. Search for the good within herself and within the world that surrounded her.

That was what she did whenever she meditated. It was her purpose in taking solitary time to aid in her healing. But tonight she couldn't find that place. There was a new goal in her mind and right now it felt closer than peace and healing. She didn't have to search for it because it was there in the room with her. In her hand and across the room.

"When I close my eyes you're there." It was a quiet admission spoken just before she took the crystal in one hand and rubbed the tip over one tight nipple.

"I'm here right now."

She hadn't expected him to speak, but with the sound of his voice, her pussy throbbed and she spread her legs wide.

"You're a distraction." Riley circled the crystal over one nipple while the fingers on her free hand toyed with her other nipple. On one she squeezed tight, pulling and tugging until her breathing came faster. The other was being massaged by the warm crystal. Her breasts felt full, sensation moving from each nipple down to her gut, settling like a pool of hot lava at her center.

A soft moan escaped before Riley could pull back. She wanted to do this but at the same time she didn't want to share too much, to show him anything deeper than a physical reaction. Her mind and her body fought to control which would be revealed.

"I can't go."

Why did she enjoy his voice so much? Her legs moved over the soft material of her champagne-colored comforter. She wanted him inside her, buried deep and thrusting powerfully until she couldn't breathe, think or care. Riley took a deep breath and exhaled in a slow but shaky whoosh of air. She moved the crystal to the slope between her breasts, trailing it down her torso and stopping at her navel.

"You can't stay." The words came out in a whimper. They needed to be said out loud because her body wanted nothing more than for him to join her on this bed, to take her to that sweet place where she'd soared a week ago. She missed that place. Every day this week she'd thought about it and missed it more. Too much. She'd berated herself for the thoughts but tonight it was a simple truth.

"Not after tonight," she whispered. "Not again."

She moved the crystal lower until it slid along the shaved skin of her mound. Riley loved the sensation of being shaved—each touch felt a million times stronger, and she experienced each lick on a deeper level. It was amazing. It was also one of the things that gave her a sense of power over her own pleasure. With one hand she parted her folds and with the other she dragged the crystal over the slickness of her clit, down past her opening and back again, letting the coolness of the crystal mingle with the heat from her arousal.

With the crystal in one hand, she slipped two fingers into her aching center, gasping at the stretch and moaning with the pleasure streaking wildly throughout her body. She lifted her legs, flattening her feet on the mattress, and pumped her fingers in and out while circling the crystal over her clit. Her head thrashed on the pillows, teeth clenched tight. He wasn't speaking but he was there. She could smell him and feel him in the heat that swirled throughout the room.

This wasn't how her meditation usually happened. It wasn't the feeling she normally sought. But this was good, too. In fact, it was magnificent. Her heart raced with the thrust of her hands. Her hips moved with the motion and Riley knew her release was near. She could feel it in every jolt of her thighs, the full sensation in her breasts. She heard it in the sound of her fingers moving against her coated walls, her essence dripping down between the crevice of her bottom and onto the bed.

"I'm right there with you."

His voice was an intrusion. A pleasurable one.

"You look so damn beautiful, Riley. So strong and talented. The way you know exactly how to find your pleasure. You didn't let me stop you. You're in your own world bringing every sensation that you need."

His words rolled around in her mind but they were hard to comprehend through the fog of desire. She was panting now, arching her back as she drove her fingers deeper.

"Damn! You're so wet. So pretty and wet. I can't stand it."

Riley couldn't, either. She needed this to end. She

needed to fall over that cliff and float once again, to let the pleasure take her away. She dropped the crystal, using fingers from one hand to work her clit faster while the other hand continued to pump fiercely inside until her legs shook and a deep guttural moan eased from her throat.

"Riley! What are you doing to me?"

His voice was clearer now, in the few seconds just before her body stilled. Her release was intense, touching every part of her body, keeping her eyes closed tight, her fingers locking where they were, her toes curling into the comforter.

"Chaz!"

She hadn't meant to say the name that seemed to be etched into her mind. She'd never called out a man's name during sex, or during meditation.

Coming down from her release was like falling onto a bed of cotton. Riley sighed into the softness, relaxing her mind, body and soul.

Loud moaning caught her attention and she turned her head to see Chaz through pleasure-blurred eyes. He had removed his jacket. His legs were spread wide, the button, belt and zipper of his pants were undone. His dick was in his hand, thick and long and dripping with his release as he made one final jerk and cursed long and loud.

Moments later he was gone and Riley closed her eyes, ready to welcome a deep sleep. It wouldn't be the first time that a meditation session had lulled her into slumber and she hoped it wouldn't be the last. But just when she started to slip into dreamland, she felt him touch her.

"What are you doing?" she asked when Chaz's strong hands and arms moved under her and lifted her from the bed.

"Helping you get cleaned up."

"No." She pressed a hand into his chest just in case he didn't believe she was serious. "I can do it myself. I don't want your help."

A muscle in his jaw twitched and Chaz continued walking. He stopped at the bathroom door.

"I wasn't going to go in with you, Riley. I know you much better than you think."

He set her down, and when her feet touched the floor, Riley backed away from him.

"I hope you don't mind but I used one of the wash-cloths in your closet."

Because he'd needed to clean up, as well. Her gaze dropped briefly to his now-zipped pants. His shirt was unbuttoned but his chest was covered by a tight black tank. She looked back at him. "Thank you."

"You're welcome," he replied, and Riley stepped into the bathroom and closed the door.

Chaz had admitted to Riley that he couldn't leave. What she didn't know was that he'd meant more than just physically getting up to leave her bedroom. By that time he'd had his dick in his hand and his desire to see how far they would go to find their pleasure was a top priority. But aside from that, something else held him to her. It was the oddest and most intense feeling he'd ever experienced. He wanted Riley physically but there was also this nagging desire to just be with her.

Chaz didn't want to "be" with any woman. Committed relationships, live-in girlfriends, long-term associations, none of those were his thing. And not just because he'd made a name for himself as one of the world's top bachelors—that was a persona he'd facilitated to grow his business. Now that Conversation Media was a global success, he didn't have to sacrifice so much of himself to sell the brand. The problem was that he'd adopted a lot of the professional persona into his personal life over the years. It worked for him because he'd watched relationships come together and inevitably fall apart. His uncle was on wife number eight and he was only fifty-seven years old. That wasn't a promising scenario for Chaz.

Riley stirred and he leaned down to kiss the top of her head.

It was morning. He'd spent the night in Riley Gold's bed, in her penthouse, with her wrapped in his arms. They hadn't had sex. The meditation/masturbation session had been enough to wear them both down. Chaz sensed their very busy workweeks had contributed to that, but he wasn't about to debate the issue.

Last night he'd watched her come out of the bathroom with a perplexed look on her face. He hated that she'd fully expected him to leave. As if he could share something so intimate and thoroughly enjoyable with her and then walk out without saying a word. It dawned on him later that he'd done that many times before with other women.

He was wearing only his boxers when she returned, and when he extended his hand for her to join him on the bed, Riley had simply walked around to the other side and climbed in. She turned out the light on her side and Chaz lay down and turned down the light on his side. Seconds later he'd pulled her into his arms and there she'd stayed all night.

"I don't know how to do the morning after," she whispered.

Chaz rubbed his hand up and down her arm, enjoying the feel of her soft skin. He'd been doing that all night. Touching her, smelling her, taking in every aspect of this woman who he'd thought he knew.

"Neither do I," he replied. "How about we make it up as we go?"

"How about we just get up?" she said and started to move.

Chaz did not want to let her go. He did not want this mood to be over. It was beyond what he'd imagined having dinner with her would be. That both unnerved and excited him.

She shocked him by dropping a quick kiss on his chest before pushing up and away from him. Her curse came next.

"I'm late. Dammit! I have a meeting with RJ and a conference call with my distributor and I'm late!"

Riley jumped out of the bed. She snatched a peach-colored silk robe from the chair and thrust her arms into it as she moved across the room.

Chaz sat up in bed. "You're an executive, Riley. You can definitely cancel a meeting."

She was already across the room, pushing a button on the wall to open the door of a massive walk-in closet. "I'm not canceling. This is important. We've got deadlines and he's trying to say he can't produce the numbers we've already presold. It's a catastrophe and I have to fix it."

She was talking while moving up and down the aisles in the closet. From what Chaz could see there were more than a dozen aisles of clothes. He could only see the first row of shoes but figured she'd have just as many shoes as she did clothes. Straight to the back was a wall of accessories. Riley came out with clothes and shoes, a necklace dangling from her fingers and a look of sheer panic on her face.

Chaz eased out of the bed. "No worries. I'll call for my car. He'll get you there in no time."

"But what about you?"

Chaz walked toward her, not giving a damn about the morning hard-on tenting his boxers until he stopped in front of her and watched her gaze dip down.

"I'll get a cab or I can wait here until my car comes back. You should get your shower. He'll be here quickly after I place the call."

She looked back up at him. "Ah. Yes. Shower. I should do that. Thank you."

Chaz grinned and leaned in to drop a quick but soft kiss on her lips. "Stop thanking me, Riley. If I'm sleeping with you I can certainly make sure you get to work."

She pressed her hands against his chest. The chilly links of her necklace eased over his bare skin.

"So we're sleeping together?" Her eyes were wide with concern but Chaz didn't detect any regret in her tone.

"Yeah. After last night I'd say we are. You cool with that?"

She swallowed and blinked and then squared her shoulders.

"I believe I am. As long as we're discreet. This cannot get out, Chaz. It has to stay between us for however long it lasts."

Her tone was adamant, which told him that was the line and he needed to decide if he dared to cross it. Not today.

"I can do a private affair with you, Riley." He

wrapped his arms around her waist and pulled her to him again. "I can do just about anything with you."

Every part of her relaxed and a smile touched her lips.

"I can do a private affair with you, too, Chaz."

She came up on the tips of her toes and kissed him, tilting her head as her tongue met his. He was instantly dragged into a heated and sensual moment that was going to change both of them forever. She pulled away first and looked at him for a few muted seconds before going into the bathroom. Chaz stood there, trying to wrap his mind around what had just happened. Then he grinned.

He was having an affair with Riley Gold.

# CHAPTER TEN

"ARE YOU OKAY?" RJ asked as Riley stood from the conference room table and began pulling her sketches together. The drawings had been spread out along the table after the PowerPoint presentation. Then the models had come in wearing the designs and she, RJ and several other members from the production team had gotten up to inspect each one personally.

"I'm fine," she said. "The beading on the Elisa gown needs work. Everything about this line rests on the details. It was in the sketch so I'm not sure why it didn't translate into production. I may just write a memo to the production team. That way they'll all know to pay closer attention. But the gown will be ready by the first show so there's no need to worry about that."

RJ was perched on the side of the table as he listened to her, and when she came close enough, he grabbed her arm to stop her from moving.

"I wasn't talking about the gowns, Riley. I'm asking about you."

Her brother was six years older than her, tall and slimly built. He had a deep voice just like their father, but he was also overprotective and prone to hovering just like their mother.

"You came in late this morning. Very late."

"So you want to dock me? I'm here at the crack of dawn every day, even on Saturdays, and I stay well into the evening every night. I don't take sick days and only one vacation per year. Come in late one morning and I'm being scolded like I'm a slacker."

She yanked her arm away from his grasp.

RJ put his arms up in mock surrender. "Whoa. I'm just asking as a concerned brother because I know how hard it is for you to go off script. Which is why I wondered what happened when I called your office and Korey told me you weren't in yet and that he hadn't heard from you."

Riley was now snatching the sketches off the table. When she grabbed the final one, she smoothed the stack and slipped them into a case.

"And now you're brooding because you don't like to be wrong." RJ chuckled. "Come on, Riley. Just tell me that everything is okay and I'll leave you alone. I can respect your privacy."

Her head snapped around at those words. "Liar. You probably already called Mom and Dad to see if they'd heard from me. And then you would have found Major and Maurice in whichever woman's bed they awoke in this morning to question them."

He chuckled. "As a matter of fact, I called Major and Maurice first."

Riley shook her head. The Gold twins were infamous for their identical dashing good looks and their prowess with almost every woman they encountered. They were also a part of the Babysit Riley Club, in which each of her brothers proudly held membership.

"That was so unnecessary. I was just a little late." She'd been an hour and a half late because she'd been sleeping too soundly and too comfortably in Chaz's arms.

"But you're never late."

That was true.

"I apologize."

"No need to apologize, Ri. You're entitled to some time for yourself. It's just that we know you, and when something changes, we worry. But I'm glad to see you're just fine and on top of things with this new bridal collection. Your reports are amazingly detailed and the plan you've mapped out for marketing is stellar. I believe we have a winner here."

That sent happy vibes throughout her body. "I'm glad to hear that because I want to revisit the specialty shops idea again. I know Dad said he didn't want to detract from our flagship stores in Manhattan, Beverly Hills and Paris, but I really think these smaller, more focused shops will hit a section of the market we're missing."

They'd had this discussion before at meetings with her father; his top two designers; Major, who was the technical developer; Maurice, who was in charge of public relations; and Janel Lindsey, the CFO. The same conversation had also been held during family dinners at their parents' house. Each time, her idea for expansion on a smaller scale was shot down, regardless of her market research on the idea. The Gold brand was big; everything they did had to be big or they didn't do it. That was what her father insisted.

"You know how Dad feels about that."

"He's wrong." She knew she was being adamant, but she couldn't help it. She was positive the idea could succeed. Riley hoped that with the successful launch of this couture bridal collection, she could convince her father that she really did know what she was doing.

"Well, let's just take on one thing at a time. The projected sales numbers for the Golden Bride Collection look great and the campaign you've outlined is amazingly thorough. If the marketing department follows through with everything you've pitched here, we're looking at a major victory for the company." RJ seemed pretty excited by that thought.

Of course he was—more sales meant more accolades for him. Not that he needed them. As the firstborn he was going to slide into the CEO position at RGF the moment their father retired. Major and Maurice didn't want that job. But Riley could see herself doing it. She'd also seen herself as a phenomenal chief executive of market research and she knew that she was ruling that position right now. So RJ could have the CEO spot, Riley planned to make her mark right here and right now.

"I have to call Sigmund again. I missed our call this morning. But I need to stress the importance of having enough stock to fill all the preorders. Once the show is over, stores are going to need dresses to sell."

"Maurice will have all the online specs ready to go so ordering will be possible," RJ added.

"I don't want there to be a wait for delivery in the first few weeks of the launch. I want brides to see these dresses, fall in love with one and plunk down their cash to buy it. And I want them to have their dresses in hand well before their wedding dates so they have more time to adore it. Especially since they'll only have it on for one day."

RJ eased off the table and went to grab his notepad and empty coffee cup. "There's my sister. For a while I was wondering why you were going so hard on this collection when I knew weddings were not your thing."

Riley picked up her half-full bottle of water. She tucked her tablet under one arm and held the sketch case in her hand.

"Oh, you know I'm never getting married. But I can relate to a woman's dream of the perfect wedding."

Probably because she'd had it once, a long time ago. Even before Walt, Riley had dreamed of what her wedding would be like. The problem with that dream was that she'd never really thought there would be a man who she wanted to marry. Blame that on the low self-esteem that had plagued her throughout her teenage years, which she'd finally overcome when she was in college. She'd taken a chance with Walt because it was a good business match and she had liked him in the beginning. The problem was marriages shouldn't be built on "like"—or infidelity for that matter.

"Well, you've conveyed your thoughts to the design team and they've come through in spades." RJ led the way to the door.

"They did. I'm really pleased with everything they've done."

"The show's going to be great. Rehearsals are already planned to start early next week."

"I'll be there," she said as they walked down the hall, past conference rooms and mini fitting spaces, where designs could be examined and altered.

"You know, Ri, you don't have to do everything. I feel like you've been trying to make up for what happened with Walt and that's just not necessary."

It was. Calling off the engagement had cost the company a lucrative deal with one of the world's top clothing distributors. On top of that, her parents had been friends with Walt's parents for a very long time. The breakup had been about more than just her and Walt. It had severed a business connection and a friendship. Right or wrong, Riley carried that guilt.

"I should have never agreed to marry him. The entire relationship was a mistake. One I plan to never make again."

"Well, you know how I feel about relationships, so you'll get no argument from me. But I would like to see you socializing a little more. Going to parties just to have fun instead of reeling in designers for the company. Taking more than one vacation. Sleeping in one morning because you work too many long days and nights in the first place. You know, stuff like that."

He nudged her when he finished and grinned.

Riley smiled back while shaking her head.

"I know you're not talking. You are the biggest workaholic of us all." Which was true. Major and Maurice were the most relaxed of the Gold siblings, while Riley and RJ took the job, the company and their family obligations much more seriously.

He shrugged as they moved to the elevators. "You might be right about that, but I do at least take the time to go on a date here and there. You're on this solo crusade when I think a little socializing might be good for you every now and then."

"Wait a minute. Are you, my big brother, telling me to find a guy to sleep with?"

"Whoa. Oh no! Full stop! That is not what I said. Let's just change the subject."

Riley chuckled at RJ's completely over-the-top but hilarious reaction as they stepped into the elevator.

"Yeah, I think changing the subject might be a good idea," she said and laughed a little more.

"What's your vision for ChatMe? Do you see yourself finding the woman of your dreams through your singles app?"

Chaz was momentarily taken off guard by the question. He hadn't custom designed a singles app. That had not been his vision at all. And the part about finding the woman of his dreams… Just no.

"ChatMe will be a hub for a certain demographic to socialize, share their triumphs, issues, goals, etc. The app was never intended to be just about dating." He gave the response in a smooth and relaxed tone even though on the inside he was irritated by the question.

Maybe because Riley had said something very similar last night.

"Okay, I hear you." The interviewer's name was Valeria and she was the owner of a popular blog and YouTube show. She was pretty and had already expressed her personal interest in him prior to requesting a formal interview.

Chaz had declined the personal invite but accepted the professional one because her blog and show had over two million subscribers.

"But you have to admit that your following in the past few years since you blew up on social media has been women. Many of whom are looking for a way to reach out to you personally."

Valeria had a sly smile, sea green eyes and a mass of curly hair. A week ago, Chaz would have slept with her. Today he was simply trying to get through this interview.

"Social media is all about making connections. Business networking, friendships and, yes, even committed relationships have been born from the many platforms out there. At Conversation Media our goal has always been to start conversations. ChatMe will do the same on a more focused level. We're excited about its formal release in two weeks and hope you'll join us for the launch."

With that, Chaz stood. He buttoned his suit jacket and said, "We're done."

Valeria stopped her recorder and hurriedly stood, as well. "Ah, okay. I hope you weren't bothered by the questions. Inquiring minds want to know." She attempted a joking tone but Chaz really wasn't feeling it.

"It's fine. Can you just let my PR people know when the interview will be posted?"

"I really wish you'd let me do a live show, Chaz. I'm sure we would've gotten thousands of viewers if we'd gone that route. Maybe you'll reconsider for the week of the launch. It'll be double exposure for you on the blog and the broadcast."

Chaz started to walk away. "As I stated before, that's not possible. I'll be tied up with pre–Fashion Week events during that time."

"Oh, right, the favor you're doing for your uncle. That's so noble of you."

"There's nothing noble about what I'm doing. King Designs is a family business that put me through private schools and college. My loyalty will always be to my family." Chaz wasn't sure why this woman was irritating him so much today. He just knew that the sooner he could get away from her, the better.

"Well then, I'll be sure to let your people know when I post the interview."

He didn't miss the bite in her tone and he understood the real meaning of her words—she would post when she felt like it.

"I appreciate that. We have a vigorous lineup of promotion on all media platforms beginning early next week and going into the month after launch, so we'd like to keep track of all of the places we need to thank for their support."

And if she wasn't one of them, he would have to accept that, but Chaz had never allowed a reporter to take advantage of him or to play him for their own personal reasons, and he wasn't about to start now.

His phone rang and Chaz said goodbye to Valeria before walking out of the room.

"I was able to move the first run-through to one thirty but we've got models, makeup artists, hair stylists and photographers on the clock," Chaz's assistant said when he answered.

"I'm on my way. Getting in the car now."

Chaz ended the call and stepped into the elevator. Minutes later, he was walking out of the building and onto the sidewalk filled with New Yorkers on the move.

Guy, his driver, had already stepped out of the black town car and was opening the back door for him to get in. Chaz slipped onto the backseat and pulled up his text messages. Nothing from Riley.

He wasn't sure if that was a good or bad sign.

# CHAPTER ELEVEN

ONE WEEK LATER, Riley walked into the 11 Howard Hotel, ready for *Saturday Style* magazine's style summit, which officially kicked off the pre–Fashion Week festivities. She wore a navy-blue wool coat that complemented her navy-and-rust geometric-print blouse, pleated skirt and calf-high cognac-colored suede boots. Her hair was pulled back into a neat bun.

One of the hostesses took her coat and Riley tucked her purse under her arm as she walked toward the ballroom alone. Since this event used the best technology on the market to showcase the hottest trends in style, Major was also attending. He had a front row seat as did Riley, but she hadn't wanted to be up front during the presentation so she'd arrived late, hoping she could avoid immediate detection and slide into a seat at the back after everyone had been seated.

Two minutes after she walked into the auditorium her plan failed miserably.

"Hello, beautiful."

"Hi." She tried to make sure her response wasn't as breathless as she felt upon seeing Chaz again but wasn't convinced it had worked.

The room was dark but with the bright blue, fuchsia and white lights coming from the stage and the large screens displaying the presentation, she could tell that he looked good. His suit jacket was dark, his jeans light, button-front white print shirt crisp.

"It's been another busy week," he said. "I didn't get a chance to catch up with you."

"Yes. I know. There's a lot going on right now. I'm just going to go and find my seat." She moved around him and was not totally surprised when he extended an arm to stop her.

"Hold on a sec. Can we just talk for a minute?"

"The show's already started."

"You knew that would be the case when you purposely arrived late." He sounded like he was making a casual observation.

His arm was extended in front of her but he wasn't touching her. She could still feel the heat emanating from him. It was familiar, and to her chagrin her body sought it.

"Five minutes, Riley. We can go out into the hall or find some other private space."

How much would she love to go off to some private space with Chaz? Way too much, to be honest.

She shook her head. "Not here, Chaz. Maybe we can meet up later."

Before he could respond Riley saw two people coming up the aisle heading directly for the spot where they stood. She moved around his arm and walked quickly to find any available seat. It was best if she sat down and got out of view.

After the show it took Riley a few minutes to make her way out of the auditorium. Reporters and photographers were everywhere and while she knew it would be good to be seen by one of them and to offer a tease about RGF's show, Riley couldn't help but hope they ignored her. Besides, Major was here—he could just as easily give a tease and a lengthy interview since he wasn't opposed to using the tabloids at every opportunity. He figured that served them right for all the times they purposely misinformed the public with outright lies.

"Hey! Riley Gold is here! We were wondering if you were somewhere in this crowd!"

Once again her plan was foiled as she locked gazes with a reporter. Riley didn't remember his name but she knew that he wrote for the *Fashion Insider* blog. He was tall and slim and wore too much product in his hair.

"Hello." Riley clasped her purse with both hands and held it in front of her as if it were a shield.

"What can you tell us about RGF's upcoming show? I know you've got something up your sleeve. The gossip mill's been buzzing, girl, so please give us an exclusive!" He looped his arm through hers and walked them past a throng of reporters who had snagged their prey and were chatting away.

The lobby of the hotel suddenly felt very crowded and Riley tried to focus on saying the words she'd typed into the notes app on her phone on the drive here.

"You'll just have to wait until the show for the full surprise," she began. "Of course, we'll be having our annual media brunch on the seventh, where you'll be treated to delicious food and face time with our top designers."

"Oh yes, I already have my invitation. But what we really want to know is if RGF will be focusing exclusively on a debonair men's collection. Or are you unveiling something extra special for the women this year?"

He was persistent. They all were, and when Riley glanced around the room to see more people stopping and talking, her heart began to race.

"RGF always offers top-of-the-line designs for everyone. We've built a platform based on quality and high fashion for a diverse world and we plan to deliver just as we have in the past."

"Okay, so you're not going to spill any of the details. You're always so discreet." He smiled at her and Riley took that moment to step out of his hold. She put a little space between them and was prepared to say her farewells and get the hell out of there when he continued.

"Unfortunately, that didn't work well where Walter Stone was concerned. We were all saddened by that breakup, but I'm sure not as sad as your parents were. That was a pretty lucrative deal hinging on those nuptials. But all that's water under the bridge now. Do you have anything you'd like to say to Walt and his new fiancée? I hear they're planning a fall wedding. Will RGF be designing the bride's gown? Or is that a little too close to home since you and Walt were once an item?"

Riley's legs began to wobble and her knees threatened to give out. She squeezed her purse as if she thought she could actually tear the leather apart with her rage. And still, she smiled.

"I wish Walter and his bride-to-be the very best. I'm sure she'll be quite beautiful in whatever she wears. Now, I'll have to say good-night."

She started to leave and he tried to grab her arm. Riley turned quickly, giving him a glare that had him immediately withdrawing his hand and attempting a faint smile. He stuffed his hand into his pocket and backed away. Riley left him standing there and headed to the bathroom. She wasn't sure she would make it out front for the valet to bring her car.

Pushing through the door, Riley went straight to the last stall. She eased the lock in place before leaning her back against it. Her eyes closed and tears threatened to fall. That reporter was an ass and he did not deserve her tears, but, oh, how that rock sat in the center of her chest, threatening to bury her alive.

She focused on her breathing and the fact that the

anxiety attack could not last forever. In very slowly, out even slower. In and out. It would end and she could continue on with her life because she was a survivor. Her fingers eventually stopped clenching her bag and held it loosely instead. Her stomach still churned but she could swallow now without feeling as if she had a throat full of cotton.

Her phone buzzed from inside the purse and Riley jumped at the sound. She took another breath and opened her eyes, feeling confident that no tears would fall. After digging inside her purse she found her phone, relieved that it was just a text and not someone on the other end. She didn't know if she was ready to talk just yet.

Drinks at my place?

Riley read the message and let her head fall back against the door. She closed her eyes again and wondered what was going on. Reporters were asking about Walt and his fiancée, when she hadn't even known Walt had a fiancée. She was sleeping with the enemy and enjoying it far too much. And Production still wasn't giving her a definite on her preorders. When exactly had her life become so chaotic?

And would drinks with Chaz make it better or worse?

She looked down at her phone and began to type.

My place, 20 minutes.

* * *

When Chaz rang the doorbell, Riley opened the door and pulled him inside. She closed the door and turned to wrap her arms around his neck before taking his mouth in a kiss that scorched every part of him.

His arms went around her waist, hands flattening over her ass and back. She tilted her head, taking the kiss deeper, and he went with her lead, stroking his tongue against hers and pressing her against his now-growing arousal. She lifted a leg, dragging it up the outside of his, moaning into him as if he were giving her everything she wanted and needed right now.

It felt good. It felt damn perfect. His body reacted instantly, dick pressing against his jeans in a hurry to get deep inside her. Her breasts were plastered against his chest. She moaned and sighed as she momentarily pulled her lips away from his. Her teeth nipped his lower lip before she sucked it into her mouth. Chaz held her tighter. He gripped her ass until she gasped, and he was just about to push her skirt down and take her against the wall right in the foyer of her house. But he stopped.

Chaz pulled back from the kiss. He kept his arms around her but looked down at her face instead of moving away.

"What happened?"

Her makeup was gone, her face freshly washed

and simply gorgeous. And her hair was down. Messy and hanging past her shoulders. He continued to survey her and noticed she'd removed her boots and taken off all her jewelry. Her eyes were dry, not red at all, but there was a weary look in them. A dead giveaway that something was going on.

"Nothing." She tilted her head. "Did we really need the preamble of drinks? Aren't we old enough to know how this is going to play out?"

"No and yes," he replied. "I'm also smart enough to know when a woman is using sex to mask her pain or discontent. Now, tell me what happened."

She pushed away from him and walked into the living room, going straight to the bar in the corner near the window.

"You can go if your plan for tonight was to talk or cuddle. I'm not in the mood."

Chaz could have figured that out without her saying so. He walked slowly into the living room, watching her quick, irritated movements as she took a glass from the cabinet and placed it on the bar top with a loud clunk. She yanked off the top of a decanter and poured more than half a glass of whiskey. He stopped a few steps from the bar and slipped his hands into the front pockets of his jeans. Riley looked directly at him, brought the glass to her lips and tilted her head back to swallow. Three big gulps and she almost emptied the glass. With a shaky sigh she lowered it and held her lips in a tight line.

"Don't you stand there and judge me," she warned.

Chaz shook his head. "Never. But I would like you to tell me what happened to put you in this mood."

"Why? So you can fix it? I'm not in the market for a savior, Chaz."

"I'm not in the business of saving people, Riley. But when I'm sleeping with a woman, I like to know she's taken care of physically and mentally. So I'm asking you again to please tell me what happened."

He couldn't phrase it any nicer, not while trying desperately to hold on to the temper brewing at the thought that someone had upset her.

She set the glass on the bar top and folded her arms across her chest.

"It's stupid." She shook her head and blinked rapidly.

Chaz knew that if a tear fell it would be the end of him.

"If it hurt you, it's not stupid."

"I'm over it," she snapped. "Over him and all his lies. Have been for a long time now. It was just that slimy reporter. He knew exactly what he was doing asking about the show and then slipping in the comments about Walt and his bride-to-be. Like

I give a damn what that woman's going to wear to her wedding."

Chaz felt partial relief in knowing that it had only been a reporter who aggravated her, and deep irritation that her mood involved her ex-fiancé.

"He's a reporter—their job is to push buttons. They get a reaction or a blurted quote and they run with it. You know how this works, Riley."

"Yeah, I do and I think it sucks."

"I agree." Chaz moved to meet her on the other side of the bar. He really needed a drink now.

She pushed the whiskey closer to him and he found a glass and poured. He took a gulp, letting the liquid burn the back of his throat before he spoke again.

"What else did he say about you and Stone?" Because that was all that mattered to Chaz. He could not care less if the jerk was marrying someone else.

"It's not relevant. I shouldn't have let it get under my skin. Like you said, I know better."

"But you continue to expect people to be better. That says a lot about you."

It also said she was probably going to continue being bothered by people who didn't have the good sense to get a clue.

"It either says I'm an idiot or I should have just punched the guy and went about my business."

"You're not an idiot." Chaz finished his drink and

turned around to lean his back against the bar. "Were you in love with Stone?"

It shouldn't matter, but it did. He was certain Riley had the capacity to love. What he didn't know is whether or not she'd given her heart to someone before.

She looked down at her glass and then up to him. "No. I wanted to be. Not just because it would have been the perfect professional union, but because it would mean that I was normal."

He shrugged. "Normal is overrated."

"Says the guy who played varsity football since he was in the ninth grade and went on to be a big shot in your fraternity."

She'd done some research on him. Chaz was flattered.

"It's much harder to be different."

She sighed. "We were supposed to be like the royal couple of fashion. Everybody was watching us and waiting for the big day. And all the time I was having daily anxiety attacks and cringing each night he decided to sleep with me."

Chaz had a rule about not knowing the past details of his current lover's sex life. But something made him want to know everything possible about Riley.

She lifted her hands and ran her fingers through her hair. What had been smooth and neat earlier was still mostly straight at the top but curling on the ends.

Chaz recalled how soft those curls were when he'd run his fingers through them. He wanted to do so again.

"I wasn't frigid in bed," she said in a huff.

"I can attest to that." He leaned over and nudged her shoulder with his.

She looked up at him with a semismile.

"Anyway, on the business end everything went very well. Stonemill Apparel was going to cut our distributing costs in half because of their global reach. At the time we had contracts with a US and UK distributor locked down. However, we'd entered into intense negotiations with Canada and China. Stonemill had warehouses and networks all over the globe. It made sense to combine all our distributing to one company. The process would be streamlined, contracts, payments, shipments would all be the same across the board instead of our production department having to navigate the different logistics of each separate company."

Chaz agreed. "A very smart idea."

"And because we were also combining our families, the company names, our brands, it was going to be a huge slam dunk in the industry."

"I remember." His uncle had been beside himself with worry over how the Gold/Stone joining was going to affect his distributing.

"And I didn't want to mess that up. I wanted RGF to not only remain on top, but to be so far ahead of the other fashion houses that they could only dream of catching up." She sighed and shook her head. "But I messed up."

Chaz rubbed a hand over her back and ignored the quick jolt of tenseness he felt in her with the touch. "You didn't mess up. You made a choice. A very good one, I would say."

She drank the rest of the whiskey, setting the glass down with another loud clunk when she was finished. "He cheated on me. I mean, I suspected all along that he had someone else but I'm not the type to hunt for clues to bust some guy. I was, however, the type to think once the wedding was over, it would stop. But there's something about having proof slap you in the face. That was a defining moment for me."

"And for Stone. It defined him as a jackass."

She nodded and turned so that she was now leaning her back against the bar just like him. "And it made me the Ice Princess. But I'm fine with that as long as RGF stays on top. As long as I continue to do a good job for our company. Next week will be another defining moment for me. The launch of our new lines, the marketing plans, the promotion, the sales, all that success will hopefully erase the whole Ice Princess title and all the negative energy that goes with it. But then this goofy reporter throws it right back into the mix and I begin to shatter like a piece of glass."

Chaz stepped in front of her. He cupped her face in his hands and tilted her head up slightly to stare into her eyes.

"There's nothing fragile about you, Riley. You are the strongest, most goal-oriented and beautiful—on the inside and out—woman I know. No matter what that reporter or any other reporter says, I know who and what you are. But more important is that you know who you are and your family—the people who love and care about you—know. Everyone else, all those people who believe what's printed on those blogs and in the papers, are idiots and don't warrant a second of your time."

Her full smile came slowly. The light it ignited in her eyes shone brightly. And the warmth that speared straight through Chaz's heart spread wildly.

"You're great for my ego."

"Oh, really? Well, I'm glad I could be of some use."

She eased her arms around his waist and pulled him closer. "I know of another way you can be useful."

Chaz grinned. He let his hands slide away from her face, moving them down to her waist, where he planted them and lifted her up to sit on the bar. "You're not the only smart one in this room, Ms. Riley Gold. I can think of more useful things I can do, as well."

"Oh, really?" She reached behind her back and

undid the snap at the back of her blouse before lifting it up and over her head. After tossing it to the floor she cupped a hand behind his head and pulled his face close to hers to whisper, "Show me."

# CHAPTER TWELVE

THIS WAS WHAT she needed tonight. Riley let her head loll back as Chaz's mouth and tongue created a scorching hot path down the line of her neck, over her collarbone and between the valley of her breasts. She moaned and whispered his name when he unhooked her bra and cupped her heavy mounds. Her legs were spread wide and wrapped around his waist, her hands plastered to the back of his head to stop him if he dared try to discontinue the sweet torture.

"Just do it," she crooned before sucking her bottom lip between her teeth and biting down in an attempt to hold in some of the desire bristling through her at the moment. The battle was lost the second he closed his mouth over one nipple and palmed the other breast.

"Yes. Take it. Take it all." Riley arched into him, loving the hard suction of his mouth and the quick scrape of teeth over her sensitive skin.

He held the other breast in his palm, squeezing and releasing. Damn, she was on top of the bar in her house, a place she'd never dreamed of having sex.

Chaz pulled back and she groaned until his strong hands found the band of her skirt. In one quick motion he lifted her slightly off the bar, just enough to pull the skirt and her panties down and off her legs. The marble top was cool to her bare ass as Riley watched Chaz remove his jacket. She reached forward and grabbed for his shirt, yanking it so hard the buttons popped free. She pushed it over his massive shoulders and down his arms. He reached back into his wallet to find a condom while her hands moved busily over his belt buckle, button and zipper. She pushed the jeans and his boxers down as far as she could reach and heard him ripping the condom packet open.

"Now," she whispered when her thighs began to tremble.

Her pussy ached for attention and her chest heaved with anticipation.

He sheathed himself and wrapped one arm around her waist to pull her closer to the edge of the bar top. She locked her legs around him again just as he thrust deep into her. They both yelled out at the quick and forceful meeting. And then he was pounding into her, taking her higher, faster than she'd ever imagined.

"You are everything," he groaned. "So hot and tight around me, so damn wet, Riley."

Riley was wet and he was easing in and out of her with a friction that touched every sensitive spot she possessed. At this moment her body was his and he was owning it completely. This was what she needed—to lose herself so completely.

"Harder!" Her hands clamped down on his shoulders, blunt-tipped nails digging into his skin. "Harder, Chaz! Take me harder!"

He obeyed her command, pumping into her so hard and fast their joining made a cupping sound that echoed throughout the room. She was going to fall right over the edge. She could feel her pleasure rising so high it had no choice but to fall gracefully. Or rather ungracefully as she yelled out his name the second her body trembled with the force of her orgasm.

"Yes!" Chaz yelled with her. "Give it to me! All for me, Riley. Give it all to me. Yes!"

She couldn't have withheld it if she tried. Her legs shook around him, her arms trembled and her teeth almost bit hard into her lip as pleasure ripped through her like a tornado. He'd slowed his thrust only marginally, his arms going around her back, holding her tight against his chest as her essence poured over him.

His quick pace resumed moments later when her body was still filled with the hum of her release. He buried his face in the crook of her neck and pumped wildly into her as if he couldn't hold back a moment longer.

"Riley." Her name tore from his lips.

His teeth brushed over her skin.

"Riley. Dammit, Riley!"

His arms grew tighter around her and Riley locked her ankles at his back. She pressed closer to him, enjoying the sound of her name in his husky tone.

"You can come for me now," she whispered, wanting him to do just that.

To empty himself into her so that they could be even and one. That was a jolting thought and before she could marinate on it any longer a painfully raw sound ripped from Chaz's throat.

"For you!" he groaned and pounded into her so fast she grew breathless. "All. For. You."

Riley's head jerked as he punctuated those last words with deep and powerful thrusts that almost pushed her right over the bar. If he hadn't been holding on to her so tightly she was sure she would have toppled over, but he *was* holding her. His arms were wrapped tightly around her as he pushed his dick into her and held completely still for endless seconds. The pounding of his dick as his release pulsed into the condom had her legs trembling.

Her back was arched and Chaz lowered his forehead to her chest. "Just you, Riley."

The words were spoken slowly as he pulled slightly out and pushed back inside her. "Just you."

She showered alone and Chaz used her guest bathroom.

After a few minutes, he stood at the sink and

splashed water over his face once and then again in an attempt to clear his mind. When that didn't work, Chaz grabbed one of the soft yellow towels from a rack and pressed it to his face. It smelled just like Riley—fresh, clean and impossibly feminine. He sighed as he pulled it away and looked into the mirror.

"What the hell are you doing?"

His deep brown eyes looked the same. The strong jaw and light dusting of a beard, the scar just above his eyebrow he'd had since he was six and the precisely lined shape-up he'd received earlier today at the barber—all of it looked the same. The man he'd always seen was staring back at him. And yet Chaz knew that was a total lie.

As he stood in Riley Gold's guest bathroom all he could think about was going into her bedroom, getting into her bed and cuddling with her until they both fell asleep. He wanted to sleep with her again. Not sex. Sleep. Him. And Riley Gold.

That wasn't something he would have even considered before.

It was insane.

And it was the truth.

He cursed.

This wasn't the type of affair he'd envisioned when he proposed this idea. He hadn't anticipated that feelings would go along with the mindless sex. And he knew that hadn't been Riley's plan, either.

Yet, here they were sharing things about themselves they'd never intended to share with anyone. It was wild.

Talking to Riley the way he had, comforting her, feeling the overwhelming need to find Walt Stone and beat him senseless, none of that was part of an affair. At least, not in his world. Chaz was about his job, his company and living a drama-free life. It was what he'd worked so hard to achieve since he became an adult and it wasn't negotiable. He had to get back on track.

At least, that was what his mind was saying. Other parts of him—the foreign part that never usually had a say where women were concerned—was leaning in a different direction. And for the first time in his life, Chaz didn't know what to do.

## CHAPTER THIRTEEN

TWO DAYS LATER, Riley was still thinking about Chaz. To be honest, she hadn't stopped thinking about him since returning from Milan. No matter how much she'd tried to deny it, the man was on her mind every day. And even more on the mornings after they'd been together. Luckily for Riley the last two days had been filled with meetings, reports and other Fashion Week festivities that had kept her and Chaz pretty busy. So busy that they'd resorted to communicating mostly via text messaging. That was why Riley's phone was now on her desk only inches away from her keyboard as she reviewed the yearlong sales projections for the Golden Bride Collection.

Riley noted the time on the bottom of her computer screen and pulled her glasses off to rub her eyes. She'd been reading and taking notes for the last three hours. It was almost four in the afternoon and she toyed with the idea of getting out of the office at a decent hour today. But there was still so much work to get done before that was an option.

She eased her glasses back into place just as a brisk knock sounded at her door.

"Come in!" she yelled and reached for the half-empty bottle of water on her desk.

"These are for you."

Riley stopped drinking abruptly, spilling a few drops of water onto the bold orange, white and blue striped sweater she wore. Her high-waist pants were beige with an orange-and-blue plaid print. Thankfully she was sitting close enough to the desk that water didn't trickle down to her lap.

"For me? From who?"

Her heart thumped and Riley fought the tendrils of panic steadily trying to creep into her mind.

Korey sat the large bouquet on her desk and snatched the card that had been attached to a long white pitchfork thing in its side.

"Let me see," he was saying and making a big production out of pulling that card from the white envelope.

Riley had no idea what came over her but she hopped up from her chair and hurried around the desk in time to snap the card from Korey's hand. She held it without looking at it.

"I'll read the card later," she said. "The hand-crafted veils were supposed to arrive today. Can you track them down so we'll be ready for the meeting with the designers in an hour?"

Korey frowned and Riley knew why. He wanted

to know what was wrong with her. While her assistant hadn't dared to ask her that question again, Riley knew he was still wondering. She could tell by the way he looked at her daily when he thought she didn't notice.

"They're beautiful." Korey watched her closely.

"They're flowers," she replied but sighed when she looked at them because they were gorgeous.

She wasn't a romantic by any stretch of the imagination, but this large bouquet filled with exotic-looking flowers and crisp greenery was exactly what she would like to receive if she were inclined to receive such gifts. Only she had no idea who would have sent them or why. She was certain it wasn't Chaz because they were simply having an affair. There was no romance involved, even though that candlelight dinner with just the two of them had been really close to a real date.

"I need to speak with you, Riley."

The booming voice had both Riley and Korey looking toward her open office door. Ronald Gold, Sr., blocked the access with his broad frame and piercing gaze.

"I was just leaving," Korey said, offering Riley an apologetic look before hurrying out of her office.

Riley slipped the card into her pocket. "Hi, Dad."

Ron closed the door behind Korey and walked the short distance to where Riley was standing in front of the desk. She'd moved in an attempt to block the flowers. Her father came close and first tweaked her nose before pulling her into a tight hug.

Riley melted into the hug, wrapping her arms around her father's expansive build. If he hadn't gone into fashion, her father could have definitely been a professional wrestler. In addition to his build, Ron's imposing stature and voice gave him an air of command. But when it was just the two of them, when his large arms were around her and holding Riley tight, he was just her dad.

"Somebody's sending my baby girl flowers?"

Riley hurriedly pulled out of his embrace and turned to look at the flowers again.

"I don't know who they're from. Korey just brought them in seconds before you arrived. But, anyway, what's going on? I thought you and Maurice were out making the rounds at all the preshow events this week." There was nothing, not even sports, her father loved to discuss more than the fashion empire his father had built.

"Probably one of the manufacturers or the boutique owners that want to carry our new collections."

She hadn't thought of that and felt a wave of relief now that her father had put that possibility out there.

"You may be right. So what brings you here? I sent the latest projections via email this morning. I'm going over long-term numbers now."

Ron reached inside his black suit jacket and pulled out a rolled-up newspaper. He slapped it down onto the desk a few inches away from the floral arrangement.

"I called his editor this morning and very strongly suggested an apology be printed first thing tomorrow. We are not here to be used for their amusement."

Riley refused to let her fingers shake as she picked up the paper and read the first few lines of the article.

Riley Gold wishes her ex and his soon-to-be wife well, but won't be designing the bride's dress.

She tried to swallow but it was hard. Instead she focused once again on breathing and surprisingly her breaths came easier, sooner, than she'd anticipated. She shook her head.

"I thought the guy only ran a blog, not that he had a byline at this trashy tabloid, as well. Anyway, I suppose he had to find something to take up space."

She dropped the paper into the trash can on her way to the other side of her desk. Ron was already pacing in the space that she'd left vacant and Riley sat in her chair.

"Not at our expense! I made it clear they would never get another interview or invitation to any of our private events if they didn't have an apology on the front page tomorrow morning. The editor is old-school but needs the readers so he was hesitant, said his guy got a direct quote from you."

"He did." She leaned forward and rested her arms

on the desk. "He stopped me after the style summit and asked about the collection. When I wouldn't tell him, he brought up Walt and his fiancée. He asked if we were designing her dress. I told him no and that I wished Walt well. Which is the absolute truth."

Riley had decided a few years ago that wishing him dead wasn't going to change what had happened.

"Don't give them ammunition, Riley. How many times have I told you that?"

"If truth is ammunition, then I might as well yell 'no comment' every time I see a reporter coming toward me. Look, Dad, I know what they're doing. They're trying to bait me, ruffle my feathers, throw me off my game. I'm not going to let that happen."

Ron stared at her seriously for a moment before chuckling and shaking his head. "Stubborn. Just like your mama."

Riley sat back in her chair, for the first time in her life truly feeling unbothered by Walter Stone and his childish antics.

"I've just got better things to do with my time. We're about to break records with this upcoming show."

Her father took a seat in one of the guest chairs across from her desk. "That's exactly what I want to hear. Tell me more about what you've done, baby girl."

Riley was happy to talk about work with her father. She wasn't thrilled that at twenty-nine years old he was still calling her his baby girl, but there was nothing she could do about that. Ron Gold wasn't the type to change until he was good and ready.

The idea to construct a runway in the center of an old railway station was brilliant. It was the perfect backdrop for the rebranded King Collection, which was King Designs's signature men's collection. Tobias King and his team of designers had always been known for their cutting-edge, streetwise men's clothes. But in the last two years that line had fallen behind women's couture and wedding wear. Chaz was aiming to change that.

"It's important to have the lighting coordinated with the music and the specific beats of the show. I don't want any lags and every model must be specifically highlighted when they get to the front of the runway." Chaz had been giving instructions all day while they worked at the venue. It was nearing six in the evening and he was just hitting his stride.

Ram, one of the three show producers, was nodding as he took notes on his tablet.

"Four rows of seats, not five. Three sections of seating and the remaining guests will be standing. We have a lot of room for people to move around, and if they're standing too far in the back or near the bar during the show, that's why we have the screens. The idea is to make this feel like a night at the club, not a high-end fashion show."

"Got it. Alexa's working with the backstage manager. They were having some deep discussion about where to place the rails and the chairs for the models. The designers are with hair and makeup, going through a hair and makeup test."

"As soon as that's complete I want everyone out to do another run-through. Have the designers stand down here and to the sides so we can get an idea of how everything is going to look. What's the status of the rest of the set? We only have six more days for construction." Chaz walked the length of one half of the U-shaped runway.

"We normally deal with the show producers."

Chaz turned at the sound of another man's voice. He held back a frown when he saw Lenzo Fuchetti, one of King's top designers.

"I know what's normally been done, but normal wasn't working for this particular line. So this time around we're switching things up." Chaz normally worked well with the staff, whether at his company or Tobias's, but Lenzo had a particularly hard time dealing with Chaz's presence and the amount of impact he had on this upcoming show. Chaz could relate to an extent. Aside from his relationship to Tobias he was an outsider. His specialty was in a totally different industry. Still, Tobias had paid for Chaz's education, which had given Chaz the tools to create his own multimillion-dollar brand. The least Chaz could do was use some of what he'd learned to help his uncle get back on top. If Lenzo didn't understand, that was his problem.

"We'll need sheer drapes at the back, pin lights as well as spotlights," Lenzo continued.

Chaz nodded to Ram, approving what Lenzo said. Ram made note of it and Lenzo huffed. There was some commotion at the front doors and Lenzo hurried off to assist.

"I have an engagement at seven. We need to get on with the run-through," Chaz told them.

"I'll get everyone together," Ram told him before walking away.

Chaz ran a hand down the back of his head and sighed. This had been a really long day. It had also been the second day of not seeing Riley. He didn't like that. And when he reached into his back pocket and pulled out his phone, he didn't like that she hadn't sent him a text since earlier this morning. He scrolled through his emails quickly, wondering when he'd become so concerned with whether or not a woman had texted him back. Normally women waited for him to return their messages. He frowned down at his phone for a few minutes more, wondering if he should break routine and text her again.

He didn't have time because they were ready to do the run-through and getting this finished in the next hour was important.

Forty minutes later they were entering the last minutes of the show. The run-through was going smoothly with two other designers on-site making a few suggestions and changes to the models' hairstyles and positioning on the runway. Chaz happily stood to the back to let them do their thing. His job was the overall picture. Making sure everything he'd been working on with the designers and his team for the last six months had been implemented. All of that made the arrival of four models on the stage wearing wedding gowns even more disconcerting.

He moved closer to the runway, where Lenzo was now directing. The shorter man was clapping his hands and motioning for the models to come to the spots he pointed to immediately. His midnight-black hair was shaved on the sides and left to hang long in a curly strip down the center, and he was constantly pushing the strands out of his eyes.

"This one should be front and center. So you switch places with her. Yes, just like that. And then turn slightly." Lenzo looked back to the booth where the lighting guys were sitting. "I want the beading to sparkle. Shine the light right on her so that she glitters throughout the room."

"What the hell is this?" Chaz asked. He'd spent a few seconds trying to come up with a less irritated way to ask why these models wearing dresses he'd never seen were on the runway, but he couldn't.

Lenzo turned to face Chaz, annoyance evident in the narrowing of his eyes and the smirk of his lips.

"It is high fashion. I don't know what these others have done to appease you and your specialty branding idea, but this is what we do here at King Designs."

Chaz didn't really have a problem with the dresses. They were fine from a cursory glance. What he didn't like was someone attempting to usurp his authority.

"The first portion of this show is dedicated to the unveiling of the men's line—fifteen new designs. There are seventeen women's designs that will follow. We specifically decided to focus on ready-to-wear designs for this showing, waiting until next year to present haute couture pieces. Therefore, King Designs isn't offering any bridal wear this year."

Lenzo sighed heavily. "It's the spring/summer season—that's precisely when we would unveil such one-of-a-kind bridal designs."

Again, Lenzo's logic was not totally wrong, but Chaz's rebranding plan called for King Designs to do the unexpected. Lenzo turned away from Chaz and continued to instruct the models. Chaz took another moment to gather his thoughts. Then he went into action.

"This run-through is over." He spoke loud enough so that everyone in the room stopped what they were doing and looked at him. "Thank you, models, stylists, supervisors. We'll see you again on Monday." He turned to look at Ram and said, "Shut the place down for the night and make sure it's locked up tight."

Lenzo, because the man really was an idiot, continued, "I'm not finished."

Chaz leveled his gaze at him and spoke with as much control as he could muster. "Yes. You're definitely finished for tonight."

Lenzo's shocked expression didn't faze Chaz as he turned and walked out. In the car on his way back to his apartment Chaz called Tobias to explain what happened and suggest a course of action to deal with Lenzo's blatant disrespect for not only him, as an executive of the company, but also for the plan approved by Tobias, the CEO. His uncle agreed. On a heavy sigh Chaz admitted he was tired and needed to unwind. He was grateful for tonight's engagement, and with that thought checked his text messages again. The one he'd been waiting for had finally come.

Be there at 8.

# CHAPTER FOURTEEN

RILEY SAT IN the backseat of the car and read the card one more time.

*208 Lenholake Avenue, 7:00 p.m.*

She had no idea where this was or what she would find when she arrived. All she knew was that after her father left her office this afternoon she'd sat at her desk staring at the flowers and wondering if they could be from a vendor or a cruel joke from Walt. Finally, she decided it was ridiculous to keep trying to figure it out when the flowers had come with a card. She'd pulled the card out of her pocket and read it, the cryptic nature surprising and irritating her. But just when Riley was going to chuck the card and the flowers into the trash she looked at the arrangement one more time.

That was when she saw it.

The vase was made of rose quartz. Faint white lines mixed with the pale pink of the urn-shaped container.

The vibrant colors of the tropical flowers—deep orange, purple and fuchsia—along with the dramatic greenery had completely captured her attention from the moment Korey brought them into her office. Riley hadn't paid any attention to the container, and as she'd reached across her desk to touch her fingertips to its cool, smooth surface, she'd smiled.

And immediately left her office to go home.

Chaz hadn't texted her all afternoon, so when she'd come out of the shower, she sent him a simple message: Be there at 8.

The car pulled up in front of what looked like a regular building around the corner from New York's acclaimed Fifth Avenue. Riley stepped out when the driver opened the back door. She grabbed the lapels of her peach coat closer as a chilly breeze blew and she stepped onto the crimson-carpeted section of the sidewalk. A green awning covered the walkway and displayed the building's address in stark white numbers.

Riley was still unsure of what she was walking into. The address attached to a lovely flower arrangement in no way expressed what tonight was about. She'd dressed according to her mood and with comfort in mind—black-and-white leopard-print wrap skirt with a peach-colored blouse and knee-length black suede boots. Her hair was pulled back in a stylishly messy knot and she carried a peach-colored leather bag she'd picked up when she first arrived in Milan.

"Good evening. May I take your coat?"

The older man had approached quietly. Dressed in an excellently cut black tuxedo complete with stark white shirt and bow tie, he looked every bit the stately butler. That was when Riley really surveyed her surroundings. The foyer was bright, with cream-colored walls, intricate molding and an immaculate marble floor. To her left was a double-height windowed gallery and a sweeping staircase.

"Madam?"

"Oh. I apologize," Riley said when the butler had stepped closer, his hand extended for her coat. She removed the coat and handed it to him.

"I believe I'm supposed to meet someone here. His name is—"

The butler had taken her coat and folded it neatly over his right arm. With his left he held up a finger, which had Riley snapping her lips shut.

"Right through there, madam. You will find everything that you are in search of."

He walked away as quietly as he'd come, but Riley watched him until he disappeared through a side door the same color as the walls. What was this place?

She walked in the direction she was told, choosing one of the two doorways that were separated by a remarkable antique grandfather clock. The room she entered was even more astonishing. The walls were a bold celadon with butter-colored floral-print wallpaper beneath the chair rail. That was just the beginning of what she thought might be eighteenth-century Parisian decor, which was definitely not her taste. The best thing about the room were the magnificent views of Central Park through each of the four large windows.

The strangest thing was the man and two women sitting on a chaise longue and thoroughly enjoying themselves. She gasped the moment she realized the man was gripping one woman's bare breast while enthusiastically kissing the other woman, who had just freed his hard cock from his tuxedo pants.

She turned and ran back into the hallway, ready to yell for the butler to appear with her coat so she could get the hell out of here. But her phone buzzed and she hustled to dig it out of her purse before it disturbed the threesome.

Come upstairs. First room to your left.

Riley read the text and her fingers immediately began moving over the screen.

I don't think so. There are people having sex in the front room.

She hit Send and looked around. It was relatively quiet considering what was happening in

that other room. Curiosity had Riley stepping ten-
tatively through the second door. This room had a
much lighter color scheme but Riley was beyond the
decor at this point. Another man dressed in a tuxedo
was standing against a wall, his head leaned back,
eyes closed, face contorted in desire as the woman
on her knees in front of him sucked his cock deep
into her mouth. Not six feet from them was a woman
wearing a gorgeous orange gown with a split high
up her right thigh. She was making use of that split
because one of her legs was draped over the arm of
the French armchair while her fingers toyed with
her exposed clit.

Riley's mouth clamped shut, not just because she
was shocked, but because of the flush that quickly
came over her skin. She felt warm and… She didn't
even want to admit it. Her phone buzzed again.

Come on up, Riley. I'm waiting for you.

She turned and walked slowly out of that room,
still trying to figure out what was happening. Without any clear answers Riley started up the stairs.

When you come in, close and lock the door and
then wait for me.

What the hell was this? And who did Chaz think
she was? Riley did not do games and she definitely
did not do sex games. She should leave right now

and let him play at whatever this was by himself. But she didn't. She walked up to the painted door and touched the bronze handle. Her hand stayed on the handle a few seconds longer than necessary as she stepped into the dimly lit room. The floor was carpeted, walls a rich mahogany filled with bookshelves and large gold-framed paintings. There were also a lot of chairs in this room. One in front of each of the three windows, a couch centered beneath a painting, two side chairs and two cherry-oak wood stools with brass legs. Across from all the chairs was an ornate bar, fully stocked.

Riley's heart beat faster, her breasts feeling a bit full from what she'd seen downstairs and her mind curious enough to have her closing the door and locking it.

"Now what?" She spoke into the room because she presumed that Chaz was here somewhere, but then she recalled his last text said for her to wait for him.

Take off your clothes.

That was the next message and Riley was already shaking her head.

"Not on your life, Chaz. If this is your idea of a date, it's no wonder you're still single."

There's nobody in this room but you and me. Take off your clothes.

Riley was about to type *no*. She was going to answer him and run down those stairs, find her coat and go home. Alone. To do what she did every night—work until she fell asleep and then get up in the morning and work some more. She held the phone in her palm and looked around. There were only two other doors in addition to the one she'd just come through. One was probably a bathroom and the other a closet, maybe.

It's just you and me?

She typed the reply, not totally sure where her mind was going.

Yes. I want you naked.

Riley read his words and her pussy throbbed.

She stood in that spot, hearing her heart pound like a drumbeat throughout the room. Chaz wanted her to do the things these other people in this house were doing. He hadn't asked her, they'd never discussed anything like sex parties or exhibitionism. She should feel offended that he would make this type of assumption about her. But she wasn't.

Riley was definitely aroused. She could picture herself sucking Chaz's dick just like that woman downstairs was doing. She'd done it before when they were in Milan and she wanted to do it again. Besides, there was no exhibitionism in this room, alone with him. Chaz obviously wanted to watch her get naked knowing there was a houseful of people. The thought had her pussy jumping again and her breath skipping as she contemplated what to do next.

I want YOU naked.

The response came to her mind quickly and she typed it before she could rethink it. Feeling emboldened she typed a quick follow-up.

Take off your clothes and come to me.

The room was silent and she moved to the coffee table to set her purse down. She rubbed her hands up and down her arms and wondered if he were just going to leave. The door across the room opened and Riley got her answer.

Chaz stepped through the door and he was gloriously naked. Riley had seen him that way before but this was different. It was on her command.

"What are you going to do with me now that I'm here?"

There was no hint of play in his tone or the way he was staring at her. There was only hunger and need, both so thick the room felt instantly full.

"You're not close enough," she said and watched him walk closer.

Every part of him was toned or muscled—his biceps, calves, abs, ass. She couldn't have sculpted a more perfect male body. Her fingers ached to touch him as he stopped just a few inches in front of her, but she refrained. Instead Riley walked around him, looking him up and down from head to toe.

"There's a scar here." She didn't touch that part of his lower back that snaked around his waist jaggedly. This one was longer than the scar beneath his pectoral. She'd felt and seen both before, but had never asked.

"Motorcycle accident when I was twenty."

She was in front of him again, noting that out-of-context question had done nothing to still the desire threatening to burn through her clothes.

"You didn't answer my question. What are you going to do with me, Riley?"

She only took a second to think before bending her knees and going to the floor. His dick was in her hand one moment, in her mouth the next. He was thick and heavy as her fingers stroked the inches her mouth did not cover. She loved the warm feel of him resting flat on her tongue. On a soft moan she sucked him in, holding him inside her warm mouth until she heard the wisp of breath come from between his lips.

He would try to hold on to control; that was the type of guy Chaz was. But not tonight. Tonight was for Riley. She was in control and she was going to get everything she wanted.

Riley moved her other hand to rub his balls while she sucked him in deeper. She increased her speed, pausing in intervals to drag her tongue up and down his length, dipping into his slit before sucking him inside once more. He tried to put a hand to the back of her head but she'd swatted it away before returning to massage his tightened sac. There was an urge inside her pushing her further, until she was making sounds and sucking him in a way she'd never known she could.

He groaned, cursed, whispered her name through clenched teeth and it made her even more determined to take everything she could from him in this moment. She needed this like she needed air. The power that was coursing through her veins was addictive, the heavy pounding of his dick in her mouth erotic as hell.

"I'm not gonna be able to stop."

His words were strained and in her mind she replied, *I don't want you to.*

Her mouth and tongue gave him the answer in another way, working over him until she could feel his legs tensing and heard the groan that seemed to come from somewhere deep inside him.

"Riley!"

His shout sounded painful just before the first spurt of his release hit the back of her throat. Riley closed her eyes and swallowed.

* * *

Chaz grasped Riley's shoulders and pulled her up to him. He moved his hands to her cheeks and lowered his mouth over hers. The kiss was no match for the way her mouth had just worked over his dick but he thrust his tongue deep inside, feeling hers and tasting himself.

The thumping in his head had to be the sound of his blood pumping thick and fast through his veins. It was loud and encouraging, pushing the desire he was already experiencing into full-blown passion. He needed more of her right now.

"Too many clothes," he groaned and pulled his mouth from hers long enough to lift her blouse from her skirt and pull it over her head. She pushed the skirt down her legs and he whispered, "Thank you. Thank you."

They worked together to remove her boots and underwear, and when she was thankfully naked, Chaz picked her up and sat her in one of the side chairs.

"Thought about you all day," he mumbled as he lifted her legs and placed each one over the arm of the chair.

She opened like a beautiful flower, her swollen labia coated with the thick gloss of her essence.

He glanced up to see that she was staring at him intently. "Is all that for me?"

"Only if you want it."

He should have known her reply would not be a submission. Still, it was sexy as hell.

Chaz grinned at her seconds before going in. He touched his tongue directly to her opening and she hissed. Her hands went to the back of his head but he followed her previous lead and pushed them away. From that moment on she was his, whether she wanted to admit it or not. Every sound she whimpered, every thrust of her hips and finally the sweet feel of her coming for him sealed the deal.

But it still wasn't enough.

He stood, hating to leave the sweetness of her, and picked up one of the condoms he'd left on the coffee table.

"I thought this would be over by now," he said when his hand was moving over his length, smoothing the latex in place. "It wasn't supposed to last this long."

She'd been staring at his dick and now she reluctantly dragged her gaze up to his. She licked her lips and stood from the chair. "I know."

Her brown nipples were hard and puckered against the creamy hue of her skin. Her waist was small but the curve of her hips and ass was generous.

"I can't stop wanting you," he admitted.

She looked like she might say something in opposition but whispered, "I can't stop wanting you, either."

Relief, desire, need, hunger all washed over Chaz

in the seconds after she said those words. It wasn't a declaration of love, which he was definitely not looking for, but it was better. She wanted as badly as he did and neither of them could explain why.

He went to her and cupped his hands at her waist before hoisting her up. She wrapped her legs around his waist, clasping her ankles at his back. Chaz speared into her and she moaned. He pumped in and out of her until she was bouncing over his dick, her arms wrapped around his neck as her back arched. Penetration was deep and felt like heaven.

He held her in his arms, easing in and out of her with his eyes wide-open so he could see passion and pleasure streak over her face. Riley was a lovely woman, but in the throes of passion she was absolutely gorgeous. He loved every sound she made, every time she pulled her lip between her teeth and the simple flare of her nostrils as she struggled to breathe. Everything, including the tight clench of her walls around his dick, Chaz loved it all. And he had no idea what he was going to do when it was over.

He closed his eyes to that thought and pumped faster until his release was pulsing into the condom and she was quivering in his grasp.

It was over. For now, he reminded himself.

The night was still young and Riley was still down for this affair. Chaz refused to think about that any further.

She fell forward, laying her head on his shoulder and snuggling closer to him. Chaz's legs wobbled slightly after the force of his climax, but he held on to her. Wrapping one arm even tighter around her back, while the other went lower so that his hand cupped her ass.

He wasn't letting go…not tonight.

# CHAPTER FIFTEEN

"IT'S BETTER IF we switch it up," Riley said. "We don't want anyone to see you at my building too many times."

Because they were having a secret affair. Riley didn't have to speak those words. Chaz had been replaying them in his mind on the drive from the house in Lennox Hill to his 92nd Street apartment an hour and a half later.

"Don't you agree?"

"Ah, yeah. That's a good point." It made sense. That didn't mean he had to like it. But when exactly did he stop liking the agreement they'd made?

"I thought you were inviting me to dinner. I'm starving."

Chaz unlocked the door and waited for her to enter ahead of him. "We can order something."

Because he definitely planned for her to stay the night.

"I'm in the mood for pizza."

He took the coat she shrugged out of and turned to hang it in the coat closet. "You eat pizza?"

She made a face—not exactly a frown and not a smile. "Who doesn't eat pizza?"

She was right. It was silly of him to think that the infamous Riley Gold didn't eat pizza. She was just so different from the type of woman he'd thought she was. In fact, everything he'd learned about Riley in the past weeks had been contrary to what he'd thought about her for years.

"I like everything on mine. How do you take yours?"

They were walking deeper into the living room and Chaz moved his hand over the wall switch to turn on the recessed lights in the ceiling. In stark contrast to Riley's cool, contemporary decor, Chaz favored warm, dark colors and minimal furniture. She stood on the cobalt blue rug and looked around at the blue Bradford sofa, matching side chairs and marble coffee table.

"Anything as long as there's lots of cheese." She didn't look at him as she spoke but continued assessing the room. "You like blue and open windows."

Chaz also had a wall of windows in the living room. His actually stretched up to the second floor. On the lower level there were no blinds, so the city was as much a part of this space as the furniture and the sleek fireplace on the wall behind him. Upstairs he did have remote blinds similar to hers but he rarely closed the blinds. Tonight he would make an exception.

"I'll order two pizzas and fries. I like fries with my pizza." He pulled his phone out of his pocket. "And yes, blue is my favorite color. What's yours?"

Chaz scrolled through his saved numbers. There were only a few things in his cooking repertoire so he knew all the best places to order food.

"Wine. The color, not the drink."

She sat on the couch and Chaz admired the soft pink of her blouse against the bold blue hue. He also loved the way the material of her skirt moved with her body, easing up her thigh as she sat back on the chair and crossed one leg over the other.

"That's an interesting color." For a very interesting woman.

When the food was ordered and Chaz had ditched the suit jacket and tie he'd worn to the party, he fixed them both a drink. They needed it. Especially since he knew he wasn't going to escape without Riley asking why he'd invited her to that party. He didn't have long to wait.

She took a tentative sip from her glass and then looked over at him. Chaz had taken a seat on the couch beside her, because there was no way he was sitting across the room from her. Pretenses between them were unnecessary.

"Are sex parties your thing?"

She lifted one elegantly arched brow with the

question and he tried to decipher if she was just curious or whether she was judging him. Considering Riley's past, he went with curiosity.

"They're entertaining. And no, not because I like to have sex with multiple people or in front of people. Not that I think there's anything wrong with either lifestyle. For me, it's about atmosphere and sensory reactions."

She shook her head and shrugged. "I don't follow. You either go to sex parties for sex or you don't."

"Life's not black-and-white, Riley. I know you believe in good and bad, right and wrong, but I've always lived in the gray area."

Chaz leaned forward and rested his elbows on his knees. This wasn't a conversation he'd ever had to indulge in before, but he wanted her to know. He wanted to see her reaction to the real Chadwick Warren.

"My uncle gets married and divorced every time the wind changes. Or so it seems. My parents had a committed and long-lasting relationship full of love and respect. I'm somewhere in between. I don't do love, but I love sex. So I go to parties and surround myself with people who love sex."

"You're the hottest social media bachelor in the world. I read that in the *Wall Street Journal*. Your net worth is somewhere around twenty-three billion. You could have any woman you wanted—one who's well-versed in the sex-without-commitment games—

in your bed every night. Why would you need to go to a sex party?"

"No judgment. No recriminations. No questions. Half the time nobody even knows who I am for that matter. And believe it or not, I've only ever had sex at a party three times. Each time I brought the woman with me and asked if she were comfortable indulging. You are certainly blunt, Riley."

"If we're talking about this we might as well talk honestly, right?"

He nodded. "Yeah. You're right."

She'd worn her hair down tonight, falling past her shoulders in a tumble of waves. It was a softer look than she normally displayed in public. He liked it.

"Sometimes I need to get away from the world I've created for myself. The world where they expect me to be the famous social media bachelor or billionaire entrepreneur. I'm not Tobias's orphaned nephew. I'm just Chaz, a man who likes and knows pleasure." It sounded so simple to him but he wondered what she thought about what she was hearing.

"Did you like being there?" he asked.

"I've never been to a sex party before."

"I figured as much. My question was did you like it?"

She ran her palms down her thighs and cleared her throat. "Yes. I think I did. Not at first. When I walked into that room and saw that threesome, I wanted to

curse you from here to hell and back for inviting me
to such a place. But then I saw a man receiving his
pleasure and a woman giving herself pleasure and
I was…aroused. Never in a million years would I
have thought something like that would turn me on."

"You're a passionate woman, Riley. You shouldn't
be ashamed of that."

"I'm not ashamed of anything," she countered.

But that wasn't true. She was ashamed of their affair. Or she was afraid of anyone finding out about
it. Either way, Chaz didn't like it and he wondered
how she was going to react when he finally told her
his feelings about their arrangement had changed.

"Thank you for the vase."

It was just before dawn. The sky was that amazing
mixture of orange and pink, and she could see daylight peeking through the pale gray shades Chaz had
lowered over the twenty-foot windows in his bedroom. The forest-green-and-white-striped comforter
on his bed was warm even if it wasn't something she
would have purchased. But what Riley really liked
about being in Chaz's bed early on a Saturday morning was the feel of his strong arms wrapped around
her, the warmth of his body against hers and the
press of his heavy arousal against her ass.

"You're welcome." His breath was warm against
the back of her neck. "I figured it would be nice if
you had something calming to look at while you're

in the office. A dildo slash paperweight wouldn't go over very well."

She smiled, something she'd been doing a lot of lately, especially when she was with him.

"That was very thoughtful. I didn't expect that from you."

"Why? Because we're only having an affair?"

Riley frowned, hating the way he said that word. Why? It was what they'd agreed on.

"Because you're not what I expected."

"You expected the billionaire bachelor who would sleep with you a couple times and move on?"

"Yes." His words were exactly right. "But I think I also expected you to be sneaky and conniving like your uncle."

"My uncle is neither of those things, and besides that, I'm not him. And we're not that feud. Didn't we already talk about this?"

"We did and you're right. We're not the feud but we're not absolved of it, either. The remnants of your uncle stealing designs from the fashion house my grandfather started that allowed Tobias to get his start affect us whether we want it to or not."

"What are you talking about? My uncle said the feud started over a woman and even when Ron had gotten the girl he'd still been horribly jealous and forced Uncle Tobias out of the company."

She'd never heard the story that way before and didn't really know if she believed it, but the fact still remained that there was definite animosity between their families and that was likely to always create friction between them.

They remained silent for the next few minutes, until she couldn't stand it any longer.

"I like being with you. I didn't think I would, but I do." There, she'd said what had been on her mind all night. Or rather the times that he wasn't inside her and she wasn't asleep.

"I knew I would like being with you," he said. "Just not this much."

His lips touched the back of her shoulder and warmth flooded her body. Why was it like that with him? It shouldn't have felt right and she shouldn't have wanted it to feel this way all the time. This couldn't be happening. Not to her and definitely not with him.

"Shower with me." She said the words and sat straight up in bed before she talked herself out of it.

When he didn't answer, Riley looked back over her shoulder. "Take a shower with me, Chaz, and then I'll fix us breakfast."

"Music to my ears!" He jumped out of the bed.

Riley chuckled and pushed the covers back. She was about to get off the bed and walk to the bathroom but Chaz scooped her up into his arms and carried her naked body. He was naked, too, so once they were in the bathroom and he set her down, Riley reached for him. She laced her arms around his neck and drew his mouth to hers for a soft kiss.

His tongue was warm against hers, soothing her immediately. Riley didn't need soothing from frayed nerves or even the fear of falling headlong into an anxiety attack, not this time. Instead she had questions that she'd never imagined having, and Chaz was the only one who could answer them.

The kiss was doing the trick. The way his tongue leisurely stroked hers and his lips slanted over hers should have started the inevitable sexual arousal. It didn't. Not this time. Instead it made Riley lean in closer and ease her arms around his waist. The urge to hold on to him was strong. The need to feel him gripping her in the same way was deep.

His arms moved around her waist, his palms flat against her skin in what Riley would swear was a tender embrace instead of a heated one. Not that she minded the heat—this morning she just craved something more.

Chaz broke the kiss. He pulled his mouth away from hers but stared down at her for endless moments. She couldn't look away from him. Not from his smoldering eyes or the thin line of his lips. When he brushed his knuckles over her jaw, she wanted to sigh. He dropped his hand abruptly and moved to the shower to turn on the water.

Riley stepped inside when he just stood by the glass doors. His shower was larger than hers.

Probably because he didn't have a tub in his bathroom and she'd insisted on a soaker tub and a large shower. The water was closer to being hot than warm, just the way she liked it, and Riley immediately stepped beneath the spray. She turned and tilted her head back, drenching her hair. Her eyes were closed so she didn't see Chaz come to stand beside her but she did hear the click of the shower stall door closing. Then his hands were in her hair, running his fingers through the thick mass just like the water.

"Oh, guess I should have asked first—do you have a shampoo with conditioner?"

He reached behind himself into an alcove in the gray tiled wall and brought a white bottle up to her face.

"Will this work?"

Of course, it wasn't her brand. She'd never found herself washing her hair without her own products, but she'd also never showered with a man before. Riley shrugged and reached for the bottle.

Chaz held it back from her. "I'll do it."

She was going to question him because she felt a trickle of fear at how serious and at the same time how wonderfully intimate this felt, but she couldn't find the words. Instead she stood there and waited while he squeezed shampoo into his hand and then put the bottle back on the shelf.

"My hair's really thick so you might need a little more," she said, then clamped her mouth shut.

His hands were already in her hair, moving until he'd built up a lather. Then he was raking his fingertips over her scalp, massaging and raking, rotating until Riley could no longer hold back her moan.

"That feels fantastic." And she wasn't even exaggerating. It almost felt sensual in a clean sort of way. She couldn't actually explain it, just knew that it was a feeling she thoroughly enjoyed.

When he was finished massaging her scalp until Riley thought she might curl up on the shower floor and fall asleep, Chaz eased her back under the spray and rinsed her hair clean. Riley reached into that same alcove and pulled out the bottle of body wash. There was a cloth on the shelf as well, and she filled it with body wash before replacing the bottle.

She touched it to his chest first, watching the big frothy bubbles cover the toned pectorals and move down his sculpted abs. She washed his whole body, wondering if he was experiencing the slow burning warmth spreading throughout like she was. After he rinsed, Chaz returned the favor and before long the shower was over. Chaz turned off the water, but they did not move. They stood in the center of the shower stall, water dripping from their bodies, and simply stared at each other. As if really seeing each other for the first time.

It was in that moment that Riley knew. It had come to her sometime during the night—this crazy idea that she and Chaz could be like this for real, in public and in private, for a very long time.

It had come to her and now she worried there was no turning back.

---

# CHAPTER SIXTEEN

ON MONDAY MORNING Riley rode in the back of the town car with Chaz. The windows were tinted and the driver, the man she'd seen driving Chaz many times before, stared straight ahead as usual. Riley wondered if he knew who she was and, if so, why he hadn't leaked to the press how many times he'd seen her and Chaz together. It was a sobering thought, especially since she'd spent the entire weekend in Chaz's apartment not thinking of their affair as a secret at all. In the privacy of his home they'd been free from any scrutiny or recriminations, something she was certain they both enjoyed.

"This week is going to be hectic for me," Chaz said. "I'm sure your schedule is similar."

She ran a hand down the leg of her pants. When it seemed apparent that she would be spending the weekend with Chaz, they'd taken a quick trip to her penthouse to grab some clothes. Still, they'd decided it was best for her to abide by her normal workday routine and drive her own car from her building garage to work.

"Definitely," she replied. "Our show is Sunday and there's still so much to do. We have the media brunch on Saturday and from what I heard parts of the show are still being choreographed."

"I had no idea how much work went into these shows," Chaz continued. "We had a situation at the rehearsal on Friday that I'm sure I'll have to deal with this morning."

"Really? I hope it wasn't anything that'll affect your show." Riley meant those words.

King Designs was a great fashion house that produced quality work. She could admit that regardless of what happened between her father and Tobias. And to be quite honest, she was anxious to see their collection this season, especially since this was the first time Chaz had been actively involved in the business.

"I'm not sure." His words and the pensive look on his face said he was truly worried about whatever had happened.

"There's always something at the last minute. Some glitch with the technical plans for a show or, more serious, an issue with a design. If things ever went too smoothly we'd probably all need to be concerned. But I'm sure it'll work out."

She reached for his hand and squeezed. When

he looked at her and smiled, Riley felt the familiar warmth they shared.

"I'm sure your new collection is going to be a big hit. Your family will be impressed, and the press will have no choice but to give you the respect you've earned."

Riley smiled and let that bit of validation settle over her comfortably. His confidence in her had never wavered and because of that she believed his words.

"I know I didn't design the gowns but I feel like this entire collection is mine. I've worked so closely with the designers and production team to bring this new vision into fruition. Usually I'm all about my numbers and reports but this time I actually had the opportunity to put all my research into a product that RGF can be proud of."

Chaz lifted her hand to his lips and kissed her knuckles. "You're good at what you do, Riley. I know that and I'm not even as ensconced in this industry as you are. And you're passionate about your work. That's what really counts."

"You're not passionate about the fashion industry, are you?" Riley wondered if once Fashion Week was over, Chaz would return to Miami and to his media corporation.

He shrugged. "I've sort of been on the outskirts of the industry all my life. Living in that gray area I like." He grinned and Riley thought how liberating it must be to create a safe space to live and not give a damn what anyone thought about it.

"But I have to admit using my skills to create a brand that best represents my uncle and his vision for the company has been fun. I mean, I never actually thought I had a place at King Designs because it wasn't like my father had built that company. I figured I'd have to make my own place in this world and I have. I love what I've built at Conversation Media and I'd never totally walk away from that. Speaking of which, the new app is launching on Thursday, the day before our show."

"Oh, wow, you really do have a big week. Well, I just might download the ChatMe app to see what it's all about."

"It's not a dating app." He said those words quickly. "Not that you would ever need an app to help find a date."

"No," she replied, a bit more sober now than she'd been just a few seconds ago. "I don't usually think much about dating."

They fell silent and Chaz ran his thumb over the back of her hand.

"We've been having a good time, haven't we?"

She nodded. "Yes. We have. I didn't really know what to expect, but yeah, this has been fun."

"Fun enough to keep going? I mean, to continue seeing each other?"

Hadn't this been what Riley thought about all weekend?

"I'd like that." The words slipped easily from her lips just as the car pulled up in front of her building. She looked out the window and then back to Chaz.

He leaned over and touched his lips lightly to hers.

"I know you have to go. The talented Riley Gold has to be great this week. And I, the outsider, have a lot to do, as well. So we'll talk about this after we've both survived Fashion Week."

His voice was a deep whisper against her lips and Riley eased in for another kiss. "Yes, we'll definitely talk about this when this week is over."

Their next kiss was longer, slower and sweeter than Riley had ever experienced. She loved it and did not want it to end.

"I'll call you later," he said when they pulled apart.

Riley smiled. "Or I'll call you."

Chaz grinned and in the next second the driver was opening the door for her.

Twelve hours later a tired but invigorated Riley pulled into the garage and parked her car before taking the elevator up to the penthouse. Her stomach growled as she walked through the door and Riley immediately thought about ordering a pizza. It was a little after eight in the evening and she hadn't eaten since a tuna sandwich at two in the afternoon. She knew there was something in her freezer that she could just pop into the microwave, but she wanted pizza with everything on it and fries.

She wanted that connection to Chaz.

Speaking of which, once she was in her bedroom and had kicked off her heels, Riley reached into her purse for her phone. No call or text from Chaz, not since earlier in the day when he'd checked to see if she'd eaten lunch, which she'd dutifully ordered as soon as she hung up with him. Her afternoon had been swamped and she figured his had been, too, so she sent a quick text.

Thinking about you.

It was honest and sincere and the first time she'd ever said such a thing to a man. Riley smiled with how good it made her feel. She was about to grab some pajamas and head into the bathroom for a shower when her doorbell rang. A giddy flutter whirled through her stomach as she hoped it was Chaz surprising her with dinner and company for the evening. Her penthouse suddenly seemed too big for just her and definitely too quiet. But when Riley walked back into the living room and excitedly pulled the door open, her happiness faded fast.

"Hey, Dad. RJ. Come on in."

"We need to talk." Her father's tone was brisk as he removed his coat and walked into the living room.

RJ followed Ron inside. His expression was somber, his tone grave as he said, "Hey."

She closed the door and followed them inside.

"What's up? Did something happen during rehearsal? Is there a problem with one of the gowns?"

RGF was presenting a record forty-two designs during this show. Ten of them were from Riley's bridal collection.

"Yes," Ron replied tightly.

"Sort of," RJ added.

Riley looked from her father to her brother and back to her father again. "Just tell me what happened." Because she was certain something very bad was about to go down.

She could see it in the lines on her father's forehead and the muscle pulsing in RJ's jaw.

"Why don't we start with you telling us where the hell you were this weekend?" If she hadn't been certain before, her father's tone conveyed every bit of the anger he was feeling.

Riley squared her shoulders and looked him directly in the eye. "I'm an adult, Dad. I don't have to explain where I was or why without knowing the reason for the request."

It was a bold statement to make to a man like Ron Gold but Riley didn't care. She didn't like her father and brother coming into her house at this time of night, questioning her and staring at her as if she'd done something wrong.

"If you would just tell me what's going on—"

"What's going on with you and Chaz Warren? Why were you photographed getting out of a limousine with him and going into his apartment building? And this morning you were dropped off here by a car registered to King Designs."

The vein in her father's head that only popped out when he was seething with rage was throbbing front and center, and Riley's fingers clenched at her sides. RJ had folded his arms over his chest in what she knew was his authoritative stance.

"I have a right to a personal life" was all Riley would say.

"With him?" RJ asked. "You know the story and you know how this looks."

"I know who makes me feel good," she snapped. "And what, are you two having me followed? Is that what we do now? Follow Riley around to make sure she doesn't mess up again?"

"But you have messed up," Ron countered. "Because not only are you sleeping with the enemy, but the enemy is stabbing you in the back as expected."

"What are you talking about?"

"That editor I know at that little tabloid—he called me an hour ago to give me a heads-up."

That giddy feeling Riley had felt in her stomach just a few short moments ago was now a heated ball of dread.

"A heads-up about what?" She said the words slowly, as if she didn't really want the answer.

"Not only are the pictures of you and Chaz going to be printed in tomorrow's paper but they're attached to a sneak peek at King's new collection. A wedding gown, Riley. And it looks very similar to one of ours," RJ said.

"Not similar," her father roared. "It's the exact same gown! They copied our gown and are offering a sneak peek before the shows so it'll look like we're the ones who copied them. Chaz Warren is behind this! He probably stole the sketch while you were sleeping in his bed."

Riley felt hot all over. Her arms began to shake and for just a second her vision blurred. This could not be happening. Not again.

RJ stepped closer to her. "What did you tell him, Riley? Did you show him the sketches?"

"No!" She could not have said the word more vehemently. "I would never do such a thing." And Chaz would never ask her something like that.

"You bring work home with you all the time. Was he here? Could you have left him alone with sensitive information? It would have only taken a second. Just like his uncle, dammit!" Her father persisted.

"He is not like his uncle!" The minute the words were out Riley realized her mistake. She saw the concern on RJ's face and unabashed fury on her father's.

She turned away and walked toward the window. Tears stung her eyes. They wanted to fall but Riley wouldn't let them. She almost folded her arms over her chest, to cradle herself and hopefully bring some comfort to the deep slice of hurt that had been opened in her. But she didn't. Instead she took deep breaths. She was way too upset for the breaths to be slow, as she'd been taught to do when threatened with an anxiety attack, but at least she was breathing. Her hands were shaking and she finally gave in and clasped her fingers together in front of her.

"Riley."

RJ was right behind her and she prayed he wouldn't touch her. After the breakup with Walt her family had rallied around her, each of them hugging her and consoling her to the point that all Riley had done for days was cry over a man she'd never loved. Tonight, the tears that burned were for a man she'd just begun to believe she could love. And she was an idiot for giving in to the dream.

"I never left any sensitive materials around him, even though I never believed he was with me just to steal our ideas." Saying the words aloud meant something. Riley just couldn't figure out what, not right now, when the pain was so raw.

"That's how they work. They befriend you and then they stab you in the back. You should have known better. You should have kept a closer eye on him."

Riley swung around. "You were friends with Tobias King for thirty-four years. The two of you worked side by side at your father's company. You didn't just leave sensitive information around him, you shared a business with him. So don't lecture me about what I should have done differently."

RJ touched a hand to her shoulder and Riley shrugged it away.

"I don't know how they got the information. Maybe the reporter is making this up." She needed to believe there was another explanation.

RJ came close again, this time putting his phone in front of her.

"Here are the pictures of you and Chaz together." He swiped left. "And these are the pictures of the gown."

Her chest caved with dread but Riley held it together. She swiped to the right to see the pictures of her and Chaz. It was Friday night when they'd left the party in Lennox Hill. They'd dressed quickly after their tryst and Chaz had suggested they go to his place. He was holding her hand as they walked to the curb to wait for the limo he'd reserved. She could still remember the warmth of his touch and how close he'd sat to her in the back of the limo. Swiping to the next picture, she cringed because it was just as her father had stated: this morning when she'd gotten out of Chaz's car in front of her building.

"Who would have been following us?" She looked

up at RJ. "We hadn't been at a fashion event and we were far away from either of our offices, so somebody must have intentionally followed us."

Ron frowned. "Yes, that's something I absolutely will not tolerate. We have to get ahead of this. I'll contact the police just to get a complaint started. Also, my guy's agreed to run the picture of our gown at the same time as the King gown."

"No!" Riley shook her head. "We don't give in to the press. We don't let them get the upper hand. Isn't that what you've always told me?"

"I also told you not to give them ammunition, Riley. Now we don't have a choice but to play this hand all the way." Ron looked at RJ.

"Send the picture to him tonight and we're pulling that gown from the show. Make it known that we're outraged at Tobias's duplicity and that we don't feel King Designs is in any way a threat to us." Her father spoke in absolute terms so that RJ only nodded.

"But we're doing the exact opposite. If we're so sure they're no competition to us why not show our entire collection on Sunday as planned? So what if theirs is hitting the papers tomorrow? You don't think people will see the difference and know which is the better product? You don't trust your clientele?"

"I don't trust Tobias King or his nephew," Ron told her. "And you shouldn't, either. Whatever you were doing with Chaz Warren, you should stop it now. He's only interested in you because you're my daughter."

All the air left Riley's lungs and she felt light-headed. She rubbed a hand down the back of her neck and sighed. "I need to be alone."

"Let's just meet tomorrow," RJ said when Ron looked as if he was going to say something else. "Be in the office at seven."

"Fine," Riley snapped and walked to the door to see them out.

RJ followed her, then leaned in and kissed her on the forehead. "It's going to be all right."

Riley closed her eyes and accepted her brother's words. He loved her and wanted what was best for her—he just didn't know what that was. And for the record, at this point, neither did Riley.

Ron stepped up to her, looking at her with his big brown eyes, his mouth bent into a frown just before he pulled her into a hug. Riley had to fight every instinct she had. How many times had she cried in his arms when she was a little girl? But Riley wasn't that girl anymore and she'd cried enough.

"I'll see you in the morning," she said when he pulled away because she couldn't say anything else.

After the breakup with Walt she'd apologized to her parents and brothers profusely for how she'd messed up. Tonight, she couldn't say those words. She'd trusted and she'd believed and a part of her knew she wasn't wrong for doing either of those things. The other part… Well, once she closed and locked the door, Riley fell back against it. She closed her eyes and whispered, "Oh, Chaz, what have you done?"

## CHAPTER SEVENTEEN

IT WAS EIGHT THIRTY in the morning when Chaz walked into his office at King Designs. He felt like he'd just left this place and now he was back again.

Yesterday had been hectic with Tobias calling Chaz into a meeting with Lenzo fifteen minutes after Chaz had arrived at the office. Chaz was still riding on the high of the weekend with Riley until he'd stood in a room with a designer who apparently hated him.

"He's not a designer. You brought him in because he's your relative, not because he has an ounce of experience in this industry. And then you expect me to stand on my head to please him. Hell no, Tobias! I've been with you for ten years and this is how you treat me!"

Lenzo's fists were clenched at his sides while Chaz stood next to his uncle's desk.

"This is my company, Lenzo. I call the shots. Whether you like my calls or not. And if you had a problem with Chaz you should have come to me and perhaps we could have worked it out. But as it stands now I'm letting you go."

"You're what?" Lenzo's eyes almost bulged from his face. "You're firing me because I wouldn't listen to this playboy's advice?"

Chaz had been called worse than a playboy.

"It's not about my advice," he'd said. "You were instructed six months ago to follow my rebranding plan. You chose not to do that."

"Security will escort you out," Tobias told him.

When that scene was over, Chaz had returned to his office, where one issue after another plagued him, including a press sheet he received from his marketing team about ChatMe. Juggling two major business events in one week wasn't the smartest plan, but he was determined to make it all work. Before long the day and night had gotten away from him. Chaz didn't get a moment to look at his phone until he'd walked into his apartment at a little after midnight.

Riley's message immediately warmed him and he'd smiled.

Missed you so much today.

He'd typed his response seconds before falling face-first onto his bed and into a deep slumber.

Now he checked his phone for the fourth time since leaving his apartment this morning. There was no response from Riley.

After dropping his briefcase onto the floor beside his desk, Chaz plugged his phone into the charger and set it near his laptop. Easing down into his chair, he tried to focus on what he needed to tackle first. He definitely wanted to go over the press sheet for the ChatMe launch one more time. Valeria wasn't publishing his interview on her blog, nor was there going to be any type of advertising on her YouTube show. He chuckled at how petty she was being but decided to move on.

His fingers moved quickly over the keyboard as he pulled up his Conversation Media account. He was about to send a message to his team when the door to his office opened.

"What the hell is this?" Tobias stormed into the office.

He dropped not one but three tabloid papers onto Chaz's desk.

"What were you thinking? We never, *ever* allow items from our collection to be photographed and printed before the show!"

The look on Tobias's face, his tone and the headlines on the tabloids all brought Chaz to a full stop.

"First, I never gave permission for anything to be printed." Especially not the pictures of him and Riley, which were staring back at him in full color.

Tobias didn't seem to hear a word he said as his rant continued. "And you're sleeping with Ron's daughter? I told you to watch out for that one and you jump into bed with her? What the hell is wrong with you?"

Chaz stood and looked his uncle in the eye. "I did not approve any of these pictures and who I sleep with is my business. Always has been and always will be."

"She's the enemy's daughter!"

"She's *your* enemy's daughter. To me she's just a woman that I lo—have grown very fond of in the past weeks. And I don't appreciate someone following us around and printing malicious lies about us." Chaz really had no idea what the articles said. All he knew was that there were pictures of him and Riley and that was enough.

Tobias pointed at the picture of a dress. "This dress right here is one of the ones you pulled from the show. How did someone get it? Was it Riley? Did you show her our collection?"

Chaz looked closer at the papers. He lined them up next to each other and stared at the pictures, thinking. "We said no bridal couture this season. That's why I took the dress out of the show."

"I know that! What I'm asking is how Riley knew."

Chaz glanced up at his uncle. "What would she gain by releasing our dress to the press early? Not that I'm saying she's responsible." Because she wasn't. Chaz was certain of that fact. He was also positive that the moment Riley saw these papers she was going to totally lose it.

"Well, somebody leaked the picture. And do you see Ron's pompous remarks? He's not at all threatened by whatever we have in our show. To hell with him and his king-of-the-world attitude!"

Chaz grabbed his phone and was headed toward the door when Tobias called to him.

"Where are you going? We've got to deal with this!"

"I've got something else to deal with first."

Tobias sighed heavily. "She is not the priority, Chaz. She's the enemy."

Chaz stopped at the door. He turned around and remembered all the things his uncle had done for him. All the money he'd spent on his education and the time he'd taken teaching Chaz everything he needed to know about being a black man in this world. Chaz appreciated all of it and he loved Tobias, but today he was going to set him straight.

"I don't care what you think about Riley, or her family for that matter. But she means a lot to me and there's nothing you, this fashion house or anybody else can do to change that."

He walked out, not giving Tobias a moment to respond. Chaz didn't care what his response would have been. All he was concerned with right now was getting to Riley before she could see these papers.

"You didn't give them the picture like Dad told you to," Riley said to RJ.

She was sitting in her office and RJ was standing on the other side of her desk. Maurice was sitting in one of the guest chairs and Major leaned on the edge of her desk. They'd all filed into her office at seven this morning, tabloids in hand. Riley had already read the stories. She'd looked at the pictures again and she'd taken aspirin to ward off the headache that still pounded at her temples.

"You were right—it made it look as if we were conceding and we'd never do that. Dad's just working on anger right now, Ri. You know he didn't mean all that stuff he said to you last night." RJ could be the voice of reason where their father was concerned.

Riley didn't know if that was because he was the firstborn or because he was the one who would eventually take Ron's place at the helm. Either way, it annoyed Riley sometimes. Last night it had pissed her off.

"But let's clarify something," Maurice said. "You are sleeping with Chaz Warren?"

There were moments when Riley detested being the only girl among her siblings. This was definitely one of those moments. Having a sister here to help take some of the heat would have been fantastic. As it was, Riley would stand on her own, just like always.

"Yes. We met up in Milan and continued the affair here." She stopped before explaining any more because she'd said enough. In her mind, however, every second of her time with Chaz had been on replay.

She'd spent the whole night lying on her bed and trying to figure out when and where Chaz had stolen their design.

"And that's why you were acting different," RJ said.

"Different how? Please don't tell me she's fallen in love again," Maurice groaned and made a face.

If Riley weren't still very irritated she would have thrown something at her forever-juvenile brother.

"To be clear, I've never been in love," she stated.

"Because you've got good sense like the smart twin," Major added.

"Where's Dad? I thought he'd want to be here to continue his reprimand." And if her brothers were finished staring at her and questioning her, Riley would really like to get back to work.

"He wasn't here when I came in, so I figured we'd see him later," RJ said.

"That's not like him to miss an opportunity to rant about Tobias King," Major said. "Speaking of which, I've gotta say this was a pretty underhanded stunt and one Tobias could have certainly pulled a long time ago. Why now? Why this line and why target Riley again?"

Riley hadn't thought of those particular questions last night or this morning. She'd been too busy thinking about Chaz.

"Those are good questions," RJ stated just before the door to Riley's office was pushed open.

Chaz came in with Korey hot on his heels.

"I tried to tell him he wasn't welcome, but he pushed right past me!" Korey practically screamed those words the moment he made it into the office.

Chaz ignored him. "Riley, I need to talk to you."

Maurice bolted up from the chair and Major eased away from the desk. The twins fell in behind RJ, who immediately stepped up to face Chaz.

"That's not a good idea," RJ told him. "Neither was you coming here. You can turn around and leave now."

"I can call security," Korey added.

"I just want to speak to Riley. I'll leave as soon as I'm done," Chaz said evenly.

RJ wasn't budging. "You'll leave now."

Chaz shook his head. "No. Not until I talk to Riley."

Korey reached across Riley's desk to grab the phone. "I'm calling security!"

She stood and snatched the phone out of his hand and slammed it down.

"You are not calling anybody and I'm perfectly capable of deciding whether or not I want to talk to someone." She walked around her desk and pushed through the barrier the twins created with their matching muscular frames.

RJ didn't move so Riley walked around him. She felt utterly foolish stepping between him and Chaz, but it had to be done or the testosterone oozing in the room would reach a boiling point and all hell would definitely break loose.

"I don't think talking is necessary," she said when she finally looked up at Chaz.

"You're wrong. It's very necessary."

"Don't talk to my sister like that," Maurice snapped.

Riley figured this situation could only get worse, so she turned to face her brothers. "I've got this," she told them. "Leave us alone."

"Oh, hell no," Major chimed. "Leave him alone with you in your office?"

"I'll be fine," Riley told them, and while she was certain her brothers were concerned for her well-being, she had a suspicion they were also concerned about Chaz being in the office and possibly stealing more of their secrets.

"Really, you can all go now. This is my office."

RJ continued to glare at Chaz.

"You and I are going to have a conversation," he told Chaz.

Chaz nodded. "That's fine with me."

Her brothers filed out of the office and Chaz stared at Riley.

Riley turned to Korey, who was still leaning against the edge of her desk. "I'll be fine, Korey. You can leave us alone."

Korey looked at her another moment before pushing away from her desk. He did that thing with his fingers pointing to his eyes and then pointing to Chaz as he passed them and walked out.

When the door closed, Riley squared her shoulders and took a deep breath. She released it slowly before saying, "What do you want to say?"

He remained still.

"First, above all else I want to tell you that I've fallen in love with you, Riley Gold. I didn't mean to and I don't know exactly when it happened, but that's that."

Her hands were shaking and she hated it. She refused to clench her fingers or cross her arms or anything like that. She was going to face him and what he'd done head-on.

"Did you steal the design?"

Chaz flinched as if she'd hit him.

"No. I would never do anything to hurt you or your company. But I think I know how it might have happened."

"I don't want to do this, Chaz. I never wanted to do this. We were supposed to have an affair. Twenty-four hours and it was supposed to be over. If we'd just stuck to that none of this would have happened."

"None of this would have happened if someone hadn't copied your design and called it King's. Nothing you or I did led to this."

His tone was serious and his voice still rubbed her in that same sensual way. Riley hated that but couldn't change what was. Instead she turned away from him. She walked back to her desk because that was where she felt safest. At her desk everything was about work, about this company and their reputation. Standing too close to Chaz when he was saying those words… It was just too much.

"I'm not going to keep saying I didn't do this because I'd like to believe that you trust me enough to know better. Or that you have a modicum of respect for me after all we've shared."

She stopped on the other side of her desk but did not sit.

"You want to talk about respect, Chaz? Just how much respect do you think I'll get in this company now? My father thinks I'm too dense to know when a man I'm sleeping with steals from me. My brothers have already planned to hover over me for all the days of my life. And now, even my assistant is going to be giving me the side-eye because I agreed to talk to you." Her headache was pounding with full force now and Riley wanted desperately to go home, close her blinds and just sit in the dark for a while. There she only had to listen to her own voice telling her how foolish she'd been.

"So you really think I'd do that to you." It wasn't a question, just a somber statement.

Riley massaged her temples. "No," she said on a weary sigh. "I don't. And that makes this even more confusing."

"It doesn't have to be, Riley. We both know what we've shared and I have an idea of what's really going on with those pictures. So just let me figure it out and you continue to work on your show."

He'd come closer so that he stood right beside her now, but he didn't touch her. He wouldn't, not until she acted as if she were receptive to his touch. She wasn't. Not right now.

"I don't need you to figure anything out for me, Chaz. I knew this was a mistake from the start. I lost my focus and I—"

He moved so that they were now face-to-face instead of side by side. "Look me in the eye and tell me that you regret every moment we've spent together. Tell me that you weren't thinking about us having a future together just yesterday. Tell me, Riley."

She looked him in the eye—those warm brown eyes that always stared back at her with such caring and understanding. The words were in her mind but she couldn't say them. She couldn't bring herself to lie.

"I do not regret anything that we've done. We're adults and we decided to sleep together. I'm fine with that and I hope you are, too. But that's done now, Chaz. The affair is over and we can both get back to our respective lives."

He didn't look as if she'd slapped him this time, but he did stare at her in disbelief. She hoped he wouldn't continue to press this issue. She'd told him that she believed him—what else did he want? It didn't matter because Riley had nothing else to give.

"Yeah," he said finally. "We can get back to our respective lives."

"Great." That was a relief. She rubbed her hands down her skirt and moved to sit in her chair. "Good luck with your show this weekend and with the app. I really do wish you much success."

His lips were drawn in a tight line as he continued to stare at her. "Same to you, Riley. I wish you the best of whatever you're courageous enough to reach for."

He didn't wait for her response but left her office, closing the door quietly behind him.

Riley sat back in her chair and closed her eyes. If she kept them closed she wouldn't think about what she'd just done or how all those dreams she'd had this weekend had walked out the door. She wouldn't think about the man who'd just told her he was in love with her, or the fact that she was certain she'd fallen in love with him, too.

# CHAPTER EIGHTEEN

TOBIAS SLAMMED THE phone down so hard it skipped over the base and he had to fiddle with the receiver to finally get it down correctly. When that was done, he slammed his palms on his desk and cursed fluently.

Chaz had walked into his uncle's office five minutes ago, catching the tail end of a one-sided conversation, but he could guess what it was about.

"That was the detective. We're pressing charges against Lenzo for stealing our product, which was the dress he made, and Ron's pressing charges against the receptionist at RGF who gave Lenzo the original design used for the dress. They'll both be charged with theft. From what the detective told me, she didn't waste any time confessing. Seems Lenzo was dating her specifically to get information. I could wring that idiot's neck right now!"

Chaz rubbed a finger over his chin. Once he'd recalled Lenzo's hostility on Friday and then again on Monday when Tobias fired him, Chaz figured the guy would have had to make only one phone call to get that story on the front page on Tuesday morning. When Chaz had left Riley's office on Tuesday, he'd gone straight to the police to share his suspicions and they'd immediately followed up.

"Exactly. But the pictures… Lenzo said he bought those from the reporter who was fired after Ron's tirade last week over an article the guy wrote."

The article about Walt's fiancée. Chaz cursed just like his uncle had.

"Can't trust anybody these days." Tobias sat back in his chair and scrubbed his hands over his face. "Well, we've got a big night tonight so we have to put this behind us."

"Got it." Chaz agreed that tonight was a big night. As far as putting all this behind them, that was easier said than done.

"Your launch went well last night. Heard you got a record number of downloads or something like that."

"Yeah, over forty-seven million in the first twelve hours." The number was still incredulous to him. "The quick influx of downloads caused a few glitches but we were able to work those out fairly quickly. So it looks like a success."

One Chaz hadn't been able to enjoy. Valeria had decided to post his interview, after all, highlighting the parts where he insisted ChatMe was not a dating service. That was where she'd added the rumors that the social media playboy had finally fallen in love with his family's number one enemy. Chaz had been tempted to call her and give her a piece of his mind. In the end, he'd refrained because what she'd published was true.

With that tidbit of knowledge, Chaz had left the office late last night and spent the rest of his launch day sitting in his apartment staring at the blinds he'd closed over all his windows because it reminded him of Riley.

"What do you plan on doing once this showing is over?"

Chaz shrugged. Working with his uncle had always been temporary, until the new men's brand was launched successfully; now he pondered what his next step would be. "Hadn't thought about it."

"You were always a piss-poor liar, son." Tobias chuckled and crossed his leg to rest an ankle on the opposite knee.

"Really. I haven't thought about when I'll head back to Miami." Or *if* he would return to the life he'd had before coming to New York. For a minute, Chaz had thought there might be a reason for him to permanently relocate here.

He could easily work remotely from Manhattan or open another office in the city. One that could be used specifically as the ChatMe headquarters. But that plan had stalled in the water on Tuesday morning.

"And why is that? Because you got cozy with Riley Gold?"

The glare he sent his uncle must have expressed everything Chaz was feeling about him mentioning her name.

"Whoa there, don't get defensive. I'm not calling her a thief anymore. You got to the bottom of all that foolishness. Which is why I'm gonna shoot straight with you right now." Tobias smoothed down his tie.

"You've been walking around here with a long face all week. Last time I saw you looking like that was when that little boy you liked having over the house moved away."

"His name was Caleb and we were twelve when his family moved back to India." He'd been the closest thing Chaz ever had to a sibling or a family member his age.

"Right. Well, anyway, that's how you've been looking. Like you've lost your best friend."

Tobias had no idea how true those words were. Chaz had told Riley things he'd never shared with anyone. She knew him better than even his uncle did. She knew the real Chaz. And had walked away from him.

"I should get over to the venue," Chaz said and started to stand.

"I'm not finished. Sit down."

Chaz reluctantly did what he was told.

"You went and fell in love with a woman who you know you shouldn't have." Tobias held up a hand when Chaz was about to speak. "And she shouldn't have fallen for you, either. Both of you knew better. You knew about the bad blood between me and Ron and, in turn, our families. But you went and did it, anyway. There's only one explanation for that."

Chaz leaned forward and frowned. "An explanation for falling in love?"

"No. An explanation for why, despite the odds and family members you knew would be against you, that you and Riley still found your way to each other. It's called fate."

"Come on, Unc. Don't start with that nonsense."

"Call it what you want, but if there's one thing I know it's love."

Chaz laughed. He couldn't help it. "You? The man's whose been married eight times wants me to believe he knows about love."

"I do. That's precisely why I've been married eight times. You see people out here running around believing that you only get one chance. You fall in love and if for whatever reason you don't stay there, you don't get to try again. But you do."

"And that's your motto. Keep trying again and again until you get it right?"

Tobias shook his head. "You get it right for the time it lasts. That's all you can be worried about.

Tomorrow is not promised, so take what you can get now. My father used to tell me and your mother that. Why do you think she ran off and married your father when she was only eighteen instead of going to college? She was taking my father's advice and now I'm giving that advice to you."

"What are you saying?" Tobias had mentioned his mother and Chaz knew he was referring to Riley when he talked about love. The only two women to ever occupy space in his heart were being tossed in his face right now and Chaz didn't know how much longer he'd be able to remain civil.

"If you love that woman, fight for her. Go through whatever hoops she wants you to, dance to her beat, stand up to her father and those Gold boys, but whatever you do don't give up. The reason I keep getting more shots at love is simple, Chaz—I'm smart enough to remain open and available for it to find me. Now, if you're smart like I believe you are, you'll accept that love has found you and you'll do whatever it takes to hold on to it."

Tobias's words played over and over in Chaz's mind throughout the night and the celebration for their show and into the weekend when celebrations continued, but Chaz's heart still ached.

Tiny flakes of white confetti rained down over the crowd as ten models wearing the first wedding gowns in the Golden Bride Collection traipsed the runway for a second time to a standing ovation. Following right behind them and walking like supermodels themselves were the three women designers and Riley.

They'd grabbed her backstage and insisted she come out with them to celebrate what her vision had created. The designers wore all-white ensembles while Riley had selected a wine-colored pantsuit and gold pumps for this evening's show. Her smile was genuine, spreading across her face until her cheeks hurt and her heart thumped wildly as her mind screamed, *You did it!*

Lifting an arm to wave at everyone in the audience, Riley and the designers took a bow before turning and walking back. Her father and RJ were up next. Both dressed in dark suits and walking as if they, too, owned the runway, the Gold men gave the crowd their handsome smiles and appreciative waves.

But the moment Riley stepped down into the backstage area she was pulled into a tight embrace.

"I am so damn proud of you, Riley! So very proud!"

Riley pulled back and kissed her mother's cheek. "Thank you, Mom. Thank you so much!"

The Gold women hugged once more and then Marva eased her daughter away from the cheers, high fives and other celebratory reactions going on backstage. They stopped in front of one of the model tables all the way toward the back door and Marva took both her daughter's hands, bringing them up to kiss.

Her mother was a beautiful woman with a glowing tawny-brown complexion and thick silver-streaked hair that fell to her shoulders in big, heavy curls. Marva wore a cream-and-gold organza gown from the RGold couture collection.

She smiled brightly at her daughter. "I knew you would find your space and shine as brightly as the star you were meant to be." Marva's eyes glistened with unshed tears.

"Thank you, Mom, for always believing in me. I couldn't have done any of this without knowing that you were in my corner."

Marva shook her head. "Yes, you could have. You were meant to do this. Your father may be the designer in this family and RJ the face that can sell anything we produce, but you, Riley, are the brains behind this company. Your analytical mind is what brought this entire collection to fruition. You saw the need, carved out a unique niche for our brand and soared with it. You, my baby, have done well."

For the first time in days Riley felt full. Warmth spread from her chest to her cheeks and she squeezed her mother's hands to hold on to all the emotion brewing inside. This was the moment she'd been waiting for—the validation she hadn't realized she'd fought so hard to receive. While it wasn't her father or even RJ for that matter, this was so much better. For some reason it meant more to have her mother—the woman who had always been Riley's role model—say she'd done well.

"You know what would make this moment better, my darling?"

Oh no, Marva had slipped in a "my darling." The nicknames her parents used for her had at one point seemed endearing. Now, as she knocked on the door of turning thirty, she'd learned those endearments usually came with pieces of parental advice she either didn't want to accept or just didn't want to hear. Tonight, Riley feared both were about to come.

"What's that? All the champagne we're going to drink at the after-party?"

As much as Marva loved good champagne, Riley knew that wasn't what her mother was referring to.

"If you could celebrate two major accomplishments in your life at the same time."

When Riley would have turned away, her mother held on to her hands. "Oh no, that's enough running away, don't you think?"

"I'm not running away. That's not what I do, remember?" Riley had stood taller, squaring her shoulders as she stared back at her mother. The actions had come instinctively.

Marva could only shake her head. "My brave, cautious little girl. You've always fought for every inch, haven't you?"

Riley resisted the urge to shrug but said, "I had to."

Her mother pursed her lips and gave Riley a knowing nod. "That was your father's fault for making you feel like you had to be even better than the boys. And my fault for not cutting Ron off earlier with that foolish behavior."

"It's nobody's fault," Riley said. Her father's apology had come on Tuesday evening, after her mother had apparently spent the better part of that morning yelling at him for the way he'd yelled at Riley. In addition to being fashion royalty, her parents were pretty good at yelling and then making up later.

"Nonsense. If we hadn't let you believe that all you needed to be happy in life was to succeed in your career you wouldn't be in the predicament you're in now."

Riley attempted another smile. "I'm not in a predicament, Mom. I'm actually in the most wonderful moment of my life. We should get out front—I'm sure the reporters are swarming."

That last remark completely gave away Riley's fake bravado and she saw the moment her mother basked in the small triumph. Riley could do nothing but sigh.

"It's okay to love him." Marva's voice was softer now, but Riley could still hear her over all the celebrating going on around them. "You don't have to feel like you're going against some ridiculous family honor."

"I should have known better."

"Nonsense. You should have done exactly what you did, reached for the love you deserve. If you love him, Riley, and he loves and respects you, that's all that matters. None of this—not the accolades at work, my or your father's validation or any amount of money—is ever going to be worth it if you don't have someone you love to share it with."

"Not every woman needs a man, Mom. We're so beyond that in this century."

"You need love. I don't care what anybody says, you will always need love. Whether it's from a man, woman or alien, you need to feel like you're loved and respected for something other than the job you do. You need to feel that you, just being you, is enough to be celebrated."

Riley had only felt that way once, or rather each time she was with Chaz. He never looked at her as Riley Gold, daughter of Ron Gold and his uncle's archenemy. He'd told her from the start of their affair that they were not the feud.

"I pushed him away." The admission that had burned in her throat for the past few days came in a soft whisper and Riley looked away, blinking furiously to keep tears from falling.

Marva released her hands, touching a finger to her daughter's chin and turning her head so that she could look into Riley's face. "Go back and get him."

It was a simple statement...one that echoed in

Riley's mind like her mother had shouted it through a bullhorn. But that was impossible, at least right now. Her father and brothers were headed their way and the celebration in the old historic building they'd rented in NoHo for the show was about to be jumping with the Gold after-party.

An hour later, loud music combined with three glasses of champagne had given Riley another headache that she wished would go away. The party was in full swing and she'd managed to find a quiet corner to hide for a few moments.

She'd already spoken to fashion editors, posed for pictures with some of tonight's models and nibbled on whatever hors d'oeuvres her mother had whizzed by and popped into her mouth.

"Be gracious. Keep smiling. Sell the product." Ron had kissed her on the forehead in between giving his instructions. "And remember that I love you, my daughter. No matter how foolish I can be it's just because I love you."

Riley recalled the moment her father had found her after his walk on the runway and it made her smile. Her father was always going to have her heart.

With that thought Riley reached for another glass of champagne from the tray held by a server. She took a small sip and was grateful for having something to hold in her hands, which hadn't stopped shaking all night. Her mother's words played on loop in her mind. Those and the words Chaz had said to her that day he'd left her standing in her office.

Lights continued to shift with the beat of the music and the hundreds of guests they'd invited to the show danced and ate and drank their way into Fashion Week bliss while Riley stood by watching. That was when she saw him.

He walked through the door across the room wearing a dark-colored suit and button-front shirt open at the neck. One of his hands was in the front pocket of his pants as he stood there looking around the room, and Riley immediately pushed away from the wall where she'd been leaning.

Her heart beat to the rhythm of the fast-paced music and her fingers gripped the stem of her glass. He was here. Chaz had come to the RGF after-party when he hadn't received an invitation.

She could leave now. Her clever little hiding place was adjacent to the exit door. All she had to do was take a few steps, push the bar on that door and she'd be free. But she didn't do that, because freedom wasn't waiting on the other side of that exit door; it was just more time in the shelter she'd created for herself after believing she wasn't worthy of love.

Riley took a step forward. She inhaled deeply and let the breath out slowly, reminding herself that she could do this. She'd proved herself to her family and the fashion world tonight, surely she could walk across this room and talk to one man. She took another step and a server almost bumped into her. Riley set her glass on the tray this new server carried and continued her trek across the room.

Chaz had walked down the few stairs from the entry and was now moving in the opposite direction. He seemed to be looking around the room, searching for someone. Riley's heart beat faster and she picked up her pace, pushing past the people cluttering the floor until she saw Chaz walk into the lounge. She excused herself and hurried toward that space, fearful that Chaz would find another exit and leave.

She bumped into a photographer seconds before stepping into the lounge area and he held on to her waist to keep her from falling.

"I'm sorry," Riley said, her hands going to the guy's shoulders.

"No problem," the guy told her and turned them around so that she was now standing in the lounge area and he was headed to the dance floor.

Riley was just about to resume her search for Chaz when she felt him right behind her. It was that heat that only they shared that warned of his proximity. The smoldering hunger that always started in the pit of her stomach before spreading throughout her body.

"Hi, Riley."

His voice draped over her like a warm blanket and Riley turned slowly.

"Hi, Chaz."

"Can we talk?"

"Definitely." And because neither of them moved for the seconds after that brief exchange, Riley grabbed Chaz's hand and pulled him through the lounge area and out into the front foyer.

There was significantly less noise and fewer people here.

"I was wrong," Riley said the moment they stopped walking.

She released Chaz's hand and looked at his surprised expression.

"I knew you wouldn't steal from me and I should have spoken up. I should have been adamant about that and about who you are. But I was afraid. I thought it was happening all over again. The betrayal and the scandal—I felt like it was all coming back and I didn't know how to handle that."

"I would never betray you, Riley. And despite how much it seems like I love the spotlight or being the subject of reports on my love life, that's not who I am, either."

She knew that. Riley was certain she knew exactly who Chaz was.

"I saw your uncle's press conference about the arrests. I'm sorry this had to happen." Tobias King had stated unequivocally that he did not condone any type of treachery or games being played with his business or RGF's. That was not the method of competition he wanted. Riley believed him, too.

"I talked to your brother."

Riley blinked in confusion. "What? Who? When?"

"RJ. He showed up at my apartment the night after the press conference. He's the one who gave me the invitation to your show."

She didn't know what to say. How had RJ known she would want to see Chaz tonight?

It didn't matter. Riley took a step closer to Chaz.

"I love you," she said, feeling waves of relief course through her body at the admission. "I should have admitted it the day you were in my office telling me that you would take care of the scandal. I should have trusted myself and my feelings, but I couldn't. I didn't know how. I should have—"

Riley's words were cut short as Chaz cupped her cheeks and leaned closer. "You should kiss me, Riley."

He paused after saying the words as if waiting for her to decide. There were people in the foyer with them—not a lot but some. They could be photographers or reporters or models, or anybody else who would love to continue spreading the rumor that Riley Gold was having an affair with Chaz Warren regardless of their family feud.

For the first time Riley didn't give a damn. People could say and print whatever they wanted. She was going to reach for what she wanted and to hell with anyone who didn't approve.

"Yeah, I should kiss you," she whispered and leaned closer to touch her lips to his.

* * * * *

# COMING SOON!

We really hope you enjoyed reading this book.
If you're looking for more romance
be sure to head to the shops when
new books are available on

# Thursday 24th October

MILLS & BOON

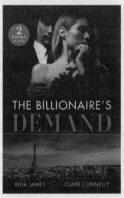
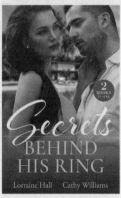

LET'S TALK

# *Romance*

For exclusive extracts, competitions and special offers, find us online:

# GET YOUR ROMANCE FIX!

Get the latest romance news,
exclusive author interviews, story
extracts and much more!

**blog.millsandboon.co.uk**